# CRAB JUICE

# CHAPTER 1

The August moon did not shine for the good alone and rolling clouds, like curtains, opened and closed on the scene unfolding in Brixton. More than ever, Triple wished he'd held his tongue – you can never unsay a thing. Too late though, too damn late for making wishes. Triple hunched into his neck until he felt it click and looked back at the six men of violent disposition. Friendly was not their style at the best of times.

In the distance, back where they'd bumped the Bedford transit van into a space only a Mini should fit, Bob Marley was pleading to the whole wide world to not rock his 'b-o-o-oat!' Someone was partying hard tonight while he led these ruthless Yardies along Acre Lane, claiming he'd forgotten the way, hoping, praying dem killing cousins would finally be convinced he couldn't remember the way and it was not going to 'come to him'.

'Yuh lost, Triple?' Jinxie spewed a jet of spittle through his teeth that splatted on the back of his neck. 'Again?'

'Well, uhm, nawman!' Triple flinched calmly and avoided eye contact. 'I only go dere one single time, Jinxie. Dat was long, long time ago, seen?'

'Oi! We dere yet?' The question leapfrogged from the back of the group, picking up a few serrated remarks on the way.

'Not yet, bredren. Near!' Triple accepted that his wrong turns and his sham uncertainty, mixed with the cool night air, were not enough. They just would not quit. The cranky crew started swapping ideas about his origins and prophesied his end.

'Wait up, bredren, I think is dis way.' Triple hung a left down Ferndale Road before they reached the town hall. Shit, he'd turned too soon. This was taking them off track again. It would have been healthier to stay on Acre Lane. Triple turned up the calm, 'Yeahmon, somet'ing familiar 'bout dis road. Might be a shortcut.'

'Shortcut draw blood, aight.' Jinxie said in his wise nigga voice, close behind. Stabbing distance.

Triple made longer strides and kept his eyes front until—
*Dis is it!*

They caught up to him, each puffing hot air and unsubtle warnings.

'Sure, dis time?' Chigger growled.

'Yeahmon! Yeahmon!' Triple proceeded up the flagstone path towards the vandalised entrance of the crumbling block of flats. The door looked new and the lock even newer.

Shit.

'Better not be di wrong door or di wrong fuckin' lock, Triple!' Jinxie scowled.

'Naw-naw-naw! See dis?' Triple pointed up at the graffiti of Thatcher's smiling head on a burly copper's body, her left hand gripped a truncheon with Union Jack colours and, in her right, she grasped a black youth by the scruff of the neck. The kid could be anybody's little brother, terror in his eyes, feet dangling in mid-air, dressed like he'd been on his way to or from Sunday school. 'I 'member dat drawin'! Seen? Dis must be di place.'

Some looked. None gave two shits. On his knees, he felt them circling him like John Crows around roadkill. He caught his reflection in their trademark dark glasses. Light glinted off Chigger's Bowie. Triple ditched the idea of breaking his lock pick in the mechanism and instead listened to failsafe tumblers resist his skills.

'Hurry up!' Chigger snarled and shifted his weight from foot to foot.

*Hurry? Rush? A lock is a delicate thing, Chigger. You can't hurry the touch. Got to take it slow. Tickle. Tease until she opens up and...* Triple kept his thoughts to himself, willing some 'concerned' curtain twitcher to notice seven black men acting suspiciously and quietly dial 999. Trouble was, he figured as he listened for tumblers yielding, any 'concerned' around here were probably *not* citizens and would want nothing to do with the Babylon.

The lock yielded.

Triple stood and applied his full weight to the metal door. It stood defiant. Jinxie called Likkle. Everyone cleared a path. Likkle rested a palm on steel and the door swung open. They piled in just as Bob Marley called across the rooftops that everything would work out fine.

The grimy, grey entrance area felt colder than outside.

Chigger lingered at the doorway. 'Hey. I'll be lookout tonight, aight.'

Jinxie shook his head at Chigger and turned to Triple. 'You goin' say you forget which 'partment?'

'Top flat!' Triple said swiftly. 'Seventh floor? I think. No, I'm sure. For sure.'

'Sevent' what?' Chigger rolled his eyes and looked wistfully towards the lift.

'Touch that lift button,' Jinxie glared, wielding a scar-encrusted fist, 'might as well blow a trumpet to say we's here, to ra-ahs!'

None moved.

'George! Outside. You on lookout like usual, seen? Clint, you da inside man, yeah? No quarrellin', a'right? Keep all tools outta sight 'less you got no choice, *aight*? We don't need no shootout wid no Babylon t'night, yeah?'

Jinxie shot Chigger a look. Chigger edged away from the lift, pursed his lips and sucked in hard.

'Kiss yer teeth all you want, wi ain't taking no fuckin' lift!' Jinxie waved Triple forward and ordered the rest to follow without another sound, up the concrete steps.

They huffed their way up through the shadows infused with piss and shit and weed until they finally arrived on the top floor. Wedges of fuzzy moonlight slanted from the windows into the hallway. Likkle went to bust the lights. That someone had already done it before they'd got there, sent a shiver down Triple's spine and he did the math. Five to one. Them was good odds. Even so, he didn't fancy their chances.

He motioned to the right door.

Jinxie signalled for him to get to it. He knelt again with his picking tools.

This lock, too, was no match and in just a couple of minutes the door squeaked open.

No one moved and it seemed they all held their breath.

A whisper of talc entered the hall. Triple squeezed his nose, trapping a sneeze that made his ears pop and his eyes water. Jinxie scowled at him then signalled them all with a Rolex wave. The fancy watch with its gold bracelet strap only came out when big luck was needed on a job.

Triple flattened out of the way. He watched Style follow Jinxie and then Likkle squeezed past and ducked in after Style. Chigger stood in the hall still, stroking Betty, his beloved and brutal Bowie knife. Triple puffed his chest, gave him a thumbs up and penetrated the darkness behind the others.

*Slap!*

Christ. He knew Mitsy could be seriously violent, especially when he'd been snoring, so he stayed quiet and clung to his sweet postcoital coma.

*Slap!*

*Come on, Mitsy, I need my sleep.*

The pungent mix of rum, sweat, stale sperm and something else tickled his nose hairs.

*Slap! Slap! Slap!*

Hell, was she trying to wake him, gagging for more bamboo? Women. One minute they're scrubbing the damp sulphur jail smell off your back, sharing giggle weed and pouring Wray and Nephew to soften up a man, and the next—

Cheap metal clinked.

*No, not Mitsy.*

He kept his eyes squeezed shut, feigning sleep, buying a few seconds in case the unlucky idiot with a death wish had burgled the wrong flat. Could be a rival or else the Babylon had followed him to where he hung his hat. One? Two? How many did he have to kill?

*Mitsy?*

*The baby?*

Thankfully, they both still seemed dead to the world.

A mix of grease and WD40 wafted his way. '*Triple*?' he almost called out. Instead, he mumbled like a man refusing to let go of sweet sleep. He opened his eyes into slits enough to study the dark.

Nothing. The darkness kept her secrets.

Then one single spot, then two pinpricks of light, flitting around like fireflies – Jinxie? With that stupid 'lucky' watch. Had to be!

He sniffed. Talc and…carbolic soap? Mitsy'd told him her Pa washed with nothing else – she'd said to hide his cheating ways. So she never had carbolic around to remind her of the bastard. But he knew a badass shooter who thought carbolic was stylish.

He listened hard, past his own deliberate breathing and into the next room. The baby wasn't crying. Beside him,

Mitsy lay naked, silent, sticky, still out cold from his freedom celebration, charged with sex and weed and too much rum.

His wits were still below max, but he carefully extended an arm anyway, feeling for his underpants. A metallic blow to his forearm reverberated through his elbow. Pain lanced into his shoulder and neck.

'No tricks, rasta…all clothes stay 'pon di floor.'

'Jinxie?' he rasped, his throat bone dry. 'Wha's up, bro?'

'Stand 'pon di bed!'

'Why? Wha's goin on?' he said, shaking off the agony. Jinxie must have used the 'lass. He felt for a bloody stump.

'Nex' time you get di blade, yeah?' Jinxie said from further away with his shiny piece of junk. 'Mi say, stand up!'

Cold steel clunked against his temple and carbolic hit his nostrils.

Style.

'Not saying it again, star! Stand up! An' Style! Drop him if he try anyting, seen?' Jinxie talked like he'd been given a promotion and a bonus brain cell. *Fuck, how'd they find him here, in this place? And how'd they even get in?*

Triple was the only one of them he'd ever brought here. One time. To hide him from the Peckham crew who were hellbent on ripping his tongue out through his arse for running off at the mouth about sticking it to one of their mothers.

'Triple?'

'Django…' Triple squeaked from over by Mitsy's clothes rail, near the door, where the shadows were thickest. The rat.

'Shut da fuck up, Triple,' Jinxie said. 'Bull make me in charge, seen?'

'You, Jinxie? In charge?' Django raised himself on his good elbow. A tell-tale click told him Style put one in the chamber. Style's impatience was as famous as his speed and deadeye accuracy. He knew that all too well.

He felt the steel nozzle jab his temple. 'Jinxie…says… stand…up!'

'Easy, Style, easy, man!' he said as though a mere fly had landed on him.

The floorboards creaked.

'Y'understan' any o' dis, Likkle?' Django spoke towards the headboard, picturing the hulk of a man with gorilla arms, frying-pan-sized hands and a head too big for its pea of a brain.

'Uhmmm!'

'Shut it, Likkle!' Style said sharply.

'Do me a favour – keep it down. You might wake my baby mother and if you wake her baby too, God help you!'

'Yeah, we know about the baby maddah.' Jinxie sounded dangerously smug. 'You always say never mix weed wi' liquor? *Tut-tut-tut*…do wha' I say but not wha' I do, eh, boss? All-di-same, yer baby maddah won't interrupt, Chief. She got somet'ing stuck in her throat.'

He turned his head towards where Mitsy still lay.

'Bwoy, Django, yu luv dem big batty 'oman, yeh? You must 'ave a big harpoon fi' poke a whale like dis, bwoy!' Jinxie said.

'Turn on di light, bro, so we can talk proper,' Django said, knowing the answer, stalling.

'No t'anks, we can see yu fine. Yu don't need to see we,' said the pupil instructing the master. Jinxie was over by the dressing table now, keeping his target guessing – it was like he'd taught the fuckers. Good.

'Likkle, help 'im up.'

Floorboards creaked towards the door. A flash of light arced into a loud slap and harsh question: 'Who's in fuckin' charge 'ere?'

'Sorry, Jinxie.'

'Shut up, Triple. Likkle, stand 'im up.'

Likkle effortlessly hoisted him like a baby from a cot and set him standing naked. Woozy and off balance was not a good combination on the springy mattress that felt slippery and wet beneath him. His feet slipped. He fell. Tried not to land on Mitsy. Bounced right up close, too close. Bed springs creaked and squeaked like they had earlier but with far less energy. She'd awaken now for sure, he thought, as her sleepy arms flopped about his nakedness in a meaty, mock hug.

'Mitsy?'

Mitsy felt clammy.

'Mitsy?'

'Mitsy?'

'Hey, hey, guys!' Jinxie said. 'Tell I dis, seen – any man know a 'oman who stay so quiet in bed you can do wha' you like to her?'

Shadows sniggered as Django raised himself up on his knees, fingering for Mitsy's face in the dark, tracing the contours of her nose, her lips, the chin he liked to nibble… following the smooth of her neck until his fingers slipped inside an open purse of flesh, wet and slippery. He pulled back, stopping the bile in his throat and tightening his jaw.

'Since you're dere, better take one las' taste of pussy… should still be warm, star,' said one fucker.

'And "Mind di gap!"…' another joined in, like he was trying out for fucking British Rail. 'You don't want to drop down di wrong hole!'

Rage mingled with more rage and Django fixed all their positions.

*Chicken merry, you fuckers, hawk is near!*

'Make 'im stand again, Likkle,' Jinxie said from a few feet away. The curtains fluttered and the moon splashed the bugger's back. More sparks flicked off his watch band and flitted about the room.

*Lucky.*

Django would have moved then, but his drugged reflexes were still fucked and Likkle's hands clamped his head and lifted him off poor Mitsy. His legs dangled and he was made to stand. His knees trembled so much he felt they might buckle.

'Why?' he wanted to shout, but Django knew these bastards all too well. He shook his head in vain. The cocktail of ganja and white rum may have reduced him to half his might, but they were about to feel the full fury for what they'd done to Mitsy.

'Dis is di t'ing: firs', di Babylon pick you up,' Jinxie was still by the window, 'an' next, they raid two of our store. Cost Bull two million...'

'Wait up, Ji—'

'No, Django! Shut it, coz the boss 'im pissed off. Him 'ave to relocate some more. Big vein poppin' in him forehead, seen? Plus, him frettin' for him special deliveries outfit too and – bugger me – four of di package – dem run off. Four!'

'What dat have to do wi—'

'How di cops kno' 'bout di stash, star. *Somebody* tip dem off an' you kno' we got rules, man. Seen?'

'Jinxie, y'all *know* me? I'm no snitch! Style, who tek a bullet fi you las' year? Likkle, who got you Frank Bruno's autograph back after you got hustled playing pool? And, Chigger, you run out of that foot cream I get for you yet?' Chigger said nothing, but the unmistakable ripeness of sweat and pus marinating the dead and dying flesh said he was close by. 'Shit, I never let any jack man o' you down. Fuckit, you'd all still be pickin' mangos in Jamaica if it wasn't for my help in di first place. Why accuse I—'

'Dat's true, Jinxie,' Likkle boomed from the depths of the size fourteens he'd got specially for him off the back of a posh lorry.

Django thought about his piece, four feet too far away, on the dresser top, next to Jinxie. Fresh and clear-headed, he could get over there easy. Grab it. Bust a few caps into the fuckers. Blam. Blam. Blam. Blam. Except Triple. Triple would get his served up slow and very painful!

Timing would have to be perfect. He knew that, hell, he had made the fuckers into the kick-ass unit they were. How else could they have caught him with his pants down and his dick dangling?

'You fuckers disappoint me!' he said with authority once respected. 'You'd all be in body bags without me, an' dis is da treatment I get. Look, you even forget to *never* leave George and Clint together on lookout. Them two will be at each other's throats, having pissing contests while the Babylon—'

Likkle, still between the bedhead and the wall, said, 'Django's right. You shouldn't never let Clint and George be lookout. Right, Jinxie?'

'Django,' Triple said, 'no one t'ink you, of all people, would ever rat us out. It's *Bull*, man. He mad like hell. Now, he only want you tell us everyt'ing what di police know about his business. Seen?'

'Wha'? 'Ow must I know dat? I don't talk to no Babylon!'

'*Don' play fool fi catch wise*, Django? 'Fess up, an' we might make a deal, seen? Or Bull want maximum hurt, un'erstan'?'

Chigger's smell grew stronger.

They were like a boxer telegraphing his best punch. Django might have pitied the bastards, but felt pumped and ready to slice them open, one by one, scoop them out and stuff them one inside the other.

'I swear, I don' talk to no pigs, Jinxie,' Django repeated. The way he saw it, the time for discussion had ended.

'Bull don't care 'bout di weed, Chief. Him want to know what you tell dem 'bout di other stuff, man? Y'know, dem packages?' Jinxie had moved closer.

'I tell dem not'ing, rasta. Triple, of all people! You know I'm no grass!'

'Well, you know how it goes, Django: squeal like a pig, roast like a hog, seen?'

Django's teeth clinked against a .45 muzzle rammed hard into his mouth, chipping bits of enamel off his teeth and crushing into his lips. He tasted blood and metal and his mind flashed back over the last time he was on the right end of a steel blowjob. Django tightened loose bowels, gritted his teeth and thought fast.

'Wait, bredren! Wait. What abou' fuckin, Twiple? The cops grab 'im first and tek him to some interrogation—'

'Talk sense!'

Django gagged. As though it had not been tough enough to use your syllables with a gun in your mouth now the fuckers wanted him to talk sense.

'He says the coppers nabbed me first.'

'So, dat true, Triple?'

'Yeah, dat's true, Jinxie!' Triple dropped the lid on what he was saying. 'But I ain't no supergrass! I tell dem I never know nothin'. Seen? So, dem let I go.'

'Not 'ow I 'member it, Twiple!'

'Django,' Triple snapped like a little dog protecting his dinner, 'quit stallin'!'

'I don't say not'ing, I swear on my baby's life. I don't say not'ing!'

Django knew it didn't matter what he said, but he needed time. 'It wasn't me, I tell you.'

'Bull insists that he wants blood for this treachery,' Style said. 'Your blood.'

In better times, everyone joked about why Style took long showers, dressed like he was too avenue to be street and loved forcing big words into small-talk. This was not one of those times.

'Hold up, Style!' Jinxie said with authority. Style kissed his teeth and retracted his .45. Jinxie went on, 'Who den, Django? Explain dat! If you never 'elp di Babylon, how come you get-outta-jail free?'

With his own Magnum on his mind, Django bought more time, 'I never talk to no Babylon 'bout nothin'! Not di stash. Not di packages. Not'ing! Somebody bail I out, star!'

'Bail? Who bail yu, rasta?' Jinxie barked, close enough now for a roundhouse to his temple, but the sopping mattress was not stable enough for the launch.

'I-man don't even kno', rasta. One minute I lay down 'pon a bunk, next minute dem say I free fi go. But I never sing fi no Babylon, star. Triple, tell dem I would never do dat!'

'We talk to Triple a'ready, Django!'

A sudden breeze fluttered the curtains, splashing moonlight over his manhood and he felt their eyes on the keloid souvenirs that crawled over his body. Like a misplaced smile, a scar ran from his chin to his left ear. Maybe tonight he would be adding a new wound or two.

'Real nice, y'know,' Jinxie said. 'Like Michael and Jello's *Daveed.*'

Two meaty hands grabbed Django from behind and clamped his arms to his side. He squirmed inside Likkle's beefy grip on his sticky wet skin.

Frayed ribbons rose from the fading orange-yellow glows over on the dresser. Mitsy had called them Mystic Ocean when she was lighting them, standing like a high priestess wearing a robe that revealed more than it concealed and complaining about him making the place untidy. Still, he'd left his piece right there, on the dresser. He could feel it already in his hand. Yes, even though some idiot in his head was saying he'd need a ton of luck to clock them all before they used his training against him.

Django appealed to his best friend again. 'Triple? Talk, man. You know me better than anyone. Bull want fi cut I out. He'll do the same to you lot, aight. Like dem firms what use all-work-and-no-pay policy. You do the job and they do you, seen? Dem man hate long division, seen?'

After a tomb-like silence, Triple's raspy voice whined, 'S-sorry, Django, but you never sh-should'a t-t-talk to di B-Babylon.'

'All right, Django. You say yu never sell out.' Jinxie sounded almost sincere. 'We can' tell di Bossman dat, seen? Don' fret. We won' kill yu, rasta. Not t'night.'

They hesitated. 'We goin' but you kno' we can't go empty handed. Bull won' like it. Giv' us one o' yu balls!'

'Wha'? Mi balls?'

'Jus' one, Django. You can choose, rasta. You always say yu'self: never go away empty-'anded!'

At that instant, it seemed to him that God and the Devil cut a deal, so Django made his move. He pulled free, dropped down and threw himself onto the floor. He hit it hard. Ignoring the pain, he barrel-rolled towards the dresser. A lucky kick found an unlucky knee and he managed to shove a shadow out of his way. At the dresser, he grabbed the box, ripped off the cover and extracted his piece.

*Blam! Blam! Blam!*

'Bumbo-clawt!' Django swore as the clip ran out. He'd preached that they should always have a full clip locked and loaded.

A hand grasped his forehead like a grapefruit and slammed his body down. His head smacked the floor and he lay like an X on the cold lino, his arms and legs held securely.

'Keep the fucker in dat chalk pose!' Jinxie stood between him and the moon with his cutlass unsheathed.

Django had always said that he'd rather die than beg for mercy. He felt his lips moving, 'Mi beg yu! Mi never grass to no Babylon! All you know me good enough. Why? I grass on you, I shit on myself.'

'You cook up deal wid di Babylon, star!'

'Deal? Mi no make no deal, bredren. Mi never sell out! Tell dem, Triple! Tell dem now, man! Oh God!'

'Too late for prayin', informer!' Style said.

A coldness brushed his scrotum. Django's mouth burst open to release a scream. It was long and loud and seemed to fill the whole wide world before it ran out of steam and shrivelled into the denseness that gathered about him, and as it did, Django watched the sunset glow from the stick of Mystic Ocean flare then vanish into a whisper of sugary smoke and somewhere behind, or above, or below him, a little baby cried and cried.

# CHAPTER 2

The minicab almost ran over her toes. Jonelle stepped back fast. Open-mouthed, she watched as it sped away, chased by the darkness, abandoning her to her stupidity and whatever lurked in the bushes. If anyone, or anything, pounced on her right now, who'd hear? Not that she was a screamer. Tyrone had told her so enough times. As usual, the thought of her ex left an aftertaste of regret. Where was he when she wanted someone to babysit so she could graft some extra pennies? It was like salt on a slug whenever she needed help or mentioned child support.

The chilled darkness thickened around her as she watched the taxi finally vanish towards Croydon, civilisation and common sense, its rear lights a last double warning. The bastard had grabbed her twenty and sped off with the change, most likely punishing her for making him struggle with the roughly sketched map Myrna had sworn would take her directly to the place.

A streetlamp stood like the last soldier holding a lost cause while kamikaze moths overwhelmed its tired aura. Three figures stood under the streetlamp; escapees from St Trinian's, they hogged the light. Where'd they appear from? Better yet, what were they doing, in the middle of nowhere? Only slightly relieved, Jonelle approached to get directions.

They reminded her of cats looking up from a discarded KFC box that someone had tossed over her fence.

'Oi, Debra! Check that thieving slag!' The gravelly voice belonged to one of the three. 'Get your own patch, bitch!'

Jonelle backed away, towards the rusting gates where the taxi man had reversed, grumbling at a small herd of girls in low tops, bum-short skirts and too-high heels that had crossed behind them, in the direction of a dead-end sign that was definitely not marked on the map. They'd fitted her customer profile for a place like 'Grilla, but with no sign of the gig and the Trinian's egging each other to go sort her out, Jonelle hurried to follow the sound of their high heels.

Earlier, she'd been listening to the kids play quietly *to allow Mummy to work on her economics essay*, when Myrna had bashed on her door, before stumbling into the flat, coughing phlegm into a hand towel, dressed in her housecoat and wearing one scarf like a bad noose about her neck and another wrapped about her in-curlers hair. Over a steaming cup of tea, that she'd plunked down on the essay, Myrna'd tearfully explained how she, Jonelle, was the only reliable person she could ask to cover her Friday night shift at a 'Grilla gig.

'Grilla? She'd always thought the word was street code used by goss-merchants with rumours to spread but Myrna, still coughing disgustingly, had filled her in, explaining that 'Grilla was really a thing; not exactly Babylon-friendly and strictly secret squirrel. Unlike in night school, where she'd learned about business advertising with billboards, leaflets, flyers, and such, this business was popular by being hush-hush. Hell, even 'escorts' advertised, but, with neither fixed address nor schedule, if you didn't know someone-who-knew-someone then you had no bloody idea.

'Why'd anyone get involved with such a thing, Myrna? If there was any bother, could you even go to the cops?'

Myrna had answered the question with one of her own, asking when was the last time she'd had a Friday night out? The answer took her back and back, way back, BC, before children that is, when she was cocooned in the care of her own parents and life was all butterflies, when things like being found dead in a ditch, half eaten by foxes and rats, only happened to 'other' people.

Why hadn't she just said no to Myrna? Her life had all too often turned on that tiny two-letter word. N.O. How many times had her fortunes turned on the inability to utter that mighty little syllable?

'I got nobody else, Jonie.' True. The other girls didn't warm to Myrna as she did, often gossin' that she had a fancy man buying her nice things.

'Come on, Jonie, you could use the money.' Also, true. She'd spent the rent on Chinese herbs someone swore would suck the pain from her young son's body, that would surely make Deen sleep, and her too. Besides that, her eldest daughter's birthday was coming up, just when she had to buy back-to-school stuff. Plus, she was determined to keep both her daughters out of the free school meal queue this term, after the bullying they'd got last time. Every spare penny was a godsend, especially with sweet FA coming from that deadbeat dad, Tyrone.

Now here she was, cloaked in darkness, wandering through a wilderness of great-ideas-gone-bad, trying to locate a club she knew was as concealed from the law as regulation and in her pocket was a jigsaw puzzle piece she was supposed to use as ID.

*The guy on the door'll know what it is and take you to the manager, Mr Maxwell. All you got to do is take coats when people come in; give them back when they leave. That's it, I swear. AND – kiss-me-neck, Jonie! – they play the best latest riddims. Dance choons you don't never hear 'pon radio. Leave you bubbling right into next week. Good money. And tips too. Please, Jonie. If you don't cover for me, I'll get the sack!*

The night air slipped under her skirt, chilling her knees and thighs. Snugging into her coat, she tied it closer. The girls, her girlies, liked to taunt her about the 50p British Heart Foundation bargain, but what this woollen treasure lacked in style it trebled in warmth. She'd told them to piss off.

*Oh God, now she wanted to pee.*

Christ, what was she doing? If anything happened to her – images flashed through her head – a chalk-outline, black-and-yellow cordon tape, newspaper headlines with Thatcher justifying her Sus laws, the Social walking off with Amanita, Kenyana and frail little Deen while reporters looked on...a pang shot through her belly.

Jonelle peered into the dark and tried to calm herself by humming a confused mash-up of Gloria Gaynor and The Temptations. Neither worked.

'Oi, get out of our way, ho!'

A shadowy group trudged up behind and bundled around her, bumping into her and each other to follow a lone torchlight. Jonelle attached herself and they made a sharp left off-road along a paved path edged with brambles and weeds.

The little torch led them down the side alley of a tin of a building. Then they stopped suddenly, and Jonelle bounced off what she figured was the well-rounded rear of the last woman of the group.

She was about to apologise when metal slid against metal and light fell on them all as a door creaked on its hinges.

Music.

The rabble piled in as though boarding the last bus out of Dodge. All too suddenly, she stood alone before a hulking scowl of a six-footer whose neck had drowned in the barrel of his chest.

'Uhm, good evening?' she squeezed out.

'You a Jehovah's Witness?'

'N-No?'

'Then get in,' grumbled twenty stone of beef wearing dark glasses. She bet herself his mother needed a thousand stiches at his birth. 'Pay over there!'

*Give it to the guy on the door, Jonie. He'll take you to a short, little man named Mr Maxwell. All you do is take coats when people come in and give them back when they leave.*

Jonelle fumbled in her pocket for the puzzle piece, feeling for sharp card edges. She handed over the ID like Myrna had told her. The man looked vaguely at the puzzle piece, shrugged and spoke as the noise level spiked.

She leaned in. 'Pardon?'

'You. Vait here!' he growled.

'Okay,' she squeaked and he was gone.

She struggled to avoid wide hips, sharp heels and pointy elbows barging in past her towards aproned women who tossed cash and coins into deep pockets before mining for change. Payees got stamped on the wrist before heading towards where the music boomed.

A makeshift partition wobbled apart and she saw a heaving, many-headed beast bathed in ultraviolet light, glowing, pulsing to Admiral Tibet's 'Serious Time', only one of her favourite dub tracks ever. Jesus! Her ears licked at the delicious loudness, and she was transfixed, watching the surge of strangers dancing like they'd hit a jackpot and wondering what lives lay beneath their fuck-off faces and playwear.

The big bass dropped.

The entire room froze for a heart-stopping moment until the boom kicked back in, rocking the room and Jonelle shivered with a deep sense of – *what?* – 'belonging?'

How did they keep this chest-pounding music from the surrounding area? In her flat, she only had to sniff and her neighbours were pounding on her walls.

'*Ssveee-t!*'

The besuited doorman had wolf-whistling fingers in his mouth and started beckoning her over. Beside him, a mini man stood behind a counter. The little Napoleon fitted Myrna's description. Looking harried, the rotund Mr Maxwell was unceremoniously threading coats onto hangers and attaching raffle tickets. Pressing her lips together, Jonelle hastily chased images of a cross between Porky Pig and Donald Duck away from her mind.

A couple overtook her and handed over their coats at the counter. People kept jostling her out of their way and, what was worse, each jolt worried her already impatient bladder.

Maxwell swiped the notes off the tabletop and hesitantly handed over a ticket with the change, taking care to place it next to a shoebox crudely labelled 'tipps'. Jonelle guessed it might have been the very box his patent leather shoes had come in, caught by the stray strobe light when he waddled over to the sagging rack of hangers against the wall behind him. A plastic card pinned to his chest read 'man ger' in embossed Dymo letters.

He regarded her like a bad smell.

'You're bloody late!' he said, looking away to take another coat.

She waited then watched as he checked the puzzle piece before handing it back with two fingers and his lips curling towards his nose. 'This's disgustin'! Where's Myrna been keeping her ID? Or was it you?' Maxwell produced wet wipes from somewhere and wiped his fingers furiously. 'Anyway, you tell 'er when you see 'er, sending someone without my *h-express* permission is not *h-acceptable*! Just like getting here late. Seen?'

Jonelle tucked the ID back in her coat pocket under his bug-eyed glare and trout pout. To top it all, she really, really needed to pee now. Since Deen, her third, life had been lived mostly under bladder control. She had complained to her

GP, expecting to be referred to a specialist. When would she ever find the time for any of those damn Kegel exercises? She tensed and a little pee squeezed out.

*Dammit.*

He made a clucking sound as he ran his eyes up and down her body. 'I 'spect we got to thank God for small mercies when we dis busy t'night! No time to piss about, yeah?'

Jonelle squeezed her thighs together. Tightly.

'Right, start on the toilets! All you need's in *there*.'

*Toilets?* Jonelle hesitated, confused.

The music spiked.

'You taking a blind bit o' notice to what I'm telling you?' Maxwell shouted.

Jonelle nodded. 'But Myrna said—'

'Move yo' ass!' he yelled. 'Do them loos properly too! *And* wash your hands before you come back. Chop, chop!'

*Myrna, you owe me, big time!*

The sign to the 'Toylits' guided Jonelle away from Maxwell, the music and towards two doors. She hurried to the nearest and ignored the scrawl that read 'Jents'. She dashed in and exhaled sharply as she passed a grimy urinal to the only cubicle beyond. Christ, another second and...she wiggled out of her skirt, yanked her pants down, straddled the metallic bowl and winced as it touched her thighs.

In full flow, she reached out to swing the cubicle door shut. No door.

Listening for impending exposure, Jonelle pressed against her bladder, urging any hesitant drippings. She spotted a toilet roll soaking in a suspect puddle by her feet. Disgusted, she shook herself dry and pulled her pants and skirt back into place.

Her hunt for cleaning stuff led her behind the door to the 'Ladys'.

None too soon, both windowless rooms sparkled in disinfectant. One sink had holes where the taps should go while the second had taps that weren't connected to anything. Only one of the three basins had working Hot and Cold with both delivering brownish cold water. With blobs of concrete everywhere, it looked like the place had either been vandalised or was incomplete. Was it even legal to occupy a building while it was still being built? Legal? She inwardly scoffed at the thought that a business that constantly changed its address from one *secret* location to another could care less about legality.

Jonelle stood outside the toilets and smiled. A bead of sweat ran down one cheek and her elbows ached. Wrists too. It was as though the place had never seen clean and she secretly wished she could see the face of the next person to come in.

Myrna would be repaid somehow, but first she had to deal with the short-arse whose name rhymed with 'hell'.

'Took your bloody time?' Maxwell said, clucking.

Jonelle tugged on her tongue, holding back the outrage at having to deal with toilet muck that included discarded condoms in both toilets and a stubborn blockage of tampons when she'd only come to check in hats and coats.

'What? No apology or nothing, eh? Bloody typical! Right. You can take over from me...' Maxwell stopped himself from leaving the counter. 'Wait. First, go clean up by the bar. Some *boogooyagga* spilled drinks all over the carpet and dance floor! Go, get a big mop and a bucket from the cupboard out back, through that door over there.'

He indicated behind him. What she thought was a closet door peeked from between the rack of coats and jackets.

'You listening to me or the music?'

'Yes,' she said. Maxwell looked fed up. 'I heard you.'

'Then hear me good: when you get to the cupboard, open it careful-like, understand. Do not go in! You listening?'

She nodded and smiled on the outside.

He continued, 'Reach in. You'll feel the mops, I'm sure – long wood with a hairy bit at one end.'

He grinned like a schoolboy. Her stomach churned.

'Anyway, grab a mop, pick up a bucket, come back here and go over by the bar before somebody slip over and cause trouble.'

Jonelle kept her thoughts on the wages and tips Myrna had talked about as she tramped over to part the coats and reveal the door. Behind her, the heavy beat dropped and lifted her spirits. Myrna was right about the music at least.

*Mmm, it's all about the bass!* Damp air flavoured with disinfectant rushed at her and Jonelle found she had entered an area with an unfinished quality that made it seem more like an enclosed alleyway, lit dimly by a brave little bulb that faltered occasionally.

The little space, or its builders, seemed undecided about what it should be. Corridor? Courtyard? Dead-end alley? It was as dim as the decision she'd made to leave her home tonight. And a wet stench stroked her nose hairs. It took her back to the first time she'd opened a freshly filled nappy. Nothing could have prepared her for such a gift. All the more, Jonelle wanted to get this night over and done with and return to her young family.

*Left? Right? What had that Maxwell said?*

Snail trails scrawled over the floor and mildew blackened the corners.

She shuddered and rubbed her arms warm.

To her left was a door blocked with crates of empty booze bottles and bulging bin-liners. Bold red painted lettering above it spelled out 'emergancy exit'.

Looking right, she saw what Maxwell must have been yapping about.

*You'll see a cupboard.*

With a shrug, Jonelle went over to the door and pulled on the handle. The door stood fast. Why was everything so hard when you did the right thing? Helping out her friend and easing pressure to find some extra cash this month. Jonelle put her frustration behind an almighty push.

The door swung inwards. Her shadow fell headfirst and disappeared as she followed. All around her wood, metal and plastic clattered. She smelt bleach and ammonia at first, then a whisper of air swirled from somewhere inside the cupboard carrying a concentrated whiff of soiled nappies.

*Reach in. You'll feel the mop. And bucket.*

Jonelle felt for a way to regain her feet and her dignity. How much easier would this all be if there were a light in this place? Surely there had to be one. She felt along the wall for a switch or pull-string.

Her hand touched something.

She gripped it and pulled.

A low moan filled the space around her, followed by a grumble and grate.

'Hell!' Jonelle withdrew as though she'd touched something hot. A red line appeared in the dark and a gap opened and grew wider, parting, like a curtain opening onto a cluttered room bathed in red. Unlike her children's bedtime story, this was no bloody Narnia.

The glow from the other place washed the cupboard, revealing a mop and pail. Jonelle reached in and grabbed them and straightened up to see two big eyes staring at her.

'Christ!' Jonelle gripped the pail and mop and thought to leg it. Something, either the look of terror and desperation, or the childlike face on the trembling little body, kept her rooted to the spot. 'Who-who are you? What's wrong?'

The girl just stood there, clutching a bundle of something Jonelle couldn't quite see.

Jonelle looked beyond her and tried again. 'What is this place?'

'Please, I change mind.' She was barely audible. 'Don't hurt me. Don't hurt me.'

'W-Who are you?' Jonelle said, holding back an urge to run and pretend she hadn't seen a damn thing. 'What's the matt—?'

'I sorry! I leave money – all of money.' The girl edged forward carefully, into the cupboard.

Inching away, Jonelle's eyes got used to the low light. The girl looked barely older than her Amanita, due to turn twelve in a month's time. Jonelle set aside the mop and pail. The shadowy little figure shrank back, cowering with one arm and turning enough to shield her possession with her body.

'No hit. No hit. Please, I change mind.'

'Hit? I won't hit you.' Jonelle stepped forward, smiling. People relaxed when you smiled at them.

'Please, please.' The girl started trembling and her eyes darted about.

'I just want to help—' Her shoulder caught Jonelle mid-chest and she lost her footing, stumbled backwards against a wall. The young woman leapt from the cupboard and her bare feet slapped slimy wet flagstones as she headed for the emergency exit.

'Wait!'

She was not waiting.

Jonelle stood up in time to watch the barefooted girl scrambling frantically one-handed over the bin bags and crates to reach the exit. It was anyone's guess how she would ever get it open and, even as Jonelle was thinking it, two things happened.

A gap opened in the pile of putrid rubbish and swallowed the girl with a sucking sound; the door back into the club flew open with a force that made Jonelle's ears pop.

Three extra-large men piled in.

'Who – *the fuck* – are you?'

Jonelle gaped up at the double-breasted speaker glaring at her while a hulking duo flanked him.

'You dumb or som'ink?' he spat at her. She glanced at where the girl had sunk into the pile of trash, realised what she was doing and looked down at the floor.

'You idiots seen *that* before?' the man growled and she looked up to see the musclebound bookends shaking their heads.

One pointed a meaty finger at her. 'The boss said, who are you, *vitch*?'

'Yeah, *whachoo* doing back 'ere?' Tweedledee piped up.

'Yeah, wha're you doing?' Jonelle recognised Tweedledum as the doorman who'd taken her to the 'man ger'. 'Ain't you that—'

The man from Armani raised both hands in surrender. 'Did I *aks* anyone to fucking translate?'

Both men shut up and Jonelle was given his undivided attention.

'I'm J-Jonelle.' She thought she saw the garbage pile twitch. She took a deep breath of the fetid air to accentuate her accursedly small chest and addressed the big man in the middle. 'I came for a mop. To clean up the dance floor?'

Unable to hold the sting of the stench from the disturbed garbage, she coughed and held her nose. The men's faces showed they were either smelling it too or pissed at finding her there, or both.

'You went *inside* the closet?' he said, counting his words like small change.

'Yes, Mr Maxwell sent me to—'

'Maxwell?'

'Yeah.' She was always telling the children that the word was *yes* not *yeah*.

'Maxwell, sent you back here?'

'Yes, he told me that—'

'Yeah, yeah, yeah, did you go in that cupboard?'

'Mr Maxwell said to reach in.'

'You touch anything?'

She looked down at the mop and pail by her feet and pointed.

'Seen anyone or anything weird goin' on in here?'

'No,' Jonelle shook her head and looked at each of the men with him. 'Nothing weird, sir.'

The big chest on the big man heaved a sigh and he pointed down at her feet. 'Pick up the fuckin' mop and fuck off.'

Jonelle grabbed the mop and noticed, too late, that dried bits dangled from it. She felt their eyes follow her to the door and did her best to ignore the trash pile where the girl had disappeared.

'Go get Maxwell!' she heard and looked round at Mr Big.

'Forget something?'

'Oh, I thought you said—' Jonelle shivered and almost dropped the bucket and mop as she hurried away. The door was closing behind her when she heard them talking.

'Think she saw anyfink, sir?'

'How the fuck should I fuckin' know? Go turn off the alarm and get Maxwell in here!'

Jonelle shut the door fully and strode away, aware of her chest pounding out of time with the booming bass rocking the dance floor, into the arrival area.

'Oi, what took you so long?' Maxwell was tapping his toes at her.

'There was no light in the closet and—'

'What did I tell you? *Reach in!*' said the barrel of sweat. 'Everything's right by the damn door. Christ! Ask people to do the simplest thing. Get over to the bar and clean that shit up and get back here. I ain't paying you for doing fuck all.'

Jonelle stamped through the scattering crowd until she came to a clearing among the revellers and a messy asterisk soaking into a wet patch of carpet.

Great. That mess was no spilt drink.

Jonelle did not do sick. She shot a death-glance towards Maxwell and spotted him being led away by Tweedledee or it could have been the Dum one.

Long before a mop, she needed a shovel. No way was she going back to that place, so she'd have to improvise with the mop and pail to first deal with the solids.

Whatever was going on here was not worth the five quid an hour plus tips, even with Myrna paying back the minicab fare. *And who was that frightened young girl and where'd she gone...into the club?*

Jonelle zigzagged the revolting slop towards the toilets.

The barn door of a man she'd dubbed The Boss stood by the counter. She felt his eyes studying her from behind his dark glasses.

'Leave it over there by the door, gyal, and get back to doin' dese coats!' His voice was low, like thunder that warned of an approaching storm. Its clarity chopped right through the music.

'This will stink up your club, yeah?' Jonelle shouted, lifting the swilling bucket and hunting for any excuse to quit for home: migraine, sudden onset of a period, a mystery virus, anything to end this madness.

'Move your arse, then!' He motioned towards the loos. 'Dump it and get back here, pronto! And no sticking that pretty nose where it don't belong. Might lose it, you feel me?'

'You know, I've got a migraine,' Jonelle started but in mid-flow a big voice slammed across 'migraine'.

'Hey, Bull,' someone called out, bashing into Jonelle. She dropped the mop and the puke slopped about in the bucket. 'Sorry, dahlin'! Phew, man, that's rank!'

Avoiding her like leprosy, the dapper dude circled her and continued his trajectory towards the bossman she presumed was still watching her.

Jonelle snatched a glance at the leggy black woman following him close at heel, and had enough time to feel pity for her, with her perfect hair and make-up, obviously well earned by favours dutifully rendered as she strutted by, clutching her purse with gloved hands and a sneer pasted on her lips. Proud that she had never sold herself for any man's favours, Jonelle continued on her way with the self-assurance of a woman whose welfare and destiny had never, and would never, depend on some penis-touting individual, even if he were handsome.

'I'm busy, TK,' she overheard the big man boom.

'Yeah, I know, but I brought you a new customer. All the way from Bristol, she is. Chelsea Lav—'

'I said I'm busy, TK.'

'Okay, don't ruffle your Armani. Prunes in da hous'?'

'Am I his fuckin' secretary?'

It was all she heard as Jonelle carefully retrieved the mop and continued towards the 'Toylits'. A sea of held noses and averted eyes parted to give her passage. Jonelle found an empty cubicle in the 'Ladys' and was soon flushing away someone's idea of a good night.

Losing mop and bucket to the nearest corner, Jonelle lathered soap into her hands surprised at how quickly the lemon freshness she had left there earlier had been displaced by the odour of piss and puke. The door opened and she watched the leggy woman she had seen with the punter that Mr Bigshit had called TK.

Instinctively, Jonelle smiled as their eyes met, but the woman responded with a sullen tilt of the head, as though looking down from atop a six-inch perch. She tottered past the cubicle where Jonelle had discarded the contents of the bucket, selecting the only other convenience.

Legs Unlimited pressed against the door.

It swung open.

'Jesus!'

Her exclamation made Jonelle spin round and rush to her side. Standing together, they stared intently into the cubicle and then at each other.

'Oh shit,' they said in unison.

# CHAPTER 3

Chelsea Laverne peered out the limo window at the rain pelting the pavement and pounding passing vehicles, glad that they were well away from that awful little club. She magicked herself back to her Bristol flat to stand under her power shower and loofah herself clean. Her clothes, her skin, everything ponged. Chanel No 5 meets 'Grilla No 1.

'Wassup, madame, rain bothering you? Bet Bristol is wetter than this, yeah?'

'TK, how many times must I say not to call me that?'

'Cool! Sorry! But tell me why'd we have to run out like somebody'd shouted fire? 'Grilla's the funkiest spot, up and down town, Cee! See how many *peeps* were pouring in? Just not 'Grilla policy to turn punters away, nahumsayin?'

The sign read Croydon Town Centre, left. He hung a right and eased the borrowed vehicle along the deserted thoroughfare.

She felt hemmed in suddenly by the space around her and wanted to open the window, except it would wet the luxurious upholstery. She still felt all those eyes, watching, studying, boring into her, regarding her like a misplaced apostrophe, gawking like she was naked and covered in bleeding boils. The personal shopper at Harvey Nicks had recommended the stylish burgundy blouse, pinstriped pencil skirt and stilettos. Harrods had done her hair and make-up. So why all those sideways glances and whispers behind cupped hands?

The last straw had been when she'd gone to powder her nose only to be confronted by a cynical smirk from a cleaner...and that young girl...squatting over a bowl...cowering... clutching her rags... It was awful and then a tiny grey foot flopped out.

Chelsea squirmed in her seat.

'Y'okay back there?'

Was it even real? Was any of it?

'Chelsea? Want me to pull over?'

'No, I'm... I'm fine!' Her words were like grit in her dry throat. She struggled to swallow. It was the Coutts Bank business pitch all over again, when they'd quizzed her on why she was as good as any of her male-dominated rivals at computerising their systems.

'Told you to let me get you a Coke before you made us run out of the place, Chelsea.'

'At £2.50, TK?' The words chipped at her throat.

'So?'

'I saw them serving up half a plastic cup, TK.'

'Room for ice, Chelsea.'

'Ice at £10, TK. It was just ice?'

'Ah, now that's where you missed it, Cee. There's ice and there's *ice*, y'see? Vodka ice is a tenner. Bacardi ice is *only* £5.50.'

'And ice-ice?' the frog in her throat coughed.

'Who wants to waste good money on ice-ice?' He laughed and looked away from the road for a second.

'TK, they should just sell Coke with your ice-ice or else cocktails – not force people to buy warm drinks and pay extra for ice, any ice. I bet they turned up the heating too.'

'Yeah, it was *hot* in there, wasn't it? Not from heating though.'

Was he salivating? Over a mob of writhing bodies, plumes of cheap perfume and aftershave mixed with sweat and alcoholic breath? She felt she deserved a medal for staying as long as she had. The 'Ladys' – the only place where they'd made an effort – seemed a haven, that is, until the unpleasantness.

'There was no aircon, TK.' If not for his inhospitable demeanour, she might have complained to that behemoth of a man who brought back memories of Shakespeare's *Pericles*, where she'd read 'the great ones eat up the little ones'. But TK had called him 'Bull', not 'Whale', as he stood there, imposing, scowling with attitude, as would she, if she had to work in such heat. And the hammering noise. Did the music, if music it was, need to be so loud? 'And what on earth was *that* dance, TK?'

'You never did a little BnG? Bump and Grind… You never do the *Bogel*?'

Chelsea snugged back into the suede sedan seat. She leaned forward to rub her ankle, which she'd rolled while being led out of the club back to TK's precious 1982 Lincoln Continental. It was a wonder it was even there when they'd got back.

'Dance's got fashion just like clothes, nahumsayin? Take the Moonwalk – and MJ wasn't the first Moonwalker by the way… and…you can't Moonwalk through a Reggae One-Drop…'

Only half listening, her eyes fell on the tawdry wristband glowing in the dark. They had insisted on shackling her with the unfashionable item in that dank little place. Chelsea tugged hard and rubbed her freed wrist.

'*Bogel* is the fashion now – you need good knees and a limbo back, man… Strick-ly BnG, me. You see how wild it got when Eek-A-Mouse came on? I got it, y'know. Want me make you a mixtape?'

'No. I'm good. Thanks.'

'Something's up with you. Tell me. If you don't want me to call you "madame" again?'

'You dare!'

'Okay, is it because we didn't find my man Prunes for you?'

'Not really.' She felt ungrateful. TK would give his back teeth to help if she let him. Admittedly, being immersed in the hubbub and writhing crowd had awoken something inside her, something indescribably primal.

'Chelsea, 'Grilla's invitation only and only word of mouth will tell you where and when. Last month there was a wicked 'Grilla in a huge container. Can you imagine it? Once, they did one in a boarded-up block of council flats in East London.'

'Ridiculous. How can anyone run a successful business on that basis?'

TK's shoulders jiggled with laughter as he checked his mirrors and pulled over for an ambulance to wail on by.

'Anyway, Bull gets full house every time; no advertising, no overheads and a shit load o' tax-free. Thing is, Prunes's always there, either chatting up the ladies or wheeling deals, nahumsayin'?'

'What if they had to cancel, TK?'

TK was checking the traffic, easing the limo away from the kerb.

She persisted, 'Fine, I may not be streetwise like you, but what if there was a fire? I would imagine that no one even checks that the numbers comply with fire regs. And why was there a young girl in the toilets carrying—'

Chelsea stopped because TK went suddenly silent.

'Young girl? What young girl?'

'Never mind.' Chelsea pushed it all far from her mind, unwilling to have him guffawing, yet again, at her apparent ignorance of the way of life he was clearly more accustomed to. Was that not why she had enlisted his help getting around London, that is, agreed to his insistence that he was the best man she could ever want to show her around?

'Okay, okay, there was young girls all over the place and – yes – some of them might be underage but it's Bull's business, Cee. Never wise to ask questions when it comes to Bull, nahumsayin'? Still, tonight was a weird one—'

'How so?'

'The place was too…what's the word?' A few seconds' thought and he came up with, 'nice'.

Reluctantly, Chelsea mentally revisited the building that looked like someone's bad idea gone wrong; the burly bouncer, the clogged entrance, the tick of a man swiping coats and hats off customers who were then being herded into what looked like a cavernous mouth that belched rank hot air and boomed big noises to pound the chest and assault the ears, and the beast that TK called Bull, who she thought might be better dubbed as Boar. No, 'nice' was not how she would have described a single thing.

'You think Bull could be your blood, Chelsea?'

Lightning cracked the night sky. Thunder followed overhead, so close it seemed to roll right over the bonnet of the limo.

'Christ!' TK jumped and braked hard. 'Sorry, Chelsea! Thought we'd been hit then for sure.'

Her body tingled as she rearranged herself in the seat. The sudden light had startled her but not as much as TK's suggestion.

Bull?

Her brother?

'You don't know this, Cee, but 'Grilla was meant to be in Purley tonight…odd that. Last minute, they switched. That's never happened before. Good thing I had my pager on.'

'Technology to the rescue, yes?'

'You'd say that. Admit it, Chelsea, you loved it, really.'

Yes, she had suffered something inexplicable when she found herself immersed in the dingy urban scene, not unlike discovering a dusty heirloom at the bottom of a box in an attic.

'It was certainly an experience, TK. Can't say I'd go again.'

'Don't be like that, Chelsea. First time of anything is always "iffy". Nahumsayin? Next time you'll feel more accepted and like one of the peops.'

It was what her mum had said in her first week in secondary school. Thinking of Mum was always like picking at a scab, making painful memories seep out…the hollow door knock, the sullen officers: *We regret to inform you that Mr and Mrs Laverne were involved in an incident at junction 32 on the Bristol-bound M4.* They'd been out celebrating twenty-six years of marriage in the West End. Four years of grieving had done little to dull the heartache.

'Chelsea?'

'I need a moment, TK.' Chelsea interlaced her fingers and bowed her head. Her counsellor had given her a mantra. *Give yourself time. Don't look back as you move forward. Time heals.* It worked. Sometimes. Maybe she should have asked him for a mantra to deal with discovering, after your parents' double funeral, that you'd been adopted and were one of—

'Twins.' The word hung on a sigh.

'Whazzat?'

'Nothing, TK…you were saying?'

TK cleared his throat. 'Yeah. Just saying now you're no 'Grilla virgin no more, next time you'll really enjoy yourself, right, babes?'

'TK.'

'Oops, sorry.' He slapped his own face with a free hand.

She huffed, unwilling to repeat her aversion to 'babes', 'baby', 'love', 'madame' and 'miss', in fact, anything that was not her name. She could just about tolerate him calling her Cee as it was, given he had such a big heart.

The limo leaned left into a turn. The signpost read Thornton Heath.

Another clap of thunder made her look. Rainy streaks rolled down the tinted reflection of features constantly awash with riddles about her origins.

'Cheer up, Chelsea. I promise you; we'll find Prunes for sure and get you a London place to rent or buy.'

'Hmm, maybe *word o' mouth* sent him from Purley to Paris?'

'Ha. Nice one, Cee. Nice one.'

'Maybe I should just try another estate agent and—'

'Chelsea, trust me. You walk – you a woman – and a black woman at that – and—'

'And what?'

TK chuckled. 'When it comes to prime real estate in posh neighbourhoods, Cee, it's a white man's world, nahumsayin?'

'TK, you're being so preposterous.'

'Cee, it not pre-pre—'

'Preposterous.'

'I'll put money on it, Cee. One look at you and they'll tell you "you're too late" or "you can't afford it" or some shit.'

'TK, that's not true.'

Had she mentioned it before? No, he could not have known that of the six estate agents she'd phoned, four had invited her to their offices. Of them, two had said she was 'too late', one regretted the seller had withdrawn the property, and the fourth claimed he'd thought she was acting for another before informing her that the property had become embroiled in a divorce dispute and, as such, was off the market.

'They'll say anything to get rid, Chelsea,' TK went on, 'but Prunes, he don't care.'

'And this Prunes character can get me something in Westminster?' she said, thinking that her last two agents may yet prove him wrong on Monday.

'Who? Prunes? West Minister?'

She decided not to correct him.

TK's shoulders bobbed as he danced about in the seat, 'Westminister to Walthamstow, Kensington to Kennington, Hounslow to Hackney…ain't nothing cookin' without Prunes inside.' TK made himself laugh out loud.

*We'll see*, she decided, but kept it to herself.

The Man Upstairs was moving his furniture again. Her dad's face shimmered in her mind and he was pointing upwards. TK chattered on through the rumbling commotion – something about club rivalry in London. Hard rain drummed on the roof of the limo.

She recognised Streatham High Street, and signs pointing the way to Brixton and the West End. London was huge, bigger maybe than the problem she'd left Bristol to solve. Just when she thought she was getting her bearings, she felt more lost than ever.

It was hard to know how she might have coped, without TK, that is. They'd become good friends since that first meeting at Paddington station. She'd been waiting for a minicab when TK'd pulled up into the kerb. She'd jumped in and it was while en route to her destination that he'd laughingly explained that he was not a minicab driver but a Meet and Greet valet who'd swerved to avoid a cyclist when she 'jacked' him. So, using a customer's vehicle, he'd proceeded to both get her to her destination, and convincingly argue that he was the best help in her quest around London to find her brother.

'Man, not even a duck would like being out in this tonight… Anyway, Cee, remember that finding Prunes was *your* fault first of all.'

'No, it so wasn't.' Chelsea fetched a handkerchief from her handbag.

The Lincoln rolled past Woolworths and stopped opposite Brixton tube station.

'You realise,' Chelsea pointed out the window, 'that you've stopped on a zigzag line?'

But he was already sliding in the other door to sit in the back next to her.

'Look, if it wasn't for you, I'd still be grafting for pennies. Instead, I'm getting paid to drive rich people about and collecting big, fat tips in a big-ass shiny Rolls-Royce limo what you leased just for me. I owe you, Chelsea. You need a nice place, the least I can do is put you in touch with a man who won't let you down. That's Prunes.'

'TK, you're parked on a zig—'

'Relax, Chelsea.' He took her handkerchief from her and dabbed gingerly at her mascara. She kept dodging. 'We been scopin' for your missing bro for months now, right. Street by street, lane by lane...what if he was one of them clubbers pilin' into 'Grilla tonight? Y'know how we black guys love checking out the sista shakin' their booty all night long, ever think of that?'

'TK, I've been busy checking electoral rolls and births and deaths. Plus statistics show that more and more people are dropping out of sight onto the streets so...'

'Yeah, I know, I know. That is why you started eliminating homeless men. I get that.'

'No, TK. You don't get it. I'm looking for someone I don't even know still exists...who might not even want to be found. Maybe all my efforts are...are...' She batted away the words 'pointless' and 'impossible' and 'insane'. She snatched back her handkerchief and used it to dab her own eyes. 'A homeless individual is still someone's son, someone else's lost one, TK, and in any case, it feels good to provide warm blue blankets to make up for intruding on their privacy.'

'But, Chelsea, half of them probably sell them blankets for fags or drinks and then you won't know which ones you've—'

'What else should I do, TK? Staple a tag to their ears?' Being on the Oxford University debating team meant she knew when she was losing an argument.

TK's eyes widened as though considering that a viable solution.

She felt heavier on the leather luxury. She'd already contacted a small army of midwives and every major hospital and clinic in the south of England up to the Midlands, interviewed the Red Cross and contacted the Mormons about accessing their records. Then she'd turned her attention to Barnardo's and every organisation dealing with orphans and missing persons. She'd felt maniacal collecting information to cross-reference with electoral rolls. Anything and everything for a single lead in locating the only blood relative she had left.

'Babes?' TK spoke softly and she felt too weary to confront him. 'You're right, I don't really get why you want to find him so much. Shit, I ain't know where any of my family is since my drunk-ass dad chucked me out. But that don't matter, you got me, yeah? You ain't alone.'

'You really think someone at the club could've been…?'

'Why not? Even that guy over there?' TK pointed out the figure hopping off the red double-decker and running for cover in a nearby bus shelter.

'Or that poor sap.' His new target narrowly avoided being run over by a van that lurched, horns blaring.

'And even one of them two.'

Shrouded in rain, the approaching pair fast-walked towards them. They looked ready to break into a run when a sudden scrawl of lightning illuminated a helmet, a checkerboard headband, and the shiny metal on their uniforms.

'Shit! Coppers!' TK slid out the back, slammed the door and jumped in to retake the driver's seat. He gunned the idling engine. A line of traffic rolled up alongside. TK banged the steering wheel. 'Shit. Move it. Fuck! Sorry, Chelsea.'

Through the rear window, Chelsea saw one of the officers speak into a radio.

'I think they're calling for backup, TK.'

'Don't even joke, Chelsea. Points on my licence is no good for me right now…or you.'

'But I warned you,' Chelsea started to say.

The two officers splashed towards them, picking up the pace as TK gunned the engine, but the Brixton traffic was standing still in the downpour with pedestrians dodging through rain and cars to cross.

'Let me in, let me in,' TK pleaded. 'Somebody let me in. Oi, get out the road!'

The two in blue ran right in front of the limo. One held a hand to indicate he should stop right where he was, then they both crossed and were gone in a curtain of sleet.

'Jesus, that was close,' TK said as he eased into a gap in the flow. She could just hear him over the horn blasts.

'You were lucky,' she said.

'What?'

'Never mind.' Chelsea fished in her handbag for the black-and-white picture she carried everywhere. The only baby picture taken of both her parents when she was born, it once brought her great pride and joy. Her dad was smiling like a man who'd just won a million-pound prize and her mum, wet-faced and grinning, was holding the swaddled Chelsea to her bosom. Mum used to say that she was trying to pull her right inside her to keep her safe, forever. Safe from people's lies and deceit, people who would do anything to satisfy their own desires.

She had her dad's eyes, they'd said.

She had her mother's smile, they'd said.

Her milk chocolate complexion, they'd told her, was a blend of his coffee colouring and her creamy Irish skin.

But they'd never once mentioned adoption.

Guilt hounded her for questioning the obvious love that had given so much. Still, she couldn't shake the feeling she'd been lied to all her life, deceived even. The line of all that anchored her had been severed, setting her adrift.

Who am I, really?

Where did I come from?

Why should where she'd come from direct where she was going or where she wanted to be?

Four years searching for answers had only brought more questions.

If only life was as simple as computers, she'd press reset, or reboot, or erase it all by overwriting with better. Yes, she could forget it all. That was always an option and a logical one. Logic was her business, after all. Or else, she could stubbornly persist with doing things properly, tying up loose ends and risking everything, including her sanity.

A tear dripped on her dad's smiling face.

She wiped it dry and tucked the picture away.

'You gone quiet again.'

'Yes. Sorry.' Her mind flashed back to a dark, grimy girl – she looked crazed, maybe thirteen or fourteen years old, if she were a day – cradling a bundle. She'd practically knocked them over, that cleaning woman and her.

'S'okay. Where to now then – we could circle Victoria – lots of homeless shelters by the bus station. Or we could…' TK was looking round at her.

'Red.'

'Wha'?'

'Lights!' Chelsea said, pointing.

The limo screeched to stop just beyond the line. A black cab driver tried to vanquish them with his death-ray stare.

'TK, you're tired. Let me drive.'

'Chelsea, my boss or one of the others catch me using the limo, I can always say you's a customer, nahumsayin? No way I can pull that off if they see you in the driving seat, get me?'

'Yes, yes, but—'

'No buts… So, tell me, do we give out more woolly blankets tonight or—'

'Take me back to the hotel…please.'

He sighed; the way people did when relieved that good sense had prevailed over a situation that defied all logic.

'TK, I *can* do this alone, y'know,' Chelsea said when the silence grew too heavy.

'What did I say?'

'I can't stop looking.'

'Of course not, Cee.'

'You might not know where your family is, but you get to choose to know them. You have no right to make me feel bad about pursuing the slightest possibility I might actually find my only connection to my natural family.'

'Easy, Cee. I never wanted to make you feel—'

'Plus…' she added an emphatic pause which he did not fill. 'You are always talking about karma.'

'Can I ask one question?'

'What is it?'

'Don't bite my head off, but what if this guy ain't bony fido?'

She decided not to correct him.

'Cee, how'd you even prove he ain't fibbin' for your pity and your purse…and what if actually *he's* out there looking for *you*? Nahumsayin?'

'You said one question,' Chelsea reminded him, more irritated by his incessant checking of her comprehension. For Christ's sake, she'd studied English, French and Latin and she programmed computers.

'Well, for sure, he ain't looking for *you* among the litter. Nahumsayin?'

'Shut up. Shut up,' is what she wanted to shout. Could her missing twin be looking for her? Chelsea simmered silently in the seat.

TK prattled on, 'They do say twins have a kind of bond, so maybe there could be some kind of homing signal, you think?'

'Saw it on TV, did you?' Chelsea said.

'Naw, barbershop,' TK said, trying to straighten out of a hairpin bend. 'One of the guys was – uhm – doin' two chicks.

Twins. I won't give any details, but while he was with one, the other...'

'Heard enough, thanks,' Chelsea said, perhaps too softly because he carried on with his story. She tuned out but then she had to tune back in.

'So, I gave them this hypo-threatical situation, yea?'

Chelsea rolled her gaze out the window and stopped herself from correcting him.

Still in full flow, TK leaned them into a left turn. 'Officially, yeah, the whole barbershop thinks that one twin is usually the evil one. I mean, your twin bro might be a banker or a traffic warden or a…a…a pim—!'

'TK! Enough.' Chelsea folded her arms firmly across her lap, squashing the urge to explain that she'd been aware of a sort of second 'consciousness', another 'mind' beside her own, since childhood. She had thought nothing of it and supposed everyone had such thoughts.

Could TK be right? Would she want to find…an evil twin? Ridiculous, she would have known it, felt it somehow. Wouldn't she?

The signs indicated Park Lane ahead. She listened to tyres strumming the tarmac. Chelsea's scalp tingled and began to itch. She sat on her hands so as not to start scratching and swivelled her neck until it cricked. This odd ritual always interrupted the nervous tic triggers whenever anxiety reached danger.

TK cleared his throat. 'Chelsea, you know I'm on your side, yeah?'

She knew but she felt bitter words lingering on her tongue.

TK took them around Marble Arch. He missed the turn to avoid a drunk who'd stumbled off the kerb and took them round again.

'These four years, I pick you up every time you come from Bristol and take you all over London – they say blood is ficker than milk or some'fink… I don't know about that, but I really hate to see you so disappointed so long about the past while the future is passing by, nahumsayin'?'

A pain shot through her head, slicing through what TK was saying.

Chelsea rocked back in the seat.

'You alright, Chelsea?' TK said, slowing down.

'F-fine!' she lied.

'Chelsea?'

'Said I'll be fine.'

'You can't keep pushing.'

'You're right, TK. I've been going about this all wrong and I'm fucking tired, tired of this whole mess! I'm done.'

'Wha'? You can't quit now! Come on, Chelsea. I's just sayin', is all?'

'What?'

'Cee, I told you nuff times you ain't alone...' TK pulled up at the hotel, deftly parking in the spot vacated by a black cab. 'I pick up some big shot from Heathrow at 7 a.m. tomorrow.'

'You mean today.'

'Yeah, laters.'

'TK, that's three hours from now. You've been driving me around all night.'

'Yea-yea-yea, I'll ditch the geezer and come get you, yeah? Nine, good? We'll find Prunes, sort you out a place, then get you back to Paddington in time for you to catch your train to Bristol, nahumsayin'?'

# CHAPTER 4

PC Brendon Bailey sprinted around the limo, wishing he could stop and give the idiot a ticket. Who was this with the balls to park on zigzag lines only yards from Brixton police station? The traffic reacted to his hand, and they were soon full pelt through the tube station alley.

His partner, WPC Murphy, matched him stride for stride with her radio to her ear. She updated dispatch with an ETA of eight minutes.

They emerged onto Atlantic Road when a barefooted figure darted from view. A bedraggled individual, about four feet tall, scrawny, possibly female, possibly carrying stolen goods. London was full of runaways trying to survive on the streets, but there was no stopping – not to write parking tickets nor investigate shifty vagrants.

'Keep up, mate!' Murphy had somehow got three strides on him.

They splish-splashed to arrive within six minutes. Murphy's tunic rose and fell with her heaving chest and he tucked his sweaty shirt back in as they looked for someone in charge.

Scene of Crime Officers were already swarming. Some were wrapping the area in yellow tape. One of the SOCOs indicated a front door where PM Thatcher was handing over a child to the officer on guard. Told to use the lift, as it had already been checked, they got to the seventh floor.

Lightning lit the corridor where they waited. Still breathing hard, Bailey remembered his first flat in Birmingham was in a place like this one. A smell of rum, weed and talc wafted out, along with a sickly sweetness he associated with death.

Tell-tale clicks and flicks of light highlighted where some poor bastard – two by all accounts – posed dead-still for cameras recording their demise.

'You okay?' he said breathlessly.

'Yes.' Murphy's tone made him wonder whether he had asked her bra size by mistake.

The detective sergeant rushed over from where he'd been standing with the senior investigating officer. Behind his back, Murphy always referred to him as a misogynistic prick, the DS that is, not the SIO, perhaps because he pronounced her name in a funny accent, so it came out 'Muff-E'. Still, the lads said the DS was not that bad, seeing that, on pub nights, his wallet was in the right place. Bailey decided to reserve judgement.

'Muff-E, that's a fine example you're setting for the new boy – dripping all over the fucking crime scene,' he spluttered, with barely a truncheon width between his mouth and the tip of her nose.

'Coming down stair rods out there, Sarge.' Bailey inched forward.

'SIO wants a team out doing house-to-house for witnesses or anyone who might know something. That's you two. Get going and stay sharp – the buggers may still be in the area. Do not, I repeat, do not engage with them on your own. Got it?'

'Yes, Sarge,' Bailey said.

'Muff-E?'

'Yes, Sarge.'

'Get going then and keep your radio on and hands off each other. Might be two or three assailants, armed. No heroics!'

'Yes, Sarge,' Bailey said to the man's back. Murphy was already waiting in the lift.

From one shocked household to another, Bailey and his partner discovered that nobody'd seen or heard anything. Murphy was convinced some were holding back information along with their tempers and rottweilers. At last the rain abated and a hole tore open in the clouds to let the moonlight stream through. Water dripped from guttering, overhead wires and their helmets and gurgled into drains as they knocked on door after bolted door. Rounding the corner onto the next street, the only real sign of life or wakefulness was coming from throbbing music, halfway down.

'Christ. Tis a wonder anyone can sleep through all that!' Murphy felt for her truncheon and tightened her belt.

'There,' Bailey said.

'What?'

'You said *tis*.'

'No, I didn't.'

'Fine, but I think *tis* cute.'

'Don't you start, an' all!' Murphy adjusted her hat and lifted her chin to make the best of her height, another touchy subject until he'd reminded her that the revered Yvonne Fletcher, the WPC killed on duty outside the Libyan Embassy five years ago, was also five feet two.

'Bailey, it's a Brixton party. We need more officers!'

'It'll be alright. These're *my* people. Besides we only want to ask a few questions, not pick a fight. Let me do all the talking.'

She gave him one of her stares.

'Look, the first sign of trouble, we call for assistance, like the sarge said.' He crossed himself.

She adjusted her hat and said, 'Fine.'

They advanced towards the music.

Bailey's feet ached, the cold air chilled his face and he felt eyes studying them.

A group of lads sat along the low brick wall, like crows on a fence. Their loud chatter died away as the officers approached, but they kept puffing smoke into pungent clouds.

'Shit, nobody said this gig was a fuckin' *pig* roast!'

'Evening, *cuntstable*, dis guy's got a big concealed weapon just fi you!'

Party people hung from windows, fanning their faces. Some started shouting:

'Oi, I know who shot *the deputy!*'

'That a truncheon or you fancying your partner, bro?'

'I'm cautioning you, girl: once you go *black*, ain't no going *back*.'

Another heckler asked to borrow their handcuffs and Bailey heard another call to Murphy, recognising she was cold. 'Come get something hot inside you, Officer.'

'Keep ignoring them, Murphy.' Bailey looked down from his six-foot height. 'They're trying to get a rise and impress their mates.'

'Can handle myself, thanks,' she said, coolly.

The music led them up a short path from the pavement to a half-open front door. After three increasingly loud knocks, a very large woman bounded out of the door, grabbed him and yanked him in over the threshold.

'Oh, dahlin'! Why you so late? Never mind that. Everyone waiting. Come show we the goods!'

'Ma'am, you might have the wrong—'

She looked him up and down. 'Wrong? No, no, no, you're alright, dahlin', just kept us waiting a bit long. Just come inside! Get your kit off!' she squealed and threw her arms around him.

'Ma'am, I'm not a stripper,' PC Bailey said, prising himself from her arms as a pile-up of excited eyes, bountiful hips and overflowing busts gradually clogged the tiny hall behind the woman.

'You want more money first?' Her eyes ran him up and down. 'Well, you're late so it all depends on what you're packing, eh, girls?'

There was cheering and Bailey thought he heard Murphy say something before he felt her tugging his tunic.

He stepped away from the woman and her leering group. Murphy inserted herself between Bailey and them.

'Madam, he's *not* a stripper and neither am I,' she said loud and clear, 'we're real police! On official business. We have a few questions to ask you and your guests. You listeneing? We're on official business.'

The woman at the door now swayed like a palm tree in a hurricane. ''Fishal binniz? What kinda 'fishal binniz? Somebody say the music too loud? Bob Marley not loud! Reggae is good music.'

'No, no, you don't understand, ma'am.' Murphy swept a wisp of blonde hair off her face.

'You calling me *stoopid*?'

'Nobody's calling anyone stupid,' Bailey said, swapping places with Murphy.

'Alleloo-yah!' the shriek cut across the scene. 'At last, the stripper's here!'

Heavy drumming grew louder and the hall of people cleared a path.

'Myrna, no! No, Myrna!' Bailey heard someone yell as he saw a figure barrel towards him and take flight. Instinct or reflex, he opened his arms as if to catch a small child. The impact knocked all the wind out of him and sent him reeling.

Sandwiched between the two women, Bailey pushed the larger off him, worried that his partner may have broken more than their fall.

While everyone laughed and pointed, the woman who had answered the door complained angrily that they had ruined her party. She helped Myrna off Bailey and wagged a finger at her. 'I was trying to tell you he ain't no stripper.'

'No?'

'No, they's *lice*...po-*lice*!'

'You alright?' Bailey helped Murphy to her feet and retrieved her hat and his helmet.

'Think so. You?' Murphy dusted off her uniform, replaced her hat and tucked her hair away.

'What a waste,' the flying woman said, and her meaty hand reached forward to stroke his cheek. Bailey backed away into something solid as a wall.

'Watch it!' the wall grumbled behind him.

Bailey turned to look up into the face of a goliath in dark glasses.

'Sorry, mate!' said Bailey quickly, overhearing Murphy warning someone that they could be facing a charge of 'assaulting an officer'.

The wall lumbered along into the party. Six others followed him, sturdy men except for the one limping with the ill-shapen paunch and reeking of talc, but this was not the strangest thing Bailey noticed.

Eddy Grant enticed dancers to his Electric Avenue and beyond and stampeded away. The door slammed shut. The two officers swapped looks.

Bailey banged the door with his truncheon until the woman he decided was the host reappeared.

'Oh, you again?'

'Ma'am, there's been a serious crime nearby.'

'Fine, fine, we'll turn the music down and—'

'Look, we don't care about your music or your party. There's been a crime and we're conducting a house-to-house enquiry. You or your guests may have seen something unusual tonight,' Bailey said.

The woman looked them up and down. Murphy stepped forward, pad in hand. Bailey looked on.

'Are you the occupant of this house?' Murphy said.

'Why you want to know?' She looked away at Bailey as though he was asking the question. 'Alright. This is my place, but I don't see why—'

'Your name, please.' Murphy scribbled as though she was writing both the questions and the answers. He knew that was exactly what she was doing.

'Don't tell them nothing, Jacinth!' someone shouted from inside.

As his partner extracted the woman's full name, Bailey peered in the open door. He couldn't see the men who had entered, not even the huge man he had backed into. Though not a frequent visitor to house parties, it still seemed odd to him that seven black men would arrive together, all wearing dark glasses.

No bag of clinking bottles and clunk of cans.

No smokes, not even a whiff of a spliff. Of course, they may have seen the uniforms and ditched anything dodgy. Talc and carbolic soap hung in their wake so they could simply have been a hunting pack looking for man-hungry women. They'd come to the right place.

Murphy waving her pen at the woman. 'You do realise we could charge you with obstruction if you do not allow us to ask each of your guests whether they saw anything suspicious tonight, Miss Morgan?'

'Look, dahlin',' she said, looking past Murphy at Bailey. 'We all jus' minding our own *binizz*, here. And it is missus, not miss? I'm a widow, y'see.'

She stepped closer to Bailey, fluttering her eyelids. 'To tell the truth, I do my best thinkin' in the marnin'...maybe you could come back later? Aroun' eleven? I cook us some ackee and saltfish and dumplins – nobody make better johnny cakes than me in the whole—'

'Thank you, ma'am.' Murphy shut and stuffed her notepad away with her pen. 'We best go, Bailey.'

'How disrespec'ful!' said the woman, muscled arms akimbo.

Bailey followed Murphy down the path. Out of earshot, she said what he'd suspected all along that, cooperative or not, half those people were off their faces and the others were higher than the London rents he'd been quoted, since his move from up north.

Brendon Bailey looked back at the house. 'We really should have talked to those seven men that came late.'

'What seven men?' Murphy asked.

# CHAPTER 5

Bull looked away from the office window at his watch. At 5 a.m., he'd expected the boys to have returned ages ago.

How long does it take to kill a man, anyway?

What if they'd failed? May as well kill themselves.

Bull patted his breast pocket and felt the shape of his P22. Insurance. His passport was there too, in the name of Dirk Manners, with a picture he'd thought his mother would have been proud of. He'd planned to show it to her on his long-awaited visit to Spanish Town, which some barbershop nutter had tried to convince him was once the capital of Jamaica. Fool. Still, until then he'd sent his ma some moolah every month and, twice a year, Christmas and Easter, he'd sent barrels bulging with clothes and shoes of various sizes as he had no idea about her actual measurements. Either way, she could make extra cash from selling whatever did not fit.

That was a lifetime ago, and Bull concerned himself with very different shipments these days. Some people didn't like the way he did business. Fuck 'em. There was his way and there was dead and, inspired by Margaret Thatcher, Bull was 'not for turning'. Democracy was a nuisance. Of course, a few fuckers who had other ideas were now fertilising the riverbed beneath Putney Bridge. These days, and nights too, the Peckham posse knew to show him and his Yardie crew respect, as did gangs from Hackney to Slough. But disloyalty, that he couldn't bear, it was fuckin' bad manners.

'Sir,' said the burly bouncer, heaving for breath after two flights of stairs.

'What is it?'

'We've a situation at the door, sir. It's Mr Williams.'

Tyrone Williams was an itch out of reach.

As he descended, Bull caught sight of the writhing crowd. Even at this time, people were bulging into the converted corrugated warehouse to swell the numbers. His mind raced back to his *business* trip to the fatherland, or *Jamdown* as they called it over there, where the dance halls slapped arse all night. Yeah. During his visit, he'd bounced with a crew that took him to catch river crabs in Clarendon one time. He'd been happy standing back with a Red Stripe for company, watching them scramble after the little critters, loading them into their car trunks. Later, they were stuffed into big tin pots and boiled to death before arriving all finger-lickin' on his plate. In fact, it was the same riffraff who had sucked crabmeat with him then that now formed his Yardie gang that looked after his respect. Until tonight, they were led by his most trusted general-turned-stinking-traitor.

'Look at them,' Bull thought, surveying the club below him, 'all them suckers all clambering over one another like crabs. Ready to scratch, claw and trample anyone, whether *mother-father-cousin-friend*, to get out of the fuckin' pot.'

His eyes finally located Tyrone Williams, a man born for the pot. Yes, having a pop-up club had been Tyrone's idea, but the guy had too many damn 'sensibilities' to do what it took to keep from becoming crab juice. Now there he stood again, clawing for a taste of the good life and being a fuckin' pain in the arse.

'Tyrone, wassup!'

'Bull, tell these meatheads to let me in, will you?' said the wiry Tyrone, backing away as though he'd got his face slapped.

'Got no time for you tonight, Ty.'

'Bull, I heard you was havin' a 'Grilla here but I had to see for m'self,' Tyrone looked around them at the building. 'Ain't this the place I found, back when we was partners? We was gonna turn it into a permanent 'Grilla, the club of clubs. When did you start fixing it up? And without tellin' me?'

'Don't need your fuckin' permission, Tyrone.' The bastard was right, they used to be partners, it was the same building and they did talk about a permanent 'Grilla. 'Point is we ain't no partners and this ain't none of your damn business no more, aight?'

'You used to *aks* my advice, Bull, and—'

'*Used to*, Tryone. Used to!' Way back. It had also been Tyrone's idea to provide club staff with ID – a piece from the same jigsaw puzzle to avoid infiltration – and to bump up the takings by selling ice, some specially made with watered-down alcohol.

'Bull, where'd you be without me?' Tyrone leant back on a steel support like he belonged. 'We was goin' to work together. Remember?'

'Hist'ry, bro. I grow up and you're still…well…not welcome here no more.'

'Why can't I come in, pay my way like any other punter and have a good time?'

'Think I don't know you're setting up a new club…what's it? The Gordon? No, the Gorgon.' The surprise on Tyrone's face was a picture. Word on the street was that he had somehow negotiated change of use of some shithole in the West End and was doing it up for clubbing, with dancing girls. 'Think you can compete with 'Grilla, eh?'

'Bull, I don't know what—'

In one movement, Bull grabbed his shirt and pulled him so close their noses touched. 'Go on, Tyrone. Let me shove that sentence back down your fucking throat. Think you can screw with me and tout your business here, you fuck?'

'Trouble, Mr Manners?'

Not recognising the voice, Bull tossed Tyrone aside like a sack of rubbish.

'Who the hell might you be?'

The besuited man with his briefcase was like a bank manager that had crossed him a while back who, now that they were on 'friendly' terms, always approved Bull's loans and served tea and biscuits whenever Bull visited his office.

'I'm here to check on the packages.'

'Hmm, I see.' Bull felt a little weak at the knees suddenly. He had expected this clown but not until Monday night, the day before delivery. He had to think fast.

Bull beckoned to the bouncer on the door.

'Take this gentleman to Maxwell. Tell him to personally escort him to my office and get him whatever he wants to drink. I'll be there in ten.'

'Make it five, Mr Manners. I have more stops and I hate to be late. Not professional, to be late or forget people are coming to see you, you understand?'

'Of course!' Bull said, keeping his chin high and puffing his chest. 'I'll be there in five. Make yourself comfortable.'

Soon as the man was out of earshot, Bull turned to Tyrone who was busy brushing muck and rust off his cheap suit.

'Tyrone, piss off. Get it into your tiny head, we're finished.'

'But, Bull, we bought this place together. My share is tied up in this and you bought it in my name and—'

'Well, I'm fucking buying you out, nigger! You ain't welcome round here no more, aight?'

'But, Bull.'

'Tyrone, I catch you near me again, bro, I'm gonna have to hurt you? Bad. Feel me? And if I hear of even one of my dancers playing at your club, Tyrone… Yeah, I know you been chatting up my bitches, fool! Now fuck off outta here!'

It was a loose end Bull already had plans to tie up and the crab Tyrone was not clever enough to see it. Now he had one more to dispatch and headed for his office, in no hurry.

*Not professional?* Shit, who did that low-life suit think he was anyway?

In his office, Bull settled behind his desk and eyed his unexpected visitor. It occurred to him that even in the dark underworld where any man, through violence, strength and wit, could determine his own destiny, a black man was still a mere messenger, and that messenger was regarding him with a look he didn't appreciate. Bull guessed he was probably pissed that he had been back in seven and not five. Fuck him.

'So,' Bull said, offering the messenger one of his top-grade Havanas and watching him reject it like a pile of shit-green wine gums. 'Fine by me, let's cut the shit and get down to business! What do I call you then?'

'I am nobody, Mr Manners. But you, you're out of your depth.'

'Outta my depth?' Bull thought him lucky they were in private, as there was no way he would have allowed him to speak like that before his Yardies.

'What I'm here to tell you – now *that* is important. So, clean your ears: my employers are expecting exactly forty packages?'

'Yes, on Tuesday. It's all agreed.' Bull felt his knuckles itch.

'And, you'll have it ready on time?' He looked up from the paperwork.

Bull put on his best poker face, his unblinking eyes bulged with equal measures of proud confidence and high-grade contempt.

'Fine, Mr Manners, but you do seem a little uncertain.'

'Forty packages. By Tuesday. That's the deal.'

'Indeed.'

'And my money? My two hundred thou'?'

The man calmly closed his case, looking at Bull in a way that no one who enjoyed pissing without pain should.

'Yes, your money… Mr Manners, may I be candid?'

'Sure,' Bull said.

'Look, I'll make it simple for you,' the man went on. Bull shifted forward to the edge of the seat. His neck veins boiled, his jawbone clenched and he felt his own breath puff hot across his forearms. 'My employers are a bit nervous right now. Between you and me, they think you can't deliver quality and on time. Too many screw-ups.'

'Screw-ups?' Bull stood and banged on the desk.

'Yes. Screw. Ups,' Mr No-Name said in a clipped manner. 'Now then,' he pointed at his watch. 'Sit…down.'

Did he think he was Barbara fuckin' Woodhouse training a dog? Bull, battling the urge to teach him some heavy manners, reminded himself that this crab was only the fucking messenger. Bull sat down.

At the same time, No-Name stood up. He tugged creases from his jacket. Bull smiled briefly at the man's bulging pecs, thinking he'd seen chickens with bigger.

'I think it's you that should cut the shit! You're in the big leagues, Mr Manners. My people pick their teeth with people like you. Play your cards right, they make you King Rat! Mess up, and – well, there's always someone who can take your place. So, what's it going to be, brotha?'

Brotha? The word was a lie coming from his mouth – disrespectful and bloody insulting. Bull reared up to his full height and struck out. His boxing coach at Barnardo's had clocked his punch at an impressive 28 mph slamming a punch bag. The calloused knuckles stopped inches short. The rush of air must have fluttered No-Name's nose hairs and yet the man did not flinch.

'Who do you fucking think you're dealing with?'

'*We*, Mr Manners, know exactly who we're dealing with. You are a man who offers Havanas, but keeps the best Jamaican tobacco for himself; a man who hates ice in his Johnnie Walker Black Label; a man who never sleeps without his watch on and favours laying on his front; who loves fucking women who don't shave. You always use your left hand when wanking in the shower and you only do this on Saturday nights; the only person to beat you in arm-wrestling now ties his laces single-handed; your father was—'

'Awright – made your fuckin' point!' Retracting his fist, Bull rocked back and walked over to stand by the window. 'I don't know who you been talking to, but don't think 'cause you know shit you can intimidate Bull Manners, aight?'

Bull looked out at where the dawn sky was spitting on the glass. Up the street, a red double-decker passed the bus stop, ignoring a waving couple and momentarily blocking his view of the street-girls with their brollies aloft in a sort of 'Up yours!' salute to the gathering storm.

'Mr Manners, how you run your...' he wrinkled his nose as though searching soiled linen, '*organisation*, shall we say?'

Bull scratched at the floor, holding back the urge to eject the man out the nearest window, or wall, come to that.

'Point is, the details are your – uhm – business, Manners. My job is to ensure you deliver forty packages on Tuesday. All healthy, fully prepared and travel ready...as agreed... Understood, brotha?'

Bull kept the four runaways hidden way-way back in his mind and far from his eyes...as well as the one they still thought was hiding out in the club somewhere. The forced relocation of the 'packages' had swept their plain-sailing operation straight into shit creek, thanks to that traitor.

'Like you said, it's for me to know, brotha,' Bull mimicked the crab.

'Good, good…then my business here is done,' he said. Bull watched him rise to his feet, ready to fuck off.

'And as you know so fuckin' much, why don't you find your own damn way out?' he was going to say when his unwelcomed visitor butted in. 'Before I go, Mr Manners,' he said, calmly threading one arm into a cashmere sleeve and lining up the other sleeve. 'There's been one small *amendment* to our deal. Of course you don't have to accept it if it is too much for you – only means we will take our money elsewhere and find some more capab—'

'Cut the shit! What's the fucking *amendment*?'

'Well, it means an extra twenty grand to you, though I personally doubt you will be able to bring home the bacon – no offence.'

As he fished an envelope from his briefcase, jabbering on, Bull worked out that, sliced and diced, he could fit the guy completely inside the damn thing and still close the lid. Of course, he would have to find somewhere else to put all that shit – he was so full of it!

'Did you hear a word I said, Mr Manners?'

Bull swiped the envelope and stood toe-to-toe, eye-to-eyeball and mimicked him: '*This special order is unlike the others. Not as young. Won't need a carer. You deliver on time, with the right details on the right documentation and the extra twenty grand will be in your* – that is – *my account.* Now, you tell me, did I hear a fuckin' word you said or wot?'

# CHAPTER 6

Jonelle felt shagged and not in a good way. After her evening of essay writing, followed by the nightmare of a night covering sick Myrna's 'Grilla job, what did she have to show for it after she'd paid out for the return taxi fare? She'd not even been able to take in the fine music, not with Maxwell barking 'fetch-this-clean-that' every two minutes. She'd got home soaking wet at 3:30 a.m. only to go fetch the kids three and a half hours later from Candice's.

Air brakes hissed loudly by her and the kids, as a passing truck paused to belch a plume of exhaust fumes before moving on in the relentless traffic.

'Bloody hell,' she stopped herself from saying, waiting with her three on the kerb.

'Amanita, hold your sister's hand.'

'But she won't let me take her hand, Mummy!'

'I can walk by myself, Mummy,' Kenyana said, with that self-willed pout of hers.

'Then you can forget about that My Little Pony lunchbox you wanted.'

Still pouting, Kenyana grabbed her sister's hand.

'Ow!'

Coldharbour Lane looked like someone had woken up long before her and washed it down with dirty water, but this was not all that left Jonelle wanting to scrub herself clean. Barely able to see the newsstand over at Miss Mattie's corner shop, she read the morning's headline and sighed within herself.

'Police baffled by local double murder!'

Jonelle studied for a safe break in the traffic and her mind flicked back to the ordeal of working at 'Grilla. Who was that girl? And what was in the bundle she'd held as though it were a baby?

*I changed my mind. Don't hurt me. Don't hurt me.*

Her tortured voice repeated on her like onions, but without that taste she loved and the embarrassing wind.

Tyrone came to mind.

Still looking left and right, she wished the lights at least would hurry up and stem the flow of traffic. Amanita was still fussing with Kenyana.

'Look, Mummy, a butterfly!' Suddenly Deen pulled free of Jonelle's hand and ran into the road.

'Deen!'

She heard the screech before she saw the black cab and the world was set to slow motion. Jonelle jumped into the road, her chest pounding with fright. She had no idea at all how she managed to yank Deen out of harm's way in time.

'Stupid bitch!' the fist-waving driver spluttered. 'Shouldn't keep pushin 'em out if you can't bloody look after 'em.'

Had she heard right?

'I'm sorry, Mummy?' Deen's big eyes filled up.

A limo tooted from behind, urging the cab to get a move on, but the traffic light had turned red.

'We can cross now, Mummy,' Kenyana called, leading the way.

Still shaking, Jonelle followed the mélange of smells that never failed to transport her to market days as a child. She led her children down aisles of bananas, sweet potatoes and yams, breadfruit, various mangos, avocados unlike any found in supermarkets as her children were probably tired of hearing, plantains (no, Deen, you have to cook them first), and stalls of sheep's guts, pigs' trotters, oxtail and bulls' testicles.

'Hey, Jonelle, look what I got for you!'

'Can't stop, Ken,' she said, not daring to look in the direction of all the excitement. Mr Music, as she sometimes called Ken, never failed to make her compromise her shopping list, only to be filled with bitter-sweet regret and have to rob Peter to pay Paul, as her mother used to gripe back in the day.

Oh shit, she was turning into her mother!

Quickening her pace, Jonelle took the lead, taking the children past Brixton station as a train rumbled along overhead. Water, or worse, dripped on her as they went under the archway at Pope's Road, into another section of the market.

Even at this distance, it was clear the salt-and-pepper-headed little man with a propensity for desiccated plums and raisins and an oversized ego was absent without leave. The rumour mill spun out that Prunes had a finger in every pie and cowpat. Today he was the rent collector Jonelle wanted to stop from turning up next Monday so she could get Amanita a special birthday present.

Market day – no Prunes.

Weird.

Very weird.

She struggled to recall a time when Prunes had ever abandoned his Pope Road patch.

'Where's Prunes?' Jonelle called, joining the queue, behind a very broad woman with her hair curlers poking from beneath a faded scarf.

'Hang on, luv. Let me finish serving this customer – so that's a tenner for the scarf and five for the bracelet, leaving you five quid change. Is that right? My maths isn't the best, sorry.'

'Thanks, and what about—'

'Excuse me, but anyone know where Prunes is?'

'Hol' on! I was 'ere firs'.' The customer swivelled to look her up and down. 'You young people of t'day, not a drop o' manners.'

'I'm sorry, I only wanted to know.'

'Den wait yu turn like everybody else!'

'Prunes ain't here today, luv,' the man said. 'I'm covering for him, see?'

The stocky little man had a strong accent. Jonelle had no idea where it came from. East End, maybe. More importantly, she had been banking on rearranging the rent with Prunes. This month, everything was falling due in the same week: rent, electricity, gas meter, and the fiver-a-week partner-throw she enjoyed with the girls. The weekly throw was always a pain to pay until it was her turn to receive the £80 payout. Shit, come to think of it, wasn't it her turn next week?

'All day?'

The man shrugged. 'Luv, he asked me to cover the stall. You know Prunes, he moves in mysterious ways!'

'Ahem, 'scuse me!' the large customer growled, grabbing up her paper bag of goods and sucking air through her teeth.

The stand-in flashed his customer a smile that said when he'd woken that day, serving her was all he could think of. 'Sorry, swee'heart, need anything else?'

Jonelle Patrick sighed at the thought that Prunes was AWOL. It seemed she'd run out of everything except bad luck.

'Daddee!' Amanita's shriek hit Jonelle like a thunderclap from clouds that were gathering into more than empty threats on market day.

Seeing Tyrone brought forward the letter from the Social that'd landed on her mat two days ago, asking awkward questions about the true nature of their relationship and living arrangements in the interest of the children. Even having chucked him out, she was still paying for his stupidity.

'Hey, kids!'

As they skipped about for Tyrone's attention, he seemed twitchy behind his forced grin. In fact, he looked ready to run.

What else was new? Jonelle thought.

'Calm down, you lot!' Jonelle said, opening her wallet and seeing only one £10 note. That bastard Maxwell had docked her pay as well as her tips – thinking about it now, the tips box had seemed a lot lighter at the end of her night than halfway through.

'What're you lot doing here, anyway?'

'Tyrone, it's market day!' she snapped, irritated by his tone.

'Nice to see you too, Jonie.' Tyrone made to kiss her on the lips. She dodged him easily and he caught an earlobe. Jonelle picked up the whiff of a woman's perfume rising off him. Her nose recalled it from a few weeks back when Prunes had offered her a sample puff, swearing that the scent was identical to the real deal from Italy, only fifty quid cheaper. She also saw a hint of something, rouge maybe, on his earlobe, or it might have been lipstick.

Trying not to think of flies on shit, Jonelle reminded herself that the children had every right to fuss about their father. Loath to admit it, they were skipping about like a maypole dance, something they never did for her after all the sleepless nights, tons of nappies and constant anxiety about feeding and clothing them by herself.

'Can Daddy come home with us, Mummy?'

'Now, now, kids, I am sure your father is very *busy* with—'

'As it happens, Jonie, I was on my way to see *you* – and the kids.'

'Were you now?'

'Yeah, how lucky was that?'

Their eyes met. She gave him a look to wordlessly remind him of their arrangement. He winked back, acknowledging that he'd not forgotten that, after he'd got picked up by the police along with his drug-dealing pals, the Social Services placed her and the children on watch. She'd assured them the kids would no longer live in the same house as their druggie father to avoid any risk of having them fostered right from under her love and care. She had still not forgiven him, because they continued to watch her kids and check up on her.

'Look, Jonie, I jus' want a quickie visit with you – and the kids, of course. They're mine too, y'know.'

Regarding him through slitted eyes, she tightened her lips to prevent herself from teaching the children words they should never use in polite company.

'Can he, Mummy?' Deen's big eyes bulged, ready to pop. 'Can Daddy come home wiv us? Pleeez?'

Amanita left her father to stand so close to Jonelle she was practically under her armpit. With Kenyana joining her brother to beg with blossoming lower lip, it was up to Tyrone to back out and not leave her feeling like the baddie yet again.

He stood there. Waiting. Waiting her out.

'Ten minutes, Tyrone.'

'Twenty, Jonie. I haven't seen them in…uhm…ages.'

Try months.

'Twelve minutes, Tyrone. Let's go, kids.'

'Yah!' The two youngest skipped around and Amanita responded by quietly taking Jonelle's hand in hers. Before the break-up, Amanita was a chatty child, so unlike the shy and reserved little helper she had become.

Shuffling through the crowded market, Jonelle ended up following behind Tyrone and the two smaller children. Amanita still held her hand as they emerged to walk towards home. Tyrone looked round and smiled at her as if to say, 'Isn't this nice?'

'Careful, Daddy.' Deen led his father around a lamppost. 'You have to wait for the red light.'

A white limousine was approaching at speed, perhaps to beat the lights at the crossroads.

'Good boy, Deen. I taught you well.' Tyrone parroted, 'Always use the Green Cross Code 'cause Daddy won't always be here to keep you safe.'

Suddenly aware she had tightened her grip, Jonelle loosened hold of Amanita's hand, mentally counting to twenty as she looked away from Tyrone. A limo was pulling up level with them, slowing to maybe make the turn.

Curious about its passenger, Jonelle caught the reflection of her little family in the windows. For all that Tyrone was a rogue, she thought, he had given her three little miracles. He was always promising to get a framed picture of them with their parents – all mouth and no trousers, that man. What would she not do for the three little devils that had brought their own magic into her life?

Soon to be a teenager, Amanita had turned from being a handful into a helping hand to look after the other two, especially when Mummy was off to night school at the poly. The two girls were forever at odds but made a great team whenever Deen needed his insulin, tried to eat something he really shouldn't, or had one of his pain episodes. Jonelle conjured up their little faces filled with dismay, watching their little brother whimper in the grips of the mysterious illness that the GP was convinced he would grow out of soon.

Bloody NHS.

Tooting horns and tinkling bicycle bells jolted her back to reality and Jonelle caught the lowering of the limo window. For a fleeting heartbeat, she spotted the limo passenger looking directly at her.

'Lucky cow.'

'What did you say, Mummy?'

'Nothing, sweetie.' She smoothed Amanita's hair back. Further along the road, two white men and a brown woman chatted on the kerb. Seeing the woman's short skirt and thunderous thighs reminded Jonelle she had forgotten to include razor blades on her shopping list. A young bobby was approaching the threesome.

'We can cross after the next car, kids. Right, Deen?' she heard Tyrone say.

'But the man is not green yet, Daddy,' Deen said with authority.

Jonelle smiled, preoccupied with the chubby policeman, looking fresh from secondary school. Like she had, the copper must have seen the woman checking out the area before slipping a packet up under her tube top.

He called out and they ran off in three directions. One scrammed left, dodging through angry traffic, the other scarpered right, at a sprint. The copper came within nabbing distance of the woman when she ducked under his arm and left him standing still, huff-puffing into his radio.

Jonelle recalled her solemn oath that, by hook or by crook, another birthday was not going to find her penny-pinching and trying to bring up her children in this hellhole.

# CHAPTER 7

'Tic Tacs?' Likkle wrinkled his brow and tilted his big head away from Bull's gaze.

'No, Likkle, not Tic Tacs!' Bull sighed, shaking his head and propping himself on his desk with arms folded. 'I said… with Django permanently off duty, every man have to sharpen his tactics. His wits. Understand? *Tac-tics!*'

To a man, they owed Django, who'd taught them to be cool operators on the cold, damp streets of London. Bull knew it, even though he had been the one who had extracted these violent Jamaicans from *back-a-yard*, enticing them away from riding the cocaine trail to New York where they'd war over home turf with Latinos, Russians, well-armed public and trigger-happy motherfuckers. He'd sold them London instead, a place to carve out fresh opportunities, where police relied mainly on truncheons and stern talk, though it was the promise of free pussy that had sealed the deal. He'd reeled them in but it was Django who'd looked after them, so they'd earn *respect* among their fraternity, who'd taken time to reason with them when homesickness or inevitable fall-outs threatened to split them up.

Shards of sunlight penetrated the gathering gloom outside, sparkling through the window. With the sun working its ass off to bring a cheery spin to the morning, Bull could care a lot less. He had enough on his plate to get through before Tuesday, and that required some heavy-duty thinking.

'O yeah yeah yeah, boss,' Likkle boomed, 'Django was real good at tic tacs.'

'Not *tic tacs*, Likkle, I said...' Bull looked up at the ceiling. 'Never mind...we all know Django was good –' *at everything, except keeping his trap shut and covering his own ass,* he avoided saying '– but the bugger grassed us out to the Babylon, seen? Now the pigs're pissing all over my parade, and I ain't hearing jack from the coppers wot I fuckin' feed from *my* own hand. Can't have that, aight?'

Bull slowed down for Likkle's sake, something he'd seen Django do. Someone told him once – *fuck knows who* – that dinosaurs with ginormous bodies had tiny brains. Likkle, he decided, should now be extinct.

Clint toyed with his .45 Magnum, while George looked on blankly. Smoke from Chigger's spliff wafted from where he sat outside the office door, after they'd all ganged up on him for putting his foot on the table and using his Bowie knife to peel away dying flesh. Slumped against a wall, Style took a swig from his bottle. Bull noted that their combined unwashed stink, even with a hint of carbolic, still failed to defeat the stench from Chigger's feet. It was a condition that Django had rabbited on about, saying that when man was a boy, Chigger used to run barefoot through wasteland in rural Jamaica, collecting chiggers. Poverty and a fear of having his feet touched meant no one could treat Chigger's festering blisters as they ripened, popped, got infected and started the cycle all over again. Jinxie, disputably the clever one among them, was slowly sinking into the sofa in the corner, gripping his stout like a hard-on and blowing smoke rings. It felt like a wake in his office. Everyone looked like they'd got bad news in the night.

'And another thing, you lot!' Bull waved his meaty hand around the room and walked over to the refreshments. 'All this is coming out o' *my* pocket. It should be a fuckin' celebration! Shit! All we need is a fuckin' coffin and a domino game – this ain't no *Nine-Nights*, aight!'

They were sheep without their shepherd and though Bull was loath to admit it, the tough-as-nails Django was obviously absent, a reality that had arrived with the dawn when the club had closed. He'd ordered Maxwell to gather them all in the office and bring drinks. Even so, a few spliffs and crates of Dragon, Red Stripe and a dozen flasks of Wray and Nephew had done little to take the edge off.

'All o' you, get over *yourselves*, aight! A traitor's got what's coming to him, and we got *nuff* to do!'

They all turned away from their bottles, flasks and smoking spliffs to give him their full attention.

'Django.' Bull stopped speaking and stared at nothing. He'd almost called on his ex-lieutenant to mobilise the troops. Shit! He could still feel the words in his throat. He coughed and started again. 'Django's loot will be shared out, get me? Stop juggling your balls, you're all getting a bonus. Now, let's get on with it!' Bull straightened his suit and tugged his tie, grateful for whoever invented eau de cologne.

He looked from man to man. 'No more screw-ups, *aight*? We got no time for screw-ups! In three days – seventy-two fucking hours – we deliver all the packages, or we can all kiss a fortune and our arses goodbye, seen?'

It was going so perfectly until now, Bull lamented privately. *If only I could ice a man twice!*

'I liked Django,' Likkle slurred. One by one, the group puffed weed and exhaled in a collective sigh.

'Yeah, well.' Bull patted Likkle. The man's back was like a slab of rock. 'When Django dug a hole for us, he was digging his own grave, aight!'

Bull walked away to sit in his high-backed leather chair.

Likkle said, 'I hate digging and gardening, I really do.'

The others chuckled. Likkle looked surprised then started grinning stupidly, displaying misaligned speckled teeth and a gap where his right canine used to be.

Bull slapped the table. 'Right! Enough o' this shit! Plus, the next man to mention *that name* in here will answer to me, got it?'

They looked at him as though they had.

'Cool, now listen up! Style?'

'Chief?' Style puffed his chest and reached into his tan leather jacket. Bull still recalled the day Prunes had convinced Style it had been imported from Milan, along with the matching leather trousers.

'Put the fucking paper and pen away, Style.'

'But, Chief, Django always used to—' Too late, Style stopped himself.

The room fell silent. Chigger looked in around the door.

Bull mentally started counting. He got to five and said, 'Yes, Style. I know that fool was always writing things down. So, where's it?'

Bull watched them all scan the room as if trying to detect who had farted.

'Come again, Chief?' Style said.

'Django's notepad, idiots! Where's it?' Bull addressed them all.

Chigger's face disappeared out of the door and everyone looked at Style, who was looking uneasy.

'Jesus Christ!' Bull stood up sharply, glaring. 'Fools! Don't tell me you left the fuckin' notepad behind!'

'Chief, the babbie woke up and started wailing! Then we see flashing lights at the windows and hear sirens!' Style avoided eye contact, his voice trailing away. 'Jinxie was in charge, boss!'

Either Jinxie was playing smart or was hopelessly suppressed by booze and weed because he sat there with the smouldering spliff in his fingers, a vacant look in his blood-shot eyes.

'Jinxie, where's Django's notepad?'

'Gave it to Chigger, boss.'

'What?' Chigger's face shot into the room while his body, with his feet, remained outside. 'Liar! I had di kid – carried di ting all di way. Me! Wid mi foot a-kill mi, to raas!'

'Is what I said,' Jinxie slurred. 'I give the likkle baby to Chi-chi-igger, yeahmon.'

'We was outside keepin' watch, boss,' Clint said, looking over to George as they both sat there, a pair of bloody nodding *bloody* dogs.

'Now listen to me, all-o-you fools! Think very, *very* carefully. Did anybody see Django's notepad or know if he hid it someplace?'

They all shook their heads, including Maxwell who was not even on the fucking job.

A knot appeared in Bull's gut. Christ, it was crunch-time and his future fortunes were in the hands of a bunch of *boogoo-yaggahs*.

To ease his pain, Bull addressed Maxwell.

'Tell me again, Maxwell. Why'd you send that girl into the cupboard after I said nobody, but *nobadie*, must go back there?'

'Someone chucked up in the club, b-boss. Sh-he was supposed to reach into the cupboard, is all! I t-told her—'

Everyone was looking at Maxwell, who uncrossed his legs and started squirming in the comfy chair. Bull opened a drawer and reached in.

'Could-a got the fuckin' mop yourself, no?' Bull said calmly, not waiting for an answer. 'So, who was she, Maxwell?'

'Uhm, I uhm, well, I don't really know, boss. It was so busy. We had a good night at 'Grilla, didn't we? Nuff people. Uhm, she was covering. That bitch Myrna sent her! She had the puzzle and everythin', and the guys on the door let her in, boss!'

'Yea-yea-yea, you said that last night,' Bull said, reaching deeper into the drawer, feeling around. 'What's her fuckin' name?'

'I – uhm – I, well, she's Myrna's f-friend. I only told her to feel inside, grab the mop and bucket and not to—'

'Well, Mr Maxwell, you don't even know her name, but you sent her into the cupboard. So explain who set off the alarm to the warehouse? Who opened the door and let one of the packages out? Cause, Maxwell, that's where we found Myrna's *friend* and she said that *you* sent her back there!'

'But B-B-Bull, Chief! I-I-I—'

'Shut it!' Bull felt the cold metal and tell-tale shape. It was right at the back of the drawer. He withdrew it and placed it on the desk.

'Could have been a fuckin' undercover Babylon, Chief,' Style offered.

That thought had occurred to Bull, except that she'd handled a mop better than any cop he knew, not that he knew many, thanks to his shit-hot, overpaid lawyer.

'Maxwell,' Bull said.

'Chief!'

'Pay Myrna a visit.'

'Yes, Bull.'

'Find out where her friend lives. Check her out. See what she knows.'

'Yes, Bull.'

'You find she been sticking her nose into my business, then...' Bull paused, drawing a razor-sharp finger across his windpipe. Maxwell swallowed hard while nodding. Bull shook his head in irritation, wishing Maxwell wasn't such a bloody good club manager. Cheap too.

Things were getting hot and they had precious little need for cops snooping around and asking awkward questions. Raids on his hidden stocks, prime stocks – *thanks to that Judas* – would have been worse had he not acted quickly to save the motherload. Bull thought of his 'packages' in the warehouse, thirty feet below them.

'Boss?'

'What?' Bull said a little too loudly.

'Sorry, boss, but you didn't finish telling me what to do if we find out that Myrna's friend was snooping around inside the cupboard.' A catch in Maxwell's voice suggested he might be getting a cold.

Bull stood up. 'Don't you get it, Maxwell?'

Maxwell looked brainward as though figuring out how many esses were in Mississippi. Everyone sniggered.

'Get over here, Maxwell,' Bull said as he went round to the other side of the desk.

Bull gripped Maxwell's trouser waist with one hand and held his zipper tab with the other. Reflexes brought Maxwell's hands down on Bull's.

Bull glared at him.

Maxwell took his hands away, surrendering his zipper.

'Now, Maxwell, looks like you got memory trouble. So, I'm helping you out *this* time.'

'Yes, boss. But I don't really think—'

'No, you don't, Maxwell.'

*Zzzzzp!*

'B-But B-Bull, I told that w-woman to reach in for the mop, to *just* r-reach in an—'

'Out with it!' Bull demanded.

Maxwell backed away, whimpering, protecting his groin. He got as far as the door and found Chigger blocking it with his Bowie knife at the ready. Maxwell shuffled back, a man condemned.

Bull calmly tapped on the wooden surface.

Trembling, Maxwell advanced until his thighs stopped against the desk. Hesitating, he eased himself free from his trousers and was barely exposed when the staple struck, its metallic fangs embedded in Maxwell's foreskin.

Tears followed the blood-curdling yelp that flew from the office, echoing down the stairs and throughout the vacant club. Someone tossed Maxwell a tissue.

'Now tell me what you're going to do, Maxwell.'

Maxwell wiped a slimy nose-drip on his sleeve and very carefully repeated Bull's orders to visit Myrna and find her friend.

'Good,' Bull said. 'And when you come back you can take them staples out. *IF* I am *sat-is-fied* you didn't forget anything. Feel me?'

Maxwell nodded.

'Style, you go with him,' said Bull, 'now who's going to tell me why Triple ain't here?'

'Triple?' said Jinxie, laughing at a joke only he heard. 'He's returning the double-decker.'

Bull recalled their story: the cops were arriving, the van wouldn't start, they gatecrashed a party, escaped out the back and Triple saw the broken-down bus on Acre Lane. Triple, who was good at anything mechanical, had got it started. He had already heard their argument that the big red give-away was all they could find at the time to take all seven of them and the baby.

'So what's it still doing outside then?'

*Come back, Django, all is forgiven!* Bull thought again.

All but one, the Yardies gathered around the window to see with their own eyes.

'It can't be,' Chigger said, remaining where he sat.

'But it is.' Likkle could sing bass if he ever joined a fucking choir, Bull thought, remembering his old mother, God rest her soul and curse his murdering stepfather's.

'He must be sleeping inside it, Chief,' Jinxie said, flopping back into a nearby seat.

'Get one of the bouncers to go check it, Maxwell.'

'Y-yes, boss.' Maxwell sniffed and walked very carefully from the room.

'George and Clint, I want to know what the cops know.'

'Yes, Chief.'

'Jinxie?'

'You were in charge last night, so I hold you responsible, seen?'

Jinxie sat up. He was having trouble holding his head still, but Bull didn't care. 'Bull, mahn, the man was ready fi we. But we stop him fi you! We was too much fi di great Django!'

Bull lifted his bottle in a toast, waiting for everyone to join him. 'Get some sleep the rest o' you. I got more work for you la'er. And, Likkle, help Jinxie downstairs.'

Likkle tossed eighteen-stone Jinxie over his shoulder and led the gang out of the room, spliffs and bottles in hand.

'Watch it!' Chigger complained.

Bull sat.

'B-boss?'

'Forget something, Maxwell!'

'N-n-no, Boss! Prunes is downstairs.'

'Yes, and I'm upstairs, fool!'

'I'll s-send him up, th-then and leave.'


'Bull!'

'Prunes!'

'Something died in here?'

The morning sun glistened on Prunes' round pate. Bull always thought he used too much coconut oil.

'You ain't sellin' me no air fresheners, Prunes,' Bull said, motioning to the soft chair facing his desk. If you ever needed a container and forty crates, padded for warmth and safety, supplied with oxygen and all you need to sustain a small child and a tiny adult on a long sea journey, then forget Harrods, Prunes was your man.

Still fanning his nose, Prunes sauntered over, sat and tossed something in his mouth.

'Hey, Bu-*urkh!*' Prunes growled, clearing his throat. 'So, Bull, why you call me away from— *urkh!*' Thumping himself in the chest, Prunes let out a little cough before trying to continue.

Bull looked on patiently as the violence increased and Prunes punched himself harder and harder. Enjoying himself immensely, he reached for a cigar, viewed his lighter then decided Prunes was still crucial, for the time being. He went over, slapped Prunes hard on the back and watched a small piece of dried fruit fly across the room from his throat, with Prunes close behind it.

'Thanks, man!' Prunes croaked, leaning on where Maxwell had wiped away drops of dick blood. 'Don't think that deserves no discount, aight? And before you give me your Santa Prunes list, what's in it for me?'

'Prunes, I'm tellin' you same as I tell 'em bitches. Don't talk with your throat full. Now, sit.'

# CHAPTER 8

Chelsea'd spent the night chased by burly men in shiny suits, dodging around rough women overflowing tight tube tops and sashes-for-shorts and the recurrent eyes of terror on the face of a girl squatting on a toilet seat in a lemon grove. The madness fell away as she opened her eyes and let the comfort of her Dorchester room.

'Room service, Miss Laverne!'

Still fastening her robe, she padded over to open the door on her order of eggs Benedict with streaky bacon, orange juice and Jamaican Blue Mountain coffee. Her mum had always insisted eggs went better with bacon.

'Did I order this too?' she yawned, looking down at the silver service with its garnished display of scrambled eggs crowned with caviar. Eggs on eggs, Dad used to say. Anyone would think she was expecting to breakfast with her parents – *Oh God*!

The porter looked confused, 'Yes, Miss Laverne, but if you want me to take it back…'

'No, no, it's okay. Mad moment. Looks tasty. Leave it. Thank you.'

He hesitated, looked suddenly awkward, then about-turned and left her alone with her breakfast.

It was not that she had ordered a breakfast fit for two, but that eggs Benedict was Mum's favourite and Dad loved scrambled eggs with caviar. A little shaken but now more awake, Chelsea helped herself to juice. She kept telling herself that it was time to move on before she drove herself stark raving mad. Some said it took five years to get over a death in the family, or at least come to terms with it. Well, it had only been four years, and she had lost two family members, not one.

Four, if she counted the parents who'd given her up for adoption in the first place.

Her appetite lost, Chelsea showered and felt soothed as she towelled dry and started getting ready. For a change, her tights slipped on without mishap before she wiggled into her navy, knee-length skirt and pulled on her plain Egyptian cotton blouse. Carefully avoiding her morning face in the mirror, she took a china cup of steaming hot coffee out onto the balcony overlooking Hyde Park.

Being in London always made her recall happier times and with that came a profound loneliness. Her cousin Gracie's face floated across the park on an icy breeze and lingered on the fringes of her mind, her voice sharp and venomous:

'You conniving, fucking bitch! Not even blood and they left every fucking penny to you! Why? Why? Why?'

She'd neither forgotten those words, nor Gracie's wish that she'd been with her aunt and uncle in the vehicle on that fateful day. Her parting salvo was to rip the photo from a family album, tear it to pieces and throw them in her face. Gracie was the final loss, even though a cousin by adoption.

Clouds were gathering thick over Hyde Park, closing in on the struggling sun and her memories as she gazed into Dad's favourite park while she sipped his favourite coffee.

'Well, you two can go walking,' Mum used to insist, grabbing her large handbag. Dad would smile and nod at her and make a quick told-you-so wink that always made Chelsea giggle, giving the game away. Then they'd wave Mum off on her pilgrimage to Harvey Nichols and Harrods 'for a few knick-knacks'. Dad loved to walk them along the Serpentine. Sometimes he'd stop at Speakers' Corner to tell her, yet again, that this was a special place for children to tell their dads how wonderful they were. From there, they would visit her favourite sight, the upside-down tree.

Her dad always called it the Weeping Beech. *Was it time to go there again?*

Thankfully, the phone rang. With her weary face free of make-up, Chelsea dreaded a time when telephone callers could see each other.

'Yes, send him up now! Thank you.'

Hurriedly freshening her face, she conjured up a smile in time to answer the door.

Normally white, TK's eyes were irritation red. 'You ready, Cee?'

'Yes, TK, but we could hang around here a while? You could finish this breakfast for me, or I can get you something other than eggs?'

'Naw, naw, we want to get there before the market gets too busy, nahumsayin'? When Prunes's in da groove, nothing will shift him away from that stall, Chelsea.'

'But you look like you need a nap!' She stopped her hand from stroking his cheek.

'Naw, naw, I'm used to it, nahumsayin'? 'Sides everybody's waking up now and jammin' up the roads wi' their cars, you get me? You know, if they ever start charging people to drive 'round London, they'll make a ton a dosh! So, you ready, Cee?'

'Yes, I'll get the porter to take my bags down to the—'

'Porter? For that?' TK went over and grabbed the two small bags. 'Let's go get you someplace to rent for your London office.'

'I really appreciate this, TK.'

'You're my peeps, Chelsea!'

*  *  *

They found Brixton drenched in tinted dreariness. TK drove towards the town hall and took a left, only to see the spot where he wanted to leave the limo taken. They drove on.

Approaching red traffic lights, Chelsea looked out at something that warmed her like sunshine for the heart. A lovely little family of five.

'After we turn here, Cee, it won't be easy finding somewhere to park and the bloody wardens are shit-hot round here. We'll have to be quick too, to get you to Paddington on time. Jesus, these lights're taking bloody ages!'

'Uh-huh!' Chelsea said, studying the man waiting to cross the junction, holding hands with a sweet little girl on one side and her adorable younger brother on the other, both having the most innocent eyes, shaped just like her own grandmother's – the one she had never met. He was pure contentment, Chelsea thought, reading the smirk on his face as they drove by. Clearly the grouch behind him was the mother, reluctant to even keep hold of her daughter's hand. She had the complete package, Chelsea mused, yet she seemed to have no idea how good she had it. As the limo inched forward Chelsea found her reflection merging with her view of the family, obscuring her reverie.

She lowered her window for a better look.

'Want me to turn up the AC, m'lady?' TK called back, with a chuckle.

'I'm okay,' Chelsea said, closing the window and sitting back. 'And we'll fall out if you call me that again.'

After a few yards, TK turned into a side street. The sign said Pope's Road. Pedestrians with raised fists shuffled out of the way. TK inched the vehicle into a spot, causing a scene with a stranger dressed in a tracksuit and armed with a squash racket.

'You can't take up two spaces, man!'

TK put an arm over the stranger's shoulder and led him out of earshot. Chelsea saw the man trying to get a look at her, but TK kept turning him away, preventing him from getting a clear look. Then the man smiled at her, shook TK's hand and took up a position by the limo, brandishing his racket as though it were a weapon.

'What did you say to him?'

'Never mind, Cee. Let's find Prunes, quick.'

Making a wavy line through shoppers dilly-dallying over decisions and haggling for deals, TK led her with purpose.

Aromatic smells rose to perfume the air. Chelsea wanted to stop and look, perhaps handle some of the exotic fruit and unusual vegetables on display. The strange chatter amused her. She recognised a few words her mum hated but that she'd heard Dad use whenever his friends came round to play dominoes.

These were his people.

*Mine too?*

'What's going on?' TK said, stopping so abruptly, she walked into the back of him. He didn't seem to notice, his attention fixed on the diminutive white man at a stall, handing over change.

The small man had a cigarette dangling between his lips with its ashes clinging on by the fingertips.

'Help you with some'ingk, boss?' he said, doing a double take upon seeing Chelsea. Obviously, some sort of pick-up tactic, she thought. Or a nervous tic.

'Where's Prunes, man?'

The man looked skyward and flashed them a gold tooth. 'Everybody's after Prunes today!'

'It's market day, yeah? Prunes is *always* here on market day.'

Chelsea thought TK was about to hop over the counter and beat more information out of him.

'Look, Prunes called me this morning – some kinda emergency – and here I am, anyfingk for a mate.' The man spread his arms to indicate they could take it or leave it and turned his attention towards her, to the annoyance of the indistinct queue gathering before the stall. 'So, you see anyfingk you like, luv? Do you a deal?'

'C'mon, Cee!' TK gripped her wrist and dived back into the crowd. Reclaiming her hand, she followed as close as she could.

'It's okay, TK. We'll catch him another time,' she said to his back, feeling a little puffed and ignoring a man calling out from a shop selling music and bric-a-brac from what she could tell. While she had not bought any music in a while, she doubted he had any Schubert or Mozart.

'Naw, naw, Cee! It's embarrassing,' she thought he said. It was hard hearing over the noise and he was facing away from her. 'Prunes's always there, you get me?'

At the limo they saw Racket Man standing a few yards away, addressing a small gathering with animated gestures. The crowd spotted them and started towards the limo.

'Quick, get in, Chelsea.'

TK locked the doors and pulled away. At the intersection, he muscled into the northbound traffic and a wall of irate toots.

They were approaching Vauxhall Bridge when the stand-still traffic up ahead paused TK's gripes about Prunes – a man who could find anything, who had gone missing.

'I'll simply re-plan, TK,' Chelsea said.

'Not the point, Cee. I let you down!' he hissed through his teeth and banged on the horn, unable to let it go. 'First, I promised we would find you a place to rent and now you need to get to Paddington and...'

TK went suddenly quiet.

'Sorry, TK. I was distracted,' she said.

'S'aright, Cee. I was saying that Prunes is tied to that damn market stall by some empirical cord. Yeah?'

'Umbilical.'

'Yea, same difference – can't imagine what could make him stay away from his wheelin' an' dealin' on a market day! Weird shit, that, nahumsayin'?'

'Uh, I suppose so,' she said, only half listening. Chelsea fished her Filofax from her handbag and opened it across her lap, exposing a spider's web of dates and tasks, each linked to carefully crafted to-do lists.

Still, mm-hmm-ing for TK, she flicked the pages.

'What's the hold up! Fuc— Sorry, Chelsea!' He craned his neck this way and that, as if being able to see the blockage might also blitz it.

'TK, I hope you don't have blood pressure trouble.' Chelsea tried to make light of it.

'I think I can see what's causing— shit! Looks like a bus parked badly or broken down. That shit's always happening, Cee. And, where's the cops, Chelsea? Where? Nahumsayin'?'

'I'll find a phone at the station, reschedule my meetings and catch the next one. Should have bought an open ticket, really.'

The nuisance did not stop at the ticket. She'd been trying to arrange those meetings for months, but thought it best to keep schtum about that.

'Bloody hell!' TK said, throwing his arms upwards in resignation before retaking the wheel and turning sharply to the left onto the A3205 towards Nine Elms and Battersea. 'Prepare to be dazzled, Cee. You're goin' to see why the lads call me *A-to-Zed*!'

'Really, TK, you don't have to—'

'Yes I do, Chelsea. Yes, I bloody do! *This* is how we do it!'

Chelsea checked her watch then the slow-moving traffic.

Thirty minutes to Paddington…in this traffic? Mission impossible, but he wouldn't listen.

TK cursed and sweated and nudged the stretched vehicle into every gap and opening in the sluggish traffic.

'Please be careful, TK.' She tried again.

'S'okay, Cee. I do this every day, remember? You do computer shit and I drive, cool?'

'Fine then, TK.' Chelsea took her eyes off what was looking more and more like an overture to a prang. Instead, she scanned the pages of her Filofax looking for the Ministry of Defence contact while scripting plausible excuses. She hoped to sell them a project to revamp their pensions system, maybe even linking it with the Stock Exchange to take advantage of emerging developments around the internet. In which case, relocating from Bristol to London was certainly justified.

The limo jerked to a halt.

'No, it's my bloody right of way, fool!' TK shouted, then lowered the volume though not the hostility. 'Sorry, Chelsea.'

As was happening all too often these days, Chelsea found she had flicked fast through her business section only to land in her personal projects. Mind maps and more spider drawings and jottings, but this time with many start but few end dates, ranging from four years ago until the present. Back home, she had boxes of paper corresponding to each heading.

Birth and Death.

Electoral Rolls and Census.

Surely her twin would share her date of birth, wouldn't he? And the first name, 'Brendon', if that was his real name, was not that common. Chelsea had started her eye-watering search almost immediately, wishing the powers that be had digitised the lot already. Her determination had failed to uncover the name of the woman who had given birth to twins and abandoned them.

'You see, Chelsea, the trouble with Londoners is they don't know London, get me? That's why everybody get' stuck and – hey! Move it!'

'Mm-hmm!'

She ran her eyes down a list headed Hospital and Birth Clinics. It indicated locations in London and many in

Birmingham, Manchester and Bristol, each a likely place where a mixed couple might safely give birth, or so she'd rationalised.

*It was all fuckin' guesswork. Christ!*

YMCA and Mormon temple: she'd found that they kept records of births from practically everywhere. Still, they were no help without a full name at the very least.

Chelsea's eyes settled on a strand of tasks for March '87 compiled after she'd read an article by a charity called St Mungo's, calling attention to the burgeoning cardboard city of vulnerable people in London. There was even mention of urging Thatcher's government to address the plight of people pouring into London to end up sleeping rough.

*Could her twin have dropped off official records because he ended up homeless, on the streets of London?*

With TK ranting in the background, she ran down the list she'd used to set off on her search of doorways, bridge arches and waysides after deciding that she would not wait on any government initiative.

*Buy A-Z.*

*Source blue blankets.*

*Tag homeless with blue blanket.*

*Update database with names, any lead data and location.*

It was always going to be a long shot…from the start! For months, while also trying to build her computer consultancy, she had continued her fruitless rummage through homeless haunts, concentrating on Lincoln's Inn Fields, Lambeth public spaces, around the Thames bridges, notably the Waterloo Bridge arches, giving away in the process hundreds of pounds in blue blankets and was still no closer to finding her twin, nor any information leading towards him.

'Stubborn is in our blood,' her mum, not her natural mum, used to say, whenever she'd grown tired of the teasing at school and remarks about her kinky hair and permanent 'tan'. She'd needed the same reminder in university when she'd wanted to quit the fencing team, the rowing club and then the ballet, frustrated with always being a sub, or the understudy. Why should she feel less or unacceptable, when she was as good as everyone and often better? Those ghosts had found her in that 'Grilla dive, meeting her open smiles with glares, susurrating and treating her as though she'd insulted their boundless bellies, blooming bosoms and butts bulging in clothes that fitted more like underwear.

The faded black-and-white photograph lined with jagged joins where she'd Sellotaped it back together peeked out from the pages of her Filofax. A bookmark to her life, it stood as testament to the love that had accepted her from the arms that had rejected her. Chelsea knew it so well, even where the rips had torn the couple from the bundle swaddled between them. If asked, she could draw it from memory, right down to the satisfied grin on her mother's face and something between pride and bewilderment on her father's.

Mr and Mrs Laverne. *Mum. Dad.* Cooing over their new-born, whose almond eyes where inherited from a mother she'd never met. Yes, she could draw it and not miss a single detail, having studied it for so long and so hard for any clue as to where and when it was taken.

'Nahumsayin', Chelsea?' TK said.

No, she did not know what he was saying this time. She'd tuned him out like the road noise. How could she be so mean, when he had been good enough to chauffeur her all over his home turf and had insisted on battling traffic to get her to Paddington in style and comfort? She'd taken a taxi once and he found out. Chelsea suspected he still hadn't fully forgiven her.

The limo lurched to a stop suddenly.

'Sorry about that!' TK glanced back at her, then waved a fist at a motorcyclist who had cut in from the small gap between the limo and the car in front, then roared away, weaving a crazy path through the bumper-to-bumper traffic on Nine Elms.

'Stupid idiot!' TK said rubbing his eyes.

Unable to help herself, Chelsea looked again at the two-toned image and for some unknown reason thought of the family waiting at the traffic lights in Brixton.

*Could the contented-looking man's name be Brendon?*

Chelsea nervously tapped the edge of the photo on her knee, moisture gathering in her eyes. Had they driven past her twin with her nieces and nephew as they stood waiting at a grimy, rain-soaked South London junction?

*Family.*

The word embodied so little joy and so much loss…so much desire. Chelsea blinked back the tears and looked up from her sadness.

Right now, TK, her first and only friend in London, was the closest thing she had to a family. Since their meeting, he had enslaved himself to her every suggestion. For reasons unknown, she had confided about mourning her parents, trying to build a business and being obsessed with finding a brother, her twin. He existed only by a suggestion from her angry cousin, but it explained the odd sense she got from time to time that part of her was missing. She sometimes sensed a second self and had read that twins do experience a shared bond from the womb. Skipping alumni reunions, dodging phone calls, accosting strangers, probing them about the slightest familial resemblance while neglecting her social calendar to follow fruitless leads had virtually estranged her from her Bristol pals, fraying the few connections she had retained from university.

'I went to the University of Life, myself,' TK had boasted proudly, when she first mentioned these things. It was one of his little sayings that made her smile; that helped her relearn how to laugh.

Flicking to the to-do list headed 'Taking my life back' she sensed that 'other consciousness'. It came innocuously and glowing like an ember about to burst into renewed light and heat.

*My twin self?*

That man waiting with his family, any of the men in that club or even the policeman running past the limo last night?

*God. This is crazy!*

Thoughts and faces flashed through her mind.

Chelsea scribbled a heading: 'all or nothing'. The line she drew under it almost scored through the page.

She realised that TK had said something.

'Say again, TK?'

'S'aright… I's telling that guy to hurry up 'cause we got a train to catch!' TK said and wound down the window. 'Move it, geezer!'

She doused his rage with, 'Actually, TK, why don't you tell me more about your mum and dad? Did they used to call you TK?'

'I told you my mum named me Anthony Kurtis, didn't I? After *him*.'

'Your dad or the actor?'

'Dad, yeah!' TK was nudging the long vehicle around a Mini with a sullen AA man looking down into the bonnet and a noticeably stylish redhead looking at him, skirt flaring with the breeze from the traffic, her arm folded across her cardigan. 'Jesus, that's why! You'd think they'd never seen legs before with all the rubber-necking…we got fifteen minutes now! Move it! Move it!'

Gripe over, TK continued where he left off, 'My dad and my mum was always at it – she telling *him* off for getting on *my* case and him telling *her* it was his job to make sure I amounted to something. He was Anthony, so I was Tony. Yeah? Don't get me wrong, I loved my parents an' that…'

If they made Paddington, Chelsea decided, she'd probably kiss him squarely on the lips.

'But together, they was driving me spare, Cee. A mate of mine came over one night, Dad smelt weed in my room and that was it.'

'Grounded?'

'Nope, he was drunk, so grounded was not enough this time...'

TK's laughter was short-lived and blasted into oblivion by a horn and the noise of metal crunching metal. Her head snapped forward and back as the seatbelt bit into her chest. Chelsea was as startled as TK.

'Oh shit, shit, shit, shit!'

She turned to look behind and her neck tightened painfully. The bump had nudged in the grill of the otherwise pristine Range Rover with its police regulation colours.

'Christ!'

'I wish,' said TK, slapping his forehead as he shrank back in his seat.

Rubbing at the pain in her neck, Chelsea saw two uniformed officers leave their vehicle. They were both about her height in heels.

The first, a rotund man who resembled a jolly Santa Claus minus the hoary beard and the jolliness, combed a hand through his hair and donned his helmet before bending down to inspect the damage to their vehicle. The second man with his pushed-in face tugged creases from his uniform, tilted his helmet and rested a hand on his truncheon as he made his way towards them.

'They ran into the back of you, TK!' Chelsea said, wondering why she was whispering.

'Yes, they did, Chelsea. Jesus – I really don't need this!' TK whispered back.

'But that's their fault right?'

'Cops're never in da wrong, Cee,' TK said as the officer signalled for him to wind down his window.

TK began apologising for the damage to his vehicle and tried to say something about the traffic and the car in front failing to indicate.

'Remain in your vehicle, sunshine. Licence?' Flatface said, his words wafting in with the cold air as he bent to look inside the car. His mother must have sat on him by mistake, thought Chelsea, trying to see the funny side like Dad would, but it wasn't working. A red Mini slowed and she recognised the redhead with the legs shaking her head and tut-tutting along with the rest of the passing motorists as they approached the roundabout to go over Battersea Bridge.

'Uhm, I'm sorry, Officer,' TK said patting his trousers and liveried jacket. 'Left it in my other outfit. But you can call this number and they'll—'

'Right! Get out of the vehicle.'

Chelsea unbuckled her seatbelt.

'No, not you, ma'am, you stay right where you are,' he told her with an overly sweet-tea deference, laced with contempt.

'Excuse me, Officer, sir, but this is my client,' TK said half-in, half-out of the limo. 'She's got a train to catch from Paddington station, y'see, and—'

'Only thing she's catching is a cold, sunshine. Stand by your vehicle. Place both your hands on the bonnet and spread your legs. Do it now.'

He was still patting TK down when the Santa arrived with a breathalyser kit.

'Blow into the nozzle,' she heard Flatface say, as Santa opened her door and looked in at her.

'Remain seated, please,' he said. 'And keep your hands where I can see them.'

Extending his torch, he flashed a light over the luxury of the interior, nodding, perhaps in approval but Chelsea couldn't tell.

Ignoring TK's admissions that he hadn't had a drink all morning, not even coffee, Flatface was advising TK to take bigger breaths and blow harder and for longer or else submit to a blood test at the station.

Santa climbed into the limo and was frantically searching for something. He opened the minibar and shoved a gloved hand into every pocket and under the seat. Chelsea decided he had lost his mind, but still her stomach churned. She felt icy cold, having never had any dealings with the police except that one time when they brought bad news to her door.

He knelt before her and reached between her legs. She shifted. He warned her to sit still.

'Perhaps I ought to check what you have concealed up there.' He fixed her with a hard stare.

'What are you doing?' Chelsea said, unable to help herself. '*You* crashed into us!'

'Did we now? Get out!'

Chelsea did as she was told and stood with TK by the vehicle watching the officers as the traffic rolled by. They fetched a dog from their vehicle and it wagged its tail happily, sniffing at everything and the both of them, before looking up at Santa with expectant eyes and, apparently, nothing to report.

'Satisfied?' TK was irate.

'We're not done yet, Sambo,' Santa said, handing the dog a treat.

Chelsea recoiled. 'Officer, I can't believe you said that.'

'Chelsea, no,' TK said under his breath but over the road noise, shaking his head in warning. 'Can we go now, Officer?'

Santa laughed, making his belly bounce inside the uniform as he pointed at the dent in the Range Rover. 'Let's be having your insurance details, sunshine. People in a rush don't roll back into a police vehicle, do they?'

'But he didn't—'

'No, stop, Chelsea. You'll only make things worse.'

'Yes, tell your girlfriend if she interrupts me again, I'll do her for obstruction?'

'You'll what?' A fire flared in her belly and Chelsea lifted her chin. Dad used to say she had his slow burn and her mum's quick outrage.

'Chelsea, no!' TK stepped forward.

With practised aggression, Flatface grabbed TK, twisted an arm behind his back and kicked the back of his knee. TK's leg buckled. Santa grabbed his other arm and they both landed on him, making TK chest the tarmac hard.

'No!' Chelsea shouted. 'Get off him! Stop!'

But they were deaf to her pleas.

'Attack us will you, sunshine,' Santa said, grunting and pressing a knee into the back of TK's neck while Flatface wrenched both TK's arms behind his back and cuffed him.

'You know what I think, nigger. You stole this vehicle and that's why you have no licence and no insurance. Stole it or some such to show off to your "bootie call" friend over there. That's what you people call it. Likes a bit of rough, does she?'

Chelsea could scarcely believe what she was hearing.

Both her parents were fans of *Beadle's About* but this was too far even for some hidden camera prank, surely.

Her head spinning, Chelsea had an urge to find a phone and dial 999.

'Stop it, please?' she pleaded, as they stood TK up. 'I can pay for all the damage.'

'It's illegal to bribe the police, miss,' Santa said, hanging on to TK while Flatface locked up the limo. 'I suggest you come quietly, unless you fancy a pair of these.'

# CHAPTER 9

It had been ages since she last had a man...*in the flat*, Jonelle hastily added in her mind when an odd scent – testosterone, she thought – floated on the steam escaping from the ill-fitting bathroom door. She had told him not to use up all the hot water, with Candice due to come do her hair later.

From the shrill noises bouncing from their bedroom down the tiny hall, the kids were playing Twister. Jonelle tried to guess how long it would be before Deen started calling to complain about his sisters cheating. Poor little guy didn't understand the game and both Amanita and Kenyana were as tired of explaining it as she was.

Her bedroom was a forest of dangling sheets, towels and clothes in various stages of dryness as there hadn't been money for both washing and drying at the launderette this week. Pulling her t-shirt off over her head, Jonelle next wiggled free of her denim jeans. Her legs seemed super stubbly. Searching, she finally spotted something comfortable and dry, a yellow gingham ankle-length smock that was draped over her full-length standing mirror – both charity shop bargains.

For some strange reason, the house felt 'right' and she experienced a powerful temptation to make fried egg sandwiches – Jonelle felt her neck for signs of fever. She absently checked her hair and make-up before going to the kitchen-cum-living space, pausing to listen at the bathroom door to see whether she knew the tune being whistled.

*Why should I care?*

She opened the fridge.

The freezer door dropped, as usual, stopped only by its tenuous agreement with its lower hinge. The egg hopper was as empty as the ice tray, and apart from half a pint of blue top, a bag of bread ends she was saving to feed the birds on their next walk, and the orange juice she was certain was empty too, the shelves were bare. Myrna really needed to bring her taxi money round before the end-of-market bargains were all gone.

Disgusted by strange 'stirrings' she'd not felt for a while, Jonelle wished Tyrone would hurry up and leave and he'd better have the decency to wash his own scum from her bath first, though she held little hope of that. She recalled the children's faces when she'd agreed he could visit with them for fifteen minutes and he'd been in there half that already.

Her mind drifted to the cupboard last night and a face filled with desperation. Where was *her* father? Mother?

Jonelle wondered if she should do something – call the police or what?

Shrugging the incident onto a mental back burner, Jonelle bent over her cassette collection. Deen had stacked them like dominoes along the skirting board, as far as the sofa and through a tunnel he'd made from her evening class textbooks and a slipper, before snaking back towards the kitchen table.

'Look, it's the midnight train to Georgia, Mummy,' Deen had insisted, with the sweetest *choo! choo-oo!*, only to burst into tears when she'd laughed. It made her feel like an evil mother.

*Bless.*

Thank God, the other five boxes of music cassettes were tucked tightly beneath her bed.

Jonelle stopped smiling when, scanning along in search of C60 minutes of TDK magic, she spotted a mixtape she'd forgotten about. A tingle ran down her spine and fanned into the backs of her knees.

'Hey, you still got that Vandross I made for you, Jonie?'

Startled and now on all fours, she turned to see him topless in the doorway, wearing her favourite towel and looking down at her arse.

'What?'

'That cassette I made you, remember? Luther Vandross?'

'Oh, forgot all about that. Bloody machine chewed it up,' she lied, scrambling to her feet quickly to go over and flick the player from cassette mode to radio.

A clipped voice buzzed from the tiny speakers: 'So far, no one has come forward to claim responsibility for this killing, though at first glance we think it is gang related. Our officers are still continuing their house-to-house, of course. However, we urge the public to be vigilant and if anyone has seen or heard anything that may assist the police in—'

'You choose news before music? With all dem cassettes 'ere? Girl, you've changed!'

'And you need to get changed, Tyrone. Have you forgotten why I let you in here? The kids have been waiting patiently for you to wash off that stink and spend some time with them.'

Jonelle tuned the dial until she heard Bobby Brown telling everyone it was his 'Prerogative' to a dub beat he'd not chosen. She'd discovered the pirated music station by mistake, trying to find Radio Caroline. Sighing, she walked over to the washing basket by the ironing board.

'Stop watching me, Tyrone. Get dressed. Your clothes are hanging by the window over there. Be careful. I'm not going outside if you get clumsy.'

'Don't be like that, Jonie. Been a long time since...you know?' He patted the towel as if he had something special hidden underneath.

Jonelle shot him a vexed expression, normally reserved for men on building sites and random motorists trying to catch her attention on the street.

'Give me a bligh!' Tyrone said, winking the way he did whenever he said something he feared might make her douse him with kerosene and light a match.

Jonelle lifted the iron.

He ducked and Jonelle patted the flat side, once, twice before resting her hand on it. She had plugged it in about ten minutes ago. She checked the socket for the third time.

'Give you a bligh? Tyrone DaSilva Williams? I've given you more chances than you bloody deserve!' Jonelle said, thumping the ironing board so hard that her neatly stacked laundry leant towards the floor.

They both made a grab for it.

'Watch it, idiot!' she screamed, holding her head and blinking away the stars.

Tyrone rubbed his forehead and nodded towards the living room door. 'Keep it down, Jonie.'

'You rock-head. Tcho!' Jonelle opened her jaws wide, trying to realign them. Great, now she'll look like a victim of violence when the Social comes round.

In her periphery, Tyrone stepped carefully over the 'midnight train' and was about to sit on the wrong end of the sofa, where a sharp point of a wayward spring awaited the unwary.

'Stop, Tyrone!'

With his tight butt inches from a possible penetration, Tyrone froze.

'Keep it down, Jonie. Jesus! You'll disturb the kids and we ain't done with our big-people reasoning. So, you been thinking any more about my offer of being part of my new club?' He did a little wiggle while waving his arms stupidly, trying to move like a woman.

She hadn't.

'I hope that isn't your idea of how I dance, mister!' she said, wishing she had let him discover the spring.

Jonelle turned back to sorting her laundry.

'Oops!' Tyrone said.

With a click the first cassette fell against the next and so it continued along Deen's creation, click, click, click…

'You better pray Deen doesn't come in here now,' she said, watching him trying to catch up with the cascade. He kept dangling from the confines of the towel. Jonelle averted her eyes and smiled to herself.

'Why don't you get him some real toys, Jonie?'

The smile banished, Jonelle sucked air through her teeth and felt the vein in her neck throb.

'Get dressed and get out, Tyrone!'

'Ain't no need for that, Jonelle! 'Sides, the kids want to spend some time wiv their old man. Back to my club, Jonie. You know how many girls I could have aksed but I *aksed* you!'

'A-S-K-E-D-*Asked*!' she said.

'Is wah I sed.' Tyrone stood up from the cassette and caught the towel as it fell. 'I only aksed. It's a chance to earn some dosh and take the kids to the zoo or some'ingk – maybe one o' them lido places? Brockwell Park lido's pretty good, I hear, and the Tooting Bec Common one's popular as shit. Listen to them, Jonie, they're bouncing off the four walls. You could change all that!'

'They're your kids too, Tyrone.'

'Why'd you think I'm busting my butt to start this new club?'

'You really want me to answer that? As you're not really here to see your kids, get your clothes on and go get one o' them sistas from 'Grilla to dance in your club. They all love baring their asses in public.'

'Family first, Jonie! 'Sides, you're the best… It's quality I want! I ain't opening no sleazy little deal. Feel me? Besides, Jonie, you really shouldn't talk about what you don't know about.'

'Oh, really.'

'Some classy sistas go to 'Grilla, Jonie.'

'Really now?'

She felt his eyes on her as she flung the freshly washed clothes back into the dirty basket.

'You really need to go, Tyrone.'

'Wait a sec, Jonie. How about I take you to the next 'Grilla and show you why only you will do for my club. Nobody got the moves like you, baby.'

'I've been to 'Grilla and seen for myself, thanks!'

'You? When?'

'Last night, if you must know.'

'You never.'

'Believe what you want, Tyrone.'

'But I was there. I never saw you!'

'Maybe you had your nose up some bird's arse,' Jonelle was about to say but it came out as a huff of exasperation.

'You're having me on, right. Jonie, you have to be in the know to even find a 'Grilla gig. I know because it was me that—'

Something flipped his OFF switch. Silently, still wearing the towel, he pulled on his underpants, inside out. His expression said there was something on his mind.

'Well?' she said.

'Well what?' He tossed aside the towel and stepped into his trousers. Too late, she spotted that delicious line of hair running from his navel downwards, disappearing under the elastic of his off-white Y-fronts.

'Aren't you going to finish what you were saying?'

'To be honest, Jonie, I don't want to talk about that place. 'Grilla is on the way down, anyway.'

'Oh?'

'Yeah. When I open Gorgon, nobody will remember 'Grilla. And that Bull Manners, he—' Tyrone said the name like an incantation for sheer evil. 'Jonelle, you have to dance for me. Please!'

Please?

Shit, he was desperate, she thought.

'No!'

'You could bring your own music, J!'

'Or I can listen to them here.'

'Jonie, Jonie-jello, Jonie-jujupes,' he said, donning his ridiculous puppy-dog face that usually accompanied those equally silly names that, in another life, used to set her giggling like an idiot. It used to work on her, dammit.

'N.O. means no, Tyrone.'

'And I got the best DJ ever, used to spin tunes for Radio Caroline.'

'N— You got a DJ like that to work for you?'

'Hey, everyone wants to be on the A-team, baby!'

Jonelle ignored the remark. 'Tyrone, what do you know about the people who run 'Grilla?'

'I said I don't want to talk about it, Jonie!'

'No you didn't!'

He reached for his right shoe and tried to stuff his left foot in it. He was still shirtless and his bristling back muscles added to the tingling in her groin that annoyed her.

'I asked a simple question, Tyrone. Either you know about them or you don't.'

'Why the fuck you want to know about that, Jonelle? Y'see, this is why I never mix business with pleasure.'

Shocked by his outburst, Jonelle looked towards the closed door. She knew Amanita eavesdropped sometimes when she was hosting big-girl chats in the living room.

They regarded each other while the dust settled. Tyrone's eyes met hers with a fixed stare. Their history flowed in fast rewind to the time he'd first spoken to her on the number 3 bus with her schoolfriends. He'd interrupted them with, 'May I have your seat, please, miss?'

Jonelle made a decision. 'Tyrone, I was at 'Grilla last night and I saw something.'

He grunted.

She ploughed on. 'It was a young girl. About Amanita's age.'

'Jonelle, stop right there!'

He pulled his shirt on and left it unbuttoned. Coming towards her, he crunched a cassette without noticing and gripped her by the arms.

'What're you up to? Let me go!' she shouted.

He slackened his grip but still held her as though she'd fly away before he was done. 'Jonelle, Bull Manners is a nasty piece of – he don't take no shit from *nobody*. He aint like me, aight?'

'I said, let me go, Tyrone!'

'Jonie, you got to un'erstand! I don't even know how *you* know where 'Grilla is, or what you was doin' there. But you can't go round *aksing* questions 'bout stuff what goes on there. Shit! And – by the way – how come you out clubbin' an' my kids are stuck in 'ere? Who's looking after 'em while you were—'

She fixed him with a look devoid of human kindness.

Tyrone let her go.

The living room door creaked on its tired hinges.

# CHAPTER 10

'Nicked!' The word was still reverberating in Chelsea's mind as she approached the chest-high counter at Balham police station. An officer bashed the top of the green monitor.

'Bloody computers,' he muttered, barely audible. He grabbed a sheaf of paper and peered over his glasses at her. With pen at the ready, he scanned the notes left him by the arresting officer.

'Sorry about the handcuffs, love. For your own protection, I'm afraid, Miss...er...' He diverted his eyes back to the form. 'L'burn, is it?'

'Laverne,' Chelsea said, noticing a quiver in her voice as a female officer approached bearing keys. Rubbing her freed wrists, Chelsea felt she'd started the day inside the wrong body. Never in a thousand years would she have imagined being in this situation. At Clifton High School, she'd been top of her Social Studies class and had never quite understood what anyone gained from contravening rules. At Oxford Uni she'd always had better things to do, choosing to solve equations and program IBM computers in preference to running with the mischief makers or participating in this or that student protest.

'Miss Lubern, it says here you were resisting arrest?'

'I was not! Your officer insulted me. I merely asked for his badge number and tried to ascertain why he—'

The man was scribbling something faster than she was speaking.

'Are you even listening to me?'

'Of course, of course, I live to listen to every sad sack that comes in here with their stories about my officers not doing their jobs properly.'

Chelsea was about to speak when a man's yelp made her jump. No one else reacted.

TK, she thought.

'Excuse me, but where have you taken my...er...the driver of the limo?' Chelsea asked. When does an acquaintance become a friend? The way he was with her, TK was somewhere in between, but she could tell from the little things he said he'd wanted them to be more. 'Mr Kurtis?' Chelsea said a little louder. 'Where've you taken Mr Kurtis?'

Poor, kind, generous TK under the full weight of the two hefty lawmen – he was battered and bleeding when they'd hoisted him off the tarmac in handcuffs and tossed him into the back of the Range Rover. Chelsea remembered her intense outrage and her utter helplessness and hated herself for it, and for sitting obediently, as they'd warned her not to try and communicate with him or pass anything between them. She could still feel the knot in her stomach.

'You've got troubles of your own, Miss Lathern. Address, please!'

She fixed him with her eyes. He returned a look she'd seen in films, indicating he wanted her to say just the right thing to bring out the yellow Marigolds and get her under a big bright interrogation light.

Chelsea gave her address.

He wrote 'The Avenue' and stopped to regard her, his head tilted right like most people do when they come in for a kiss or say 'pull the other one, it's got bells on'.

'Clifton, eh?' he said, smacking the pad with the pen.

'Yes,' she said, mentally replaying her words.

'The Avenue, Clifton, Bristol?' Eye to eye.

'Last time I checked.'

'Fine.' With an exasperated huff, his pen scrawled away.

'Look, I'm director of TechnIQ Solutions. It's my company and I was in a hurry back to Bristol when—'

'Of course you are, dear!' He expelled a deep, heard-it-all-before sigh. 'You might, at least, concoct a more believable story, Miss Lobbern. We can check all these things, you know. Actually, you could use your computer powers and fix this bloody thing,' he said, clipping the computer around its non-existent ears. 'Then we can check whether you've any priors.'

'Priors? What priors?' Chelsea was hardly able to believe her own ears.

Ignoring her question, he kept reading.

'My officer says here that you kicked him? Company director or not, you cannot kick an officer of the law in the shin. That's assault!'

'I did not *kick* anyone! *He* pushed *me* into the police vehicle and caught my heel! And that was after hauling me from the limousine and flinging my suitcase and Filofax to the floor and shouting at me when I tried to retrieve them...' The officer was clearly unmoved.

'Fine, may we get on. I need to sort this and know where you have taken Mr Kurtis?'

'Hear that, Debra? She needs to get *on*. And *we're* late for tea at the palace!'

The shrill remark made Chelsea turn around to see three scoffing women sitting on the floor with their backs against the wall. Until that moment she'd felt alone before her inquisitor. How long had they been there; listening, laughing at her, not minding their own damn business?

Like they were in their living room, two sat cross-legged in short skirts, fishnets and very neon-bright panties. The third, in the middle, clutched her knees with folded arms, allowing her tartan skirt to gather about her hips.

'Quiet, you lot!' said the officer. 'I told you before, keep interrupting me and you'll be there a sight longer. And stop blocking the passageway!'

'But *we're* regulars, John!' said the chubby one, scratching her crotch in full view of everyone.

'Shut it, Debra!'

'Typical. Some new pussy turns up and he treats us like trash.'

The officer pointed his pen at the woman in the middle. 'You can shut it an' all, Veronica. Show some dignity and put your knees down. Nobody wants to see what you had for breakfast.'

'Should'a seen what we 'ad for supper!' the skinny Veronica guffawed, sticking her middle finger up at him before using it to stroke herself. She winked and Chelsea turned away, disgusted.

She watched two policemen manhandle a struggling youth towards a nearby cell. They opened the door and told its occupant to stand well back.

'Hey,' the youth protested, 'I ain't sharin'!'

They shoved him inside.

Remembering TK, Chelsea tapped on the counter. 'Please, can we get on?'

'Ooo! Y'hear *that*, Debra!'

'Wait-a-fuckin-sec, isn't that the bitch from Croydon?'

'You *know* this lady?' The officer looked over at them.

'Lady? She's no *lah-di-dah* lady! Innit, girls? She was slidin' into our patch las' night. Thievin' little slag!'

He regarded Chelsea curiously. 'So, you *know* these women, miss?'

'I have never seen these...' Chelsea hesitated, perhaps a little too long.

'These what?' One of them shot to her feet, fists bunched. 'Wan' a piece, do yah?'

'Cut her, Debra,' the lanky Veronica said, then raising her hands in surrender towards the officer. 'Sorry, John. Mistake. It don't mean nothingk, K?'

Chelsea stood stock still, lost for words and so shocked by the absurd accusations that she was having trouble filling her lungs. The sergeant was refusing to accept her word over that of the arresting officer, and now he seemed keen to accept the confession of three vile strangers over hers. 'I tell you, Officer, I don't know these people, nor would I want *anything* they have!'

'Well, we shall see, won't we?' the officer said.

'I swear she was in Croydon selling pussy wi' us, John.'

'That's enough, Veronica,' he said, writing something down.

'Oi, I told you to call me Ronnie,' Veronica said.

Chelsea looked round to see all three were now standing.

Outrage piled upon confusion. One moment she was hurrying to catch a train home to Bristol; the next she was standing handcuffed in a London police station and arguing with prostitutes.

*And where had they taken TK?*

'So, you still insist the gentleman was no more than a *friend* and you have never seen these women?' The officer waggled his pen, waiting for her response.

'Yes, Mr Kurtis is a friend, a *very good* friend who was kind enough to—'

The three women erupted with laughter.

'A *very good* friend!' one said, mimicking her. 'Wonder how much her *very good* friend makes for each trick, eh Ronnie?'

'Not a lot, he's her *very good* friend,' said the lanky one, setting them into peals of laughter yet again.

Waving his pen like a conductor's baton, the officer said, 'That is it! One more outburst and you three can wait in the cell back there, *capiche*?'

He turned back to Chelsea. 'Sorry, Miss Laburn.'

'Laverne, L.A.V.E.R.N.E,' she reminded him.

'Ooh, listen to the educated cunt.'

Chelsea did not look round.

'Right.' The officer called for his female colleague to take the rowdy three into a cell.

'It's chock-a-bloc, Chief.'

'What?'

'We're full up, Sarge! No room in the inn.'

'Where the bloody hell am I going to put this lot?' He waved his arm in a wide arc Chelsea saw included her.

She shuddered and leant forward against the counter.

'Constable?' she said.

'Sergeant!' He indicted the stripes on his uniform.

'I insist on seeing someone in charge.'

His face fell, and it became so quiet, you could hear a low moan from down the hall and the rumble of passing traffic.

'WPC Rockwell,' the sergeant beckoned.

'Yes, sir?'

'Take this suspect to the interview room and search her!'

'What?' Chelsea said.

More cackling. 'Better check everywhere, Rockers!' said Veronica. 'You know we women can hide things in all kinds of places.'

Inspired by the trio, he added, 'Yes, strip-search the subject, Officer Rockwell.'

'Why?' Chelsea stood back and a shiver ran down her spine. Part of her wanted to attempt a dash for the door, but she obeyed a more rational part and said, 'I demand to see your superior!'

'I *am* in charge here, miss!'

WPC Rockwell grabbed her arm.

Chelsea backed away.

'Best go quietly, luv,' they chorused behind her, laughing, all three wiping their eyes.

'I demand to know why I am to be searched,' Chelsea said.

'Strip-searched!' Ronnie reminded everyone.

'Well, I think I can smell alcohol on your breath. Our narcotics team will measure that for us and WPC Rockwell here will check you're not concealing anything on your person for your *very good friend* back there.'

'Not back there anymore, Sarge,' Chelsea heard the WPC mutter.

'No?' he said, lowering his voice and bending closer for his colleague's discretion.

Leaving her side, the WPC walked to the far corner of the counter and stood on tiptoe as the sergeant leaned towards her.

'We lost him.'

'Lost him?'

'Needed a few stitches, Sarge.'

Chelsea was always good at lip-reading; sadly, this was one of the ways she had known what other girls were whispering about her in school.

'Why'd TK need s-stitches?' Chelsea stuttered, recalling the yelp and fighting back panic. 'Tell me why. I want to know why.'

'Do you now?' the sergeant straightened to his full height and rolled up his sleeves.

'Better tell her, Sergeant John.' Chelsea knew Ronnie's voice now.

'We won't let her hurt you, Johnnie boy,' growled Debra.

'Be quiet, all of you… Rockwell, do your job,' he said motioning to Chelsea.

Chelsea heard her dad's voice in her head: 'If you're ever in trouble and we're not contactable…' Then he would have her recite the number and a name he'd given her. Swimming, riding her tricycle, skipping or while he was tickling her into a frenzy of laughter, she had to get it perfect, forwards and backwards. He never told her why that number nor why that name. Until now, she'd never had to use either.

'I insist on making my telephone call.' Chelsea stood her ground.

'Got some fancy solicitor, do we?' the sergeant shot back, ignoring noisy requests from the three women to also be granted a phone call.

'Fine, Rockwell, give her the call. And, Rockwell?'

'Sarge?'

'Be *very* thorough with that search, understood?'

'Yes, Sarge!' said Rockwell.

To her consternation, with a finger in the dial and the handset at her ear, Chelsea found her mind a blank. It took three misdials before she got a ring. She prayed it was the right phone.

With a cheery, 'Bristol County Court!' a Ms Meryl Mercer said that she was the one speaking, '...and how can I help you?'

Chelsea introduced herself and asked for the person her father had named with the number. 'Parker-Richardson?'

'I'm afraid the judge is in Chambers, Miss Laverne,' his secretary said. 'May I take a message?'

Chelsea swallowed hard.

# CHAPTER 11

'What?' Jonelle shut her eyes against the dribble of water escaping from the damp towel around her frowning forehead.

'Did you ever have an orgasm? 'Cause I never did. Not 'til last night,' Candice said, towelling so vigorously, she pressed Jonelle's neck hard against the cold porcelain. 'Sorry Jonie.'

''S'okay. I like it a bit rough.' Jonelle grimaced, desperate to change the subject and realising her mistake too late. The wonky chair arm slipped away, again. It had been one of Jonelle's less successful charity shop deals. As usual, they jiggled it back into place and Candice helped Jonelle apply fresh wrappings of Scotch tape before retaking their places. Jonelle leant back slowly until her neck was once more hanging over the basin rim. The little distraction had arrived in the nick of time.

'So, about that orgasm,' Candice said, attacking knots in Jonelle's hair with a plastic comb. 'Met this guy, right? Nice. Tall. Brown eyes. Big hands. Me and him went to that new restaurant in Streatham last night. Him wearing Gucci and the biggest fake Timex you ever did see. Asked me if I wanted one. An orgasm, I mean.'

'No?' Jonelle said, too high.

'Yes!' Candice screeched, a decibel higher.

'So, what did you say?' Jonelle asked quietly, considering the children were only in the other room, doing homework, after her inconsiderate sperm-provider had finally left. The bugger got them so overexcited she was fighting a headache by the time Candice had arrived. The windows and walls in her tiny bathroom were still steamed up, even now, and she'd only noticed the scum around the bath when they'd come in to wash her hair. Next time, if ever there were a next time, he could take *his* children to the zoo, or the lido, instead of being a bloody nuisance in her life.

'Cheeky monkey! Fancy asking a girl *that*…and on a first date! Ohmygod! Don't know *who* he thought I was.' Candice paused to attend to a particularly resistant knot and then continued, 'Girlfriend, I told him I was definitely driving home *alone* if he was going to start that kind of chat.'

'Disrespectful or what, eh?'

'Telling me!' Candice said. 'Jonie, I was *well* ready to walk.'

'Good on you, girl,' Jonelle said.

'The devil laughed and shoved this thing under my nose. I felt such a fool.'

'What!' Jonelle sat up and faced her.

'Vodka with Baileys in it!'

'Oh no!'

Candice licked one lip then the other.

'You're too *bad*!' Jonelle slapped her gently on the hand. 'Stop it.'

'No, Jonie. It's an orgasm – in a glass!'

'Like Sex On The Beach?' Jonelle said.

'Uh-huh.'

'So, you tried it?'

'Tried it? I ordered two more. Couldn't hardly walk after… Took a taxi home.'

'Got the real thing?'

'Jonie! What kind of girl you think I am? Now, brace yourself, here it comes!'

Something landed on her scalp, molten, warm, soothing all her troubles away and smelling of toasted almonds and honey. Waves of serenity ran across Jonelle's head and down her neck and shoulders. She gripped the chair to keep from relaxing right off it. 'Mmm!'

'I know…' Candice said breathily. 'Feel free to doze off.'

'Mmmmm.' Jonelle wallowed in the deep sense of care and comfort. 'You think I don't see your evil plan, dontchya? *Send Jonelle to sleep, snatch her kids and steal her fortune.* Right?'

They laughed. Candice gave her an oily slap on her bare shoulder.

'Very funny. Settle down. Oil's getting cold.'

Jonelle resumed her position and Candice continued to apply the warm oil. She was like an unexpected gift. They'd sat in the same Business Studies class for almost a term before crossing nodding distance to shake hands and share tea. A Jill of all trades, Candice had brewed the perfect cuppa right there in Jonelle's kitchen after they'd decided to study together. It was during one of those sessions that Jonelle's dry scalp issue had met Candice's hot oil remedy.

'You know one treatment won't be enough, right?'

'Of course not!' Jonelle had agreed.

'Don't nod off on me. I brought an extra treat for you.'

Jonelle watched Candice reach around the saucepan of hot water she was using as a bain-marie to warm up the jar of oil. She tugged her handbag carefully towards her and lifted out a small floral tin.

'Here, my dear, I always have a facial, manicure and pedicure when I get my hair done, so—' She waggled the tin at Jonelle.

'Candy, I think we should get married!' No sooner'd she said that Jonelle became conscious of an unnatural silence, different than the quiet of children reading and drawing. She sat up abruptly.

'Wassup? Oil too hot?'

Jonelle listened hard and then the bathroom door flew open.

'Mummy! Mummy! Come. Quick!' Amanita's voice made the window rattle.

'Whazzwrong!' Jonelle stood up, rushed towards her. Her foot kicked something, but she ignored the pain.

'It's Deen! It's Deen!'

Jonelle pushed past her eldest daughter and ran into the children's room. Kenyana stood in a corner crying. Her little son lay on his back, clutching his throat and writhing. Jonelle threw herself on the floor beside him.

'Deen! Deen!'

Candice appeared the other side of him. 'He's choking, Jonelle. He's choking!'

As Jonelle kneeled closer, Candice pointed towards the hall.

'Jonelle, quick! Go call 999. I used to be a nurse. Let me attend to him, you get an ambulance! Hurry!'

The words refused to translate into action. Choking? Why? They were doing homework, how'd this happen?

'Hurry, Jonelle!'

Amanita hugged her little sister and the two were in floods of tears. Jonelle saw Candice shouting something.

'Go, Jonelle. Get an ambulance and come back and tell me!'

Snapping out of her paralysis, Jonelle ran down the hall and out of the door still wearing a towel for a top. Desperate, she tried to remember where the nearest phone was. Descending the stairs two at a time, she slammed into the entrance door to the block, yanked it open and ran out.

Nearest telephone! Jesus, where was the nearest phone?

She ran towards the launderette, praying with every stride that nobody was hogging it. She burst in, narrowly avoiding a small child with a bin liner over her shoulder.

The phone was free. Dangling from it, a hand-scrawled sign read: 'fucking owt of orda agane'.

'Shit! Shit! Shit!'

The image of Deen's skinny little body jerking and gagging was suddenly replaced by a picture of a payphone in a wood-panelled hall. Jonelle sprinted for all she was worth towards the Duck & Diva pub.

Something, oil maybe, was running down her cheeks and over her forehead and into her eyes. Wiping her vision clear, she ignored the raindrops sprinkling her bare shoulders and wetting the towel. Her bare feet slapped the pavement with every stride and still she couldn't get to the pub quick enough.

*Get to the phone.*

*Get help.*

*Deen was choking.*

Nothing else mattered, not the slippery pavement, not the towel getting wetter and heavier, not Kool Kurls barbershop with its Saturday morning customers cheering her on like a winning racehorse, nor Oswald, the owner, yelling, 'Oi, darlin'! Lookin' fit as usual!'

Everyone was creasing up and shouting over each other.

'That's plenty fit enough for any man, eh?' said one customer, as they all crowded the door and shopfront window for a better look at the running girl's legs splashing her way past the shop.

'Wish that towel would fall,' one said.

'Oh yea,' another yelled. 'Then wha'?'

'I'd lend her mi shirt, of course!' They all laughed so loud Triple was sure the noise would be heard all the way down to Brixton police station. Shit. Feeling exposed, Triple hunched into the barber chair and angled his face away from the window.

'Stop squirming, boss!'

'Okay, sorry.' Triple eyed the razor hovering by his right cheek.

The banter continued full volume.

'Had a filly like that once,' said one, puffing his chest and licking his lips.

'Only one?' someone else whistled. 'Blouse-n-skirt mahn, I 'ad two! Di mother for breakfast an' her daughter for dinner! Innit, Triple?'

'Don't call out mi name, man.' Triple ducked as though caught in a shoot-out. 'A man come in here for a good haircut and get bloody noise an' abuse!'

'Coolit! Coolit!' said Oswald, raising his hands. One held a red speckled towel and the other the razor he'd just scraped down Triple's neck.

'Coolit,' Oswald said again. 'Triple's a regular. None o' you better diss 'im, get me?'

The sudden quiet was worse than the big noise they'd been making. Kool Kurls barbershop was always a trading post for crudeness, betting tips and insights on the meaning of life.

Triple wanted to go, but there was still half a head of hair to shave away.

'Oi, Triple, what's with the skinhead look?' someone finally asked.

With the cut-throat razor blade skimming his temple, Triple neither looked round nor acknowledged the speaker. Someone advised the room that women found bald men very sexy, kicking off a noisy debate. Oswald kept his attention on the hairline on Triple's forehead.

Someone out of sight shouted, 'You must be on di run, Triple!'

His flinch was ill-timed, involuntary. Triple felt something brush his forehead, above his right eye.

'Jesus Christ, Triple-man!' Oswald stepped back from the chair, looking both annoyed and horrified, with blood on his blade. 'Why you move? I tell di man fi sit *still*! All-di-same, no-problem, no-problem. Sit there, press your hand right here and…do…*not*…move! I'll be right back.'

'Jesus, man, another inch an' it woulda be your eye, Mr T!' another customer said.

With a hand pressed down on his forehead and his head tipped back as Oswald had told him, Triple felt a wetness running over his closed right eye and down his face.

'Look! Look!'

He heard chairs scraping the floor and shoes scuffling towards the entrance and windows.

'Ozzie! Come out here, quick!' one said.

'Ozzie, you going to miss 'er, man! She's coming back! Ooh, check dem legs an' that ass, swee-eet!'

'You lot are *pathetic, pathetic!*' Triple recognised Oswald's voice. 'Triple. Hang on a sec! Be there in jus' a minute! Now, move over you lot, this is *my* shop. Get outta mi way!'

Someone called out for her phone number.

Triple wondered what she did to make them laugh and jeer.

Their conversation turned to whether she already had a man, and if she had run down to the pub to put coins in the condom machine.

Triple's neck was starting to hurt, but it was the stinging pain over his eye that worried him.

Waiting alone, Triple closed his other eye and pictured them all jostling for a grandstand spot to watch some fuckin' girl run by. He retreated into his most private thoughts, grateful for the brief distraction.

Bull must have seen the bus by now?

*Go someplace far, far away where nobody knows you. And stay out of trouble.* They'd advised him to avoid banks and, with the sizeable payoff, they'd also urged him to get himself a new name, a new identity and a new passport. What the bastards never told him was how he was supposed to stay alive until then.

'Right. Back to work,' Oswald said, standing next to the revolving chair.

*Psssht*! The tell-tale sound of a bottle being opened made Triple open his eyes to see Oswald raise the Dragon Stout to his lips.

'Want a sip?' Oswald held the bottle towards him.

'I's awright,' he said, tasting a bit of shaving foam.

'Good,' said Oswald, 'cus I need every drop. I *'ate* the sight o' blood, me!'

Ignoring raucous requests for sips, the Kool Kurls owner proceeded to clean away the blood from Triple's face, pausing for gulps of stout. Then he swapped the bloodied cover for a clean sheet to protect Triple's shirt.

Beneath the giant bib, Triple gripped the chair as Oswald wiped something over the cut.

'Only one thing for it,' Oswald said.

'Yea, man, Mr T. You can't walk roun' with one single eyebrow!'

Ignoring them all, Triple told Oswald he may as well remove the other brow and sat very still as the blade scraped away his remaining eyebrow before completing the job of giving him a hairless head.

The chair reclined and Oswald busied himself foaming up his face.

With each ding from the door, Triple flinched.

'Might be your nose next time, you keep doin' dat! Wassup wi you today?'

'Sorry, man!' Triple said, hearing shop talk shift back to the local news.

'They said there was blood everywhere, man.'

'Yea, so much…you never expect it on your own doorstep, man.'

'Yeah. Police release 'im name yet?'

'No, dem tryin' fi locate relatives, man. Dem always do that first, no?'

'Yea, mon, but everybody know who, already.'

'How?'

'People talk, rasta!'

'Den who?'

'Is Django!' someone shouted too loudly.

'Triple, you know why they call this a cut-throat razor?' Oswald said, taking another swig for fortification and almost missing his mouth.

Triple kept very still and very quiet as they all prattled on.

'Baby?'

'Well, mi friend live in da same block. He say da girl keep herself to herself. Big-chested. Big-boned. Sweet. Shame they killed her.'

They all sank into a moment's silence. Four men bowed their heads in contemplation, waiting beneath the sign saying 'In God we trust, everybady else must pay cash'.

'You finish, Oswald? Mi haf fi leave, man,' the words waited on his lips. He felt he was on a bed of nails.

'Dem say Django was in jail, right, yea?'

'Wha' for?'

'Dunno. Don't ma'er! 'Im was in the nick. When him come out, he catch somebody poking his woman an' t'ings get ugly.'

The youngest guy broke the silence. 'Why die for a piece o' pussy?'

'What you think, Triple? You did know him, right?'

'Look,' said Oswald, steadying himself against the chair and pointing his razor from man to man, 'N-nobody talk to Triple, seen? I...seen enuff blood for one day!'

'Oi, Ozzie! That's not a bad look you give Mr T, y'know. I want one o' dem, but without the gash down the side.'

'Very funny,' Oswald said, dropping the empty stout bottle in the bin and searching among his table of cologne, aftershave and assorted oils. 'Man, I could do with a good cigar about now.'

'Cuban?'

'What else, eh?' someone said and added, 'Dem say that in Cuba dem roll di cigars 'pon di thighs of virgins. Bet none o' you ever know dat!'

A voice way at the back yelled, 'Dat's why dey can't never make dem in Englan'!'

Uproar exploded in the room.

Unable to help himself, Triple chuckled along. The job done, no one would recognise him easily after this. He glanced in the mirror, pleased with the transformation.

'So, you off fi get a head rub, Mr T?' someone snickered.

'Remember to put a *cap* on it,' someone else snorted and once more the room was in riot.

Triple smiled. Though the joke was not lost on him, he considered a hat was a very good idea indeed.

Triple made to leave the chair.

'Hang on, boss!' Oswald rested firm hands on his shoulders and Triple sat back, remembering the ritual immediately.

Oswald fetched the mirror.

Triple took the briefest glance at the three bony bulges on his skull and gave Oswald the thumbs up. 'Thanks, Mr G.'

Nodding triumphantly, he watched Oswald wash his hands and unscrew the bottle for the finishing touch.

Triple relaxed for the first time since he'd come into the barbershop and wondered what sort of hat would complete his new look. His thoughts floated back to the previous night and hovered, watching himself and six others piling into the van to find it wouldn't start. Chigger was carrying the infant and – God knows – nobody could figure how he'd kept it so quiet. With the cops swarming the area, they'd spotted a party and gatecrashed, walking right past two people in fancy dress. Some of the party people said the two cops were strippers, and others said they were real. He'd got his crew to see sense and they'd sneaked out the back before Chigger got shot for whining about his fuckin' foot. They found the abandoned bus and got it started right after he'd puffed air through the starter motor. What a godsend that was.

The Babylon had even waved them on, like they were a night bus with passengers. With that, Triple settled his head back into the chair. He felt silly now for worrying when someone-up-there was clearly looking after him.

He closed his eyes as Oswald's big hands massaged oil into his smooth cheeks, jawline and chin, down to his neck, front and back, before splashing cool, aromatic aftershave onto his freshly shaved head.

Triple hit the ceiling.

# CHAPTER 12

Myrna already felt like death and now someone was banging down her door. Whoever it was had some choice words coming, especially for hauling her away from her medicinal fry-up, juicy and ready.

'Go away.' Her whisper was still too loud in her head.

My God, how much rum had she drunk? Maybe she should've stuck to the Babycham without the brandy, but it was far too late now for regrets. Only a good breakfast, and maybe another little lay down, before taking a good long bath and gargling with some Listerine was going to help. After that, she planned to see how Jonelle had got on at 'Grilla. Come to think of it, it was Jonelle's turn to receive the partner money! With a hand to support her throbbing head so it wouldn't fall off, Myrna swatted at the banging, hissed her teeth, and glanced at the clock.

It was nearly time to take the partner money round… with a little extra for last night so Jonie could get some proper shopping, poor thing.

*Good people, that Jonie. Salt o' the earth.*

The banging grew more urgent, like they were trying to bash their way in. Myrna decided it was not JW's or one of the girls escaping a beating.

'Awrite, good God, awrite!' she called out, sighing and

resting a calming hand against one temple. In the other, she lifted the dripping spatula from the sizzling pan.

*Jesus, people should really learn to wait!*

'*Tcho*! I'm comin', I'm comin'!' she called down the hall. Trouble was, you couldn't leave chicken livers frying for too long as they cooked so quickly. They were already lovely and brown clinging to the onion rings in her special blend of coconut oil, bacon dripping and Kerrygold.

Myrna unchained the door, released the double lock, and yanked it open.

'Yes!' she said scowling and brandishing the oily spatula.

'What took you so long?'

Wishing they were JWs, Myrna rocked back at the sight of the two men – one looked vaguely familiar but the other was the last person she expected to darken her doorstep.

'M-Mr M-Maxwell!'

'Don't you M-Mister M-Maxwell me, Myrna!' He pushed right past her without bothering to wait for a 'come in'. The other man followed, and they stopped in the hall. Myrna looked at them, then at the open door behind her.

Maxwell was walking strangely and was still in the suit he always wore at 'Grilla. Perhaps it was all the clothes he owned, she thought. The other man looked smart and wore a jacket she recognised, but for the life of her, she could not recall from where.

From the kitchen, her liver smelt like it had passed perfect.

'Comfortable place you have here,' he said, looking around like he wanted to buy it off her, complete with the fine things she'd grafted so hard for.

'Thanks,' Myrna said, looking from man to man and willing her brain not to come bursting out of every orifice in her head.

'Something smells nice.' The man sniffed *her* air and licked his lips. If they thought she was going to feed them too, then they had another think – *Jesus!* – her liver was burning!

'Myrna, you weren't at 'Grilla last night?'

'I know,' she said, wondering why two men came all this way to tell her something she already knew. 'Can we make this quick! I've got something on the stove and—'

'That's the trouble, y'see. You sent someone and – *ow, Christ Almighty!*' Maxwell winced and crumpled against the wall to the amusement of his friend. His knees buckled inwards as if he was carrying something as fragile as a raw egg between them.

'You need to pee?' Myrna asked, aiming the spatula at the door by the entrance, but really wishing the two of them would simply piss off.

'Never mind him.' The stranger's gaze made her feel like she was the sizzling pan of liver, onions and bacon. Myrna shivered.

'We need to know more about your friend, the one what took your place last night. See, she did such a fine job, we need to pay her a little visit. Give 'er a bonus. Is there somewhere we can sit and chat like civilised people, Myrna?'

Like an usher in some fancy place, he stood aside to let her lead the way.

The spatula fell.

'Pick that up,' the man told Maxwell, who was still having trouble standing up straight. 'Myrna, tell Maxwell where he can come find us.'

A bad feeling raked cold and sharp down Myrna's back.


Triple rested his shiny baldness on the headrest, adjusted his designer dark glasses, unbuckled his seatbelt, and waited for the pretty hostess to come by. Maybe he could have her buckle it again for him later, he thought.

Feeling anonymous behind his darkers and enjoying a weightlessness from loss of worry, Triple listened to the lullaby of Rolls-Royce engines transporting him to the paradise his payoff had promised. With Django's ghost back in London, nobody was smart enough to locate him. There would be neither sleepless nights nor hounded days. He'd left it all, taking only his new look and new identity, along with all the *bills* he needed to live comfortably.

'Sir, your seatbelt?' the stewardess said with a face as fresh as morning dew and the friendliest smile. 'The pilot's turned on the landing lights.'

Triple shrugged awkwardly. He had fins for fingers as he fiddled with the seatbelt buckle. The stewardess leaned across, singlehandedly positioned the two halves and slotted one into the other. Click. Before she straightened up, Triple inhaled enough of her perfume to fill both lungs and inflate his dick.

'The landing lights are on now, sir. Please put your seat in the upright position.'

What a sweet ride. He had arranged it surprisingly easily too and here he was, descending to kiss Swedish soil. No doubt, the coppers had expected he would choose Jamaica or Jamdown as he liked to call home.

Fools. For all he knew, those Judases might have set him up with a sexy M16 so he would arrive to 'Hey Triple, man! Welcome back!' and then – *bla-blam*! – brains splattered all over the front page of *The Gleaner*.

Well, his mother never gave birth to no fool. He'd popped into the Tate library and found an atlas and did a little checking. Who'd ever look for a black man, a Jamaican at that, in a freezing place like Sweden? If anyone wanted to pay him a 'visit', they would go south for sure. So, Sweden it was. Iceland seemed safer still, but he figured that would have been suicide.

Bull must really be missing him right now. Admittedly, thoughts of Django had sneaked up on him a few times too. He wasn't proud of what he'd done, but this was a dog-eat-dog world and Django would have done the same to him.

Wouldn't he?

Straight up!

Triple felt the cabin shiver as softly as the bounce in that hostess's butt.

Landed.

New life.

No more being pushed around. Triple savoured the pine-fresh scent of freedom. It was not every day you got the chance to start over and with a pocket full of 'fuck off' donza. Well, it was all in the special account he had opened in the new name.

The passport officer said something, but it sounded like he had hot porridge in his mouth.

'Sorry? Mi ears nah work!' Triple said, shrugging his arms wide.

'Remove your glasses, sir, please,' the passport officer said again, lifting invisible spectacles from his own face.

*Sir? Sir Triple!*

Nodding and smiling his best, Triple removed the dark glasses. The man mouthed the new name Triple had chosen. Someone told him once – *shit! Django!* – that *Brown* and *Smith* were so common they practically filled phone books, so it was a bloody nightmare to locate any bugger with either name.

Now the man was taking his bloody time looking from the passport photo to him and back again – *dammit* – why hadn't he shaved his head *before* he took the passport photo?

*Fuck!*

'I'm having chemotherapy,' he was about to say, but the man smiled almost as openly as the SAS stewardess and Triple stopped feeling cold.

'Welcome to Stockholm, Mr Smith Brown. Enjoy your stay.'

'T'anks!'

Strolling through Arlanda Airport, Triple looked for signs to a taxi rank to whisk him off to begin his new life and meet some Swedish chick and settle down. He spotted the same hostess from the flight pulling a case, probably going off duty. He thought he might ask her to join him for a drink, but changed his mind. First things first, find a good hotel with a hot tub and room service, and *then* check out the skirts.

Know how you spell *trouble*, Triple? – *w.o.m.a.n.*

*Fuck off, Django.*

Smith Brown had a skip in his step as he passed hugging arms, kissing lips and suits shaking hands while boards looked for the names that were written on them. With his head high, he was certain his own mother, wherever she was these days, would walk right by him.

'Hey, Triple! Is dat really you, bro?' a voice echoed all through the hall.

# CHAPTER 13

Style angled his fedora and brushed off the raindrops clinging to his tawny jacket. They'd ducked under the Kool Kurls
awning as the heavens opened.

'Maxwell, you's actin' like Dracula dat stay out too late at
the fuckin' ball.'

Maxwell looked pained. 'You mean Cinderella, dontchya?'

'Sure, you can be Cinderella if you want.' Style kissed his
teeth and glanced behind through half an inch of shatterproof
glass. He clocked members of an unlikely testosterone club,
sitting like devotees before an altar of mechanised chairs,
lounging and laughing, each awaiting a turn to sacrifice their
locks to one of three busy clippers. Style lifted his hat and
patted his Afro with a free hand.

'We didn't have to hurt her, Style!'

'Naw?' Style said, trying to see the haircut rates through
the condensation and rubbing the stubble on his cheeks. If he
could be bothered, he'd explain they'd – *he* – would have to
turn Myrna's friend's lights out as well as she'd probably seen
plenty, plus women talk. Hell, she was probably blabbing to
the wrong ears already.

'Naw mahn! I mean, she pissed me off a lot, but she's a
good worker! *Was...*' Maxwell retched. 'Gawd-damn, so
much blood!'

'Yeah, say it louder so dem people in dis barbershop can hear!'

Maxwell pulled his jacket closer, wincing as his hand brushed against his fly.

'You leavin' that staple in your dick?'

'You heard Bull!'

'Gonna get infected and drop off!' Style chuckled.

A number 3 bus rolled by. Style saw the puddle and calmly sidestepped. Maxwell's groin took the full effect of the splash.

'Christ Almighty!' Maxwell yelled as he backed away into the glass window.

The mini tsunami left him dripping from his chest down.

'That's gotta hurt, bra!' said Style, trying to feel sorry for the bugger.

Laughter erupted from inside Kool Kurls barbershop as Maxwell carefully pulled his trousers away from sticking to his crotch.

Style checked the waterproof watch Prunes had sold him, telling him that it was water resistant to '3ATM', whatever the fuck that meant. Prunes had sworn it was all the rage with pilots, the US Navy Seals and even the British SAS, but he'd only bought it because it was shiny.

Maxwell wiped his wet cheeks. 'Fuckin' bus nearly drowned me, innit!'

'Can't believe you didn't see that coming.'

They'd talked about waiting inside the block of flats for the woman, but that helpful Myrna had disclosed that a key was needed to get in, and to get out. Like Django used to say, *Never go inside where you can't get your arse out again.* So they'd been left standing out in the cold and rain to watch and wait and wait.

Style was still savouring Myrna's tasty liver-and-bacon cooking, but the overcooked onions were repeating on him now. Slightly overdone and greasy, it had taken him right *back-a-yard*, where gals played with skipping ropes while bwoys chased bicycle wheels with sticks and played keepy-uppy 'donkey' with stuffed milk cartons.

The glass door opened, a bell dinged and the volume went up as someone stuck his head out the entrance to Kool Kurls.

'Hey! You guys don't have to stand out in the rain, y'know.'

Faking a grin, Maxwell straightened up.

'Very kind of you,' Style said in his best BBC news voice, doffing his hat like he'd seen Clint Eastwood do playing The Man with No-Name, a thousand times. 'Thanks, all the same. We're waitin' for someone.'

# CHAPTER 14

The door swung open into their office.

'Finished that report, Bailey?'

'No, Guv,' Bailey said, swivelling away from Murphy. They'd been debating about the vices of community policing before the chief burst in. 'Almost done.'

From the guvnor's face, Bailey suspected he'd got off the phone to his accountant who'd given him bad news about his precious pension plans. The man lived to retire and was all the keener now that policing was fast becoming more about form-filling, gathering crime figures, and typing up notes to feed a monster pile of bloody paperwork.

'Hell's bells! What's taking so long? I need you two back out on the streets bringing my crime stats down, not gazing into each other's eyes, wasting precious policing time.'

'Yes, Guv,' said Bailey, focusing on the piles of paper and ignoring chuckles rippling round the office.

'And there's a transfer form to process – Balham's dumped on us 'cause they're full up, would you believe it?…and another woman in Interview 2. Bailey, you take one, Murphy, the other. And have that report on my desk within the hour. I don't intend to miss my Sunday roast.'

'Yes, Guv.' Bailey responded to the chief's back. Murphy's eyebrows were in scowl mode as she threw a pissed-off stare at their retreating boss. The guvnor always knew how to ruffle her feathers, then *he* had to deal with the fallout. Bailey let her choose which room, hoping it would calm her down. Still biting her tongue, she managed to grumble, 'You take Interview 2.'

Bailey finished his cold coffee, ditched the cup, and took a sheaf of paper towards interview room 2.

The woman sat, head bowed, staring, arms cuffed to the chair. She seemed out of place to him, somehow. They always did, Bailey sighed. He'd become used to his colleagues' over-zealous attitudes to certain, shall we say, segments of society. Well, some of his colleagues at any rate.

'I'm PC Bailey.'

No reaction. No offence taken.

Bailey closed the door behind him and decided not to lock it. Speed-reading down the chit: Assault: gave nurse a bloody nose; gave doctor a black eye; shoved a wheelchair into porter. Property damage: hospital furniture and windows.

'Miss Jonelle Patrick?'

There was nothing of her – somebody was either exaggerating or misrepresenting the facts, surely.

'Will you confirm your identity, please, Miss Patrick?'

Closer up, he guessed her weight. Eight stone, give or take, under her baggy trousers and ill-fitting jumper – both sleeves stained, right shredded to expose a bony arm. Height: five feet ten inches standing? A scraggly mess of oily curls framed a gaunt face. She reminded him of that new singer named… Whitney *Something*. Texas? Dallas?

*It'll come to me.*

'Been arrested before, miss?' Bailey asked, looking back at the chit to double-check her name. There'd been no time to look up priors, but he'd do that later.

'No!' She shot him a white-hot look.

Either she wanted to tear his eyes out and suck out his brain or she was in a great deal of distress with no idea why she was in Brixton police station being processed. It was a look he had come to recognise ever since the Sus imperative became essential policing. Bailey braced himself for the usual 'How could you sell out your own people?' to come railing out at him.

'Water?' Bailey offered, attacking the heat and the tension in the little box of a room with its barred window. The only other way out was through him and then the door.

'I want to go get my kids!' she growled. She tensed, her fingers like talons gripping the arms of the chair as she lurched against her bonds before falling back hard to glare at him like a wild cat.

Bailey often felt handcuffs were unnecessary, removing dignity from people who ended up walking free to resume their normal lives as innocent citizens. 'Respect' ranked high among *his* people and aggression simply bred more aggression.

'Look, I can take those off, Miss Patrick. But first, you have to calm down, answer a few questions and allow me to assist you in any way I can. Yes? This can take a few minutes or a few hours, it's up to you. Cool?'

Her heaving jumper fell into rhythm with her flaring nostrils and the claws slowly became hands again. She looked away, deflated.

Show a little mutual respect, he always believed, and they'd now have enough of an understanding for him to conduct the interview speedily and go finish that report to slap down on the inspector's desk.

'Now then, do we still need those cuffs on?'

'No,' she said, avoiding his eyes.

He stood motionless by the chair, key in hand, waiting.

She looked up, her eyes meeting his.

'No,' she said, with more cotton and less crowbar.

'May I get you some water now?'

'No, you can get me my son!' she said, almost snarling. Making a fist with her free hand, while Bailey uncuffed the other.

Bailey straightened up. 'Look, miss. It is *miss*, right?'

She shrugged and rolled her eyes upwards.

'Fine, *miss* then – I'm here to help. So, let's try and fix whatever got you into this mess. Deal?'

She slumped at his words and stretched an angry expression over her pretty face. Bailey took in her vulnerability and felt more determined to help.

She stood sharply and refused to meet his eyes.

'Please sit back down.'

He caught her looking at the door.

'I'm big and I'm fast,' he said, keeping his eye on her. 'Sit down, Miss Patrick.'

Bailey reached for the cuffs. 'Look, we have to get on, miss.'

Rubbing her wrists, Miss Patrick proceeded to prowl the room. She stopped by the window. Could she squeeze through those bars? Bailey wondered. And what would happen if she did slip through and take off?

*Houston! That's it, Whitney Houston!*

'Miss Patrick?'

'So, you want to help me, do you?' she said, finally sitting, scraping the chair closer to the table.

Leaning forward, he readied his pen.

'Says here you were at King's College Hospital when the assault occurred?'

'Assault?' she said, and her eyes burnt into him.

'Miss Patrick, why don't you begin at the beginning? Let me take your statement so we can sort this all out for you.'

Then he made the mistake of looking discreetly at his watch. She went ballistic.

He leapt up and threw himself between her and the door. She slammed into him in an effort to get out. The bang was certain to bring officers rushing in to see what was going on.

With Bailey's body blocking her way, the suspect backed up.

'Sit down, Miss Patrick!' he said firmly, breathing hard.

It seemed she wasn't half as vulnerable as he'd thought. 'I'm afraid we'll need those cuffs again!'

'Fine, fine!' she said offering her wrists in abject defiance. 'Nobody'll listen to me anyway.'

Bailey picked up the cuffs but set them down again, near the pad and pen, then retook his seat. To his surprise nobody had come in to see what was happening.

'Are you ready to give me your statement?'

'I went to the hospital to get my son…' She began as Bailey sat on the edge of his chair and grabbed for the pen to start writing. '…and the bastards told me they couldn't find him anywhere!'

'What?' Bailey said, his pen hovering above the pad.

'Exactly!'

Bailey set the pen down.

'King's College Hospital?'

Suddenly unable to speak, she stared over at the window and placed a delicate hand over her mouth.

'Please go on, if you can, Miss Patrick.' Bailey wanted to wrap it up before the guvnor stormed in and made him hand over to one of the others. 'You were saying you lost your son!'

'*I* didn't bloody lose my son!' She stood and slapped her chest with a hand, over her heart.

He decided to let her do all the talking and he would do all the writing.

'I left him at the hospital!' She was counting out each word. 'They told me to go away and come back for him and when I did…'

She sat again.

The door opened. An officer looked in.

'You okay in here, Brendon?'

'Uhm, yes!' Bailey looked from his colleague to the suspect and back.

'What was that noise?'

'My chair slipped. But we're alright in here, aren't we, Miss Patrick?'

With her head hung, she nodded. He could tell she was crying, and he hoped the officer at the door would understand and think she was simply being emotional about the arrest.

'Get you a coffee? Tea?'

'No, thanks,' Bailey said. 'Miss Patrick? Coffee? Tea?'

They both waited on her response. None came.

Bailey motioned 'no'. His colleague signed that the guvnor upstairs wanted him to wrap this up quickly because they needed the room. Or so he guessed. Bailey rolled his eyes and nodded acknowledgement.

The woman looked up as the door closed. Her face glistened. There was usually a box of tissues on the table. Shit. It would take precious minutes to go looking for one. Miss Patrick swiped her sleeve across her dripping nose and continued, 'My son was chokin' yesterday morning, right? I ran down the pub, called an ambulance and they took him to King's College Hospital for a check-up.'

He'd usually get addresses, times and other particulars to establish a few facts to go on and identify any witnesses, but Bailey decided not to interrupt her.

'We waited for bloody ages in A&E. Christ, if Candice had not been there—'

'Candice?' he interrupted, instinctively.

'My babysitter.'

He quickly jotted that down.

'She used to be a nurse. Deen would be dead now if—' She looked out the window. 'Deen hates rain! He says it makes his body hurt more.'

She started sobbing.

'Excuse me, Miss Patrick,' Bailey said softly. 'I know all this is very upsetting, but we must get through this. Perhaps we can find a way to—'

'Okay, okay!' she said bringing herself back into the room and turning away, fanning her eyes.

'You were saying that you were waiting for ages in A&E, but can you back up and tell me what happened before the ambulance. I mean, why did your son – Deen?'

She nodded.

'Why'd he start choking? Had you been eating or was it some—'

'His *bloody* dad. That's what choked him,' she said, stamping a foot, making to straighten up. 'Don't worry, I'm not going to *assault* anyone again, except that bloody Tyrone when I see him – I *told him* that useless…that useless… I told him to *never, ever* give the kids money, especially coins! No coins! Shit, he never gives *me* anything to buy clothes, shoes, food…'

'You saw him give them the—'

'No, I didn't!' she said sharply, returning to the table. 'But I never have enough money to leave it laying around for kids to put in their mouths, get it?'

Bailey kept quiet, jotted 'Tyrone' and put 'Deen's dad' next to it and kept writing.

'The girls – *my two girls* – told me Deen was doing a magic trick that their dad showed them with the coins before he gave them the money. That was when he started convulsing and Amanita, my eldest, came to get me. Candice sent me off to call the ambulance and she got him breathing again by the time… by the time…sorry! I'm alright! Give me a second, will you!'

He gave her sixty before saying softly, 'So the ambulance took him to King's?'

'Well, Candice recovered the 50p coin, see?'

Bailey nodded.

'But Deen still had a £1 coin inside him somewhere. So, the ambulance people said they'd best get him checked out properly. That's why the ambulance took us to A&E. They don't take chances with kids, they said.'

Bailey nodded occasionally, writing furiously.

'So, when they finally got to Deen – *bloody NHS!* – this nurse took one look at him and said he was fine and we could go home. *God, why didn't I bloody listen?* Anyway, then a kids' doctor came to sign him out. Jamaican, trained, whatever anyway, he said he didn't like the look of Deen – said he looked anaemic – wanted him to stay the night and Deen was really tired.'

'And you left him?' Bailey said before he could stop himself.

'This doctor was saying he still didn't like the way Deen was breathin' and wanted to do some tests. I *told* him Deen always looked that way and – well – but – anyway, he was talkin' like he knew what he was talkin' about.'

She seemed to be waiting, perhaps for him to catch up, so Bailey looked up from his notes.

'I went back for Deen first thing this morning.' She made a fist. Two fists.

'And nobody could fucking find my son!'

A gut feeling told Bailey this was why it took six grown men to restrain Miss Jonelle Patrick while they waited for the police.

'They couldn't find him?'

She looked at him as though he was responsible, and Bailey lowered his pen.

'They checked the ward, and he was not there!'

'Surely, he had to be *somewhere* in the hospital?'

'Said he'd been playing hide-and-seek with some of the other sick children and nobody could find him.'

Her eyes glazed over, looking without seeing.

'Miss Patrick?'

Before he could get off the chair, she closed her eyes and seemed to flutter to the floor.

# CHAPTER 15

Petrified at what she might see, Jonelle squeezed her eyes shut. She was lying naked on a concrete bed. Her head was resting on a pillow that felt filled with rocks. Her belly was big as the whole world and her legs spread east and west. A tearing pain lanced through her, jagged and deep. Hovering above her own body, she watched in horror as a pair of hands parted her, reached inside, grasped her unborn foetus and pulled, hard. Falling back down, into herself, she started screaming, loud and long, but the sound was stuck in her throat. She yelled for her mother and shouted for her father as the heartless hands pulled. Her desperate cries echoed and died against the walls of her own mind. 'No, no, don't take my baby. No!'

'It's okay, it's okay!' the kind voice soothed beside her head. 'You're okay. My name is PC Bailey. You fainted.'

Strange brown eyes looked down at her. She shrank from him, unable to understand where she was, her eyes darting about, searching for answers finding herself in a room with two police officers.

'Here, drink this?' The man hovered over her.

The mist cleared. The horror returned. This was Brixton police station.

Right?

Deen?

Jonelle sat up quickly and pushed the PC away.

'I want my son!' she said, knocking the paper away and spilling water on the floor beside them.

'Charming!' A woman officer sighed.

She looked beyond them to the doorway and an older officer in a fancier uniform, looking at her. He introduced himself as the detective sergeant and told her that, while she'd been out cold, his officers had phoned the hospital.

'What?' Yes, they'd lost her son, her boy, her precious boy.

'Yes, we phoned King's and your son is there! He's safe. Okay?'

'Really?' She stood up and found someone had put a jacket about her shoulders.

'Really.'

Thank God. A tension receded from her body so totally her knees buckled. Strong arms caught her under her armpits.

'Steady, you best sit down!'

The PC dragged a chair from under the table, set it behind her and bid her sit.

'I'm okay.' Jonelle swayed on her feet. 'Can I go now?'

The two officers looked to their DS who cleared his throat.

'There's paperwork to complete, I'm afraid… Have we got enough information to contact Miss Patrick later on?'

'Yes, Sarge.'

Jonelle's hands shook as the details of the last few hours came into sharp focus. Deen was lost and now he's been found, this was all she needed to think about. They were talking about her now as though she wasn't there. The world was still spinning slowly so she shifted her weight from foot to foot, trying to keep from falling and fighting back the urge to run and run and run all the way to King's College Hospital and Deen.

'It's decided, Miss Patrick. One of my officers will drive you over in a minute!'

'No, I'll get there myself. Can I go now?'

'It's peeing down out there, love,' the woman PC said. 'And the hospital may still be pressing charges. It's better one of us takes you to collect your son and—'

'Fine, fine, but can we go now?' Jonelle edged towards the Way Out. She had no idea how to feel. The joy and relief of knowing Deen was waiting for her was as disorienting as the moment her insides turned to treacle when they'd lost him. She wouldn't settle until he was back in her sight, in her arms, in her care.

'All the cars are out, Sarge,' a man called.

Everyone looked across at the counter to where he'd popped up out of nowhere. Looking at a green screen of information, he explained he had sent the last car off five minutes before.

The DS banged the counter. 'Check again. You know those bloody computers can be damn slow to update!'

'Not using the computer, Sarge. Bloody thing locked up and I can't get it going. I called the engineer, but you know how it is...' He shrugged towards the deluge outside the window. 'A little rain and everybody's stuck.'

'I'll examine your computer for you.'

'And you are?' the DS asked.

'She's the Balham prisoner transfer I told you about, Sarge. That Judge Parker-Richardson call to the chief?' Murphy replied before the woman could.

The DS raised both eyebrows and rubbed at a discomfort in his midriff. 'Yes, again I am very sorry you were arrested, Miss Laverne, but the Balham station officers were just doing their job, investigating anything suspicious—'

'Officer, if it'll hurry things along, I could fix your computer.'

He shrugged away her offer and continued, 'Unfortunately, miss, your driver still needs to produce his driving licence at this station. As to the drugs we found in the limo and the cost of repairs to our vehicle, well... I am prepared to release him to you on police bail.'

'Bail?'

'Well, yes. I think that's reasonable, considering... You'll only need to pay if he runs off and fails to turn up tomorrow morning, that's Monday morning...of course, he's free to stay over here once the hospital's released him. He'll be fine with a Band-Aid or two – these things do happen when offenders resist arrest, I'm afraid.'

'No, no, bail's fine.'

'Good. Is someone taking you to visit the offen– your friend?'

'It was offered...'

'I see,' the DS noted, looking to his officers. 'Miss Patrick and Miss Laverne need to get to King's in a hurry, yes?'

'Sarge,' Murphy nodded.

Everyone waited while the man behind the counter went closer to the green screen, scratching his head with both hands.

# CHAPTER 16

They'd found a retired vehicle under tarpaulin in the police station car park and eventually got it started. Now Jonelle's eyes followed the rain spatter that meandered down the dusty window like teardrops. Two old biddies hung from brolly handles watching her watch them as they waited anxiously to cross the road a few yards from a pelican crossing. Blurred pedestrians overtook the cop car as it inched past a bus stop where a barrel-shaped woman sheltered a small boy from the wind and spray with her coat.

Jonelle's heart leapt and she ached to feel the tiny body of her special little man in her arms again.

'Did you say nine minutes, Officer Murphy?' Miss Laverne asked from the back seat across from her. She'd seemed patient, calm and sickeningly self-confident at the station only minutes ago.

'It is what it is, Miss Laverne,' said the woman driver. Jonelle wondered whether PC Bailey would make better time if he were behind the wheel.

She caught Laverne looking at her and turned back to the scene beyond the window, wishing she'd had the energy to ask what she was bloody staring at.

'You know, I still fail to understand how Mr Kurtis ended up in hospital!'

PC Bailey spoke. 'You heard the super, Miss Laverne. He was resisting our officers. We follow strict guidance on Stop-'n'-Search these days and I'm afraid that when your friend did not—'

'I was there! He did not resi—'

'Miss!' The WPC was firm and braked hard. Everyone lurched forward. 'We cannot discuss the case. You and your friend can always file a complaint that will be investigated properly in a timely manner. The super has released your friend to your recognizance. Our orders were to simply get you to King's College Hospital and see that he is released from the officer there.'

Deen's face floated through her mind. Jonelle's anxiety had long exceeded the scale of 1 to 10, 10 being 'are we fucking there yet?' The policewoman had said they'd make Denmark Hill in under ten minutes. That was right before someone let them into the sluggish queue and she got arsey about why people were clogging up the roads on a Sunday morning.

'Sorry about the traffic, Miss Patrick,' PC Bailey said, looking round at her. 'These things happen, eh? At least your son's safe and sound and waiting for you. You must be so relieved.'

He was probably trying to be 'helpful' or some shit like that, but it pissed her off that people were always assuming they knew her, or had a clue about what it took to bring up three kids on your own, battling to find a way forward while some bugger kept changing the road signs and tripping you up whenever you felt you were getting someplace. She just wanted to scream, 'Mind your own fucking business and stop talking to me like you give a shit. Turn on that bloody siren and blast the damn traffic out the way, if you really want to get me to my son faster!' The bitter words bashed into Jonelle's tightly closed lips. She gulped them back down.

*How could anyone simply lose a child, like he was a sock or a bunch of bloody keys?*

'It's fine,' Bailey went on, 'we don't have to make conversation. I only wanted to take your mind off the traffic and let you know us cops like it when missing persons turn up, especially children. The first forty-eight hours are the most crucial, you know. After that, well, *–oop!'*

Jonelle saw Bailey rubbing his ribs and giving his colleague a narrow sideways look.

The vehicle claimed a mere three inches of tarmac.

Shaking her head, Jonelle lifted her eyes to the greyness when her attention was caught by a wiry man, a turbaned woman and six little people, three in pristine head coverings, all in billowing white robes. They scurried towards a dirty brown building with its doors open to receive them out of the winds and driving rain. Her dad was a deacon in church. He would insist on family devotion to the Almighty with unstinting service attendance, whether sleet or sunshine, homework or no homework, flu or no flu, period or no period.

'So, you know all about computers do you, Miss Laverne?' Bailey was saying.

'It's my business to know. Computers aren't only in our future. They're *today.*'

WPC Murphy, at the wheel, made a disapproving noise and craned her neck, trying to see ahead of the car in front. 'Bet there's nothing causing this hold-up. Happens every time there's a little rain! Might turn off – go up Herne Hill way or sit here for thirty minutes.'

Miss Laverne – who Jonelle was convinced was sleeping with pretty important people after she saw how they were swanning about her in the station – kept gassing about how computers could speed up crime detection, especially as they didn't need sleep or have homes to go to.

'Take missing persons, for instance!'

'You say that, Miss Laverne,' Bailey butted in, 'but computers will never have that human touch, nor recognise faces in a crowd. I read that if you tried to build a computer to do what the human brain does, the size of it would fill a few huge buildings and still not get close!'

Laverne tried to get back in, 'Ah, at the same—'

Bailey wasn't giving up the cause: 'And a lot of good people will lose their jobs to them boxes of tangled wires and flashy lights.'

*What a pair of gasbags!*

Jonelle thought about the last time she'd ridden a noisy car. She'd taken a minicab to collect her three from Candice's. They'd all wanted a window seat. Before she could stop them, Amanita had settled it by choosing to sit in the middle.

Shit! Amanita and Kenyana! They must be worried sick not hearing from her all day. When they'd all arrived to collect Deen only to find him missing, something animal had burst out of her and she forgot she had two other children until the police had her restrained and started talking about Social Services keeping her girls during her incarceration.

*Is there somewhere we could take them for you? Or someone to come and collect them, Miss Patrick? A relative? Their dad?*

*Tyrone? No bloody way. With the eyes of the Social on her, waiting for her to slip up, just once?*

Tyrone was bad news. *Don't kick me out, Jonie! I swear, I won't deal no more drugs from now on. They didn't even convict me.*

*Family?* A lump formed in her throat as she remembered her own father, a man of his word, had told her never to darken his doorstep again. Even so, she'd sneaked back to the family home with Tyrone, to snatch up a few possessions and found he'd changed the locks. Standing in a cold telephone booth, she'd begged her mother to speak to her dad or leave her clothes in a bag by the bins, maybe some money for food and those pills she'd read she needed for a healthy pregnancy. But instead of her mother, a strange voice repeated that the number she'd dialled was not in service.

Family was not an option, either.

That left her looking to her girlfriends again.

Candice, there for her yesterday, a new-friend-turned-old-faithful, had not answered her phone. Myrna too had failed to pick up and nobody'd seen her. She was probably still sick and in no condition to help a soul but herself.

Keefah's voice had found a way to her ears, over all the din at the hospital. Ironically, Keefah was the quietest among her girlfriends.

'Jonie? Jonie, it's me!' There she'd been, tilting her bandaged head quizzically from beyond the barrier of nurses and porters holding everyone back. Keefah's husband drank on Saturdays, religiously, so, Keefah'd be in A&E Sundays, with his blessing. That's how Myrna'd whispered it in the launderette anyway. Jonelle had once sworn that if she ever met the bastard she'd hit him upside the head, see how he liked 'walking into doors'.

Jonelle'd tried to wrench away from the officer. 'I want to talk to my friend over there!'

They'd held her fast, but let Keefah through.

'Jonie, I heard them nurses talking about Social Services having Amanita and Kenyana—' Keefah'd mumbled out one side of her swollen lips, and winked conspiratorially. 'I'll take the girls to your *mother's* and tell Miss Mattie you'll be along soon. No trouble at all. Don't worry.'

On launderette day, Jonelle and the regulars often discussed the maternal Miss Mattie, how Mother Mattie might be grieving the loss of a child or sickening for a daughter of her own. It explained why, Jonelle sometimes thought, she'd always clung to her with conversation and hers were the only children she offered free sweets and to babysit, if needed. 'A young lady must be able to go out now and then for a bit of livin',' she'd giggled into her cupped hands. So she'd accepted Keefah's suggestion to give Miss Mattie a try.

'Yes, please, Keefah. Tell *Mother* I'll be round to get the girls quick as I can.'

Jonelle closed her eyes, trying not to think what would have happened had Keefah not been there.

'Hey! Are you alright over there?' The words came with a hand resting gently on hers. Jonelle pulled her hand away, opened her eyes, and saw her fellow back-seater looking directly at her.

'I'm fine!' she said, folding her arms across her chest.

'Sorry, it was just that you – never mind,' she said, settling back and looking away, forward. 'Constable Bailey?'

'Yes, Miss Laverne.'

'What if a person goes missing for a number of years?'

'Pardon me, Miss Laverne?'

'Earlier, Constable Bailey, you said the first forty-eight hours were crucial. What about the first twenty-eight years?'

'Hmm, twenty-eight years?' Bailey picked up the thread and started weaving a tale about a long search for someone who would have grown and changed beyond recognition. 'So, hair colour might change. Nose. Voice, perhaps. After such a long time, most people are likely to become unrecognisable, let alone anything else…you only have to consider yourself and how different you were last year, last month, last week…'

Jonelle tuned them out but what she really wanted to do was cover her ears and shout lah-lah-lah repeatedly. What if she'd lost Deen? What would she tell people…his sisters…her circle of girlfriends…the regulars in the launderette, Tyrone? Jonelle rubbed circles into her temples. After twenty-eight years would he recognise his own mother in some sad-faced old lady, all crooked, wet-eyed and grey, leaning on a stick and calling him Son? Would she recognise him?

This ember of thought found enough tinder to set off a blaze of panic.

'Officer, can't you do something to get us there faster. Please!'

# CHAPTER 17

Bull was feeling stink. It was a two-part stink, if anyone wanted to know. First off, he'd been forced to break into a sweat and move his cargo to Prunes', to stay ahead of the cops; secondly, he was now hanging about on Prunes' patch, everything moving at a snail's pace while the clock ticked his chances away. He'd needed all hands on the wheel, or deck, or whatever, ready for the final move, the end game, the money shot. Trust that lazy sod, Triple, to bugger off whenever there was heavy lifting to do. But at least, this time, there'd be no Django to stand between him and what he had comin'. Bull imagined the absent Triple drunk and slobbering over some sorry skank's tits, trying to feel better about giving up his best pal's address. Bull tut-tutted, but he honestly didn't give a shit. The waster would show sooner or later and get a proper bollocking. With four out on errands, he'd only had five guys to clear out 'Grilla and he'd had to drive one of the sodding vans himself thanks to that knobhead going AWOL. Scratching at his groin, Bull felt so much anger bubbling up, he wanted to growl. So, he did, low and guttural.

*Fuck you, Django!*

Plus, with the clock ticking, he had to be waiting on bloody Prunes, who was working on Jamaica time.

Things'd be sweet if he came through, but Prunes'd screwed up his face like his nut sack was in a clamp and griped about short notice. Shit, it's not like he'd asked for the earth or nothin':

*Two containers, each with concealed compartments.*

*Forty packages – scratch that – thirty-four plus a special single, an older child and a minder.*

*Food, water, chemical waste disposal, nappies.*

*Transport to Docklands for loading.*

'For Tuesday? Shit!' Prunes'd said, looking at his fake Rolex and spilling raisins for yet another six-second rule pick-up. 'You don't ask much, do ya, Bull!'

'Stop blowing smoke up my arse, Prunes!' he'd told the weasel.

'Bull, what can I say? You think I'd miss a market day to… Wait.' Prunes puffed on his second Jamaican cigar and shook his head. 'Ah. Thing is, it might be too rich for your blood, Blood! Plus, be risky – damn risky – for me too, aight? Naw, forget it! Forget (puff), it (puff).'

'Cut the crap, Prunes!' Bull'd snorted, tightening his jaw so hard his gums were still feeling tender right now.

'Listen me, listen me.' Prunes'd paused to swallow, then reload. 'Bull-man, I'm taking *gi-normous* risks using my place of business…it's bloody short notice, aight. Cost me personal losses letting down my loyal punters on market day… I got overheads… I gotta pay Tom, Dick and his mate Harry… don't want to rush you or *nothin'*… No way I would profit from a brother man's misfortune…not even making anything for myself as such…me, with mouths to feed an' t'ing an' t'ing…of course, if you don't think it's a fair price?'

He'd bit down hard on his Jamaican, sucked in a big drag, ready to ram it up Prunes' nose, lit end first.

'Alright, Prunes, I'll give you a bigger cut!'

Even while they'd shook on it, Prunes had gone on, 'Everybody want to ship with Prunes, Bull, but you're right to come to me. You know I'd always give a brother first dibs, aight. What are friends for, eh?'

'I won't forget this, Prunes!' Bull'd told him, bumping knuckles instead of shaking hands like wankers. But he knew Prunes had shafted him, the money-grabbing little hustler. He'd only have to put up with it for forty-eight hours before he'd burn the little crab along with that fool Tyrone.

Prunes'd scuttled away without looking back, without bothering to help pack up the place and transport the packages; even though the fool knew that moving fast and low was the only way to stay off the police radar.

*Fuck you, Django!*

Bull rubbed at tight knots in the bulging muscles of his shoulders and neck. He knew a girl once who'd ease them knots in a flash. Too bad her man had found them in his bed. Bull felt constricted in the clutter of Prunes' office. One wall was lined with a stack of barrels, ready to topple. On another wall hung a large red, green and gold flag hanging like tapestry.

*Ah, Jamaica, land we love.*

Many yesterdays ago, he'd made that first visit to his mother's homeland, to Spanish Town in the parish of St Catherine to see her and reveal himself as her anonymous benefactor of ten years. Prunes'd found her and set up the deal sending barrels, stuffed with clothes, trinkets – all gifts – 'cause no mother of Dirk Manners was going to live poor or walk about in rags, no matter what she'd bloody done.

Prunes'd made all his travel arrangements, right down to the taxi that got him to the dusty shanty address in the middle of the Caribbean island. It was as clear as if it were yesterday – the fresh food, the spliffs, the sing-song way people talked…

'Yu say you's her son? Jesas! Den, how come yu never tell nobady yu was comin', Son?' his gap-toothed stepfather had chirped. 'Wi could'a send *s'maddy* fi pick yu up fram di airport!'

'S'aright. I was gonna surprise my mum. Where's she at?'

Bull remembered his stepdad's bulging eyes and his rum stink. The jerk had rocked back on his heels trying to recall where his wife – Bull's ma – had gone. It only took one gentle squeeze of the bastard's turkey neck to refresh his memory and find out that the shit-for-brains had been collecting the barrels using his ma's signature – 'she told me to do it!' – and because they'd kept on arriving, he'd kept on signing for them and selling the contents after 'she fall down, hit her head and got dead'.

'Dead?' An odd feeling had bubbled up into his throat, but Bull hadn't shed a single tear. Crying was for sissies – a lesson he'd learnt in Barnardo's where boarders bawled about having no mother or no father and no people to foster or adopt them.

Fuckin' losers.

So, he hadn't got to see his mother for the first time and hadn't found her sitting, as he'd imagined, wearing one of the many outfits he'd sent, three times every year, for a decade. He couldn't ask her about his pa – what he did; who he was; did he kick ass? Ask her what had threatened her so much that she'd left him behind to be brought up like a fuckin' charity case.

Bull yanked his gaze from the flag, searching for where Prunes kept his smokes or drink or stash.

Water under the bridge now, Bull huffed, feeling the tension tighten his neck and shoulders even more as he relived the rage, hearing echoes of the lying toe-rag Bertram shouting from inside a barrel floating into the darkness, down the silvery Rio Cobre River, as it meandered away, through the lush St Catherine countryside to eventually flush into the Caribbean Sea.

# CHAPTER 18

'Miss Laverne, people leave home all the time and don't want to be found. Even the police must respect that. Might be very upsetting to have someone walk up to them and drag them twenty-eight years back in time, don't you think?'

Thank God Deen'd been found if that was their attitude, Jonelle sighed. She'd been focusing on the conversation to avert the anxiety. A passing motorbike farted a plume of fumigated dampness into her face, causing her to gag and cough.

'You alright back there?' The WPC stretched her neck to catch her in the rearview mirror. 'Want me to pull over?'

'H-how long…' She tried to sound okay mid-cough.

'You numpty!' The WPC tooted the horn at a motorist darting in front of them. 'Sorry, miss, only a few minutes if this engine keeps running. They should have replaced these wrecked cars by now – been four years since the riots, right, Bailey?'

Bailey and Laverne ignored the question, still gassing about missing persons. Jonelle decided she would too and tilted her head to catch the time on the bejewelled watch her fellow passenger wore. She worked out the diamond dots were the 12, 3, 6 and 9 and the gold dots covered the numbers in between. Reflections off the glass made it impossible to distinguish the hands, upside-down.

'It's twelve twenty-seven!' Laverne offered, interrupting herself.

Oh shit, three minutes till Deen's next medication. Had he even had his first dose?

'Seriously, can't you go any faster?' Jonelle huffed.

Murphy said something about breaking rules and reached for a switch. An intermittent wail barged through the traffic before them, flicking precious minutes off their journey. Jonelle allowed herself a discreet smile of relief when she saw a sign welcoming them to King's College A&E.

They hadn't quite stopped when Jonelle tugged frantically at the door. It remained locked.

'Those doors open from the outside, Miss Patrick,' Bailey said. 'We'll let you both out and escort you in.'

She willed him to hurry up as he alit from the vehicle. He opened Laverne's door then hers. Jonelle scrambled out, hitched up her skirt and fixed her eyes on the hospital entrance. 'Actually, *you* lot bloody keep up.'

She ran, ignoring calls for her to wait. Too late, she spotted an approaching ambulance and, leaping to safety, she kept going, dodging around a white van in her way.

'Waitforusplease!' she heard behind.

'Oi, watchit!' came from a pair of white overalls at the van's side doors, hoisting a container off a trolley that was laden with other containers marked Hazardous Waste. Too late to avoid it, Jonelle bumped the trolley, rolling it into one of the men who, as luck would have it, stopped the thing with his foot.

'Sorreee!' she yelled above the eruption of cuss words she'd only ever heard from Jamaican street thugs brawling about turf at 2 a.m. some nights.

Finally, she found the ward.

'Ah, Miss Patrick!' It was that doctor, the same one who'd said he didn't like the way Deen was breathing. 'I've got the test results back! How's that for speed, eh?'

'Sorry.' Jonelle sidestepped him.

'You need to come this way.' The too-cheerful man, pointed with his clipboard.

'You have him?'

'No, but I've got his results. What a coincidence seeing you just when—'

'Thanks!' she said, rushing ahead, vaguely aware of some commotion behind her. She started to feel heady from the potpourri of sweat, disinfectant and urine she associated with hospitals. 'I can't stop now, where do they have Deen now?'

'Paediatrics, of course,' she heard his quick strides behind her. 'Wait up. Don't you want to know about your son. Deen?'

'Can't stop.' She made a quick double-check she was following the correct floor markings. 'I came for Deen this morning and they'd lost him. I've come back to get him and... ah-ah-ah!' Jonelle rubbed at the sneeze with her hand.

'Lost him?' The doctor looked perplexed. 'We don't lose children at *this* hospital. I'm sure there's been some mistake. Come with me.'

Shaking her head, Jonelle followed. The sooner she collected her son, the sooner she'd end this madness and get back to her life.

Nurses beckoned for his attention, but the doctor castigated them for not seeing that he was busy. Jonelle felt guilty for noticing the width of his shoulders, the strength in his stride.

They circled cordons where workmen were installing new doors and replacing large panels of glass where a mini tornado must have blown through recently and Jonelle felt shamed.

'What's your name again?'

They'd stopped at a nurses' station. He puffed his name tag towards her. She read the name but didn't fancy trying to pronounce 'Erasmus-Esteves'.

'I know. Just call me Dr Eric, like the children do.' He beckoned a nurse away from her paperwork. 'Nurse Gabon, this is Miss Patrick. She's here for Deen Patrick – sorry – Williams. Deen *Williams!*'

With a smile that made her lips thin out, the nurse came over and removed her glasses.

'Ah, Miss Patrick! We've found your son.'

'*Found* him?' The doctor looked confused.

'Yes, doctor. Uhm, the last shift told me that Miss Patrick had been in earlier. They reported the boy couldn't be *found* on the ward…' Her voice tapered and she drummed a pen on a pad in her hand.

'Christ!' Dr Eric stepped back as if the nurse was suddenly infectious.

'Look, please take me to Deen now so we can leave—'

'Miss Patrick!' The two police officers closed in fast, their boots squeaking on the tiled floor. PC Bailey was leading and looking more than a little peeved. 'Miss Patrick, we called for you to stop and wait. Do I need to remind you you're here under our escort? There are complaints from this hospital against you. You shouldn't run off and—'

'Fine, fine!' Jonelle shot at them and waved at the nurse. 'This lady can tell you what I was telling you all this time. Go on…'

The nurse shrank away, folded both arms across her breasts and cleared her throat. 'As I was about to say, Miss Patrick, I understand that – and this was before I started my shift a minute ago – your son'd been playing hide-and-seek…hid a little too well and…anyway, that's what my colleagues told me. We're very, very sorry for the inconvenience—'

'Give him back to me now,' Jonelle spoke firmly and as calmly as she could with the two officers flanking her. 'Please.'

'Yes, yes, of course. Wait here, please.'

'*In*-credible,' Dr Eric said, gaping at the retreating nurse. 'Miss Patrick, it's most irregular. Believe me. Can't think what I'd do if any of mine went missing!'

His manner and tone slipped past all her defences. Jonelle

felt stumped for anything appropriate to say. Instead, she kept her eyes trained eagerly in the direction the nurse had gone.

'Miss, maybe this was a silver lining, as I'm a research fellow here.' Dr Eric sidled into her line of sight. 'I've been analysing Deen's results.'

She wondered what was keeping that nurse.

'There's still no cure, Miss Patrick,' Dr Eric went on.

'What?' Jonelle's knees lost some power.

'The good news is that these days the prognosis is much better than a decade ago.'

Jonelle hated words like *prognosis* when plain language was enough. 'What're you saying?'

The doctor addressed the two officers, 'Perhaps, Miss Patrick and I may speak privately about her son?'

Not really wanting to go anywhere except to collect her boy, Jonelle tilted her head to read his notes between his fingers: '*chron...in...aem...ickle ce*' and '*hered...(?)*'

He was still trying to convince the police it would only take a second and he was sure she wouldn't run off while learning about her son's health.

Meanwhile, Jonelle tried to fill in the blanks and make sense. *Sickle*?

Christ, Candice had told her to make her GP check Deen for something called *Sickle Cells*! She tried to see more.

'*Incurable*.'

The words hit like a punch to the stomach. The Laverne woman suddenly appeared from nowhere.

'Officers, you both seem very busy and reception is getting crowded with sick people. I don't need to be here, so why don't you tell me where I can find Mr Kurtis? I'll go see him and you can meet me there when you're ready?'

Bailey looked at her then at his partner. 'Murphy, you take Miss Laverne to Mr Kurtis and release him to her. I'll wait here with Miss Patrick.'

Murphy nodded and led Laverne away.

Jonelle watched them leave. Her stomach churned and her attention bounced around the corridor. More than ever before, she yearned to complete her business course and earn enough to go private for Deen.

*Bloody, bloody NHS.*

# CHAPTER 19

Bull thought Prunes' office could have way more room for a body to move about if not for all the stuff. He tutted at the shelves bending and bulging with box files, the small teak desk, a big brown leatherette wing-backed armchair and a futon-cum-lounge seat. Still, he had to hand it to Prunes, he knew how to live and do business. Most of all, Prunes was reliable…so far!

Prunes' office door creaked, ripping Bull out of his reverie. A small girl entered carrying a tray. Bull smiled at the array of liquor and then at her. Good ole Prunes! When it came to 'demand', he was the crown prince of 'supply'.

'Come in, sweetheart!' Bull said, eyes popping.

Watching her cross the room to set down the tray, Bull's eyes didn't linger long on the unopened bottle of Scotch beside the gleaming lead crystal tumbler. He also ignored the box of Cubans to trace the curve of the jeans and t-shirt that clung like a second skin.

*Prunes, yu dawg!*

She looked about twenty-three, twenty-four, with the low mileage of a sixteen-year-old and Bull licked his lips and found them bone dry.

He reached out.

'No, sir. Wait—'

Bull clamped a hand over her mouth. 'Darlin', some men like to talk and shit. I'm not one of them and I don't want to know your name or nothin'. I've got a lot of energy to dump. Get me. No use for chit-chat. Show me what your momma gave you.'

Like a pro, she struggled, pleading eyes and all, so much so Bull almost believed she didn't want any part of him. Pulling a testosterone-powered grin, Bull braced himself against her best efforts bouncing off him like the rain that was now drumming the skylight.

'That's it, bitch. Gimme all you got!'

With one powerful arm restraining her by her face in a long reach, he decided to unzip her first, yanking away the stone-washed denim and tossing it before ripping white cotton pants from the softness beneath. Out of respect, Bull forced a smile at her feeble fight as she scratched and kicked. His biceps bulged against slender resistance while he carefully unleashed himself.

'Swee-eet! I like your spirit, girl!'

He felt a new energy surge into her chest and thrashing limbs, as though she'd been holding something back. This is when a pro distinguished herself from a novice, he thought. The distraction made him slacken his grip.

She was wriggling free!

'No, no, no, you stay put!'

'Mmmf! Mmmf,' her breath puffed warm and wet into the hand covering her mouth and nose. Working her jaw and twisting her neck, she somehow managed to take his little finger between her teeth and bite down to find bone.

'Fah-ckin'!'

He yanked his hand away from her bloodstained teeth and sent it back, open palmed, with interest and a forearm used to pressing 120kg in the gym. The calloused to tender connection produced heat and sound that sent the girl's head spinning. Her body followed with a twirl, then she fell backwards, half on, half off the futon.

'Blood's pumping now, bitch. No more foreplay.' Bull looked down where she lay with her lips bloody and parted and quivering, her chest heaving and her limbs resigned, outstretched like a wishbone. 'You can cut the act now, bitch. You have to know when to quit the pleasure-pain thing.'

Not that Bull minded people getting hurt for taking it too far. So, he ignored her eyes, looking about all terrified at the sight of his hardness, and her pretty mouth moving but making no sound.

'Look, I don't munch carpet or kneel before nobody, you feel me?'

He wasn't really asking. Bull reached down. He hoisted her like a sack of feathers and caught her on his chest. The force caused her arms to flop about his neck and Bull suspended her with an arm beneath each bare thigh, parting her.

Taking aim, he lowered her for his upward thrust.

'Damn!'

Bull began to think what such a moneymaker might bring to his stables. No, to steal her from Prunes would be bad manners. There was a joke there somewhere – another time – right now, this chick was showing him rare skills. Besides, come Tuesday, he'd be able to buy and sell Prunes, lock, stock and this pussy too.

Bull flexed, holding her tight and pushed for home.

She yelped, bucked, tightening on him in a powerful spasm, all the time pushing against him as though she wanted to be anywhere but riding the Bull.

'Damn, girl!' Bull grunted. Maddened by the superb friction this clever little bitch was generating, he walked them to the nearest wall and slammed her hard. With every advance, banging her head on the wall, pumping air from her body until Bull shuddered violently, pressing her warm softness into the cold, solid brickwork.

She hung from him like clothes on a line. Bull walked over to the futon and dumped her there. Looking around, he spotted her torn t-shirt on a shelf and used it like a samurai cleaning his sword. Seeing red, Bull shrugged. Some women couldn't handle all that meat he had down there without special training. Besides, he didn't do gentle. Gentle was for pussies.

'I've had better,' Bull said, packing up his equipment and pulling on his trousers. 'Don't get me wrong – you're good. Got potential. Had more time...' He paused, waiting for the head rush to pass. That's the trouble with having massive legs and thighs, he found. 'Yeah, if I had the time, we could see what else you got under that hood, girl. Unlucky for you.'

She lay, not speaking. Not even a word of appreciation. He wondered whether that was how she earned big tips and favours from her 'customers'. Well, she'd done enough and deserved an Oscar or some other big-ass award for acting like she'd never got the Big-D before.

'Ain't you gonna get dressed?'

She didn't look up.

The fun was gone and he was starting to get pissed. Maybe he'd got cum on her clothes or some weird shit like that. Who knows? Women.

'Tell you what? You ever get tired of Prunes, come see me, y'hear?'

Bull had been feeling all screwed up. It had all been such a mega wind-up with all the stress of cops turning up when they shouldn't, losing stock and messing up profits while having to relocate operations in no time flat, then finding out your number two was a double-crossing, two-faced supergrass... but right now, he felt renewed. Ready for...whatever comes next. Damn, that bitch was good treatment. Rebalanced, maybe like some fuckers felt after taking a joint or some other kind of medication. Knowing what people want and providing what people need was a talent he'd respected in Prunes.

Once, in the beginning, he'd tried to recruit Prunes into his crew but either Tyrone or Django, or both of them, had put Prunes off. Now that the dreamer and the two-faced git were off the scene, maybe…

The office door swung inwards and banged against a coffin-shaped box Bull hadn't noticed before. A large label on the side read 'Fireworks'.

Prunes walked in, looking pleased as a man who'd pulled up a garden weed and struck oil.

'You like the little treat what I sent up, Bull?'

'Prunes, you spoil me!' Bull said, clocking a loose-hipped bird in a cat suit following Prunes into the room.

'But you haven't touched it!' His host's jaw dropped as he looked over at the tray.

Bull laughed. 'Hey, hey, Prunes. After that main course, you bring dessert too?'

The pussy beside Prunes winked and Bull winked back.

'Uhm, well…' Prunes looked a little like he'd missed the joke then regained composure. 'Anyway, I's got a little surprise treat. Never say I don't know how to—'

Almost inaudible, a whimper floated up from the futon and Prunes advanced further into the office, locating the source of the tiny sound. He stopped mid-chew. Bull used to warn that he'd someday crack a crown on a pip.

'Cara?' Prunes rushed to stoop beside the crumpled, trembling figure on the futon. She'd pulled on her jeans, but they still gaped open at the waist, and she held her bloodied t-shirt over her bare chest.

'Uncle?' was what Bull thought she said as he grasped the whisky bottle by the neck and wrung the cap off.

'Bull, man!' Prunes said, eyeballing him. 'She just turned fif-*fuckin*-teen today!'

Bull poured two fingers of whisky, lifted the glass and said, 'Happy birthday!'

# CHAPTER 20

Chelsea followed Murphy onto a mixed ward and past bed after bed of patients, some moaning, others complaining or looking up at the ceiling. Relatives were dotted about beds eating chocolates or fruit, touching hands or stroking foreheads. Tubes and wires connected some to devices that blipped or dripped.

'Who is this man to you, Miss Laverne?'

The question was innocent enough, and Chelsea wondered why she had no ready response. 'Uhm.'

He was a friend, plain and simple. Why couldn't she just say that? In fact, if she had said that Judge Parker-Richardson might have extended whatever he'd said to the superintendent to include TK, a man who was only in trouble for having done her a favour.

A bloodcurdling wail ripped through the hospital hubbub as if someone had stepped on the tail of a bobcat and back down the hall heated voices mingled with the crash of metal on a tiled floor.

Chelsea met WPC Murphy's surprise with a shrug. A flow of staff surged through them, towards the noise. Murphy edged away, following them, indicating to a doorway beyond Chelsea.

'He's in there, on that ward, Miss Laverne. There should be an officer with him. Remain with them until I return. Yes?'

'Yes, yes,' Chelsea called after the policewoman.

On the ward, sad faces surrounded one sleeping old woman, another bedded woman in a web of wires stared at the ceiling while a man and small boy ate grapes. They looked up as Chelsea walked by, following her with their eyes. She scanned the beds. No TK. Two were curtained off and the noise of cackling came from one of them, so she chose the other.

Slowly pulling back the curtain, she peeked in.

'TK?'

The glint of a handcuff caught her eye. Then she saw the plastered arm. Chelsea covered her mouth, sucking in shock and outrage. He lay on his back with his face flopped away from her and he was snoring gently.

Looking around, Chelsea hunted for a nurse, doctor, someone official who could say whether she might proceed beyond the curtains. A scruffy figure looking more like a homeless beggar than a patient stumbled towards her, seeking attention from distracted hospital staff, rebounding from one dismissive hand to another. Chelsea supposed she had broken ranks, probably fed up with hanging around the A&E. In any case, she'd have no information about TK's condition.

More white uniforms leaked from doors and adjoining halls to rush along the corridor in the wrong direction. Sighing, Chelsea siezed the moment and slipped between the curtains, drawing them closed behind her.

A puff of cotton covered TK's left eye. His chest rose and fell, making him less corpselike in the bed.

*Oh, TK. What did they do to you?*

Resist arrest? No, he did not.

Policemen don't lie, surely?!

Tearful and careful not to disturb him, Chelsea noticed a tray. Orange juice, a piece of toast, baked beans, a single rasher of bacon and what looked like an ellipsoid of potato. Breakfast, she decided. There was no steam rising from the dirty brown liquid in a paper cup, a string dangling over its side.

Stewed tea.

Untouched breakfast.

*Oh, TK! This is all my fault!*

There were no police guarding him. Perhaps gone for a toilet break, or something better than watching a grown man sleep, she thought, and decided she too might leave TK in peace. How was he able to sleep, at any rate? Who knew hospitals were such noisy places? When he woke, the first thing she'd do was buy him a decent meal. Backing through the curtains, Chelsea decided she'd stay in London and get TK back on his feet. *Why'd she think to do a thing like that?* The grateful half of her mind told the dubious half that she owed him that much. More.

Chelsea drew the curtains after her.

'Prease!'

'Jesus!' Chelsea jumped away from the grimy hand. The arm tugging her sleeve extended from the diminutive person with sallow skin visible beneath her ragged hood. There was something about her expression as she looked up at Chelsea, with obvious anxiety and clutched a bundle of rags to her chest.

'*Médecin! Médecin!*'

'No, no! I'm no doctor.' Chelsea backed up against the curtains around TK's bed and lowered her voice.

'*Aidez moi!*' the figure said, peeling back her makeshift hoodie enough to make eye contact. '*Elle est très malade! Vous devez m'aider!*'

Sunken and wild, her eyes checked about them continuously. Long, dank jet-black hair hung from under the ragged cloth she wore as a combination headwrap and shawl. She smelled as though she'd walked far, and her bare feet told Chelsea she had encountered broken glass along the way.

People were looking at them.

'But I'm really *not* a doctor!' Chelsea looked for someone qualified in the vicinity.

Stupidly, she was replying to French with English!

Chelsea rifled through her brain for some French vocabulary, some way to say, 'I can't help you, but I will find someone for...'

Once confident in the language, she felt irritated at how hard it was to remember simple vocabulary and grammar. Perhaps it was the pressure, but all she could think of were swear words, the sort that the boy in her French exchange *famille* had peppered his speech with, not when *maman* or *papa* were about, of course, but especially when *mes amis* dropped by the chateau to meet his English student, the one with the same name as a football team.

Chelsea looked back down the corridor for hospital staff.

The girl looked too.

Two security men appeared in the corridor doorway.

'Du!' the bad little word shot from the elfin face, and she ducked into her grubby hoodie. Last time Chelsea heard this expletive, a Vietnamese college friend had been whacked on the shin with a hockey stick. When Chelsea looked down, the jittery stranger had vanished and the curtains behind her fluttered gently.

One security guard stopped to inspect a tall cupboard, the other entered the ward, checking behind the door and stooping to look under the first bed. Who had they lost?

Chelsea ducked back behind TK's curtains, looked down and caught a fleeting glimpse of a blackened and shredded sole. She stooped and looked under the bed.

'Get from under there!' she said firmly enough to mean business but not wake the sleeping TK.

Crammed in the cleft where wall met floor, the small stranger shielded her bundle. She could have been fourteen or twenty-four.

'Come on,' Chelsea beckoned more energetically, 'you can't be here!'

At that, she wriggled further away with a look of weariness and desperation.

'You?' Chelsea gasped in a penny-drop moment, recalling the dingy 'Grilla club ladies', reeking of disinfectant. 'It was *you* in that cubicle!'

There were voices approaching. Chelsea heard someone being asked whether they'd seen a small child on the ward.

*Christ!*

'No, polis! Preas! No, polis!' Terror glistened in her eyes.

'You speak English?' Chelsea whispered.

'A *rittle* bit! A *rittle*! Preas, no polis!'

'Shh!' Chelsea put a forefinger across her lips and pointed up to where TK still lay sleeping and handcuffed to the bed. Whatever this was about, she wanted to keep TK resting, undisturbed. Then there was the policewoman, Murphy, who might be back any second. 'Quickly, uhm! *Vite!* If you don't want to be found, come out. *Please. S'il vous plaît! Je vous l'aidez!*'

Slowly, the nodding stranger inched out but refused Chelsea's outstretched offer to help her with the bundle. Keeping her eyes on the gap between the curtains, she backed away from Chelsea.

Using her basic French, Chelsea tried to confirm her suspicions. '*Vous êtes Vietnamien?*'

'*Oui.* I fro' Vietnam,' she said. Then, in a tortuous mix of English and French, she tried to explain. Unable to follow her *Franglais*, Chelsea whispered that she should continue in French only. Her listening comprehension had always been superior to her oral anyway. Outside the curtains, doors were being opened and closed and the metallic slide of metal on metal grew closer.

'Excuse me, have you seen…' The officious voice was close, loud enough to be three beds away if not the very next one.

'Can't you see she's sleeping,' someone replied angrily. Chelsea pictured the woman staring at the ceiling with her two spectators.

The little Vietnamese explained that she didn't want to cause trouble for her family back in Vietnam; that a violent gang wanted protection money. They'd threatened her family, her father if he didn't pay what he owed. She was only working for them to save her family and prevent them being ejected from their smallholding where they grew *des cacahuets* – peanuts or cashews?

Peanuts.

Chelsea picked up that she'd given up a chance to – do something or other – and attend the Ho Chi Minh City University of Information Technology and she missed her family.

'*Ils m'a dit que je pourrais devenir une prostituée dans Vietnam ou être une nounou en Europe sinon ma famille seraient les rembourser en sang,*' she explained, flooring her verbal accelerator.

Chelsea flagged her down. '*Trop vite! Encore, s'il vous plait.*'

The stranger slowed down and, in a low whisper, continued to explain that the bad men had given her a choice: work as their prostitute to get her passport back and to earn a ticket home or... Even repeated, Chelsea struggled with *nounou*.

The girl pointed at her bundle and rocked it.

'*A nanny*! Of course,' Chelsea nodded, miming a babe in arms.

The girl nodded furiously and told Chelsea they were called 'packages', kept in dark rooms, given babies and told that if the babies died, they would die too but if they took good care of them, then they and the families they'd left behind would be very well cared for. She said she'd met other girls from Vietnam and from Thailand, the Philippines and Indonesia. Sometimes, a girl would run away, and when they caught them...

It seemed incredible. Chelsea wondered whether the girl had absconded from under the care of the Maudsley Hospital, next door, where mental health was treated. But if her story were true, then had she run away from these people and found sanctuary in the toilets at 'Grilla, if this really was the same girl.

'So, why do you need a doctor so badly?' It was not quite what she'd meant to ask, but Chelsea felt disoriented from translating and sifting for logic and a way of helping the girl without disturbing TK.

The girl peeled back the swaddling.

Chelsea gasped.

The girl told her the child was very sick, but she'd hidden this from the men for as long as she could.

'They kill the sick babies?' Chelsea wondered if she had translated correctly.

'Oui!'

Chelsea was considering making a second call to the judge when approaching footfalls whisked the girl's attention away. The curtains flew apart like startled birds and a security guard regarded them quizzically.

''Cuse me,' the man huffed.

Chelsea stepped towards him, wagging a furious finger towards the snoozing TK.

'Shush!'

'Sorry, but have you seen a small child around here...' he said, whispering, hovering a palm about three feet off the floor, '...about yay high?'

'How dare you barge in here, with sick people resting?' Chelsea whispered tersely, forcing him back and pulling the edges of the curtains closed behind them. 'What's your badge number?'

'I'm so sorry, ma'am. We've got an emergency situation. I'm just doing my job, right!'

'Badge number, please.'

'Fine, you haven't seen anything,' he said, stomping off, muttering to himself.

Chelsea re-entered behind the curtains to find the girl stroking the child, her cheeks wet. She looked up at her and Chelsea saw someone supporting a weight of responsibility far beyond her strength and resources. If it were as she'd said, then this tiny girl, squatting there in rags, was risking everything to get treatment for the baby.

'Okay.' Chelsea reached out with her best French. 'I'll try and help. First, let me take the baby and—'

The girl drew back, taking the bundle with her.

Sharply, Chelsea whispered in her best French, 'Look, if I'm to help, then let me have the baby.'

Chelsea told her she'd pretend she'd found the child abandoned on the doorstep.

The girl protested furiously.

Realising her error, Chelsea corrected it, assuring her that she was not going to leave the child on the doorstep, but pretend she had *found* it on the doorstep. It was something she'd seen in news reports and besides, it would attract far fewer questions and less suspicion from the authorities. The baby would get the help she desperately needed, and it looked like they had no time to waste.

TK rolled his head from one side to the other and mumbled something unintelligible before releasing an embarrassingly long whoosh of air beneath the sheets.

The girl, looking more resigned than convinced, extended her arms as though offering her heart and soul.

'*Tốt*,' Chelsea said in Vietnamese, adding quickly in French that 'in college, I had a Vietnamese friend named Dung and she taught me how to say a few phrases. I am sorry if I said it wrong. It was a long time ago.'

The girl's eyes twinkled and cracked lips managed to smile. She seemed to grow a little taller.

Chelsea felt the baby stiffen suddenly. She parted the curtains and, before hurrying away, told the girl to wait there for her, that the man in the bed was her friend and if he woke up, to tell him in English: *Chelsea is coming back soon.*

'Chelsea?' TK pulled the covers off his face.

'How are you feeling? You look...' Chelsea tried not to say, 'white as a sheet'. She noticed his eyes were darting around and beyond her as he painfully raised himself up on his elbows.

'You alone?'

'The police brought me here.'

'Bull's men.'

'Bull's men?'

TK was shaking. 'Chelsea, some weird shit's going down. They were wearing white coats, pushing a trolley...what's Bull's boys doin' in here acting like hospital people?'

Chelsea wondered whether he was delirious.

# CHAPTER 21

The hospital security man looked up at her from the screen. 'Are you sure that's *not* your son, miss?'

Jonelle looked left at Murphy and right at Bailey and decided not to repeat herself.

'I can make the image a bit sharper, you know, by reducing the noise and adjusting the contrast with this little knob here!'

Jonelle's toes curled inside her shoes. Earlier, WPC Murphy had suggested she might be overreacting to the situation: *Miss Patrick, stop, you'll hurt someone!... We accept your son's not playing hide-and-seek...he's missing and not vanished into thin air!... We're all here to help! Please, calm down!... Look, I understand... I'm a mother too!* That was what had allowed them to take the bedpan off her. Now here they were going over security footage of the hospital exits and entrances.

'Look,' she said in a sub-zero tone. 'I happen to know my own son. That's *not* him.'

'Wait!' said Bailey. 'Go back a few frames!'

'Piece o' piss!' the security man said, scanning his audience for signs of disapproval before returning to fiddle with the equipment. 'This is a real good piece a kit.'

They watched as he toyed with knobs, sliders and buttons to stop the tape reeling forward. The start–stop clicks and winding spool reminded Jonelle of a time when she'd make cassette tape recordings off the radio. The only music she craved right now was Deen's voice.

'Ready, folks?'

Jonelle scowled at the idiotic grin on his sodding face. Remembering Murphy's wisdom, she breathed deeply and let it out very slowly as they all regrouped to peer over his shoulders. The two officers positioned themselves to allow her just enough space to see but not reach the man or his precious surveillance equipment.

'Here comes the ambulance again,' the man commentated.

Yet again, they all watched the Jonelle of an hour ago run into frame.

The ambulance braked, narrowly avoiding knocking into her. Funny that, she hadn't realised it had come that close.

There she came, around the white van…side doors open… two men…one hefting the enormous bin off the trolley.

Big 'BioHazzard' sign.

'That's odd?' the security man said.

It was like watching someone else, seeing herself bash into the trolley and shove it out the way, sending it rolling.

'See that?' someone said. Sounded like Bailey.

'That's *really* odd,' said the security man. 'What day is it?'

'See what?' Murphy said to Bailey.

'Sunday!' Jonelle said from the back.

'Can you show that again…slow it down?' Bailey asked, pointing at the small screen. 'Back to when the trolley bumps into that guy's foot!'

'Are you joking, Officer? Prepare to be amazed,' the security man started pressing buttons.

The reel went back, everyone moved closer: Jonelle looked ridiculous to herself as her onscreen expression wrinkled at a snail's pace, while the trolley took forever to roll into the man by the van, only to touch his foot ever so slowly and…

'This bit, watch that trolley,' Bailey said. 'Keep your eyes on that lid!'

Jonelle focused, waiting for the slow rise of the lid on the bin marked Hazardous Waste.

R-i-i-i-p!

'Oh, shit!'

First something tore, then Jonelle heard a bird flapping in the room somewhere, except there was no bird.

'Hate it when that happens. Bloody cheap tapes! Not to worry. I'll have this fixed double-quick.' He pulled scissors and half a roll of tape from a drawer in the desk. The splice won't take long, he assured, and we probably won't lose anything important. 'Happens every soddin' time you switch to slo-mo. Not to worry, you have me.'

'Why'd you want to know what day it was?' Jonelle asked the security man, pursuing her curiosity to lower her frustration.

'Well,' the security man said, standing up from hunching over the desk and stretching his back. 'It was those two guys.'

'What about them?'

'Well, I've *never* seen them before. Plus, nobody told me they were starting to collect waste on Sundays... Okay, here we go...showtime!'

The splice had broken right into the scene where they watched Jonelle jump away from the approaching ambulance. The scene twitched and she vanished from the screen, immediately reappearing in slo-mo past the stubby man in white overalls, holding the hazardous waste bin.

It looked like a sealed container.

Then a line appeared and slowly thickened into a thin black wedge.

'See, right there, the top is—' PC Bailey started.

'Shush! I'm trying to see!' Jonelle peered more closely at the growing gap, unsure what she was seeing and unable to turn away. Light bounced on something shiny, silvery and the opening grew to show something with stripes inside the bin.

'What's that?' Bailey said.

Jonelle squinted to focus.

'Not sure, but as the picture's in black and white, the two tones could actually be anything…blue and silver, or red and…' The security man grew quieter when he looked up at her.

'Green and gold!' It had to be, she started to shiver as she recognised the pattern.

'It could, miss. Yes, it could be green and—'

'That's Deen's!' Jonelle backed away, grabbed her head to stop it exploding and prowled the small room. 'It's Deen's jacket! It's Deen's!'

'That's not bloody likely!' said the security man, looking back at the screen. 'Excuse my French.'

Jonelle pushed through between the two officers. Bailey grabbed for one arm and Murphy caught the other, to hold her back from the security man, who leaned away, wide-eyed, pointing at the screen. 'It's a hazardous waste… It flipped open! It shouldn't do that! What's going on?'

'He's right, Miss Patrick,' Murphy said, tightening her grip. 'Try to stay calm.'

Bailey left Jonelle's side to lean on the desk next to the security man, who kept Jonelle in sight. He bent close to the screen, rubbing his chin.

'Yes, why didn't it stay shut…when it contains hazards!'

Jonelle looked at the still image, but her focus went far beyond the screen. 'I'm telling you, it's Deen's jacket!'

# CHAPTER 22

A sad, wailing front gate alarm made Prunes jump and rush out of the office. Bull went over to look out of the window and saw that Prunes was already down and outside. He bet himself that his short-arse had scrambled down the three flights of stairs, four-at-a-time.

Bull reckoned Prunes' place had once been three detached properties – he'd probably demolished one to make more space, used this one for business and, shit, fuck knows what that third one was for? He regarded the tall, long fence interrupted by the eight-foot fuck-off wooden electric gate that had admitted them earlier. On the left was a neat six-foot hedge over which Bull spied very flat, grass-green turf that looked proper ready for something poncy like golf or planting fuckin' flowers… Bull couldn't put it all together with Prunes…a market trader with a few dodgy connections on the side!

'You think you know a person…' Bull watched Prunes bark instructions to his guys, trying to find the right angle to manoeuvre the white van between the buildings and through to the back. Triple had been the only one who could handle anything bigger than a bike. That is, him and the man who'd taught him how, but he didn't want to think about *him* anymore. Not now. Not at all.

Prunes went from pushing at the air to drive them backwards, to fanning himself to bring them forwards, only for the vehicle to gently crunch a piece of brick from the corner of the building, sending dust flying and adding colour to the rainbow of past mishaps.

Bull guessed that when Prunes slapped his forehead, closed his eyes, and lifted his face to the skies, he was not praying. When Prunes opened his eyes, he made eye contact with him. Clearly unimpressed, Prunes went back to flapping about frantically to guide the van safely through the gap into the backyard, where they'd already parked Bull's BMW.

Served him right, seeing that Prunes had another, wider gate, one he'd claimed led directly into his backyard.

'Why don't you use that?' Bull'd asked earlier.

'Got a deal with neighbours, Bull. Them gates are kept shut at weekends and evenings.'

'Tcho,' Bull had kissed his teeth, 'I keep telling you, Prunes. Join my crew and nobody give you no shit!'

Bull turned and went over to the back window. Shaking his head side-to-side, he tried but failed to figure out why Prunes was holding out.

'You know me, Bull. I'm like a lone wolf, man. Ah-wooo!'

Ha ha fuckin' ha! There he was, offering the fool a chance to run with the big boys, so he could tell his neighbours to shove their deals and watch them cower behind drawn curtains as he unchained those gates any damn time he damn well wanted to.

*Hell. Yeah.*

From ground level, Prunes was waving, beckoning up at him – probably thinking he ought to be down there himself, in the damp and cold, sorting his Yardies out.

Yeah, right. Like he wasn't paying him enough – *sh-i-i-i-t!*

From the lofty perch, Bull scanned across Prunes' Whyteleafe operation.

*Bet he ain't never seen no white leaf, neither.* If he could ever give a shit, he'd ask Prunes why a black man would ever want to set up in any place so white.

Bull cast his eyes over ranks and files of barrels and covered crates, netted pallets, neatly parked vans, vehicles, one flatbed and some big-arse tanks Prunes'd said were for refilling gas bottles. There was a small forklift and a loader thing – who'd think the dog had started life as a handcart boy, fencing stolen mangos and ackees in Jamaica's Linstead market!

According to Prunes, people saw trucks arrive full and leave full regularly, all the time. But never after 8 p.m. and never on weekends. It was why Prunes was having the squits over their weekend deal but – *fuckit* – way he saw it, the fucker was getting enough pie…with cream.

Bull took a long slurp of whisky, lifting his eyes towards a small plot behind it all, where scrub and trees bowed like old men climbing uphill towards skies that had gone from weeping like a bitch to plain fuckin' moody.

He caught Prunes' frowning face down below where the van was parked askew between two containers. Though he wasn't looking, Bull gave Prunes a cheery thumbs up and unwrapped a duffle coat from a box marked 'Exklusives' and pulled it over his Armani before heading out and down all the bloody stairs. Prunes'd explained that an office on the ground floor meant no time to tidy away if, say, *unexpected visitors* dropped by to, say, *ask him to help with their enquiries.*

At the foot of the stairs Prunes met him and led the way through a kitchen and out into the backyard.

'Fuck, Bull, your guys are bloody shit drivers!'

'Chill! It's a bit o' plasterwork.'

'Tcho! They even got them licence?'

Bull almost laughed, but scowled at him instead.

'Well, I got a guy who can teach them to drive proper. I can even get them driver's licence. Special group discount.'

'Bet you got a guy to sort out a bit o' plasterwork too, Prunes. My treat! Wait! That ain't it – you're still pissed I stuck it to your niece. Right? Blame yourself, bro. Shoulda told me you was sendin' her up wit' refreshments.' Bull had a mind to tell him how *refreshing* she'd been, but maybe a Positive Prunes was better than a Pissed-off Prunes when you wanted every-sodding-thing to be good-to-go in less than forty-four hours. Bull double-checked his watch for confirmation and threw a friendly arm about the shorty, putting Prunes in a playful half nelson.

'Urrk!' Prunes gagged and dribbled a pulpy mess. 'You're choking me, Bull.' Bull let him go.

'You're too stressed, bro. Better not have a fucking heart attack 'fore Tuesday. Or I'll kill ya.'

'Funny, Bull, funny,' Prunes rasped, rubbing his neck. 'By the way, what time on Tuesday?'

'My people –' the words felt good, and because Prunes was distracted brushing half-chewed raisins down himself, Bull started again '– my people…my peops keep the exact details on a strictly need-to-know basis, get me? That way nobody not invited will turn up, seen? Know what I'm sayin'? They tell me where and when on the day. Gotta get everything ready to rock 'n' roll. Seen?'

'I got the message.' Prunes abandoned the raisin gunk stuck to his trousers and waved urgently at the freshly parked van. 'Look! It's still wonky! Get your guys to straighten up, Bull. Think I could pack all this shit in here if people don't fuckin' park proper?'

Bull raised an eyebrow. Jinxie nodded back, straightened the magnetised 'BioHazzard' sign he'd caused to slip when he'd leant on it, and jumped into the driver's seat next to Chigger who sat with his back to him with both feet extended out the open passenger door.

The engine grumbled. The van lurched forward and

stopped so hard, the BioHazzard sign flew off. The passenger door swung with force.

'*Blood fire!*' Chigger's voice filled the yard, climbed the hill and announced to every Jamaican in earshot that he was ready to wring a neck.

'Cut di shit!' Bull restored peace and walked up to where the clean patch left by the 'BioHazzard' sign had been. 'Open up!'

Chigger limped round, shuffling keys, looking for the one that opened the side of the damn thing.

'What's up wi you two jokers?' Bull said.

Jinxie was stifling a laugh. 'So, Boss…everything go smooth like butter…perfect…and right at the end…'us' when we was ready fi leave, some bitch run straight into the trolley, di t'ing ram right into Chigger bad foot!'

'Gimme dem.' Jinxie snatched keys off the grumbling Chigger and tried the smallest one on the bunch, before continuing, 'An' Chigger was holdin' that heavy bin we was liftin' off the trolley still!'

'So yu t'ink it *rass-claat* funny!' Chigger yelled, pointing at Jinxie with his machete.

'You dropped the bin, Chigger?' Bull interrupted sternly.

'Uhm, no, boss.' Chigger lowered the machete and his voice.

'Open the fuckin' bin.'

'Yes, bossman.' Jinxie called across the yard, 'Hey, Likkle! Come help mi wid dis while Chigger check out 'im foot!'

Everyone stood back as the big man set down a large box and came over to heft the bin marked BioHazzard out of the van.

Jinxie raised the metal cover, pretending not to hear Bull's questions as to why they'd not locked the lid and what would they have done if anything had got out.

Green and gold caught Bull's eye.

'Wait up! I s-sell them jackets,' Prunes said, taking a step back.

'We got a problem 'ere, Prunes?' Bull looked from the jacket to him then to Jinxie and back again.

'Naw, man, naw, man!' Prunes stepped forward. 'J-just dat them is...uhm...quality jackets...fly off the stall. Use to be one of my exclusives, I'm tellin' ya!'

'Hmm.' Bull cast off the comment like lint. 'Nice work, Jinxie. Your plan was good, then?'

'Course, boss, it's not Django alone can strategysize, yeah?'

Bull went closer, lowering his head into the bin. 'Look, he's all curled up – must think he's back in his ma's belly...what's that smell?'

'Prob'ly wet hisself!' Jinxie said then sniggered, 'Or maybe is Chigger-foot!'

Prunes was unusually quiet now, Bull noticed.

'Cool. Get it packaged away and ready with the rest, Jinxie. Make sure the nurse looks him over, seen?'

'*Yessah*, boss.'

'Prunes, my man,' Bull patted his host on the back as gently as he could, 'you'll have a' early grave if you don't stop fretting 'bout stuff you can fix wit' plaster and a lick o' paint or fuckin' nosy neighbours... Course, you could always join a winning crew, eh?'

Prunes said nothing.

'Suit yourself.' Bull shrugged. 'I ain't askin' again, bro.'

Prunes stood, head bowed, staring at the ground like he expected something to crawl up out of it. A sudden gust blew over the yard with an oily breath. Snuggling deeper into the duffel, Bull snapped his fingers.

Prunes looked up. 'Sorry, Bull... Come, let me show you what your money's paying for!'

Prunes led them through the rows of large containers, each festooned with markings indicating they'd seen ports in Belize, Jamaica, Hong Kong, Brazil, Antwerp and a few more. With a wide stride, Bull narrowly avoided a greasy puddle.

Chigger didn't, by the sound of it.

Finally, they arrived at two large containers and went inside the first one.

'Shit, bro,' Bull said, 'it even smells clean.'

'My own secret concoction,' Prunes said. 'Sniffer dogs smell it a mile off, but then they get high. So high, they can't tell east from west. Know-what-I'm-sayin'?'

Everyone found that funny. Bull praised Prunes for lightening up.

The levity died as a siren wailed, approaching fast.

What now?

Prunes hustled everyone out of the door, ordering them to go inside the house and—

'Wait,' Chigger said, listening hard. 'Fire engine!'

'How do you know?' Prunes said, wide-eyed.

'Yeah, he's right,' Jinxie said.

Bull told Prunes to carry on with the inspection of the containers. More than ever, he looked forward to being shot of them all. The second container was as immaculate as the first with the same sweetness in the air that Prunes assured Bull wouldn't get into the cubicles and affect the packages.

'I got everything covered, Bull. Matter of fact, only thing now is a picture to go with the papers for that last package. Then we can sort out all the documents.'

'Documents?' Bull's stomach fell and his muscles became a bag of knots.

'Bull, quit jestin', Django collected the documents from me Wednesday morning gone.'

'All of them?'

'Yeah. All of 'em. Every single one… You sayin' I diddled you?'

Bull shook his head. 'No, it's not that, Prunes…'

Prunes spoke over him, 'I'm telling you, Bull. My guy got all the pictures off Django and sorted out every jack one of them with fake birth certificates. Passports, too. I checked every single one, personally, when Django come round. Twice, I check them! Last Wednesday, it was. Didn't he give them to you?'

Bull spread his arms. 'Wha' do you fuckin' think?'

Prunes popped more dried fruit in his mouth with practised ease. 'Then he must'a put them some place safe and sound. Just get them off Django. Where's he at, by the way?'

'Fuck! Fuck! Fuck! Fuck! F-U-U-C-K!' Bull threw a wild punch that narrowly missed Prunes and banged the container wall.

'Be cool, we got some time. We just have to ask Dja—'

'We can't fuckin' ask Django nothin', Prunes!' Bull stomped a foot hard before trudging off.

'Bull, sir?' The voice hit him like a ball of cotton. He didn't know when the nurse'd arrived. It was her job to just be there, do her thing and be gone, like a silent little fart in a lift. She was always 'the nurse' as he hadn't bothered to remember her name – hell – with no right-hand man, he had to deal with all these 'little' people.

'Excuse me, Bull?'

'Not now. Not fuckin' now!'

Chilling little eddies whipped up as air swirled about the containers.

'Bull, hold on, bro?'

'What!' Bull faced Prunes, ready to charge at the first man who said the wrong thing.

'I was thinking...' Prunes tugged his zipper all the way up to his neck. 'Well, if *Batman* ain't about, why don't we check with *Robin*?'

'What?'

'Just ask Triple about the documents, bro!'

# CHAPTER 23

In the hospital reception, Chelsea finalised arrangements with the police.

'Yes, yes, I understand my responsibilities, Officers. I do run my own business and very well if I say so myself.' Chelsea wondered whether she might end up eating her words, especially as the officer was giving her a look that was saying 'Then why, in God's name, are you taking such a risk?' After all, TK she knew well enough, but the Patrick woman had been a handful for two trained, uniformed officers and by the damage she had caused…

'Then they're yours, Miss Laverne,' WPC Murphy said with PC Bailey looking on, holding the paperwork to receive her signature. 'One, or even both, fail to appear at the station tonight and… Well, let's say I wouldn't like to be you!'

They pointed. She saw Jonelle Patrick watching from near the exit, fiddling with her hands and pacing.

Chelsea signed.

Her throat was dry and she felt light-headed. When had she last eaten? For that matter, when had any of them had any nourishment at all? TK hadn't touched his food and, like the little Vietnamese girl, his breakfast tray had long gone.

Miss Patrick didn't seem to have food on her mind. Her eyes were watery and her shoulders sagged as the two officers addressed her. Chelsea listened on as they checked Miss Patrick fully understood the terms under which she was being allowed to collect her girls and report back to the station.

'Yes.' She understood she was still on police bail.

'Yes.' She understood she needed to get to the station and make a formal complaint about her missing son and that they would get the ball rolling to find him.

'Yes.' She understood that Miss Laverne would have to pay if she didn't show.

Finally, Jonelle Patrick looked at her like she was a table-spoon of cod liver oil – *sans* honey.

'Of course, you could wait and return to Brixton with us to—' Bailey said.

'No, I'll go with her,' Jonelle told them, stepping closer with a subdued 'Thanks'.

'No need to thank me, really, Miss Patrick. I'm sure you'd do the same for me.' Chelsea wished she had said something less ingratiating. 'It was good of the police to let me take you to get your girls. You must be out of your mind with worry!'

'Yeah, okay, okay. Let's go, eh?'

'Mrs Liverne? Mrs Liverne?'

The entire waiting room looked around. Chelsea decided it was close enough to her name and waved at the minicab driver.

TK kept insisting he was able to walk.

'Hospital rules, boss.'

The porter paused to tilt the chair over the slight lip at the threshold. 'Rules are rules around here, all to keep you people safe, y'see!'

Chelsea looked over to see Jonelle looking back at her.

*Safe?*

The minicab driver took over and they all followed him to his vehicle. Thankfully, the only rain lay in puddles in the car park and was running along to find the nearest guttering. He held the chair while TK stood and used his plastered arm to nudge Chelsea away.

'Hey, hey, I ain't no invalid here!'

'TK, I'm trying to help.' She backed off and let him open the passenger door, one-handed and one-eyed – the eye bandage needed to remain until tomorrow. Meanwhile, she climbed in the back with a very sombre Jonelle Patrick, sitting like a rumbling volcano.

Chelsea heard a kettledrum roll and decided it was thunder as she pulled on her seatbelt. Negotiating with the two officers had been very different from sealing a lucrative computing contract. It had taken all her skill and at least one high-stake threat to be allowed to take them away and bring both TK and Jonelle back to Brixton station later that night.

This, she had pointed out, would be good damage control, freeing them to study footage with the security man and his machines. They could interview hospital staff for every shred of detail around the 'alleged' kidnap of the small boy in their charge, who must be found most urgently. Especially as *nobody*, not even the police, had bothered to follow up Miss Patrick's earlier complaint about the hospital 'losing' her child after they had arrested her for trashing the place. Thus, she'd gained a break for Jonelle and got them to agree to file a missing person report immediately.

'Where to?' The driver gunned the engine and waited for a woman to waddle across the exit, hotly pursued by a man laden with a small suitcase in one hand and a small child under his other arm.

Chelsea looked to Jonelle.

'C'mon, c'mon,' the driver said.

'Miss Patrick?'

'Brixton, please!' she told him and turned to Chelsea. 'And you can call me Jonelle.'

'Chelsea. And that's TK.'

At the sound of his name TK looked round. 'Yeah?'

'Nothing. Relax,' Chelsea said.

'Please, will somebody say where we're going?'

'Oy, oy! We're payin', so chill out, man!' TK said up front.

'Ain't got all day. Calls're backin' up. Where to?'

'Know where Miss Mattie's is?' Jonelle said to the taxi driver.

'Yeah, everybody know Miss Mattie's!'

# CHAPTER 24

'Quit telling me what I already know.' Bull thumped Prunes' office table like he owned it. It had taken over a week for Prunes to get the forgeries done, so there was a snowball-in-hell's chance he would get new ones by Tuesday, barely two days away.

'Where's Triple at?' he bellowed, using decibels to jog their sorry-arsed, weed-induced memories. 'Think!'

They just sat there, watching him finger stab his own temple in a further attempt to get them to go deep for some answers. 'Think!'

Fuckin' fact is Django woulda hidden the damn documents real good. He was a bastard like that, which was why he'd trusted him...once. Even if the crabs could find Triple, what good would it do now?

Bull eyed them, his breath puffing hot from his nostrils, Django's boys sitting like dumb-ass kids in school without their homework done. George perched on the side of the desk, Likkle took up more than half the futon with Jinxie on the other end and Clint squashed between them, avoiding a wet patch they were all viewing with suspicion. Chigger was out on the landing, listening at the crack in the door, with orders to not allow even a fart through, unannounced.

They sat and stared.

Bull heard Prunes say something from the corner where he'd wedged himself when they'd all piled into his office. *No, no, you stay, Prunes. Me, you and them – that makes two heads!*

'Speak up, bro!'

Prunes made a noise like a car trying to start with the choke still in.

'E-Hrrmm— Sorry,' Prunes said. 'Must be coming down with somethin'… Uh-hurm, I'm only sayin', Bull. It took weeks to get them documents, right? And… Uh-hum-*Uh-hum*, we could take *new* pictures and such, but *not* by Tuesday? Why not call off *this* Tuesday? Go for the next week?'

Bull saw red, made a fist and carried it over to where Prunes stiffened to attention. Precious minutes had ticked away since they'd sat here passing around the same damn, useless information, and now…

'Check it, Bull.' Prunes looked up from under his nostrils. 'Y'see, I'm thinkin' dat if Triple had a woman, she might know *something*? Like where them papers is?'

'Course!' Bull dropped his fist. A second ago he'd wanted to fuck Prunes up. He turned and wagged a knowing finger at his minions. 'A dick's just a dick without a pussy!'

The room came alive with nodding dogs and rumbles of agreement.

'So, who knows where Triple's girl's at?'

Silence.


As far as Style was concerned, it was somebody else's turn to hang around with Maxwell, waiting for some bitch to show her face. The Myrna woman had been fun and all, but he'd done his bit already.

Style rubbed his eyes, thinking how the Kool Kurls guy, that people were calling Ozzie, had insisted they come in this time. They'd told him they didn't need no haircut, but Ozzie'd told them he'd always hated people hanging about outside like gangstas, putting off his customers. That meant his long leather jacket was only a little damp still, but the purple trousers he'd worn this time, 100 per cent genuine polyester according to Prunes, had been saved from a drenching. Plus, coming inside had got them out of the sights of two Babylon he'd spotted coming towards them. Another fucking bright side, as Style supposed Django would say, is that while Bull had bellowed at him for not making Myrna take them directly to her friend, it was Maxwell who had spent Saturday night with staples fucking up his todger.

He'd chosen the green plastic chair facing the door and left the three-legged stool for Maxwell, who'd borrowed a cushion off the bench that looked like it used to go to church once.

The barbershop crowd were banging on about politics. In Jamaica, poli-tricks, as it was known, was not his game and Style found the noisy debate hard to blank out. He casually studied the windows from the flats across the road and everyone going in and coming out. He'd already seen four women who seemed to fit Maxwell's description of the Jonelle woman. One of them had walked too much like she had balls, big ones.

'See! My point is making even this stranger smile?' Ozzie was looking right at him. Style wiped the sneer off his face and refocused. What was keeping that bitch?

A couple of cop cars wailed past, and he shook his head at a man leading a woman carrying a baby while one-two-three-four-five kids followed behind like little ducklings. Every jack one was dressed turban-to-toe in white, like they were going to a ghost gig.

'Yahman! Take Milk-Snatcher Thatcher, right?' Ozzie waved his shears around the room talking shit about shit.

The banter picked away at violent tendencies that had made him 'wanted for questioning' back in Jamaica, where nobody had liked his answers too much. Style felt for his weapon, making sure it hadn't peeked from its hiding place. People got jittery when they saw you were packing heat. Understandable, he supposed.

'Tcho! Don't mention that Thatcher woman round here, man!' Someone objected up to the ceiling, right in Style's ear, making his trigger finger itch.

Maxwell motioned in the direction of the sign marked WC. He rolled his eyes and Maxwell shuffled off.

'Peace, bro. Peace! Hear me out, nuh!' Ozzie pointed his shears at him. 'Or yu can stan' outside 'til mi done!'

That shut everyone up and they all watched Ozzie take another cool sip of Dragon stout before going on.

'Now. See dis bredda here, smiling, dress-up proper and lookin' stush?' Style looked up, straight-faced. Ozzie's shears aimed all eyes at him. 'Thatcher comes on the scene and ev'ry jack man get di chance fi betta himself, right? But 'ow much take di chance fi betta we-self, eh?'

They all nodded and Style shifted uncomfortably, half expecting someone to shout 'Amen' and start singing. Style was starting to wonder what was taking Maxwell so long in the toilets.

'Yah but, consider dis, mi bredren!' a voice cried out from the far side of the lounge that was the shop. Grateful for having all eyes off him, Style sat forward, half listening, half wondering whether to go check Maxwell had not done a runner or some shit like that.

The speaker was saying, 'Di worl' no level, mi tell yu! Is all "who yu kno' an' wha' kinda *hedge-u-kay-sion* yu have", mi bredren! *Privalidge!*'

'See wha'-a-mean, bredren?' Ozzie butted in. 'Nuff come to Englan', a land o' opportuni'y fi big-up we-self but 'ow much o' we take dat opportuni'y?'

Ozzie was looking at him. 'Where you frien'?'

Style, pointing with his lips, indicated the curtain of red, green and gold beads.

'Oh yes, 'im gone a really long time, eh? Maybe flush himself down the toilet.'

Style shrugged. Not that he was bothered really. He only wanted the woman Jonelle to show up real soon so he could get the fuck out of Kool Kurls and get the job done.

'All-di-same, yu mind if mi use yu as *h-eggsample*?'

He sat back in the chair and shook his head, pretending he didn't care one little bit.

'Bredren, wha' you see 'ere is...' Ozzie said, puffing his chest and holding them in suspense. 'Style!'

Style twitched, his body tightening for action. Had he and Maxwell been made? Bamboozled by a rival crew? Shit! Had Maxwell figured it out and scarpered, leaving him to face the music alone? Fucking mongoose! With a full clip and his two blades, Style felt sure he could clear a way to the door and save himself.

At that very moment, Maxwell parted the beaded curtain, poked his head in and all attention swivelled off Style.

'You were gone long,' Ozzie chuckled. 'Mi nearly sen' some scissors to cut the crap back dere, breddah.'

Maxwell slowly entered the room to carefully retake the stool next to Style.

Style pulled his jacket closer and checked again his pistol was still well out of sight.

'Why you take so long,' Style said quietly to Maxwell, adding a discreet elbow to his ribs.

'Bloody staple fell out in the bowl!'

Style stifled a laugh. 'Hope you washed it first before you put it back in!'

Ignoring the remark, Maxwell attempted to cross his legs and immediately stopped himself. 'Seen her yet?'

'Think I'd still be sittin' 'ere?' Style nodded towards the

group. 'It's *like* sitting with a bunch of bitches, *to-ras*! Chat, chat, chat!'

Then Ozzie said something that made them both perk up.

'Take Triple,' Ozzie announced. 'Di guy always try fi mek life better. Thatcher said get on yer bike and what he do?'

'Thatcher never say dat, nahumsayin'!' a dissenter heckled.

'Who says?'

'Not Thatcher! Tebbit or some other shithead!' It was the same youth Ozzie had tried to eject earlier.

'I swear, Rickie, if you wasn't mi nephew, I'd...' Ozzie was saying when Style cleared his throat.

'Yo, Ozzie?'

'Yeah, breddah man?'

'Please, continue,' Style said in his best diction, eyeballing the young Rickie. 'I think we can all learn somet'ing important 'ere, if we listen instead o' interruptin'. Go on, bro. You were saying about somebody named Triple?'

Ozzie told them all about a man who was constantly running from one crew to the next, an expert with anything mechanical.

'I used to know 'is maddah!' Ozzie had a faraway look in his eyes talking about Triple's mother, so soft and sweet. 'I try fi help her out but, in the *h-end*, dere was just too much competition... H-anyway, back to Triple, right. I always tell 'im he can mek somet'ing of 'imself when 'e leave school—'

'And where is he now then?' Maxwell interrupted, earning a scowl from Style and the room.

'I's getting to dat!' Ozzie said. 'Triple jus' keep on driftin'. Fool wouldn't take one single opportuni'y – I even tell him to come learn fi cut 'air – then all o' a sudden – 'im turn it all round.'

'Yeah?' Style stroked his stubbly chin. 'How, bro?'

Ozzie shrugged. 'He never like fi talk 'bout it, but one day he clean up him *ack*. Pay off all him bills. Start comin' in for 'aircut and shave, full works with the mos' *esspensive*

aftershave and calogne – used to say dat nobady understan'
'im head like Kool Kurls.'

'And when you see him las', then?'

Ozzie tilted his head at the question and waited. 'You guys
know Triple, den?'

'No, no,' Maxwell said, looking around the room. 'You
mention 'im name, right? Y'know, whatever became of 'im? I's
only curious is all.'

Style overheard one of the other young men whisper to his
neighbour. 'Hey, man, Rickie, ain't tha' dat geezer we see las'
Friday at 'Grilla? Check out dat suit and everythin'!'

'Bwoy, wish I knew weh Triple woz right now,' Ozzie said.
The man in his chair straightened and started massaging his
neck with both hands. Ozzie pushed his head back into the
ninety-degree neck-bend and buzzed his shears in readiness.
'Any o' you see Triple lately? He was actin' real jittery yesterday
marnin, like him gone get 'imself in trouble?'

Style chuckled along, making mental notes for Bull. Until
now, none of the crew knew Triple visited this place. Seemed
fuckin' suspicious when it was right across from where that Jonelle
woman lived. She shows up at 'Grilla. He disappears. Smelt fishy,
for sure. Style wondered whether Maxwell had made the same
connection. No doubt Bull would be glad of the information.

Two coppers strayed into view, stopping where he'd been
standing earlier with Maxwell, rainwater dripping off their
helmets. Style willed them to walk on.

Myrna had sworn there was nobody else involved but the
Jonelle woman. Not that he trusted her, even after making her
moan as he rode her across her thick bedroom carpet, even
after she was sprawled on her king-sized bed letting him tie
her to the four corners.

No, for sure, that Myrna hadn't mentioned Triple even once,
but the three of them could still have been up to something? But
why wouldn't she have given him up? Style couldn't figure it out.

Was Triple worth having frying pan oil dripped all over your body while you screamed into big-arse drawers stuffed down your throat...even if you were into that kinky shit?

No, he decided, the tasty Myrna would surely have sung after her skin started blistering and definitely when the hot pan was pressed up against her sensitive parts.

The gas should have filled the flat by now, waiting for the first person – please God, let it be the Babylon – to bust down the door and investigate.

Ding!

The glass doors swung wide and two blue uniforms stepped in.

# CHAPTER 25

Jonelle crossed then uncrossed her legs, wiped her hands up and down her jeans and sank back into the minicab seat. The constricting seatbelt seemed determined to throttle her rather than keep her safe. She felt bloody helpless…in a box, compressed, struggling to breathe, taunted. She wanted to scream. Scream long and loud.

How could she escape this sinkhole that had opened beneath her? If only she could close her eyes and sleep, and sleep and sleep, then awake to find that it had all been a silly nightmare, that it was not real, like she always told Deen.

*Oh, Jesus. Where the hell are you, Deen?*

No, this was no dream. She fought to overcome a numbness – a terror. It was hard to think, to feel, to breathe.

So hard!

She had to find a way…for Deen's sake!

For Kenyana.

Amanita.

Jonelle's hands shook involuntarily. Suddenly she was fifteen again when the school nurse said words that would turn her entire world upside-down. 'Jonelle, are you pregnant?' And here she was again, battling to stop strangers tearing her from her child.

Since leaving the hospital, she'd fought a sense of panic, feeling half in the world, half out. Her tired eyes searched the faces of every small child they drove past.

Starting at her brow line, a rank of pain marched north across her forehead and laid siege to her entire head. Thinking hurt. A million questions marshalled, from what to do when they finally found Deen to what to tell people when they never found her son… Her thoughts found myriad jagged paths leading to utter despair. Her ears itched. Her palms felt wet, sweaty, but she knew she had to get a grip, somehow.

Up front, the cab driver and TK argued about which way was fastest and had fewer lights.

The cab hit something. Jonelle bumped her throbbing head on the roof of the vehicle.

'Told you this road had too many bloody sleeping police-men.' The driver's tone slithered between rude and bloody rude.

'Yeah, well, they never wake up when I drive over them,' Chelsea's friend TK said, his voice competing with the sound of gears crunching. 'Look, I know these streets, nahumsayin'? Turn here, man!'

'This is *my* minicab, right? This is *my* job!'

'*And I'm paying*, so make the turn like he said, okay?' Chelsea sat up straight, rubbing her head like she was hurting too.

They all leant into the sudden turn.

For what seemed the umpteenth time, a big container lid flew open in her mind, and Jonelle saw the familiar flash of green and gold. She'd handwashed it often enough because Prunes had claimed it was 'exclusive'. *Surely* she was mistak-en, wasn't she? She did worry too much – Tyrone was right! Deen had fallen asleep somewhere while playing hide-and-seek – wouldn't have been the first time. *Please God, don't let it be Deen's jacket.*

'See, told you!' TK said in triumph, as they emerged in front of Miss Mattie's corner shop.

Jonelle opened the door.

'Oi, let me park first!' the driver called out.

Jonelle sat forward on the edge of the seat. As the hand-brake crunched, she alit into the cool air and ran for the shop front with the big CLOSED sign on the door.

Peering through the glass, she saw no sign of life among the darkened aisles nor behind the counter. Jonelle stretched an arm through the burglar bars to bang the door.

Keefah'd promised!

*I'll take the girls to Mother Mattie! It's no trouble at all.*

Maybe the old woman had taken them to the park or some-where? Jonelle wished it had been Candice at the hospital, utterly reliable, sensible Candice, more bloody reliable than all her friends put together! *Bless 'em.*

'Jonelle, maybe there's another door?' Chelsea was behind her.

'Shit, I'm so stupid!' Jonelle bashed her head with the heel of her palm and ignored the extra pain. Miss Mattie had hailed her from her other entrance, the access to her home above the shop many times. 'It's around the corner.'

She hurried away, Chelsea trying to keep up.

Jonelle was about to hammer on the door but saw a slip of paper jammed there, at eye level. Jonelle snatched it and unfolded the message.

'No! No! No!' Jonelle said, tossing the paper behind her.

'What?' Chelsea was grasping at the fluttering note.

Jonelle felt her knees go and slumped into a squat. The paper slipped to the ground.

Chelsea picked it up and read aloud:

*J, Miss Mattie not home. I think gone to church. Girls at mine. Can stay the night, if you want to come get them in the morning. Keefah.*

It began to spit and a cold breath of air blew a pungent odour in their faces.

'Why's this happening?' Jonelle's dad's condemning face flashed across her mind. *Bad things happen to bad people, Jonelle.* She sniffed.

'Hey! It's okay.' It was Chelsea, stooping next to her. 'We can go to this… *Keefah's?*'

They stood up together.

The minicab idled on the corner.

TK said the new address was not far, only about ten minutes round the road diversion. The minicab driver argued it would take twice as long, with the bloody traffic.

'I can walk it in three minutes,' Jonelle insisted, shifting from foot to foot.

'Okay, you two drive. We'll walk,' Chelsea instructed, straightening up from the passenger window and cautiously patting TK's shoulder.

Perhaps it was a trick of the light, but seeing those two together made her think of a couple she'd spotted on her first and last ever visit to 'Grilla, looking like a pimp with his pro. She mentally dismissed the thought – there was no time for trivia right now.

Jonelle was strides away when she heard the vehicle pull away. A relentless rhythm came up behind her.

'You didn't have to, y'know,' Jonelle threw behind her.

'I wanted to.' Chelsea was breathing hard.

'Why'd you want to?' Jonelle said. 'Think I'll run off, get you into trouble with the cops?'

Chelsea matched her stride for stride.

'Look, I can't imagine how you feel right now, Jonelle. Must be any parent's worst nightmare! But I'm not your enemy, okay?'

'Look, I don't know you and I don't want to know you. I only want my son back and—' Jonelle's chest tightened, worse than when she had an evening school assignment to hand in, or a surprise test. 'Actually, we're here!'

A man opened the door and stood wearing a dog collar, slippers and the focused expression of a man trying to do long division in his head. 'Yes?'

'Keefah here?'

'Ah, you must be Jonelle.' He craned his head to see down the path. 'This your sister?'

'No.' Jonelle tried to peer over his shoulder into the hall. 'We're not sist— Look, is Keefah here? She's got my girls.'

A smile revealed too-white teeth and he seemed to be waiting for something…a handshake, a bloody peck on the cheek or the kick in the balls she'd been saving up for this moment for all he'd put poor Keefah through.

'Erm…may we come in, Pastor… Sir?' Chelsea said from behind her.

'Yes, yes, of course! So sorry…seeing you both has given me an idea for the sermon I was working on.' He stood aside and waved them into a wide hallway and a whiff of pub, offering a hand first to Jonelle. 'Reverend John. You may call me Rev, but plain John is fine.'

Jonelle ignored him and Chelsea reached for his extended hand. 'Pleased to meet you Plain John.'

That made him chuckle.

'Please excuse Jonelle, she's had a shitty day – pardon my French!'

'No, don't apologise.' He waved both palms. 'Having a shit time of it m'self. I'll call Keefah for you… Keefah!'

Jonelle looked past the staircase, hoping the door under the stairs had a toilet behind it given the state of her bladder right now.

'Keefah!' the reverend tried again, went deeper into the hall and had a third blast before turning back to them, looking embarrassed. 'Forgive my beloved – deaf as a doorknob sometimes and always walking into things…'

The rev lifted his face heavenwards and pumped up the volume. 'Keee-faah!'

One of the hall doors swung open. Long black boots carried a willowy body into the hall. Mentally, Jonelle removed the sprayed-on denim jeans from under the familiar tartan skirt, added heavy make-up, a lamppost and a couple of schoolgirl-looking mates.

'You!' Chelsea said beside her, recoiling.

'You've met?' said the rev, his expression bursting with '*What a small world this is!*'

'Uhm…sort of!' Chelsea said, while Jonelle stood dumbfounded.

'Veronica! Come say hello,' Reverend John said cheerily, calling her under the ornate lamplight in the hall. Yes, it was her, Jonelle thought, noticing Veronica and Chelsea were facing off like they'd arrived at a gig in the exact same gear.

'Veronica.' The rev broke the awkwardness. 'Be a dear and call your cousin for us. You know she can't hear a thing from the top of the house! God help us if we ever have a fire down here when she's up there.'

Jonelle watched the boots and denim mount the Paisley-carpeted stairs.

'You can wait in the lounge.'

'No thanks,' Jonelle said.

'We've a minicab coming, Reverend,' Chelsea said at the same time.

'Suit yourselves… If you'll excuse me – Keefah'll be down with the girls in a minute.'

Soon as he was gone, Jonelle turned to Chelsea.

'How do *you* know her? Veronica.'

'We got arrested at the same time.'

Jonelle stepped back from her.

'No, no, not like that,' Chelsea said. 'They – she and her two friends – colleagues – whatever – were prostitutes, I think. TK was driving me to Paddington station when the police pulled us over, took us to the station, and – anyway, that's how I know her... What about you? You seem to know her too?'

'I was going to work Friday night, saw her and her two mates – nasty pieces of work – they thought I was stealing their johns or some such shit! One of them wanted to—'

'Mommy!' The child was nowhere near the bottom of the stairs when she launched herself, arms outstretched.

'Kenyana, no!' Jonelle said too late, but just in time to catch her daughter against her tummy.

'Mommy, Mommy, why were you *so* long!' Kenyana sobbed into her shoulder.

'I'm sorry, Kennie. Don't cry, hon, you'll set Mommy off,' Jonelle said.

Amanita was studying them, staring strangely at Chelsea. When had her eldest come to be so 'grown up'? She seemed miles away, standing there at the bottom of the stairs, just feet away, inserted between Keefah and...that Veronica.

'These two were good as gold, Jonelle.' Keefah was beaming.

'Where's Deen, Mommy?' There was a catch in Amanita voice.


Chelsea thought Kenyana was the cutest little thing. Her elfin face bore hints of Jonelle, while Amanita was her spitting image, in miniature. Seeing Jonelle shrouded in the low light of the hallway, cradling her daughter in her arms, Chelsea's mind flashed back to the 'Grilla club and the ladies' toilets. A veil lifted from her eyes and given where they were, in Brixton, had she seen her before?

Jonelle, the young Vietnamese, Veronica – it was just too many coincidences to contemplate amidst the riot of emotions in the place, on an empty stomach.

Feeling observed, Chelsea caught Amanita looking at her still, taking her in with eyes just like the child she'd seen somewhere…the limo…at the traffic lights…but they were with a man then…their father perhaps…he'd surely be here if it had been them.

Jonelle's shoulders visibly sagged, and Kenyana slipped a little. She hefted the child back into a close embrace and started clearing her throat.

'You must be Amanita.' Chelsea edged towards Amanita, who took a half step backwards, away from her offered hand. 'My name's Chelsea.'

Amanita looked up at her mother. 'Is she from the Social?'

'No, sweetie. I'm not from the Social,' Chelsea responded. 'We – uhm – your mother and I – only just met. Today. At the hospital. Your brother, Deen – we left him playing at the hospital.'

'Playing?' Amanita's eyes met hers with a look that said, 'get real', mirroring a look Chelsea had read before in Jonelle's.

'Yeah. 'Nita, you know how your brother loves to hide-n-seek.' Jonelle held her shoulder and pulled her daughter towards her. 'Deen'll be home soon, 'kay. Good news too – I met a doctor today who knows why Deen's been so unwell too. Isn't that wonderful?'

The child wrinkled her brow and narrowed her eyes, then a smile balanced precariously on her lips, her face caught somewhere between joy and sadness.

A flash from outside lit up everyone's face as, what sounded like a plague of locusts, attacked the roof and windows. Thunder boomed down the hall. Kenyana covered both ears with her hands and buried her face in her mother's neck. Amanita flinched but remained where she stood.

'That was a close one,' Keefah said, relieved. 'Any sooner and the note I left on Mattie's door woulda got well soaked, Jonie. Can't believe I didn't remember Miss Mattie went to church every Sunday, rain or shine. Silly. Anyway, John didn't mind. Plus, Veronica – did John introduce you already – yes? Anyway, Ronnie helped entertain the girls, while I cooked – you *must* be really hungry, no? I did enough for—'

Keefah and her cousin shared the same height and bony features. Chelsea hoped that was where the similarity ended, especially for the rev's sake.

'No, Keefah, we're not stopping.' Jonelle adjusted her daughter in her arms as she slipped again. 'When did you get so heavy, Kennie darlin'?'

'Wot? Keefah 'n' me not good enough company fer ya?' Veronica said in her husky smoker's rattle. Chelsea spotted small dots and puncture bruises on Veronica's inner arm, by the veins near her elbow, as she placed a hand on Jonelle's daughter's shoulder.

'You'll eat wiv us, wontya, Amani'a?'

Chelsea listened for one of the vehicles splashing along the road outside to stop. *TK, what's taking you so long?*

'Come over here, 'Nita, honey.' Chelsea saw Jonelle's eyes darken as she beckoned her daughter closer.

The door behind Veronica swung open and the reverend's smile brought extra light into the hall. 'Thank God, you're all still here! I've brewed tea – enough for everybody. Bring your friends into the lounge, Keefah, dear. I've got digestives, children. Chocolate ones.'

Keefah stroked Kenyana's hair. 'Will you have a cuppa at least, before you go, Jonie?'

Chelsea saw Jonelle's features sag and she looked pale. 'Jonelle, the car isn't here yet. We could wait in the dry, yes?'

'It's on the table getting cold.' The reverend dunked a digestive into his cup of tea. 'Come on, kids. There's Horlicks, Ovaltine and Milo with condensed milk.'

Kenyana wriggled free of her mother.

Amanita looked momentarily conflicted before taking her little sister's hand. 'I'll take her, Mommy.'

Thunder rolled across the sky and into the hall.

'I got no time for this.' Jonelle started towards the smell of chocolate and of tea brewing.

Keefah blocked her. 'Jonie, what's the matter? We've been mates for yonks and—'

Jonelle glanced at Veronica before responding, 'Keefah, you are a good mate. I really appreciate you having the girls. I owe you one.'

'Yes, but why're you being all...' Keefah looked like a tortured angel. Her cousin moved to flank her so Chelsea went and stood by Jonelle.

'Not here, not now.' Jonelle held her ground.

'Fine, let's join the kids.'

Keefah led.

They followed.

# CHAPTER 26

Bull felt horny standing naked in Prunes' en suite shower cubicle, water pounding him like a million tiny fists, and, as he was on the third floor, he found the pressure satisfying.

Bad enough the Babylon had suddenly cracked down on his establishments, interrupting the order of things. Bad enough the traitor turned out to be the last man on earth he'd suspect, and it was fucking unfortunate that his Yardies had not taken the time to search around for Django's grubby little notepad, full of *information* and incriminating scribblings – to be fair, the traitor'd probably sold the contents to the Babylon, anyways – *now this*! How the blouse-n-skirt was he supposed to deliver the 'packages' without them bloody passports and bloody birth certificates?

Bull cupped handfuls of water and washed his head and face. His elbows kept poking the plastic-sheet shower curtains. He decided he'd had enough of the cubicle made for midgets where every manoeuvre brought his biceps, back or butt into contention with a cold, wet surface. Reaching forward, he turned the knob to OFF. A soup of scum swirled at his feet, draining down the plughole. He felt muck clinging to him, still. Bull's horniness grew more intense. It was the kind of rampant desire that usually spelt trouble for somebody and had precious little to do with the fact that Prunes' tight little niece was only a few doors away.

He wanted – needed – to stab something or someone.

Real bad.

Tonight.

Like a hulking matador, Bull swirled the towel around his dripping bulk and buffed himself dry.

Looking around, he saw that the place doubled as extra storage, but, behind the door, it seemed more like some sort of school chemistry lab with large bungs everywhere, racks of test tubes and stacks of boxes containing assorted bottles. With the swish of the towel, Bull toppled a pipette sticking out of a towering tubular contraption labelled 'Dior blend'. He stopped. But the weight of the damp towel was enough for gravity to finish what he'd started. Dior Blend was all over the floor but the stack of bottles that shared the shelf clinked and stayed put, caught by an unseen hand.

'Tcho!' Bull kissed his teeth and continued dressing.

Using his shoed foot, he brushed the larger broken pieces out of his way and stepped over the aromatic puddle. Prunes had tried to flog him an aftershave with 'summer' in its name. *Newest au de toilet from Paris, bro. Straight up.* It smelt just like this mess.

Bull looped the tie around his collar and his shoulder nudged another shelf, tilting it enough to send racks of bunged bottles marked *Original Samples* sliding away from him. Ignoring the tinkle of glass on glass on the bathroom floor, Bull emerged into the office and headed for the exit and the stairs.

He'd taken his eye off the ball for far too long, entrusting the untrustworthy with his future. Enough. It was high time to fix this thing...himself.

*Gotta up m'game 'fore every gawd-damn t'ing turns to shit!*

Arriving at the kitchen door, Bull stood looking out across the yard, still doing up his cuffs. 'Everybody ready?'

They were skulking, blowing into clasped hands and rubbing them together before toasting them near the open mouth of the blazing drum he'd seen Likkle carrying earlier, black smoke curling out from it.

'Tell them to put that damn thing out, man.' Prunes hurried over to him, wagging a finger back at the Yardies. 'Bull, I *gots* to keep my neighbours sweet, y'get me? Make your guys kill dat bloody fire! JEEZASS! I pay nuff money fi them big signs, man: *Beware: No smoking. No sparks. No* fuckin' *flames*? Can't they read? Tell dem, Bull. Tell dem...or else—'

'Or else what, Prunes?' Bull said, neither shaken nor stirred.

Breathing heavily, Prunes looked up into his face. 'This place goes up, Bull, I won't be the only one losing a bloody fortune, get me? Man, I knew I shouldn't a brung you lot here... Knew it, knew it, knew it!'

'Chill, Prunes! Chill!' Bull patted Prunes on the back and brushed by him, stepping into the yard but remaining beyond the smoke and soot. 'Oi, put the bloody thing out before you give our guest a heart attack... What're you lot gassing about anyway?'

Their expressions dripped with what Bull *knew* they'd been muttering about and feeling. Hell, to some of them *he'd* been like blood, but so what! They'd better not let him catch *his* name in their mouths, and they knew it too.

'Not'in', boss!' Likkle said with a face like some bitch had caught him sneaking a peek. 'Wi ain't talkin' 'bout nobody at all.'

Jinxie came over. 'Chief. We're all ready and Maxwell – he jus' get back.'

'So, where's he at?' Bull looked around in the dirt.

'With the taxi, Chief?' Likkle said, blocking his view of half the yard. 'He went to Croydon first and saw the note we left him, he say can you lend him a tenner to help with the—'

Jinxie punched Likkle on the arm.

'I'm talking to da boss.' Likkle looked down on the two fivers Jinxie held out to him. 'Oh...'

'Tell Maxwell he better pay me back later.'

'And tell him to hurry up,' Bull added, pulling his jacket so close you could see the outline of the weapons it concealed.

'Fuck, it's turned cold. Jinxie, whoever's driving, tell 'em to bring the car up to the door here and make sure it ain't no ice box, and hurry up with that fire and y'all go saddle up. I want every jack man in the van and ready to follow me 'fore I buckle up, understan'. And, Likkle?'

'Yes, Chief?' Likkle stopped and stood as if balancing a pint of beer on his head.

'Do up your fuckin' flies. Jeez!'

Bull went back to stand in the kitchen doorway, away from the smoke and chill. Prunes eased around him, carrying a dripping cloth. He watched the midget toss it at the tongues of fire licking out from the mouth of the drum.

'Fuckin' hell!' Bull whispered, watching Prunes feel for his eyebrows and backing towards a stack of gas containers marked *Beware: No smoking. No sparks. No flames.*

'Bull, can't you control these-these-these…?' Prunes spluttered from across the yard.

Bull gave him a withering head-to-toe. 'They put the fire out, didn't they?'

'You mean *I* put the fire out!'

'We're going in a minute and after tomorrow we'll be gone for good, okay? Now stop whining like a bitch, aight?'

The drum puffed on, reminding everyone it was not quite done burning yet.

'Sorry, Bull, but, well…' Prunes lowered his brow and his tone, 'Y'know what I mean – it took me a long slog getting set up 'round here. Tough time, trying to get people to accept a black man living close, let alone have a business in this leafy residential area.'

Bull said nothing, watching Jinxie walk over to the black BMW and climb in the front passenger door while Clint ran round to the driver side. The other Yardies piled into the van.

The Beamer rolled up to the kitchen door where Bull waited. Prunes waited for Bull to clear the doorway.

'You won't regret this, bro. You helping a brother out and shit. Aight? I'll tell them no more fires. Relax.'

'Upsetting people's bad for business, Bull. Why can't you wait and let me sort out some new passports personally?' Prunes mumbled.

'Listen up,' Bull tapped out his message on the smaller man's forehead with an index finger and Prunes edged back with each syllable. 'I got a d.e.a.d. line, get me? You always deliver, Prunes, but this may be the one time they tell you no.'

'Never, Bull.'

'Never say never, Prunes.'

'But, Bull—'

'I'm getting them new documents, seen? No way I'm missing that Tuesday delivery, Prunes, aight?'

'I get it, bro, I get it.' Prunes rubbed his forehead. 'They're the bes', but you can't rush artists. Gotta give 'em time, bro… An' it's me they'll blame!'

'For what you're chargin' me, bro, you can afford a bad name, aight.' Bull held out a hand. 'That address?'

Prunes held the folded paper like a cigarette. 'Bull, these guys don't like new faces? Gets 'em all jittery, understan'? Go easy.'

Bull snatched the scribbled address. 'We all got problems. Mine's gett'n' 'em documents by tomorrow. I got no more time for fartin' 'round. They gimme what I want, they get no shit from me, aight?'

'B-But, Bull…' Prunes hung his head in resignation. 'Promise me you'll go easy. Victor and I go way back too, man.'

'Oh, I see.' Bull grinned. '*Victor*, eh?'

'No, not like that.' Prunes shifted his weight. 'But we help each other out now and then.'

'Your personal life is your bizniz, Prunes. Can they do a good job in the time or no?'

'Why's you think I sent Django there, Bull?' Prunes stepped back. 'Everyone use them, bro. They's *quick* and *damn* good. Passports, birth certificates, driving licences, you name it, they been doin' 'em for years. Family business – safer that way an' they don't come better. Word on the street's that they make the real ones by day and the fake ones by night. They'll be real pissed, but they like cash too. Will cost me plenty to get back in their good books.'

Bull made sure he could read his damn handwriting. 'Chill, Prunes. They do what I ask; I do what you say; everything's copacetic?'

Maxwell waddled in, bandy-legged.

'Where's Style?' Bull asked.

His lips moved and words fell all over the place.

Bull said, 'Zip it!'

Maxwell zipped it.

Bull pulled out his P22, remembering Django didn't think much of the Walther, which was good enough for James Bond. Then again, Django had no style…and no loyalty!

'Exactly where is Style, Maxwell?'

Maxwell recoiled, looking at the weapon. 'I l-left him at the barber's, Bull.'

'What?' Bull's P22 dipped. Maxwell attempted to cross his legs. 'Tell me you two have *not* been—'

'No, ssah! Wait, no!' With his eyes fixed on the handgun, Maxwell had a sudden attack of verbal diarrhoea. 'We was waiting…waiting for the woman… Myrna's friend that was in G-'Grilla… Friday…across the road, we was watching for that Jonelle P-P-P—'

'So she's still drawing breath is what you're sayin'?'

'Uhm, well, we knocked, b-boss. Nobody was at home, boss. We was waitin' in the rain and – then, somebody recognised me from 'Grilla and S-Style said I better—'

'Said you better get back here while he staked out the fuckin' place.'

Maxwell nodded vigorously.

'Give me strength!' Grinding his teeth, Bull holstered the P22 under his jacket. 'Make yourself useful, Maxwell. Go double-check that all the packages are wrapped up and ready to go, understan'? I want everything perfect for Tuesday when we leave this place and not a damn thing else going wrong, right? Or else… Well, you don't want to know what'll happen. Feel me?'

'Y-yessah!'

Maxwell was almost out of the door, taking unusual care to step over the threshold. 'Maxwell?!'

'Sir?'

'You still got that "reminder" I gave you?'

Maxwell looked at Prunes.

'What, you think Prunes knows what goes on in your pants?'

'Yes, I mean, no. Well—'

Bull sighed. 'Which is it, Maxwell?'

'Yes, Bull, I didn't remove it. I swear!'

Bull took something from his pocket and tossed it. Maxwell caught it instinctively and then dropped the staple remover. 'Do it yourself or ask the nurse to give you a hand. Make damn sure that all the packages are fit and ready for delivery. Laters, I'm goin' to *aks* her about your staple too. Get outta my sight!'

Bull got in the car. 'Drive.'

The Beamer eased safely between the buildings. Bull heard a scraping noise as the van followed them out.

Fuck Prunes.

As they nudged through the traffic, Bull felt he was leading the final charge. Those documents were all that remained for the handover. There'd be no further cockups – hell, anyone'd think the fuckin' circus had come to town!

Clint was doing fine behind the wheel doing Triple's job. Wherever he'd gone, he'd better fuckin' stay there.

'Clint?' Bull looked down at the time.

'Yeah, boss.'

'Drive like you goin' to a cricket match at the Oval, seen? Then hang a right and head for Peckham.'

'Peckham, boss?' Jinxie said from the passenger seat upfront.

'Yes, fuckin' Peckham.'

'But, Chief, Django mek a deal. Peckham stay outta Brixton and we stay outta—'

'Do the maths, Jinxie, how much fucks do I give?'

Liquid silence flowed through the vehicle.

'And what did I say about mentioning that name?'

'Sorry, Chief.' Jinxie kept his eyes front.

Bull patted his jacket pockets in turn.

Spare clips? Check.

Knuckleduster? Two. Only for show; he felt happy enough with the damage he did with his bare knuckles.

Pliers? Check.

Then Bull felt for his good luck charm, the very first flick knife he'd ever used to make a point in an argument over turf, back in his Barnardo's days.

'You boys must be hungry?' Django used to water the jackasses before setting them to work. *Stupidition*, as far as he was concerned, but why tempt fate, eh? These idiots were used to shit like that and *If it ain't broke, why fuck wiv it, eh?*

It was left to Jinxie to crack into the awkwardness. 'Well, I-man could murder some curry goat, y'know, Chief. But business first, right?'

'You know that patty place in Camberwell?'

'No, Chief?'

'Cool. I'll tell you when to stop... You boys want to hear some jokes?' Bull said. 'I know you lot like a good laugh before a job.'

'Yea, Chief. But is alright. We's loose enough, yea?'

'What, you think I can't be funny too?'

'Uhm, no, boss!' Jinxie fiddled with his seatbelt and traded a glance with Clint.

Bull told them both an old joke, forgot the punchline and stopped talking.

Both men laughed anyway and said they'd tell the others when they stopped.

'Funnies' thing I ever heard, Chief,' Clint said.

'Year, right,' Bull grunted. 'Pull over there.'

'But it's an Indian, Chief?'

Bull attributed the stupid remark to low blood sugar and Clint being dropped on his head at birth.

'Now, Clint… Pull over!' Jinxie advised.

The van screeched up to stop behind them.

Bull led the way.

# CHAPTER 27

A startled Asian gent welcomed them into a mist of Madras curry and Singha beer. Bull brushed him aside while being informed that a table would be free in about thirty minutes and offered drinks by the bar while they waited; on the house of course, please.

Bull grimaced into his face. 'Listen me. Did I *aks* you a damn thing?' Bull looked behind at Clint, Jinxie, George and Likkle. 'Where's Chigger?'

'He comin', Chief,' Jinxie said, pointing down and mimicking Chigger's limp.

Bull looked left. A fine woman sat facing a black man looking like he'd either just arrived or was about to leave. Bull clocked a highchair and a child, maybe hers, or theirs. Who cared?

To the right, six raucous skinhead youths sat with enough skirts for four of them, unless they were into sharing and shit. Palace supporters, from the look of them. One flung Bull a dirty look and mumbled something. Lucky for him, there was no time for small fry tonight.

'We'll sit over there.' Bull nodded towards where eight people were already gathered around a birthday cake with a fire hazard on top.

'So sorry, sir, but that table is…' The man called from behind Bull and his men.

'Whose birthday's it?' Bull demanded of the eight unsure but merry faces.

'Humphrey, you're such a card. Is *this* the entertainment?' The squeal came from a large woman at the head of the table. Her gaze found Bull's eyes and then slipped right down his chest to his crotch, where they stayed.

Bull moved closer and smiled. 'So it's *your* birthday, luv?'

Looking up from her seat, the rosy-cheeked woman licked puckered lips. 'Why yes, honey.'

'Twenty-one again?'

'You can surely come again.' The woman reddened, fluttering long eyelashes.

Bull withdrew the smile. 'You want to see twenty-two?'

The woman nodded tentatively. The restaurant din died. 'Get lost then.'

'Come on, Maggie.' A man popped up like a jack-in-the-box from his seat. 'I think we'd better go. Everyone, I know a nice little place around the…'

Everyone watched her party escort the woman out, her coat half on, half off, for trying to pull it on in a rush.

'Watch it!' Chigger said, pulling attention to the doorway, as the last of the birthday group exited. 'Step on mi foot and I'll gut you, I swear!'

Four waiters filed in, bearing trays of orders. They stopped short, confused, with spiced steam rising from rattling containers on their heavily laden trays.

Bull beckoned them forward. 'Bring it here and keep it comin'!'

The waiters looked anxiously from Bull to their guvnor. He told them something in their language that Bull figured meant 'hurry the fuck up and serve them' in English.

'Eat up, boys. All you can eat in five minutes, aight? And no drinking on the job! I need you boys sharp tonight.' Bull turned to the nearest waiter. 'Oi, take that fire hazard away.'

'Yessir, mister, and will there be anything else?'

'No, no!' Bull pulled out a large roll of banknotes as he went over to the guvnor. 'What's the damage for this shit?'

'Uhm,' the man looked cornered and raised both his hands, 'on the house, sir. All on the house.'

'Fuck me, your chef working his nuts off for you back there and you're givin' this shit away for free?'

'No, no, no. I don't mean to offend.'

'Well, if I was your people, mate, I'd be fuckin' offended. Wait up! You sayin' my money ain't good enough, aintchya?'

'No, no, *NO!*'

'I'm offended.' Bull lifted his chest to full height, watching the smaller man frantically flick through a well-thumbed little receipt book he'd fished from his back pocket.

'It was ninety-five p-pound, sir.'

'That so? Well, I make it ninety-five quid and a big-ass tip that you won't see now, mate.' Bull looked at his watch and waved him away, out of his sight. 'Eat up, boys, three minutes!'

Conversation slowly returned to the other tables and something or someone at the footie table made all those Palace supporters laugh out loud.

Bull went over to the couple by the door.

'Hey little one.' Bull's hand completely enwrapped the baby and lifted it from the cot. The woman started towards him and was swiftly stopped by her man's hand. 'What's his name?'

'Trudy,' the man replied.

Bull looked at the man still tethering the woman.

Her voice shaking, the woman said, 'It's not a boy. Her name's Trudy.'

'Trudy's a girl's name? No kidding.' Bull held the child aloft and then lowered her to face level, fresh eyes locking onto eyes that had seen way too much. 'Hey, little Trudy! Who's a little cutey? Cutey-cutey-coo! Who's a little cutey, eh?'

The child gurgled and blew bubbles that hung like grapes from her bottom lip. Bull thought she felt as light as a bag of weed and was as cute as hell. From the corner of his eye, he saw Trudy's mother growing all huffy and pull herself away from her man's restraining hold. He also checked that the guvnor had not been tempted to dial 999.

Replacing the child in the cot, Bull lowered his face to hers and tickled her chin with a finger.

'Trudy, you be a good girl, y'ear me? Listen to your Uncle Bull: don't you ever let me catch you doin' drugs. And don't let your parents fuck you up. You're ma tells you she's goin' on holiday, ain't takin' you and she'll come back soon, don't you fuckin' believe that shit, y'hear me? As for your dad,' Bull lifted his face from the child's and looked hard at the man and then back at the child, 'you memorise his face, Trudy, 'cause pretty soon he'll be off someplace he can be forgettin' all about you, get me? So, don't you ever trust nobody, hear? And when you get to eighteen, come look for Uncle Bull.'

Bull kissed the child's forehead and checked his watch.

'Time's up, boys!'

Cutlery clinked on china plates and chair legs scraped the floor. Bull was following them out of the restaurant when he stopped beside the group of red jerseys with blue stripes and yellow sleeves. They all avoided his eyes except the large lump of a lad beside a little blonde tottie in a red and blue miniskirt and yellow woolly scarf round her neck. Beside her, a young boy had his shaven head on the table surrounded by a small forest of Singha bottles and plates of spicy food.

Bull remembered a tough guy in Barnardo's who'd dissed him. Funny thing, he'd had a shaven head too and thought he could say and do whatever the fuck he wanted.

Bull grabbed the back of the chair and dumped the sleeping lad on the floor so he could sit right up close to the blonde, throwing an arm around her shoulders. The manoeuvre wedged her chair up against the large mouthy lump, clearly her boyfriend. With a wall behind and beside, he was forced to sit there, cornered.

With one arm on the girl's shoulder Bull weighted her down and grabbed a chilli pepper off a serving plate, juiced it into his own mouth.

'Hot stuff!' he said, licking his lips, catching her eye. She looked away disgusted. He gestured at her trapped hero. 'Yours?'

'Git your arm off m'bird!' The lad tried to stand, but he remained wedged. His hand caught a plate and tipped red curry down his Palace shirt.

'Tut, tut, tut,' Bull said, as his Yardies filed back in and circled the table with murder in their eyes. 'That stain'll be a devil for your mumma to get out. Okay, this is how this works: one of you's goin' to apologise to all black people in here, and everywhere, especially little Trudy over there, then we'll leave you to your little – whatever this is!'

The boy on the floor stayed where he fell, face down on the dusty carpet while the others sat back, fists tight and lips tighter. Bull placed his peppered hand under the table.

'Get off me!' she flinched.

Bull looked at her casually. 'Another move like that and you'll need surgery, y'hear me?' He gave Mr Madras a look reminding him to stay well away from the telephone or whatever the hell alarm he might be trying to reach.

The girl sucked in sharply and grabbed her boyfriend's arm, whose sleeve was rolled up to reveal a bicep wrapped in a razor wire tattoo. Bull figured he might push fifty kilos without much trouble.

'Get off her, bastard!' Razor Wire said, still struggling to get out the corner in vain.

'Nobody up to apologising then?' Bull kept the girl stuck in her seat. His face blank of expression, he kept his hand in position. 'Think fast, cause I ain't got no time to waste. Who's going to 'pologise.'

'Yeah, you talk big wiv your *girlfriends* wiv ya,' Razor Wire said, chin high, face red.

Bull looked over at Jinxie. 'Get the engines warm, boys. I can handle this.'

Jinxie gave him an are-you-sure-boss look.

Bull nodded. 'It's cool. I'm goin' to settle this little misunderstandin'. Get Clint to pull up out front. Save time and shoe leather.'

It had been Django's thing to never use their right names in public. *Well fuck Django and this piece of shit for dissing him.*

'Now about that apology?' Bull asked, feeling the conflict between control and scorching outrage.

'Please, Trev, just fuckin' apologise!' Blondie was flushed and squirming, still clutching her Razor Wire.

'Yes, Trev,' Bull taunted. 'And be quick about it.'

'He didn't mean nothing, mister.' One of the other girls shrilled.

'Just tell the fucker you're sorry, Trev!' one of his boys added, but Trev ignored his people, concentrating on pushing the table over but Bull'd weighted it down with his free arm. Feeling her moisten and grow slippery, Bull retracted his fingers and began to stroke. Covering her mouth too late, the blonde gasped and juddered, digging red-and-blue-striped nail polish into Razor Wire.

'What the fuck!'

Bull brought back his hand and licked a finger. 'Mmm, tastes like chick and the chilli brings the flavour right out! But, being honest here, that wasn't as good for me as it was for you. Trust me, waxing beats shaving. Like stroking a bloody porcupine, that was!' Bull wiped his hand down Blondie's chest and watched jaws drop. 'Now, Trev, how about you apologise to me and take your porcupine here out back and fuck it.'

Trev exploded, straining every muscle. Bull let go of the table and heard Trev growl, saw him grab a half-full bottle of Singha and swing. Bull ducked, Trev's spikey girl didn't.

Blood burst from her forehead all over the table.

Amidst screams, Trev's boys found their balls and were converging. Bull took out the nearest lad with a pulled punch to the head. Two more grabbed an arm each. Emboldened and unperturbed by his girl's bloodied face, Trev pounded Bull's midriff. It must have been six of his best.

'Not bad,' said Bull with a sniff. 'My turn now.'

Bull brought his arms together and the heads of his two restrainers with them. They landed on beds of rice and curried dishes.

Trev and his last two mates came at Bull, brandishing cutlery.

'Guys, you're makin' a meal o' this!' Bull said, thinking there might be a joke there to take away to the car for the guys. 'Trev, time's up. I'm busy. Apologise now before you get a lot sorrier, you piece o' shit.'

'I ain't fuckin' 'pologisin' to no *wog*. Fact, I'll say it again even better. *Good riddance, nigger!*'

'Hmm, I hear you…and you added special emphasis too. You know I have to quit playin' now, right?'


Clint was finding it hard to drive for laughing, still tickled from hearing that Bull had seasoned the girl with chilli with her man sitting right there.

'*Making a meal* – nice one, Chief. And he really said *nigger* to your face, boss?' Jinxie asked, chuckling and checking for Peckham posse lookouts he knew would clock them rolling along Lordship Lane.

'Naw, I made the whole damn thing up!' Bull said, annoyed, deciding not to bother telling them he'd taken a fork off one tough guy and skewered his thigh while another had lost his bottle and left Trev alone armed only with knives that got shoved up his arse.

Clint and Jinxie were still sniggering as the Beamer slowed for the traffic lights.

Bull spotted a familiar briefcase with its owner and lost all sense of humour. 'Stop! Stop the fucking car!'

'Wha!' Clint crushed the brake.

Jinxie jolted forward to headbutt the dash and whip back into the headrest.

'Fu-uck-me-roughly-sweetheart!' Bull rasped, his eyes wide in disbelief.

No-Name was unmistakable, but who was he standing there gassing with so intently? Bull edged forward in his seat to focus on the hulking figure wearing an all-weather purple boiler suit, his shiny dome protruding like an island surrounded by dazzling white hair, swept back into what Bull decided was a ponytail, long as any girls. The fucking thing dangled down to the middle of his back. Christ, he knew chicks who'd kill for that thing! The big fat Timex, the Nikes, it had to be the King Rat of the Peckham posse standing on a street corner jawing with No-Name. Bull sneered.

'Ain't that Silk over there, Chief?' Clint looked round at him. 'Got to be. Same hair tie up wit' a ribbon and—'

'I know who Silk is, fool! What's he doing shaking hands with...' Bull let his voice trail away. 'Be quiet. I want to see this.'

'But, Chief, the lights.' Clint looked round.

'Fuck the lights. You move and I'll show you loadsa lights. Matter of fact, Clint, kill the engine, get out and open up the bonnet!'

Clint started on about Triple being the one to fix engines, but Jinxie interrupted, 'Just lean over it, bro. And don't touch nothin', cool!'

'Jinxie.'

'Yeah, Chief.'

'Tell the boys to drive round us and wait in the van on the other side of the lights.'

'Yes, Chief.'

'That fuckin' Rat,' Bull whispered to no one, fogging up the tinted glass and wishing he could hear what they were talking about, standing out there in the open.

Another two red-amber-greens and a heavily tinted Rover pulled up. No-Name climbed in, and it drove off.

Silk walked away.

Bull ordered Jinxie to get himself and Clint back in. With the lights still on red, they drove on, turned and followed Silk discreetly.

'He's gone into that building,' Jinxie said. 'Camberwell gym.'

'A gym? Open this late?' Clint asked the question Bull'd already answered.

Bull told them to park up and he stomped up to the front door. They followed.

A man peered round the half-opened door as if he wasn't wearing any trousers and asked them if they were with Mr Silk's private party because the gym was closed otherwise.

'Who else?' Bull stepped in his face.

Apologising for not having recognised them, he opened the door fully and pointed them in the direction of the weights room, reminding them where the fresh towels were and to please-please-please not pee on the sauna stones.

As they walked down a darkened corridor, Jinxie leaned towards Bull.

'Chief, can I say something?'

'No!'

Silk was lying on a bench while two other men, each with an arm full of iron, handed him a barbell. Silk's forearms bulged as he took the strain, his chest pumped full as he lifted both legs and crossed them at the ankles.

'I like to keep my feet on the ground, myself,' Bull said.

With the barbell hovering above his chest, Silk wobbled slightly. 'What the hell! Who let you in here?'

'This is a private gym.' The dumb ass squared off with Bull.

'Correction.' Bull gave him a finger jab to the chest that sent him cowering away. 'It's a private session in a public gym. Right, Silk?'

'Yeah, what of it, Bull.' Silk regained his composure and managed one full bench press. 'Django off duty tonight?'

'Could say that!' Bull brushed the other goon out the way and approached the bench. 'Saw you shootin' the breeze with an old mate o' mine just now.'

'Don't know what you're on about, mate. What the fuck're you doin' here and I don't like you pushin' my people about neither.'

'Hmm, I figure you got 40kg on each end right there, and when you add the bar weight, that's about what? 100 kilos? A shitload on them shoulders, *mate*.'

'You could say tha—' Silk started, going into a fifth press.

Bull grabbed the bar as if he were spotting and added a few more kilos on the down.

'Fuck!' Silk croaked, grimacing, sweat pouring immediately down his face, soaking the edges of his silvered ponytail and dripping onto the bench. His eyes bulged from the effort of avoiding a chest full of barbells or worse. 'What're you doing?'

'You were about to tell me what business you have with cashmere-coat-and-briefcase?'

'None...of your...fuck...ing—'

Bull figured he'd added about 20kg to the 100 that hovered inches away from crushing his windpipe.

'I'd talk if I were you, Silk.'

'Go...to...he...hel—' Silk's arms popped extra veins and he struggled to breathe. His feet had long dropped to the floor as every muscle in his body strained to keep 100 plus off his neck, while Clint and Jinxie stood by keeping watch over Silk's two idiots.

'Al…ri-right! G-G-Geezer…said…' Silk rasped. Bull eased off slightly. 'Said he…had a prop-prop—'

'Prepasition?'

'Proposi – never mind… I dunno! I dunno!… Lift it off me!'

Bull pushed down again, adding about 60kg. Silk was wilting dangerously fast.

'No…no…stop!'

'So stop yankin' my fuckin' chain!'

'He only told…me…to be…ready…Wednesday…morn-morn… I can't take…any…more, man!'

'Then hurry up!'

'B-Bull… I swe-swear. He don't tell me noth…ing, just said…be ready for a big job… Wednesday morning. Something 'bout fixing som'ink!'

Bull's head and heart were racing, but it had nothing to do with the weight he was still dangling above Silk.

*Fixing, eh?* Bull asked himself. People only fix what goes wrong, so what was No-Name up to? More to the point, could he trust what Silk was saying to save his neck?

'Yeah, fixing is what he said.' Silk was awash with sweat and blowing hard.

'I don't believe you, Silk!'

'Better Adam and Eve it.'

'I got stupid tattooed on my forehead?'

'Bull, no!' Silk's eyes bulged with terror as Bull hoisted the weight from out of his slippery palms.

'You two.' Bull pointed at Silk's guys. 'Tie him with them ropes.'

Silk's men hesitated. Clint pulled out his Magnum and Jinxie produced his long blade from his jacket.

'Make it tight!' Bull insisted, watching the two work the ropes into knots about their boss's musclebound body. 'Feet too!… Hurry up.'

They worked faster and when Bull'd waited long enough, he lifted the weighted barbell high. 'Right, Silk, let's see how long we can discuss your street meet before my arms give out and I have to let this go, shall we?'

'I'm telling you *truth, Bull.*'

'What's his name?'

'Don't know!'

Bull jerked the heavy dumbbell. Silk closed his eyes and swore the man never gave him a name. He'd kept asking, but he just kept saying it was not important.

'How'd he even find you, Silk?'

'I don't know. The man knew things about me only my GP knows. He found me and the boys working out, said he had some business for someone like me and that…'

'What did he mean someone like you?'

'How the fuck should I know? – sorry! He just said it, yeah?'

'Something you're not telling me, Silk.' Bull raised the bar, moved it down a few inches from Silk's neckline, dropped it and caught it late. 'Oops! That's why I never trust spotters.'

Wheezing cuss words, Silk tried to get air into his pounded chest, eyeballing the iron Bull held above him.

'Hmm, this thing is getting really heavy now, Silk. My arm's feeling such a burn from all the fuckin' galactic acid I might just—'

'Bull, stop, wait, no!' Silk rasped. 'I never…seen this man… be-before…'

'You know, gyms always make me sneeze. All that testosterone, you think?'

'Bull, no, I'll talk… I'll tell you…*everyfingk!*'

'Talk!'

Silk spilled the beans: No-Name had approached them; he'd never seen nor heard of him and his 'group' before, but they needed some cargo taken to Gatwick and guarded—

'Gatwick?'

'Yeah.'

No-Name wanted him to gather a team with guns and vans and shit, like that.

'How many men, shithead?'

'T-told him I could get thirty soldiers for sure, and another t-twenty, if the price was right?'

'So you growed a pair!… Was the price right, Silk?'

Silk's eyes darkened. He looked away from Bull, lips like a frog's pussy.

Bull shifted, wobbling the weights. 'Man, I got an urgent need to scratch my arse right now.'

'F-four! Fuckin' *FOUR!*' Silk said, eyes like saucers. 'Alright?'

'Four quid? Four hundred?'

'Four hundred grand! Four hundred grand! Deliver some packages to the airport. Satisfied?'

Bull dropped the barbell.

# CHAPTER 28

Amanita was expressionless, watching her little sister tilt her head back, using both her tiny hands to hold a large mug. Steam rose from a big cup of chocolate-coloured liquid on the table before her. Jonelle shivered at the sight of Kenyana's milky Milo moustache.

"Nita, you haven't touched yours.' Jonelle reached out to brush her daughter's hair with her hand, the way she calmed her whenever she arrived home from school upset.

'It's too sweet.' The child leaned away from her hand.

'What's wrong, 'Nita?' A blend of shock and despair shot through her.

'Nothing.' Amanita said towards Chelsea.

Jonelle felt life had been *jacked* and she was being driven towards insanity. She steadied herself against the sofa and looked away above Keefah's and the reverend's mantelpiece to see an exact replica of a picture in her dad's study. She'd grown up looking up at that same frozen scene with a robed and bearded Jesus cradling a lamb to his chest.

*You're like that lost lamb, Jonie.*

She'd never told her dad about the recurring nightmares his words had given her, like the one in which she searched for home and couldn't find her parents. Right now, she'd never felt more lost and alone.

A loud knock made them all start.

Amanita got up.

'No, stay, honey!' Jonelle said, too late. Amanita was already by the bay windows, parting the nets. 'Someone's at the front door, Mommy. A man. I think. Should I go and—'

'No, honey. It's Keefah's house.' Jonelle watched Keefah and Veronica follow Chelsea from the room. 'We got to go, anyway. Leave these nice people in peace.'

'Amanita, you didn't touch your Milo.' The reverend held out the mug. 'Too hot?'

'She's fine,' Jonelle said without looking round, 'thanks for looking after them, but we got to go.'

Jonelle ushered her daughters from the room, walking behind them, prodding them towards the sound of voices by the open door, allowing a cool, damp draught into the warm interior.

A warm familiar hand found hers and she smiled down at Amanita.

'Don't worry, Mommy.'

Kenyana jumped between them. 'Are we going home now, Mummy? I want to go home.'

'Yeah, we're getting you home, little one.' A smiling TK stepped forward just as yet another flash of lightning lit up the street outside and Veronica hurried away, upstairs.

From where he stood dripping on the welcome mat, TK introduced himself to Amanita and Kenyana.

Kenyana dodged behind and hugged Jonelle's thigh. Still holding her hand, Amanita stayed put and tightened her grip.

'Oh, Kenyana,' Jonelle worked her face into a half smile, 'it's okay. Be nice.'

'I understand, shy one,' TK said, lifting his plaster-casted arm. 'It's this thing, innit? Bet you can draw a nice picture on it for me, eh? Got a pen, anybody?'

'Did you say home, Jonelle?'

'Yes, home.' She turned round to meet Chelsea's gaze.

'Hmm, okay…but you must be starving, I am.' Chelsea regarded Amanita and Kenyana. 'Why don't we all grab something at a restaurant?'

'I'm fine! We're fine.' Jonelle gathered the girls to her and started towards the door.

'You like burgers?' TK grinned down at the girls. Kenyana remained half-hid behind Jonelle. 'I bet you could eat two whole Wimpy's all by yourself!'

Kenyana giggled.

'Also…' Chelsea blocked Jonelle's path towards the door, 'we've got that *appointment* in Brixton, remember?'

'*I said*, we're goin' home!' Jonelle felt a fire flare in her belly as she thanked Keefah one last time and asked her to thank the reverend for the Milo, promising to return the brolly she'd forced into Chelsea's hand, although she'd said they'd be okay.

Her girls were still waving back at Keefah when they left the gate.

'Told that taxi driver to wait.' TK was looking up and down the road. 'He's gone, the silly sod. I wasn't going to tip him anyway.'

'Come, girls.' Jonelle pointed her nose in the direction of home.

'Wait, I can order another taxi,' Chelsea called after her. 'I'm sure your friend will let us use her phone.'

'Do what you want. We're off home.' Jonelle led her girls away, with Kenyana sandwiched between her and Amanita, as they often did to help the little girl keep up.

The rain-washed pavement, water gurgling down the drains and the cool evening air made Brixton feel like it had been rinsed and left to drip dry. Jonelle felt she was in a spin cycle. To make matters worse, she'd left Keefah's without dealing with her bladder situation.

'I'm cold, Mommy?'

'We'll be home soon, Kennie! Walk a little faster, honey.'

'I'm trying, Mommy.' Kenyana was getting her legs entangled with the large umbrella she'd insisted on carrying after Chelsea'd handed it to Amanita.

Home was Jonelle's sanctuary. Besides, she needed to wash and change her clothes. Maybe then she'd think about doing the Wimpy thing. Get someone round to watch the kids sleep in their own bed while that Chelsea delivered her, and TK, to the cops later.

Listening to the rhythm of her own steps, Jonelle's thoughts floated about in her mind, reminding her of the kids' bubble maker – a gift from Candice. Candice? If anyone could help her straighten out this mess, it was quick-thinking Candice. If only she could get hold of her. Prunes too, maybe? She'd see him tomorrow because Monday night was rent night and Prunes would never miss that. Come Tuesday night – *please God!* – she'd see Candice at evening class as usual and they'd be able to sit at the back and whisper about all this madness. Maybe even laugh a little more than usual and be asked to leave, this time.

'Amanita, why don't you take a turn carrying the brolly?' Jonelle heard Chelsea say behind them, somewhere.

Up ahead, three lads approached. Each had fresh haircuts, but their clothes hung as though professionally crimped and crumpled. Their raucous laughter echoed down the street and parted curtains.

Jonelle braced herself.

She was in no mood for this – not helped by the feeling that she was a dam ready to burst. The tension was dialled down when the trio went by without any hassle. Moments later, she heard them hassling Chelsea for her name and number and daring TK to do something about it and calling him a cripple.

'Don't look at them, 'Nita...you too, Kennie...and be careful of them puddles!'

Two roads from her home stretch, it dawned on Jonelle that they'd be going right past Myrna's.

The streetlamps popped to bathe them in sepia as they neared familiar surroundings. Jonelle envied the people putting their children to bed inside council houses that PM Thatcher was giving them the right to own. That will be her one day, exercising her right to own her home, for her and the kids. Soon.

Kenyana splashed into a large puddle. 'Kennie, be careful.'

'Sorry, Mummy.' Kenyana started to cry. Jonelle calmed her, ignoring her complaints about squelching shoes and wet socks. Deen would have done the same, but deliberately.

'I know I'd carry Deen, honey, but your brother's much smaller than you,' Jonelle replied, taking care to avoid the word 'lighter'.

'And *he's* the baby, isn't he, Mummy?' Kenyana said triumphantly, stretching her little body, elevating her head and puffing her chest.

'Yes, and you're a little lady,' said Jonelle.

They stopped at the next kerb.

There was a flicker of movement to Jonelle's left, up ahead. Jonelle remembered the times her own shadow had scared her while walking home from evening classes.

'Kids, get behind!' Her arms shot out to block both girls.

'What is it, Mommy?' Kenyana balanced on one foot with the other hovering, frozen in mid-step. Jonelle set herself between her daughters and the figure that emerged from the hedge two houses away. Amanita dropped the brolly.

'Excuse me, Mrs.'

He was well dressed but still made her uneasy. It was too early to be thrown out of the pubs. Then again, the Duck & Diva was not far behind the unsteady man.

'You got the time?'

'Everything alright there, Jonelle?' TK called from a few paces back.

'Jonelle?' The stranger perked up and wobbled closer to where she stood, still protecting the children. 'You're never Jonelle? Myrna's friend? That Jonelle?'

'Who's that man, Mummy?' Kenyana tugged on her arm.

'How come you're so late?'

'Late for what?'

'Everybody gone…(hic) but if you hurry, there might be a few *strugglers* hanging about still.'

'Strugglers?'

'Down the D & D? Everybody turn' up to drink to poor Myrna. Who could do a thing like that to such a nice sweet, sweet, swe(hic)eet, lady, I never know?'

Chelsea and TK caught up.

'Make sense, man.' Jonelle wished he'd stand still before she threw up. 'I've no idea what you're on about.'

'Look,' he pointed down the road. Lines of black-and-yellow tape fluttered just outside, near the house where Myrna always entertained her, and their girlie group, that same Myrna who still owed her a taxi fare and much explaining, with apologies. The very same Myrna who was also holding this month's partner payout that she was counting on for food, back-to-school uniforms and a present for Amanita's birthday.

The stranger burped, looked like he might be sick but then regained his composure, of a fashion. 'Poor Myrna – the Babylon say it was suspicious cercum-*hic* circu-*hic*—' He took a deep breath, backing up as though about to do the long jump… '*sushpishus* happenin's! But…everybody know it was murder!'

'Murd—?' Jonelle gasped and covered Kenyana's ears.

'Ye-e-s! Plain bloody murder!' the stranger continued. 'Poor, poor Myrna. Can't believe she's gone. The life and soul of the party she was on Friday night! Should've seen her when those two police strippers turned up!'

'What? Myrna?' Jonelle looked down into Kenyana's eyes staring up at her. 'Party? Friday?'

'The same,' he said and turned to TK and Chelsea. 'You know Myrna too? Well, yer all very late but you might catch some *strugglers* still down the D & D. I still feel them should 'ave gone to the Prince Regent, as it was Myrna's favourite pub. Remember how mad she was, when she got all dressed up with her big hat. Security wouldn't let her near Lady Di when she was opening that AIDS clinic las' month in Tulse Hill? Ah...that Myrna with her royalty!'

Whatever he was thinking made him chuckle as he walked away, swaying as though trying not to fall off a balance beam.

'Now there's a man who's had a skinful, at least enough for a man three times his size,' TK said.

'Who's this *Myrna*, Jonelle?' Chelsea asked.

'Oh, yes!' The man stopped within earshot, stumbled backwards two paces, then forwards again. His voice bounced off the closed windows and shuttered doors. 'Forgot to tell you...there's some stranger asking 'bout you. Good-looking, stylish, nice haircut, nice jacket. Funny thing though, he never *knowed* Myrna and kept pestering people about when youse coming. Never want to leave no message and then he keep sayin' he don't mind waitin', like anybody care 'bout that. No offence, but we was only there for poor Myrna, right? All the same, you might still catch 'im if you hurry...'

He started walking back towards the pub, realised he was going the wrong way and did a one-eighty, mumbling as he went, 'Didn't even know Myrna but he still turn up, his coat reekin' of liver and onions, pushin' 'is busybody nose where it don't never belong. No respect. Poor Myrna... Poor, poor Myr—'

Jonelle stood rooted to the spot, stunned, trying to take in what she'd just heard.

A hand grasped her arm.

She jumped.

Chelsea let go. 'Christ! What do you want to do now, Jonelle?'

# CHAPTER 29

The nurse moved with experience and care in the small space at the far end of the container.

'Brace yo'self…it's only a little prick.'

Maxwell saw the familiar tremor running down her arm into the hand holding the needle like a spliff. She aimed the business tip towards his spongy flesh cupped in her other hand and he flinched, losing his balance on the crate he sat on with his trousers and bloodstained boxers down around his ankles.

'Oi!' the nurse chastened.

'Wo-ah!' Maxwell flailed his arms to keep from falling backwards. 'You're high again, aintchya?'

'Nope!' she snapped, pointing the loaded syringe at his crotch. 'And I told you: *don't* move, Cuz – 'less you want a dick kebab.'

'But you're sh-shakin' – and don't call me *cuz* 'round here, you crazy or wot?'

'Never mind them.' She gestured behind, down the short corridor of hatches towards the door to the outside. Maxwell was sure he'd heard her slur.

'Stop squirming!'

'I'm not even movin'!' He kept a sharp eye on the needle circling him for a second stab at a landing site. She was holding the syringe like a throwing dart this time. He squeezed his eyes shut, took one last breath, and held it.

'Hmm, I need a magnifying glass...'

'What? Why?' he gasped.

'Too messy.'

'Messy?'

'Infected – big time. You use a rusty stapler? Hope you kept your tetanus up to date.'

Infected? His dick? He'd never signed up for that and didn't need her stories about what weirdness people did in the privacy of their own kinkiness. 'Didn't ask for no lecture, aight? This was no game, so just get on wiv it, will'ya – you locked the door?'

'Naw,' she chuckled. 'Makes it easier for them packages to run off...again!'

'You wot? Another one of them legs it and it'll be my f—'

The penny dropped when she stuck her tongue out at him. He looked narrowly up at her. 'Oh, grow up, will ya!'

'Chill, where's...?'

'What's the newspaper for?' Maxwell interrupted whatever she'd started saying as she opened a copy of the *Sun*.

'Catch any blood and pus. Took all afternoon to clean this steel box for your precious packages? Can't think why you lot put people in filthy places like this and think you can keep them healthy.'

'You just keep page three outta my sight, understan'?'

She shrugged, looked confused and laid topless Linda Lusardi at his feet anyway. 'So, what was wrong with the last place, anywise? Bet I know whose bad idea this wasn't. So, where is Mr Hard-to-Get?'

'You ask too much question...just get the bloody staple out.'

The nurse peered through the magnifying glass. 'Get a grip, Cuz.'

'Stop calling me cuz – 'round these people we ain't no relation, aight? You're the nurse. I'm Mr Maxwell, 'cause what Bull don't know won't hurt me, aight?' Maxwell ducked down, lowering his voice to a whisper, 'Django taught me that!'

The name hung like forbidden cigarette smoke in the closet space for this *little op*, as she'd laughingly called it when she'd agreed to help and told him to drop his trousers.

'So, where's Django, then?'

'Seriously, don't ask!' Maxwell looked away and gripped the crate, taking care not to move with his reviving python being probed, up close and too personal for comfort.

'Control that slug.' She squeezed firmly.

Maxwell held his tongue and kept his mighty beast against his belly. A red and yellow fluid splatted on the newspaper and a rancid odour found his nose.

'There we go… So, *why* can't you tell me where Django is?'

'Shush!' Maxwell laid a finger across his lips and looked down the short corridor, towards the exit. 'One o' them might be out in the yard…or the house!'

She retreated again into her torture bag, behind her feet. 'I was only asking about Dja—'

'Sh-ush!' Maxwell stiffened. 'You really *doesn't* know, do ya?'

'Know what?' She rummaged in her first-aid bag and returned with two objects, like a chopstick and a pointy tweezer, far too close to his ball sack, teasing hair away from not-hair.

'So, nobody's told you, eh?' Maxwell spoke slowly, careful to not distract her. Truth is, it didn't seem right to him that, of all people, she didn't know. She and Django were always trading banter made to look like love-talk, cute at first but it quickly got annoying to everyone but them two. Surely someone should have told her *something* about that fuckin' traitor. He'd caused Bull and him so much grief and pain. Because of Django, he'd had to run around doing Bull's dirty work, like he was one of them *yagga-yaggas*, as he called them Yardies, inside his head when no one was looking.

Bloody Django.

Would things ever get back to normal so he could get on with being the manager of the best touring night club that nobody ever heard of? Suddenly, Myrna popped up, right in the middle of his thoughts. Maxwell shuddered violently.

The nurse shot him a stern look, laced with annoyance.

'Sorry, sorry.'

'You might be if you do that again…and if you don't hurry up and say what it is that nobody's told me.'

Seeing that Bull hadn't told her, Maxwell decided it was not his place to blab. He burped. Those onions he'd finished off while Myrna and Style were 'having a chat' in her bedroom had awoken his irritable belly.

'Listen me good, aight!'

'Mmm-hm!'

'*Don't* mention that name 'round here or anywhere no more, get me? 'Specially 'round Bull.'

'What name?' She slanted her head at his groin. 'Django?'

'*Him*. Yes! Bull's orders, seen?' Maxwell said loud and clear. 'So don't let *your* mouth write a cheque *your* arse can't cash!'

'Know what I think?' She winked. The syringe reappeared, as if by magic, and squirted an arc of fluid that just missed his face. 'I think you're delaying the inevitable. Now hold still, Cuz, and think: *Django!*'

'Wait!' Maxwell bristled, mentally pulling away to run screaming. A sting of pain punctured his flaccidity. 'C-CHRIST Almighte-ee!'

'You're more of a baby than Bull's precious packages, up there!' She disposed of the syringe into a yellow box and unsheathed a fresh scalpel from her doctoring bag.

'Oh, yeah?' Maxwell said in tears. 'Let me stick something in you – see how *you* like it!' That didn't sound right to him, but, 'That fucking *hurt*, right? What's wrong with just using a bloody staple remover? It's wha' it's for, aintit? *Shit.* No, you got to whip out a scalpel and antiseptic?'

'*Anaesthetic.* Antiseptic comes later and, yeah, I could do it without anaesthetic, but any trained nurse will tell you that every operation has risks and, fine, give me that staple remover you had in your *sterilised* pocket and I'll yank out the staple imbedded in your—'

'Ah'right, ah'right, made your fuckin' point! Get on with it!'

It was hard to see anything of the staple now, but he knew it was still there, somewhere, under swollen flesh, matted with hair, blood and pus.

She told him to relax, that she was only wiping the area with mercury.

Maxwell sat like a stone statue, looking away from the approaching razor-sharp blade.

'Control your thing, y'hear – won't be my fault if it jerks and – *slicey dicey!*' Her hand was still not steady enough for his liking.

The numbness had left him feeling disjointed. Maxwell held his tongue and his nerve, deciding not to even breathe.

*Slicey dicey?*

'Stop!' Maxwell yelled, pointing, casting caution to the wind.

'What now?'

The exit door swung wide open.

'Shit!' The nurse shot to her feet.

'Stop them!' Maxwell stood quickly or he tried to, at any rate. Three of the four girls cradling their tiny bundles had eyes focusing out of the exit to the yard beyond. 'For Chrissakes, don't let them out!'

'Lucky thing I was here, eh!' Prunes was standing calmly by the container, chewing, as the packages huddled together. 'Back inside, you lot! Tomorrow you get your freedom, and we all get paid. Or you can run now and be dead instead. And what about your families, eh? Thought about that? Yeah, you think about that while you pretend you don't understand what I'm telling you.'

One by one, they retreated to their cubicle.

'What if I wasn't doing my rounds?' Prunes glared at them both and then directly at Maxwell with his trousers and pants down by his ankles and a needle and thread dangling from between his thighs. 'And put that thing away! This ain't no fuckin' time for a hard-on.'

Maxwell covered himself with his hands as best he could. 'It's the antiseptic what she give me!'

'Yeah, right.' Prunes angled his face away from him. 'Nurse, you done your work here?'

'Y-yes!'

'New arrival in the container next to this one?'

'New arrival?'

Prunes looked heavenward. 'Maxwell, you got a death wish or—'

'B-But B-Bull told me to—'

'Look, I got no time to piss about wit you lot. Maxwell, get decent and go sort out that new arrival. I'll be back in a bit… and make sure you lock this bloody door.'

Prunes was gone.

Maxwell gave it a minute's silence before telling the nurse to tie a knot or do whatever, because they or she better see/ check on the new package.

'Up to you.' She shrugged. 'And don't give me that look. I was sure they were all locked up.'

'Don't care.' Maxwell felt stinking mad. He watched her snip the thread and heard her say about it dissolving and staying clean, like he couldn't figure that out for himself.

She tossed him a bundle and he caught it.

'What's this for?'

'Nappies, in case you have any embarrassing mishaps while the anaesthetic's still working. And here, catch!'

He did.

'Painkillers later tonight and tomorrow. Antibiotics, just in case.' She kissed her teeth muttering that she didn't see why she cared when he clearly didn't.

After a few failed attempts to get his pants up, he stuffed himself into an adult-sized padded nappy and pulled up his trousers very, very carefully.

'Cuz, I don't need this shit. This is it for me.'

'What? You know you can't work anywhere near hospitals. Not schools. Not no place with kids, right?'

'I'm starting up my own business. Just a few more evening classes and I'm all set. Might even give you a job. You could quit Bull too, Cuz.'

'Dream on!' Maxwell tried to work out how to walk straight with the tightness in his trousers working against him while checking, for his own peace of mind, that the packages were secure. 'Let's go sort out that new package.'

They went out to the next container and found its door hung wide open.

Like the other one, they used a steel bar to remove the metal façade concealing the inner entrance. Eventually, he accepted her help, and they entered the corridor and air-conditioned space with the low emergency light.

'Bit dark,' he heard, misjudging the distance between them.

'Jesus…' Maxwell winced.

One of the first 'Grilla nights was in a massive container, like this one. Bull had rented that from Prunes too. If memory served, there was a master light switch under a panel behind them. 'Okay, you keep going…be right back.'

He felt for the panel and found the switch.

Maxwell found her standing in the rear compartment, looking down at a cot, with both hands covering her mouth. She was shaking.

'Bloody hell! Not again!' Maxwell hobbled over to her side. 'Cuz, it's your *harmones* or some shit, breathe. And don't think about it – what got you in trouble in the first place. Calm down. Breathe.'

He held her by the elbow. 'Look, because of you, they'll get a good home, aight? Think about it – good people are paying thousands for 'em. They'll have the best life they'll ever have... and it's all down to you! Get me?'

Maxwell felt pride in his own words, the very words he'd used to persuade her to do these little *jobs* for Bull, in the first place. Then, in case Prunes was eavesdropping, he said softly. 'Remember what Django told you?'

He did, and she should: *This is the best way to say a big 'up yours' to the bloody NHS what kicked you out, when you was down! And it's tax-free.*

But she wasn't listening – just stood there. Eyes bulging and throat going lumpy, as usual. Happened every time. Next would come the waterworks and he'd have to remind her, yet again, that she couldn't keep even one of them. They weren't hers and never could be.

Maxwell kept his voice soft but firm, like he always did when he needed to talk sense into her craziness.

'Fight the feeling, aight?' She was rubbing her eyes and stroking her neck. 'You don't wanna know what Bull'll do if he gets back to find things ain't ready – get your shit together, Cuz!'

*Thanks, Mother Fucking Nature.*

# CHAPTER 30

Jonelle felt intimidated and uncomfortable in Chelsea's hotel suite. It was the kind that only ever appeared in her dreams – vast, with champagne on ice, two sparkling crystal glasses and a slipper bath filled with bubbles, her and Denzel.

The tops of the picture frames, in the loo, above mirrors and lamp shades – every sneaky finger-swipe came back dust-free. She eyed Chelsea, wondering who she'd slept with to get a suite like this, let alone two? Chelsea had insisted that her and her girls needed this one for themselves alone, and she felt too worn-out to argue.

She sat back down before her empty wine glass. If there's one thing she remembered from night school, it was that it's bad business to owe what you could never pay back. So, why'd she come here?

Was it because some drunkard had told her a stranger was looking for her, or the news that Myrna was never going to tell her why she'd hauled her sick self to a party last Friday because she was now dead? Or the four pairs of tired eyes that were waiting for her to accept the offer of a chance to step back from the brink and think?

Jonelle placed a hand over her ribs and rubbed at the tightness making every breath feel like her last.

'Stop.' Chelsea covered her glass with a hand and TK lifted the bottle away, just in time. Any slower and… Well, it probably would have made a very expensive puddle.

'Suit y'self, Cee.' TK swivelled over to Jonelle's glass and tilted the bottle to pouring point. 'Ma-dam…Jonelle?' TK waggled the bottle, tapped her glass with his plaster cast and raised his brows.

'Oh.' Jonelle nodded to the bottle. 'Yes-yes, please.'

'Say when,' TK instructed, pouring, watching the torrent of redness swill around in the potbellied glass. He looked up at halfway but kept going.

'Okay, *when*!' Jonelle raised a hand when the glass was nearly full.

'Sure?' TK froze and looked up at her.

'Okay, just a tip more.'

Jonelle watched him top up just short of the rim. Chelsea'd called it a flute, but it was as big as the vase she'd got down the market that Deen later dropped on the kitchen floor. She tried to remember the last time a man had waited on her without leaving her pregnant. She wondered what Tyrone was doing right now, while she was in all kinds of shit, her life spinning around like hell on ice.

'Cheers!' said Chelsea. 'Flowery bouquet, but do you think it's quite room temperature, Jonelle?'

She'd been trying to make her feel comfortable since they'd arrived. Asking whether the room was airy enough, whether they wanted anything more from room service and could she hear any traffic noise that would disturb her or the girls? It'd started to get on her tits when Chelsea'd wanted her to choose their bloody wine! Why? Not like *she* was bloody payin' for a damn thing!

'You chose well, Jonelle,' Chelsea said.

TK found that funny for some reason, even though he'd only been on juice. Jonelle viewed him through narrowed eyes.

'Looking sleepy there, Jonelle?' TK mimicked her expression.

'I'm not, TK.' Jonelle turned from him to Chelsea. 'Anyhow, I didn't choose. You told me that *Jayer… Yager?…* guy was a good wine bloke,' Jonelle said, with a sip that slipped into a slurp. She covered her mouth.

Chelsea slurped hers too, swivelled it like mouthwash then swallowed.

'It's what wine boffins do.' She held the glass up to her nose. 'First, they *breee-eathe* in the wine, smell affects taste, you see? Then they roll it round their palate at the back of their throats.'

'Of course.' Jonelle rolled her eyes and wanted to giggle.

'Yeah,' TK said. 'Then they spit it out – what a waste!'

'When you're buying wine for your customers, you want to know it's great stuff, TK.' Chelsea sipped from her glass. 'Been to any wine tastings, Jonelle?'

Bloody hell.

'Once-a-month, *don't-choo-know.*' Jonelle set down her wine to fold her arms across her chest.

'Lucky you. I'd love to go to one.' Chelsea took another sip. 'My parents used to go wine tasting when we went on holidays in France. Left me with my Filipino nanny, Divina, while they got squiffy and full of stories.'

*Squiffy?*

Jonelle chuckled nervously.

'*Squiffy*, Cee?' TK guffawed.

Chelsea looked down into her wine. Wistful. Pensive.

'Yes, anyway, TK. Everything I learnt about wine, my parents taught me. They'd open a bottle at every evening meal. Of course, until I was old enough, my wine glass was filled with grape juice.'

Jonelle sipped more wine. 'But you're hardly drinking, Chelsea.'

'You're right.' Chelsea lifted her eyes and raised her glass with a forced smile. 'Here's to parents, eh?'

Jonelle hesitated, but then clinked glasses with her and TK, who joined in with his orange juice.

'Cheers,' they said together.

Jonelle looked over at the phone.

'We called them from Brixton underground station, remember?' Chelsea softened her voice. 'They had no news on Deen, not yet.'

Jonelle looked away from the phone. 'Why didn't you just give them this number?'

Chelsea looked over at TK, then back at her. 'Jonelle, you all needed rest. I thought if they knew where we were it'd risk you spending the night in a police station, away from your girls and worried about your son.'

TK extended his legs, stretching them all the way from his vocal cords to his toes. His audible relief cut across their conversation.

TK spotted them watching. 'Sorry.'

'They're still looking, okay? But PC Bailey's pissed about me asking for an extension – threatened me – but I still got him to agree to me getting you and TK in by 10 p.m. tonight, but there's no way we can do that now. We'll just have to sort it out with them in the morning.'

'If you two had kids you'd…' Jonelle wiped her eyes and didn't bother to finish.

'Someone'd lose their teeth if they lost my kid.' TK waved a fist. 'If I had a kid.'

'Jonelle,' Chelsea said, 'you're a good mum to those kids but you really need to rest now, get your strength back. Have you seen your eyes?'

'I should be out there, Chelsea. Looking.'

'Can't, Jonelle. You're on police bail, remember… TK too… At least this way we all get to sleep in a proper bed – get fighting fresh for tomorrow. And your girls have you for the night too. Yes?'

'Fine, fine!' Jonelle glugged wine and didn't bother smelling it or swilling it about in her mouth even a little, like *Mummy used to do.*

Jonelle adjusted herself. The seat cushion that felt marshmallow soft was beginning to get uncomfortable.

'What we need around here's some good *choons!*' TK sat forward, wincing as his plastered bandage hit the arm of the chair. 'Can't wait to get rid of this *bloody* thing!'

'Language, TK!' Chelsea motioned towards Jonelle's children with her head.

'Sorry, Jonelle!' TK exhaled forcefully, aiming the remote control at the television. Chelsea'd told them it was not only a TV but also a radio, cassette recorder and Betamax player rolled into one.

Jonelle settled back, kicked off her shoes and folded one leg beneath her before realising that Chelsea had done the same and she was now watching her. 'Told you it was the only way to sit on these chairs.'

'Well, you were right.' Jonelle half smiled, unable to recall hearing such a suggestion.

In the next room, she heard familiar squabbling, which, at least, seemed normal. Like her, they'd never been in a hotel before, let alone washed in a whirlpool bath. She imagined them sitting where she'd left them, like a couple of clouds in the fluffy robes, huddled on a sofa as big as their beds with cartoons flickering on the huge screen in front of them.

'But I want to watch Peppa Pig!'

'Shush, Mum said if we started fighting, we'd have to go to *sleep*! And it's my turn to choose!'

'But I want to watch Peppa Pig!' Kenyana said, a decibel lower.

Jonelle felt suddenly very, very tired.

'You know *all my life*...all I ever wanted to do was the right thing, especially for my parents. Make them proud.' The words that were meant to stay firmly in her head tumbled from her mouth.

*Please, let nobody hear that...*

'I bet they're proud of you,' said Chelsea. 'After you gave them three wonderful grandchildren.'

*Shit!* Too much red wine – Christ! – when'll she ever learn?

Jonelle felt her tongue revving up and did her best to take her foot off the pedal and turn off the ignition. 'The thing is...' Her mouth kept going, with TK and Chelsea waiting to be told what the thing was. 'The thing is...is... I was only fifteen. That's too young. I knew that then just as I know it now. I needed my mum, and where was she, eh? Answer me *that*?'

Beyond the end of her finger, TK sat like she'd asked for Jesus's middle name. To help him answer, she gave him a finger prod to the chest.

'Uhm.' TK rubbed at the jab and angled his injured arm away from her.

'*Presactly*, TK!' They both looked puzzled, so Jonelle explained. '*Precisely* and *exactly*. Presactly!'

Edging away from more prods, TK turned back to tuning the radio with the remote. Jonelle was pleased he bypassed the chatty LBC station and that poppy-poppy Capital.

'Your mother didn't come to the hospi—'

'Nope.' Jonelle shook her head so violently her eyes felt like they wobbled in their sockets. Chelsea sat forward. 'What about their da—'

'Nope, *not* my mum and *not* their bastard father, just we three – me, myself and I!' Jonelle tightened her lips and her grip on the neck of her wine glass. Yet, being her own traitor, she could not shut up. 'So there I was, fifteen. Throwing up in class. People saying I had an eating disorder and calling me fatty. Didn't tell nobody I was pregnant 'cause it was none of their damn business.'

'Nahumsayin'?' said TK.

Chelsea leaned closer. 'Oh no, Jonelle.'

Jonelle edged away. 'More wine please, TK. You know, Chelsea, this is *really* good shit what I chose!' *TK, where's that music? Something good and loud enough to drown out the drunk talk!*

'My waters broke. All down my leg, into my shoes, right there on the street corner when we was just hanging out, my friends and me, having birthday smokes.' She waved her free hand frantically. 'Not me! My girls. They'd got me a cupcake with a candle stuck in it. One minute they was singing and the next— Woosh! Thought I'd shit myself. Shitted? Shat? Wha'ever!... Oh hell! I'm sorry, you two don't need them details, do ya? After that, Myrna runs off and "borrows" her mother's gas money. It was her that got me to King's in a cab... couldn't even come in with me 'cause if *Corrie*'d finished... *Coronation Street*, Chelsea! TK, don't tell me *you* never watched it neither?... Anyway, if the tea wasn't ready before *Corrie*'d ended... Well, *you don't wanna know*! Besides, I promised Myrna I wouldn't tell a soul that her mother hit her.'

Jonelle paused for a sip.

'Oh, Jay,' said TK.

The crimson fluid went down with a soothing sting and Jonelle felt her eyes grow heavier.

'Jonelle, you went through all that...'

Jonelle watched Chelsea unfold her legs, walk over to look out the large window into the night, towards where she'd got her daughters all excited about visiting the special places in Hyde Park in the morning. 'And you didn't give up that baby.'

'Give up my child?' Jonelle made a fist. 'I could've whacked that bitch from the Social. The nurse had just put my baby on my chest and she was there with her: *You're so young, where's your support? Can't bring a child up all on your own, without a home, without family to support you. What about your education? Does the dad even know you're here? Do you even know who the father is? Have you considered adoption or fostering? We can arrange it all for you, for your baby.* That bitch!'

Jonelle paused.

Took a drink.

Took a breath.

Coughing, she continued, with TK looking at her wide-eyed and Chelsea still over by the window, looking out. From behind, it was hard to tell if she was even listening. Jonelle hoped not, seeing she'd blurted out far too much already.

'TK, I don't need no pity, aight. So you can just wipe that look off your face right now, *know-what-ahmsayin*'? Now you got me saying that!' Jonelle sip-giggled and spilled wine down her chin. Wiping it away with the heel of a hand, she waved the glass towards the bedroom door. 'I got me kids. See 'em? Do they look like they're starving? Do their clothes stink or got holes in 'em? And I can tell you they're doin' fine at school too!'

Jonelle flipped to King's College Hospital and the doctor going on about test results. She stopped and stared at the floor.

*Bloody hell, shut up, Jonelle.*

'Jonelle, any fool can tell you're a good mum.' TK's face was a picture. Anyone'd think his painkillers had worn off.

'Aw!' Jonelle drained her glass and waggled it for a refill, so he set down the remote as a catchy beat trickled from the speakers.

'Mmm.' Jonelle grabbed up the remote and turned up the volume on Gladys Knight's nocturnal rail trip to Georgia. TK croaked along to the refrain.

Jonelle heard Deen, playing on her living room floor with his train, going '*choo! choo-oo!*' She jabbed the 'OFF' button and tossed the remote, narrowly missing Chelsea.

'Hey…' TK lifted the Perrier from the ice bucket, 'you two're having water from now on, *nahumsayin*'?'

'More wine.' Jonelle pensively raised her empty glass.

TK shook his head, looking for support, but Chelsea downed the rest of her own wine in one. 'Fill mine up as well, please, TK.'

Jonelle's eyes met Chelsea's with a smile. It was clear that TK was sweet on Chelsea. She'd clocked it from the first but much harder to figure whether TK was a 'good friend', 'brother', or – whatever. Jonelle liked the way this man was with Amanita and Kenyana, helping them feel at home in a strange place.

It had been TK's idea to pass by the Duck & Diva and take a sneak peek inside while they waited with the children, out of sight, around the corner. He'd recognised the man waiting by the bar as being from the 'Grilla. *One of Bull's boys, Jonelle: every one's a nasty piece of work.*

Jonelle thought she heard something, like a struck match, at first. Now fireworks.

Kids.

'Mummy, Mummy!'

'Wha' is it, 'Nita?' Jonelle looked towards the bedroom door. 'Quick, Mummy!'

'Grown ups're talking, honey.'

'But, Mum!'

'You go. Sounds important.' TK pointed the bottle towards the bedroom. 'We can wait, Jonelle.'

'I've got to pee, anyway.' Chelsea rushed towards the door to her adjoining suite.

Jonelle shoved her feet into the soft hotel slippers. TK lifted his knees out of her way and put the radio back on. Jonelle felt as though her dream destination had switched to another track. Was there ever going to be a way to get her life back on course.

Amanita sat on the edge of the bed, pointing at the TV.

'Where's your sister?'

'Dunno.' Amanita shrugged. 'Look, Mummy!'

'What d'you mean: you don't know?'

'She was here a second ago... Mum, look, the TV. It's you.'

'Kennie?' Jonelle shouted, panic pecking at her chest.

'Quick, Mum, before it goes!'

'Amanita, you're supposed to be watching your sister.'

'But, Mum!'

'Kenyana,' Jonelle raised her voice above annoyed and slightly below panic. 'Kenyana!'

Chelsea came up behind her, adjusting her skirt. 'Everything all right?'

'Amanita Patrick, where's your sister at?' Arms akimbo, Jonelle spoke softly, aware of a tingling sensation washing over her scalp.

TK joined them, pulling the door to shut out the music. Two big eyes grinned up at them from between a pair of bony little knees. Kenyana's small hands covered her mouth, useless against the fit of giggles trickling out between her fingers.

'Kenyana!' Jonelle pulled her from behind the door.

'Mum, Mum, you're on TV!' Amanita pointed, frowning in frustration.


On the TV screen, a ramrod of a nurse, eyes accessorised with saggy circles, blinked into the camera. *Very nearly knocked me over to get to the passing intern – insisted she was not taking a ticket because the baby needed immediate attention. People just don't want to wait their turn like everyone else, you see. Claimed she'd found it at the door... You tell me, who'd leave a baby at the door to a hospital?*

Off camera, a man's voice asked whether she would describe this person for the *Crimewatch* audience.

The nurse cleared her throat, rolled her eyes up and to the left: 'I think she was about five foot eleven, six foot, something like that, slim...white, wait no, sort of – uhm – coloured – can I say that on TV?'

'You mean mixed-race?'

The nurse nodded furiously: 'Yeah – half-caste! Took the child—'

The nurse listened to a question about the baby and responded:

'Poor thing was wrapped in rags. No cot or basket. Filthy, it was. Took it straight up to the A&E doctor on duty. Demanded attention. Shoved the baby at him.'

'And what did he do then?'

'He took it, of course. She was very bossy, though! Well-spoken and bossy, she was. Didn't want to wait like everyone else, y'know what I mean…?'

Looking frightened, Amanita spoke over the TV. 'They had a picture of you on there before, Mum. They said that you—'

'Shhh!' Jonelle stopped her daughter. 'Let me hear what they're saying, 'Nita!'

The scene flicked away from the hospital to Brixton police station where a flustered inspector faced the camera and questions.

'As I said before, I do not believe this has anything to do with the spate of child-snatching up and down the country. The Force is committed to bringing those responsible to justice, but first we are concentrating on finding all these children and returning them to their f—'

The camera panned to a pretty redhead in a lime-green jacket. The lens ran down her outfit as she spoke, zoomed in on her question, then flicked back up the steps to the inspector.

'This live?' TK asked.

Chelsea and Jonelle turned in unison. 'Shush!'

*'No, we have no evidence that these children are being taken to order. This is mere speculation on the part of the press. I will not be drawn to comment on an ongoing investigation.'*

The inspector looked fed up with the entire thing and while he spoke, images of workmen sweeping up glass and carting away broken hospital furniture flashed across the TV screen: 'Yes, there was an incident earlier involving another woman. We can't rule out a connection, though we had two officers on the scene at that time… No, the women haven't escaped or gone missing…we'll be interviewing them in good time to assist with our enquiries.'

Two head-and-shoulder images filled the screen.

Jonelle waved frantically at TK. 'Turn it off! Turn it off!'

As he aimed the remote control, Chelsea snatched it from TK's hands. 'No. Wait. Wait!'

A tearful couple had their faces pressed up against the glass partition of the hospital Intensive Care Unit with a reporter poking a microphone under their noses to find out how they felt when they'd received the news.

'We're…we're…' The woman, dressed in Harvey Nichols, was unable to look into the camera.

'We're elated,' the man beside her declared, stiff-lipped. 'We have had months of hell, I can tell you.'

Mingling words with tears, the woman regained enough composure: 'Things like this should never happen to people like us.' A disembodied hand appeared, offering a handkerchief. The woman dabbed her eyes. 'We thought we'd never see our Tristram ever again. Can't wait to have him back home and safe in Dulwich where he belongs.'

The camera brought an emaciated little baby face to the screen.

'It's him, Jonelle.' Chelsea pointed.

'What?' Jonelle said. 'Who?'

Chelsea signalled they best talk in the other room, seeing that the girls were listening, and Jonelle replied with both thumbs up.

'Okay, girls,' TK said. 'I think your mum wants you to get some sleep now. Long day tomorrow.'

'But I don't want to sleep.' Kenyana started crying and demanded she wanted to stay with her mother. Chelsea and TK retreated to the living room.

'Go to sleep, honey.'

'You come to bed too, Mummy.'

'I'll be with you soon, honey. 'Nita is right here beside you and don't you roll into my spot.'

'I won't, Mummy. Can we have a big bed like this at home, Mummy?'

'Hush, Kennie. Close your eyes and go to sleep.'

'Are the police upset with you, Mummy? You can hide behind the door too. I'll show you how.'

'No one is upset with me, Kenyana. It was just silly telly. Go to sleep, everything'll be different in the morning.'

'Mummy?'

'Yes, sweetie?'

'I want Deen.'

'I know, sweetie. It'll…be alright…soon.'

# CHAPTER 31

PC Bailey's Timex confirmed he was checking it about every two minutes, but the phone just sat, like a tight-lipped suspect. What was she playing at? They should have come in thirty minutes ago, according to the previous phone call. Miss Laverne had either lost their number or British Telecom were playing 'upgrading' the exchange, again! She'd refused to give him a number. If she had, he'd be on the blower finding out where the hell they were, instead of just sitting here like a – what time was it now?

Bailey wondered whether his watch needed winding up. From across the open-plan office, flurries of tap-tap-tapping flew from the fingers of the only other person not presently responding to an avalanche of 999 calls. WPC Murphy'd called 'heads', winning the task of updating their records on the testy newfangled computer. Between his watch and the phone, he avoided her glares. Thanks to Patrick, Laverne and Kurtis, there were plenty of notes, not to mention all the witness statements from the hospital. Computers, they'd been told, would power them to a paperless society, saving many trees, so now everyone was scribbling in their notebooks, copying them with the typewriter, to make them legible, so that someone could two-finger-type their information into the computer.

This technology was all clever stuff, he supposed, looking over at his partner-in-fighting-crime. She caught him this time and he smiled. Murphy shot him one of the two looks he'd come to recognise. One meant she was bloody disgusted she'd had to beg her ex to collect their daughter from the childminder, the other was textbook Murphy for 'I told you this would happen, stupid!'

His watch said 10:57 p.m., but the phone was saying nothing.

Chelsea Laverne could still phone or turn up before the window of opportunity was fully closed. They never let on, but there was usually some leeway for people with trouble sticking to the punctuality rules, or if they could show they had been beset by insurmountable problems preventing them from—

'BAILEY!'

'Yes, Guv?'

'You!' The chief inspector's long arm ended with a finger pointing directly at him before hooking back his way. 'My office. Now! And bring your secretary with you.'

'Yes, Guv.'

Murphy's face flushed, going from 'pissed off' to 'fucking pissed off' as she pushed her seat back and shot to her feet.

'Stay calm. Don't take the bait!' Bailey whispered to his partner as they walked abreast down the hall.

At the chief inspector's door, Bailey tugged at his uniform. Murphy ran a hand through her hair to neaten it, he thought, until he looked.

The door was ajar. Bailey knocked anyway.

'Get in here, dammit!'

The guvnor stood by his desk, folded arms resting on his belly. 'I got the press camped outside. And now, Downing Street's taking an interest in what we're doing about these child kidnappings in the borough...and in the rest of the country, like I am responsible for it all!'

He started prowling between his view of Brixton and his desk.

'Christ, kids get nabbed – they grill you over what you're doing about it. One of them gets found – they grill you over what you're doing about it. Tell me you clowns 'ave heard from that Liverne woman?'

Bailey opened his mouth to respond, but the chief punched into his left palm with his meaty right fist. 'I knew she was trouble, I just knew it. People with names like that – hard to pronounce, let alone spell – nothing but walking, talking troublesome fuckers!'

'Guv, Miss Laverne's probably been delayed or...' Bailey began.

'Has...she con...tacted...this...office?'

'No, sir,' Murphy was curt.

'Exactly. You two assured me that Miss Levirne would produce the Patrick woman, along with her friend, Kurtis, by 8 p.m. Then you said they'd be here 22:00...because "they were getting children safe and fed" or some tale like that. It is now...' The inspector pointed up at the wall clock.

Bailey already knew the time, but he looked anyway.

'Eleven-bloody-o'clock, Constable! Even during the riots, I was never here this late.' The inspector hammered on his desk. 'Important people want answers. Big, very important people want to know what-in-blazes is going on at *my* bloody station. Frankly, so do I.'

'Yes, Guv.'

'Take Murphy here and get me some bloody answers. I teamed you up so you could learn a thing or two from a more experienced officer, goddammit. If there's any truth to all the speculation, this department has bloody aided and abetted kidnappers in stealing yet another child.'

'Guv?'

'Have you even got *any* proof that it *was* the Patrick woman's son?'

'But, Guv, the hospital—'

'Only has *her* word that she brought her child there at all.'

The chief tugged at his own jacket. 'Think this uniform came from some fancy-dress shop?'

'No, Guv, but—'

'Tell me something, Bailey?'

'Yes, Guv?'

'Where's that twenty quid you owe me?' the chief inspector went over to stand facing Murphy.

'Guv?' Bailey replied, confused. Murphy looked tense, making eye-to-chin contact. 'Uhm, I don't think I owe you twenty quid, Guv.'

'Really, Bailey?' His boss turned to face him. 'And what if I shout about it, start throwing things about and act like a maniac, screaming to everyone who'd listen that you owed me twenty quid and won't pay up?'

'With respect, Guv. Not the same thing. I believe Patrick did actually take her son to the hospital, but I didn't actually borrow any money from you.'

Murphy spoke up. 'Guv, Bailey was not the arresting officer and the notes said—'

'Yes, Murphy, we all know how it is with you and your partner here.' The inspector continued towards the window.

'Excuse me, sir?' Murphy said, stiffening. A small vein appeared in her forehead.

Bailey felt like someone had flipped open his head and stirred his brain with a whisk. He started sweating under his jacket.

'Don't get your knickers in a twist, Murphy.' The chief inspector returned to his desk. 'Look, Bailey. Just because a person makes a claim at the top of their lungs and throws things about, doesn't make it valid. Got it? The boy could have been sick and they had to get him better before they could sell him on. I'm calling time on Patrick and Kurtis. You two lost them, you two go find them. Apprehend them tonight. Bring them in, understand?'

'But, Guv, our shift's already—'

'Been extended, Bailey. It's *your* mess and I'll be damned if I'm going to clean it up for you. Besides, I'm short-handed and you two would recognise them far better than anyone.'

The inspector sat and reached for the telephone receiver. Taking a sideways glance, Bailey saw that all colour had drained from Murphy's already-pale face.

'Look, I've got all sorts of high-ups breathing down my bloody neck right now. You have to expect me to pass on the benefit,' the inspector said. His index finger selected numbers and started dialling. 'But just so you don't think of me as a total bastard, why don't you two get a drink and a bite to eat before you get down to catching those baddies?'

'But Murphy's little daughter, Guv.' Bailey looked up at the clock.

With the phone pressed up against one ear and both eyes studying something on his desk, the inspector grunted, 'And I've got two sons and a daughter wondering why Daddy's never home to have dinner with 'em...hello?'

He waved them out of his office.

'You alright?' Bailey braced himself for the reply.

'I'm fine,' Murphy said calmly, three times. 'Fuck it, I need a drink.'

He didn't think it was a good idea, given they were in uniform, but Bailey followed anyway. He deduced she'd been leading the way to the Duck & Diva when Murphy turned sharply towards a big red Wimpy sign.

She ordered a Wimpy, with everything. And chips.

He ordered a coke. Everything else seemed an assault on his appetite.

'Anything else, sir?'

'No.' Bailey turned to see Murphy fold her arms and pull her shoulders tight. 'Just a sec... I'll have one of them with the coke.'

'The spicy bean burger?'

'Yes.'

'Chips?'

'No, just that.'

Murphy let him pay.

They sat around a plastic table. Bailey sipped his coke and watched as Murphy tucked in.

'Seriously, don't you find everything in here a bit...*plastic*?'

Murphy shrugged and licked her lips. Bailey glimpsed pearly-white teeth and a pink tongue slip through to wipe thick sauce from small lips. He looked away.

'Okay, how do we go about finding those two?' Bailey sucked icy-cold coke up his straw and wished he hadn't.

'Fuck knows,' Murphy shrugged, still chewing. He watched her open wide and rip the guts out of her burger.

Bailey decided it was best to wait.

'Someone's left a perfectly good brolly!' One of only two attending staff said, looking enquiringly their way. 'Yours?'

Bailey shook his head.

'I saw it first,' the other declared. 'If nobody comes back, I'm having it!'

'You going to eat that?' Murphy motioned, pointing a chip at his bean burger.

'In a bit.' Bailey sipped coke and listened to the brolly banter.

'You sure it was that cute little girl's? Looks too big. Could get four people under that thing.'

'What little girl?'

'Don't you remember...?'

Clearly not, Bailey thought, placing a napkin over his burger as though it were a murder victim. Murphy looked to be halfway through her fast-food frenzy.

'She was with the guy and two women?'

'Two little girls?'

'Yes, that's them!'

'And the dog, we had to ask them to leave the dog outside?'

'No, no, the dog people came in after them.'

'Oh, the kids with the two model types?'

'Now you say it… Well, the little girls were definitely sisters, but the two women looked related too, you think?'

'Anyway, yes, this must be *their* brolly.'

'Chelsea!'

Bailey sat up, tapped the table to catch Murphy's attention and signal with his eyes to get her listening to what he was hearing. She looked up, puzzled, and went back to finishing her chips.

'The short guy with the cast, was he with them, or was he with the dog people?'

'No, he wasn't with the dog people…looked like he was in a fight or some'fing, innit? Couldn't make up his mind, kept talkin' about bad hospital food. Anywho, the one he called Chelsea made him hurry up. I'm sure that was her name 'cause Chelsea's definitely making First Division this season! Go, Blues!'

# CHAPTER 32

'It's like playing tug-o-hearts with that Kenyana,' Jonelle sighed, returning from tucking in her girls and sinking to the floor opposite Chelsea. She used the single seater as a backrest, drew her knees to her chest and made a crown out of her interlaced fingers. 'Oh God! How can things go so *effing* wrong? One minute I'm trying to help out a friend and the next...!'

'It'll be alright, Jonelle.'

'No, it won't, Chelsea!' Jonelle pulled her head down between her knees. 'Now the whole bloody world will see me being a bad mother on TV. Feels like everyone's watching... waiting for me to mess up so...so...they can say *I told you so...* and take my kids away. I do my best for them...with no help from nobody and...!'

TK started pushing a recharged wine glass across the table, towards Jonelle. Chelsea remembered the time when she took solace in drink, thinking it would dull her pain and turmoil and finding the opposite. She gestured for him to stop and take it back, but at the sound of glass on glass, Jonelle looked up.

'Thanks, TK...' She reached out for the glass, and downed it in one, almost missing the table as she set it back down again. 'I'm being pathetic, aren't I? I bet *your* parents were always there for you two.'

'Me? Naw?' TK pushed back into his seat. 'You got that wrong, Jonelle. Always on my case, they was. I was bad. My friends were no good what I used to run wiv. Do this. Don't do that – nahumsayin'? Parents, huh.'

'Jonelle's a parent, TK,' Chelsea reminded him, perhaps too soon, but she felt she had to break in and limit the damage. 'So, not all families are the same, right?'

'Yeah, I bet you could call yours right now, Chelsea, and they'd come running – no matter what kinda trouble you was in.' Jonelle's wet eyes found hers.

'No they wouldn't, Jonelle,' TK said.

Chelsea forced the lump from her throat and raised an I-got-this hand. 'Thanks, TK. What he means is, Jonelle, that my parents are dead.'

The words lacked the usual sting. How strange.

Jonelle hugged her knees, silently staring down at the shag pile.

'You didn't know, Jonelle. But you're right, they'd come running.' Chelsea drew her legs up onto the sofa and hugged her own knees. 'They sent me to the best schools that money could buy, put me through university and helped me set up my business. No, I never wanted for anything. They were always there to love and protect me.'

'I'm so stupid. Sorry, Chelsea.'

'Don't be sorry, Jonelle, you didn't know. You give your kids something no money can buy. Isn't that right, TK?'

TK nodded furiously. 'Word, Chelsea, word! Now, how about we put our heads together. Sort this shit out, yeah? Your son swallows some money and… Where'd you say he got the money? No, that don't matter. You take him to KCH and they lose him, so – obviously – you trash the place and they arrest you. Am I right so far?'

Jonelle reached out to pour herself more wine. Chelsea watched her, anxiously, wanting her to slow down. 'Jonelle, do you mind us going through it with you? See if we can help?'

'No, no, TK's got it right, so far.' Jonelle spoke slowly and carefully, concentrating on lining up the bottle with the glass.

'Cool,' TK went on. 'The important thing is they still don't got your son and then you see his jacket in some sort of waste bin that two guys were taking from the hospital.'

'It was Deen's. I can just feel it in my waters, y'know?' Jonelle used both her hands to bring the overfilled glass to her lips, spilled some and proceeded to lick the wine off her hands. 'Can't get anything right, can I?'

TK looked on, deep in thought.

Chelsea unwrapped her arms from around her knees and sat on the edge of the seat, trying hard not to feel so helpless. Surely every puzzle had an answer on the back page, didn't it?

'Bullshit!' TK shot to his feet as though stung.

'TK,' Chelsea said in a scolding tone.

TK surrendered with one hand, 'No, I mean it's got the smell of Bull all over it.'

'Bull?'

'Run's the 'Grilla, right, Jonelle?'

'You mean Mr Maxwell?'

'Naw, Maxwell don't own 'Grilla.'

'Jonelle, did you ever have any dealings with this Bull character before?' Chelsea was speaking while TK was telling them about the man in the pub.

Jonelle started rocking back and forth, in silence.

'You okay, Jonelle?'

'All I did was cover a job for my friend.'

'We know, we know, Jonelle. TK, could you be wrong about this Bull character?'

'Naw, man, Chelsea, that gangsta'll do anything to be Mr Big, nahumsayin'? And with his main man, Django, he's gonna do it too. Still can't think what he'd want wiv your kid. That bit don't make no sense to me, nahumsayin'?'

'We need to logically debug this mess.' Chelsea went over to the desk in the corner where she located an A4 pad among the complimentary hotel bumf, then fished a pen and a fresh packet of Post-Its from her handbag. 'I'll explain...in my line of work, programming computers, my programmers often get stuck when things get complex or problematic. So, we do what we call *debugging.*'

TK said his whole damn life needed debugging and poured himself more orange juice.

'Anyway,' Chelsea went on, 'we walk through each logical step sequentially and, sometimes in reverse, trying to see what we can discover. Do you mind, Jonelle?'

Both TK and Jonelle looked at her, blankly, so Chelsea explained that they should reverse the timeline, retrace their steps through each *function*, no, each event, over the last day or two.

'Back to when you were last with Deen, Jonelle.'

'No, let's go back to when I saw Myrna at my door sayin' she was sick.'

She didn't see the point, but Chelsea agreed just so they could get started and hauled furniture to clear space. 'No, Jonelle, I've got it... Sit down, TK...you're still injured, remember?'

Chelsea made a big canvas from sheets of A4 carefully laid edge to edge. She scribbled locations, names and drew main event circles, and each person became a Post-it with concentric relationship circles, like data attributes, she told them. Lines with arrows, Chelsea concluded, will link people with the places to chart how they flow.

TK looked up at the ceiling, scratching his head with his free hand, so Chelsea pointed out that the inner circle was for close relationships, like family, and the outer circle would show any significant associations.

'Can we call them something else coz it's all making my head spin, nahumsayin'?'

'Fine, we'll call them rings inside circles – that better?'

TK said he was happy. Jonelle clapped. Chelsea took an awkward bow.

'Now then, Jonelle, I'll just add the kids to your inner circ— Your inner ring, okay?'

'Sure.'

'And your mum and dad?'

'If you must.'

'And the kids' dad. What did you say his name was again?'

'Who? Tyrone? No way. That toerag ain't comin' anywhere near my inner ring ever again.'

Chelsea decided to make an exception and give Jonelle a 'middling' ring, for people who did not fit into her inner ring and were not quite 'outer ring', like Tyrone.

The rewind took them back, across the River Thames to the Duck & Diva pub in Brixton where Chelsea and Jonelle's circles briefly separated from TK's.

'Yeah, that's when I did my I-spy bit.'

Bull's man in the pub, Chelsea and Jonelle thought, should be called Bull #2.

'No, call him Leathers,' TK offered. 'The pub was steaming hot, but that geezer kept his jacket on, stunk of liver and onions, ignored the small group drinking and crying for that Myrna woman you was tellin' us about, Jonelle.'

Chelsea crossed out Bull #2, and wrote Leathers as his name. Chelsea then wrote Bull in his inner circle and drew a line connecting him to Duck & Diva and 'Grilla.

'So Myrna goes in his outer circle?' Chelsea hovered with her pen.

'I 'spose.' TK nodded towards Jonelle, who shrugged. 'Jonelle said the drunk guy told her Leathers was waiting for her.'

Chelsea wrote Jonelle's name next to Myrna's.

'Jesus!' they said in unison. Standing together on the safe portion of carpet, they peered down at the emerging map. 'So, if Leather is in Bull's inner ring and therefore, 'Grilla, why's Leather looking for Jonelle?'

'How should I know, Chelsea?'

'Know what I think?' TK rubbed his chin, clearly about to announce a revelation. 'This looks dodgy...real dodgy, nahumsayin'?'

'Let's keep going...' Chelsea sighed and tiptoed carefully around her makeshift chart, reminding everyone that their aim was to locate Deen and help Jonelle.

They argued whether to include taxi man, Miss Mattie, Keefah's husband, and the drunk who'd told Jonelle about Myrna.

'Fine, I've added them,' Chelsea told them, drawing rapid circles on Post-Its and scribbling the names inside them. Chelsea felt like a four-legged spider reaching in to build her web of circles on the floor. 'Okay, now we're all at the hospital event...'

*WPC Murphy*

*PC Bailey*

They all had the police in their circles. 'That's interesting.'

'...and painful, Chelsea.' TK raised his plastered arm, carefully.

*Girl with baby*

Chelsea and Jonelle both had her in their intersecting outer rings and linked back to the 'Grilla.

'We're at the hospital now, but maybe we should debug some more?'

'You sure it was the same girl we saw in the toilets, Chelsea?' Jonelle asked.

'Toilets?' TK held his head.

'At 'Grilla.' Jonelle told them both that she'd first seen the frightened girl while searching for a mop. 'There was a big room, behind a closet. A warehouse, I think. She looked so frightened and ran out, carrying something.'

'A baby,' Chelsea confirmed.

'I guess so. That's when Bull and his apes came in.'

'But you said you didn't have anything to do with Bull, Jonelle.'

'I didn't,' Jonelle bristled, 'I don't.'

TK sat forward, rubbing his chin, 'If you was working at 'Grilla, Jonelle, you had something to do with Bull.'

'No, I was working for Mr Maxwell.'

TK looked at Chelsea and turned back to Jonelle. 'Hmm, must'a seen you in his warehouse or wherever…was there any guards or alarms?'

'I was only looking for a mop like Maxwell'd told me,' Jonelle explained.

Chelsea lifted a hand. 'Stop. We haven't got to that bit yet, you two. We need to stay in logical sequence.'

'Life ain't logical, Chelsea.' Jonelle added a full stop in the air with her index finger.

'Please, Jonelle, bear with me a little…' Chelsea waited.

Jonelle reached for her glass of wine, changed her mind, and folded her arms. 'So, now we're where you and a Vietnamese girl were under TK and he's sleeping, right?'

'Two women overlapped with me,' TK sank deep into the single sofa, 'and I slept through the whole damn thing – dreaming about bloody Bull's men hobbling around the place. It's proper depressin' – and my arm's throbbing now. Time for a couple of them painkillers, maybe four.'

Chelsea shook her head, shared a look with Jonelle that either meant 'typical!' or 'men!' or both, and they continued working the sequence, adding 'the security guard watching monitors'. Jonelle insisted the 'doctor running tests on Deen' might be relevant because he'd actually seen Deen.

Chelsea wondered whether he was the very last person to see the child, but said nothing as she added 'Deen's doctor' to the hospital circle and drew a line to Jonelle.

Without anything definitive, Chelsea recommended they extrapolate still further, as something obvious may just reveal itself, as often happened in these exercises. Jonelle agreed, fanning herself even though the aircon was on.

The network of coincidences brought them back to the moment they stood, face to face, in the 'Grilla toilets.

'Why'd you look at me like that, Jonelle?'

'I was exhausted and – to be honest – it was not my sort of place and – don't hate me – you looked tarty.'

'Thanks.' Chelsea tapped the pen on her right cheek, thinking. 'Well, you seemed out of place too, I've got to say.'

'Men kept looking at me like they hadn't eaten for weeks while the women—'

'Me too. Like wearing your true size was weird, right?'

'Exactly!' they said in unison as Chelsea caught another image in her flashback.

'So, it was you carrying that bucket of—'

'Puke!' Jonelle finished her sentence.

'Oh my God!' they said in chorus, with Jonelle slurring.

'Told you: I was covering Myrna, see? Was her job. I was s'pose to be taking hats-'n'-coats and she drew a map and – never mind – let's keep doin' the buggy-thingie.'

'Debugging.'

'Yes, that.'

Jonelle made her add a taxi man that she called 'Croydon' and they were back to when sick Myrna asked her to do her a favour.

With Jonelle swaying gentle by her side, they looked down at the carpet-map-of-occurrences revealing they'd met each other at 'Grilla, narrowly missed an encounter in Brixton market when she was with Deen and was now with her, trying to find him.

'On the CCTV I saw you crashed into the hospital trolley, Jonelle. One of the men looked seriously pissed when you ran off.'

'I saw it too on the video. But what I want to know is, how'd they got hold of my son's jacket?'

'Hmm, picked it up by accident?' Chelsea tapped the pen on her teeth, thinking it was curious that a girl with a baby was discovered at 'Grilla and a young child had gone missing at the hospital. She thought about the young Vietnamese woman and what she'd said about why she'd escaped to the hospital. She decided it was both unwise and unsafe to tell Jonelle, just yet.

'And what bloody connection did poor Myrna have with Leathers, anyway?'

Chelsea shrugged. 'Paying respects to an employee, maybe?'

'So, why'd he be asking about me?' Jonelle rubbed goose-bumps off her arms. 'What if I'd gone in, to pay my respects… with my kids at my side?… And, Chelsea, look at who all our lines lead back to.'

Chelsea made a thick line under Bull.

# CHAPTER 33

Jonelle nestled into the downy welcome of her grandma's bed. Wrapped like a gift, she felt secure under the weight of material, nuzzled into the marshmallow pillow with its faint smell of bleach.

'Always boil, bleach and iron your sheets, pillowcases and knickers,' Nanna would tell her.

Nanna's? Surely, she couldn't be there. Nervous about opening her eyes, Jonelle squeezed them tight shut. A relentless drumming grew louder, accompanying a throbbing in her head. Another weight, heavier than a pillow but soft as an arm, lay across her forehead. Tyrone?

Without opening her eyes, Jonelle wiggled a toe, then a foot, then a finger. It was as if there'd been a great party in her body and when the music had stopped and everyone had left there was an unholy mess to clean up. Had she been gargling sand? Unsure she was even alive, Jonelle held her breath and listened. She heard none of the usual cussing nor bottles breaking. There was no noise of dustbins being kicked to spill rubbish into the road, no sirens, no thumping rhythms forcing her to miss party nights. Only throbbing in her head. She was no longer a little girl at her nanna's and this was not her own bed in her own home.

So, where was she and whose arm was this across her forehead?

Cool air fanned across her face and her lungs ached.

'Aaah!' Jonelle resumed breathing and stared into the unfamiliar darkness, while a dizzying wheel of images spun through her mind: Deen's face... Deen wearing his favourite jacket... King's hospital... Brixton police station... PC Bailey, Myrna... Tyrone, Tyrone again...circles and rings with Bull in them all. The thick duvet covering her started to feel like a steel net.

'Oh God!' As the fog cleared, the return of feeling meant the dead weight was not Tyrone's, but her own arm. She wiggled her fingers, regaining control, trying to turn, but her stomach lurched forcing bile up into her throat.

She'd been drinking, she remembered now. Wine, it didn't seem a lot at the time. Still, why'd they make her drink so much, so fast, when she barely drank at all?

Sliding back down, she tugged the warm covers up under her chin and curled into a ball and hugged her head. She'd kicked out Tyrone, because of his dodgy wheeler-dealings bringing the Social to her door. Now she'd brought police bail into their lives, spilled her guts to people she barely knew and let them get her drunk...while Deen was still missing...and Myrna – hard to believe full-o-life Myrna could be dead – and some leathery stranger was in a pub with their names in his mouth, Myrna's and hers...and – Jesus Christ – Deen was still missing!

In that very instant, more of a candle of an idea than a light bulb flickered in her mind. Feeling so worked up, she might easily have missed it, but there it was: why not just disappear? Vanish off someplace, with the kids, of course. If no one could find her, especially some strange man in the Duck & Diva, they'd leave her alone, surely.

So now, all she needed was a damn good plan, but first, the loo.

'Ow.' Jonelle tried to sit up, but her head didn't like it. She decided to roll and felt for the edge, too late.

The floor came quickly.

Crushed boobs triggered a coughing fit she hoped would dislodge the gritty bitterness from her throat. She lay naked on the carpet, trying to recollect where she'd put her clothes, or even taking them off.

Her eyes adjusted to the shapes of lamps and a coffee table at the edges of the lounge. She felt around and found a damp patch before her and, the sofa behind, clearly not a bed at all, her fingers found no clothing among the sheets and duvet.

Bits of the conversation lingered in her mind, like faded lipstick:

*No, Jonelle, the girls're still here…asleep…safe and sound.*

*Yes, yes, I promise to call Bailey first thing in the morning… stop worrying.*

*No, you stay there, Jonelle. Don't move. I'll clean it up. TK'll get you a towel.*

Balancing her aching head on her neck, Jonelle stumbled in the direction of the bathroom, feeling ahead for anything she couldn't see.

Her feet padded onto warm tiles and she reached for the light switch. Her clothes hung like ghostly shapes from the shower curtain rail and the towel warmer. They smelled a little sour but were nearly dry. She emptied her bladder, splashed cold water on her face and dried herself with one of the little towels, the sort that Prunes would try and sell as exclusive.

A discoloured ball of paper with yellow slips overflowed from the bathroom bin. Jonelle recalled puking straight into a circle around the name Bull. Horror and embarrassment flushed through her. Jonelle's throat resisted the memory but her pounding head wouldn't let her off.

Bracing herself, she hurriedly stepped into damp undies, clipped her cold bra to her warm chest and pulled on her trousers and jumper. Body heat would dry everything soon. On a wedge of light, she left the bathroom towards the bedroom door to check on her girls.

Unlike those at home, the suite doors never creaked and neither of the two lumps in the king-sized double bed stirred.

A flickering television, with the sound turned right down, watched them sleep. It was probably serving as a night light for Kenyana, who was afraid of the dark.

Kenyana was sucking her thumb and her hair was braided. Jonelle had no memory of doing that and 'Nita couldn't. 'Nita was hugging a pillow as though trying to smother herself. It was her favourite sleeping position.

Jonelle felt her lips quiver at the sight of them both. She wanted to cuddle them, closely, tightly, but she stayed at the threshold. Amanita was a light sleeper at the best of times.

Back in the lounge, Jonelle's kernel of a plan was harvest ready: get home, get the kids' birth certificates, get Deen, get lost so that nobody, but nobody, and most of all Bull, could find them. She'd finally take her three children away from this South London dive to somewhere they could grow up happy and enjoy a life she'd never had – and be safe.

Simple.

Her business class tutor'd talked about a simple theory – 'Offams Razor' or something like that – Candice would remember the name. They'd been the only ones to argue, objecting that men always thought problems were solved with sharp implements. Anyway, 'something-razor' seemed to fit because 'the simplest idea was usually the right one' and her idea was simplicity central, for sure, plus multi-talented Candice, who'd do anything for her kids, had all the smarts to help her make it happen.

She shoved her feet into her shoes, grabbed a small packet of cashew nuts from the tiny fridge in the desk, slipped out quietly closing the suite door behind her and walked briskly along the corridor, through a fire door, down a set of stairs and out of an emergency exit into the West End night air.

\* \* \*

WPC Murphy and PC Bailey managed to sneak past the siege of reporters undetected to get back into the station by the side door.

'Don't journalists ever sleep?' PC Bailey whispered. 'Christ, it's after midnight.'

Murphy didn't respond, so Bailey tapped her on the elbow. 'Look, I know this is only a small lead, but it's sure to get us back in His Nibs' good books.'

'Yes, you go tell him those bail absconders were practically under our noses in the Wimpy round the corner while we sat on our arses, waiting for them to turn up. If you're bloody lucky, Brendon, he'll charge you with wasting police time.'

PC Bailey looked out the corner of his eye at his colleague as they mounted the stairs to the offices. Murphy was clearly pissed off, seeing as she had a strict last-name-only policy while they were in uniform.

'But it's relevant, Nyree,' he said, bracing for a further reprimand, which didn't arrive. 'Seems clear to me that, as they were seen at about 8:30 p.m. by the Wimpy staff, they must have been on their way and were delayed with sorting childcare.'

'But it's now nearly 1 a.m.,' she retorted with a shrug. 'Look, it's your funeral. Trouble is, we're partners. You go down and I get buried with you.'

'We're doing our job, Murphy,' he said, pushing on the emergency door. As they entered the main corridor, the incident room door flew open and it seemed half the department flowed out in a gush of blue.

'What'd we miss?' Bailey asked Collins and Carmichael, who were coming towards them.

Collins adjusted his large helmet on his legendary over-large head. 'Where've you two been? Out back...inspecting the vehicles together again?'

Carmichael found that hilarious. 'Think yourselves lucky the guv'nor didn't miss you.'

'He's the one who sent us to— Oh, never mind!' Murphy snapped and blocked Collins. 'Are you going to tell us what's going on or not?'

'Not,' Collins said, tucking his helmet under his arm. 'No time. Guv wants us out the station before the paps figure out what's happening. He's still in the incident room, go ask him.'

They found the chief inspector studying a map of the south-east, with a familiar scatter of flags and irregular markings representing people and places of interest to the police.

'Guv, got a minute?'

'Tell me you have Patrick and Kurtis in holding!'

'Uhm, well, no, Guv, but—'

'Better be a bloody big *but*, Bailey.' The inspector folded his arms across the barrel of his chest and settled on both heels, all ears.

'Sir, we've a lead you should know about…' Bailey recounted for him the conversation he'd overheard in the burger bar between the two workers and why he was convinced that they were referring to Patrick, Kurtis and Laverne.

The inspector gave him a blank look, like the lads did when he told a joke, only his superior added an Arctic feel to it.

'Don't you see, Guv?' Bailey said. 'Proves they were telling the truth…she had her two daughters with her, like she told us about. Her son must be missing. Yes?'

Bailey looked over to see his partner's shoulders drop as she breathed in deeply, stretched her lips tightly together.

The inspector started slow clapping.

'Bravo, Sherlock,' said the inspector. 'Now, while you two were busy stuffing your faces…'

'Excuse me, Guv,' Murphy broke in, looking straight ahead at no one, 'you told us to get something to eat.'

'Well, while you two were stuffing yourselves, listening to dubious chitter-chatter, we got a solid lead in Camberwell. A father reported that his child was almost snatched from their baby's pram in a restaurant, but for his quick thinking. And that's what? A mile from King's College. Plus, hotel staff in Paddington think they've seen the suspects. Policing, Bailey, is about following leads, gathering evidence and providing proof. I expect you're still new to how things're done around here. Murphy, you should know better. Really. I'm taking you two off the case.'

'But, sir!'

The inspector fixed Bailey with a look that advised caution and shut him up.

'Effective immediately, you're both off the Patrick and Kurtis case. I've drafted in help from the neighbouring boroughs – with more officers assisting we can get this thing wrapped up before the shit gets any deeper. I need the bloody politicians off my back. Then there's the press – everybody forgets how much crime we've taken off the streets! No, this missing child thing has to stop and stop tonight.'

Murphy expelled a long, slow breath.

'Look, I'd send you both home, but it'd look bad to the others. Dispatch told me about a domestic disturbance a few hours ago, a 999 caller concerned about strange comings and goings at a gated property in Whyteleafe. Burglary, no doubt, but they'd be long gone by now. You shouldn't need backup. Everyone's out. Just make a list of what's missing. Probably an insurance scam.'

'Yes, Guv.'

'That decommissioned vehicle still running?' The chief stifled a laugh.

'Yes, Guv,' Bailey said.

'Good job – the rest are out on assignment. When you get to the address, you can use that to explain the delay. Chin up. You two did a reasonable job on the door-to-door recently – I do read reports, y'know – so, run along and talk to Dispatch for that Whyteleafe address.'

'Sir…?' Bailey began.

'Yes, PC Bailey?'

'Nothing, sir. No, nothing at all.'

'Good. Get going.'

# CHAPTER 34

Bull had always been taunted by whether midnight was 12 a.m. or 12 p.m., but he'd never let on. It bothered him even more watching the wipers squeak-squawk over the dry windscreen, reminding him of dry-humping. It was getting on his tits.

'Kill 'em wipers will yuh, Clint!'

The wipers died.

Now that the rain had pissed off, the two jokers upfront were making out the road signs better using Prunes' directions via Peckham to the East End. It was yet another area that someone he'd once called his right-hand man had advised him not to take his 'Grilla business, talking of *respect* for the local crews, but Bull thought he'd just been chicken-shit scared.

Bull found the stink of that rat, Silk, was still clinging to him, even with Peckham long behind him. Why would Silk prefer kilos of iron bouncing on his chest, over telling him what No-Name and he were up to? Maybe it was high time for him to take the Peckham boss's head in one hand and No-Name's in the other and scrape their teeth together until one of the fuckers fessed up about their secret meetings and fuckin' secret handshakes. That is, if only he knew where to find Mister-fuckin'-No-Name.

Bull kissed his teeth at that thought.

'You say somet'ing, boss?' Jinxie looked round from reading out instructions and Clint looked round too.

'Watch da fuckin' road an' hurry-the-hell up!'

Bull flipped his gaze to the rising skyline over the City of London, thinking the job was a piece of piss, really: get forty babies, attach a trafficked pair of tits to each, deliver them for shipment, get paid a shed load o' dosh.

So, a couple of the girls'd run off, so what – some fucker had said everything happened for a reason and when one door shut, another opened. More shit on shit from Barnardo's. Hell, No-Name shut any door on him he'd just kick the fuckin' thing down and shove it right up his arse 'cause everything could be fixed one way or other, and this work was still easier than warring over turf to make big bucks on drugs and pussies.

If he'd not stopped to feed the *dawgs*... If he'd not paused to give that sweet baby Trudy life advice: 'Don't you ever trust nobody wiv your shit!'... If he'd not taken the time to teach them curry-lovin' youths some manners, would he have caught them standing there like pimp and hooker? Bull glared heavenward thinking that someone-up-there must be looking after him.

The car jerked.

Clint's driving was so shit, Bull wondered again where-the-hell Triple was as he punched down into the empty seat beside him. 'Yeah, where?'

'Whazzat, Chief?'

'Clint, just fuckin' drive!'

The signs were showing The City.

He was hours away from a fortune that he'd invest to make an even bigger one...it was all about deals within deals...and nobody'd better get in his way.

Bull nodded, agreeing with himself. The graffiti had died out the closer they'd got to the City and the air had tasted of money.

'How far are we now, Jinxie?'

Jinxie scratched his head. 'Boss, uhm, about an hour I tink or maybe twenty-five minutes or so?'

'I'm hearing ten minutes.'

The vehicle accelerated. Bull was pressed back into his seat.

'Right!' Jinxie suddenly said, wagging a finger under Clint's nose. 'Turn right there.'

'Where?' Clint looked left and right but kept going.

'Turn, turn!'

'Turn where?'

'Right, I said, turn right.' Taking hold of Clint's chin, Jinxie turned Clint's head to the right. 'Right. There! And now you missed the turn, bro.'

Clint jammed on the brake and the van behind screeched up behind them.

'Oh, right. You should'a said! And, Jinxie, touch mi chin again, you and me'll have words, seen?'

Jinxie jumped out to explain to the van behind.

They all waited for a giant bug of a road sweeper to scuttle towards them on its little rotating brushes and pass by. The van reversed, Clint reversed and turned right off the main trunk road, leading them to roll up to their destination.

'Make sure it's the right place.' Bull ignored Clint's apologies. 'I ain't getting out to discover you idiots can't read.'

Bull watched them bang on a door and wait. He did up all the buttons on his jacket ready to get out. His men waited three minutes before banging on the next door where someone eventually opened it. There was much arm-waving and lip-flapping, during which he saw Clint feeling for his Magnum. A hand pointed. Every eye followed it over the road to a tired place with peeling paintwork and an aging board that read: Hindermann's Food and Liquor Import Export Emporium and Haberdashery.

Jinxie gave the van the thumbs up.

Checking his pockets again was a ritual he always did before a job. This wasn't a job, but you never knew. Wondering why that fool Prunes'd not simply named the place on the address, he joined his men now congregating on the pavement where the air smelt of spoilt fruit, old vegetables and bargains.

'Clint, stay here. Watch my wheels. They get pinched, you get pinched. Feel me?'

'Yeah, boss.'

Jinxie bashed the haberdashery door. As Prunes'd said, they waited exactly two minutes then kicked it, and after another two minutes, exactly, they rang the little bell at the side.

It opened a crack and a dead-eyed face peered out at them.

'Prunes sent us.'

The door swung wide. 'Come *in*, come in!'

Jinxie went in first, much to Bull's annoyance. He recalled Django drilling them to never throw the boss into danger, like he couldn't take care of his own damn self.

They played follow-my-leader through a maze of racks overflowing with material, while the leader explained why they had to walk in darkness.

'Police patrols, nosey parkers, chancers, we get all sorts around here and you never know who's looking, do ya? There's more light in the back...walk in the middle more and watch your feet...them wheels on the fabric racks can trip you up. You been warned... Now, watch your heads!' their guide stifled a yawn.

They did, except for whoever was at the back.

Thud!

'Ras'!'

Finally, they arrived in a dimly lit area with shadowy figures surrounding them on every side.

'Izza trap, boss.' Jinxie had his piece out first. Bull reached for his as the others pulled weapons.

'No, this is where we keep the suit fabrics: pinstripe, tweed, houndstooth, wool, gaberdine and even silk, we got the lot and some. I'll show you...'

'In the dark?' Bull could think of only one reason to not bash his face in.

'Feel this...finest tweed...even Savile Row buys from us. You name it and we'll supply yards and yards—'

'Made your point... Now, fuckin' get on with it. I ain't got time to waste.'

With his eyes now adjusted to the dark, Bull watched him stretch up to a high shelf, bring down a small box and reach into it. Bull readied himself. He wasn't born yesterday, and this guy was about to find out the hard way.

'Whoever's coming in with me? Put these on.'

Bull barged in front of Jinxie. 'What's that?'

'*These* go over your shoes and *those* for your hands and *that* for your hair. We don't stay ahead of the cops by being sloppy, mate. If you're comin' in, you keep your shoe dirt, fingerprints, and hair follicles to yourself, *capish*?'

'This kinky shit better be worth it,' Bull said, after ruining three latex gloves and two disposable caps.

The man shrugged, grabbed an iron bar behind him and threw all his weight against it. The whole wall slid apart, half into the ground and half towards the ceiling.

'Get inside – and quick. Just you. Rest o' you stay out here.'

'What about us, boss?' Jinxie said, poking his piece back into his trouser waist.

'You heard the man. Wait here.' Bull stepped forward, into the gap.

'This is where the magic happens,' the man said, grabbing an inside lever with both hands. With a grunt, he leaned on the lever.

The door slammed shut and Bull looked around at a pristine, floodlit room with four desks facing each other in the middle, surrounded by walls of filing cabinets and shelves holding labelled boxes. He saw no windows, no way in or out, apart from the way they'd come. The air had a sweet smell to it, not like incense but something Bull couldn't quite place.

An old woman sat hunched over one of the desks, knitting maybe, it was hard to tell as her back was partly turned to them and the sudden daylight brightness was dazzling. Dressed in black and wearing a black armband, she didn't look up from whatever she was doing. He figured she should be rocking in a chair somewhere, telling her grandkids bedtime stories or some shit. If he cared more, he might pity her.

'Sorry, I should've warned you. The scribes need to pick up every detail when they're working. I have some dark glasses you can borrow…'

'I'm cool,' said Bull, soft and low, determined not to squint.

'Suit y'self. You'll have to speak up for her,' the man pointed with a lift of his chin. 'She's got eyes like a hawk but is deaf as a bat.'

They walked up to stand before the desk.

'Ma'am! Visitors!'

She looked up first at the man before her, then at Bull and back again, chewing on something, reminding him of a little market trader he knew.

'Why you bring him in here?' Her teeth were as black as her armband.

'Prunes sent me.' Bull stepped closer. 'He said you could do a rush job. Must be done tonight! Now!'

'Louder,' the man said. 'Place is soundproof so nobody outside'll hear – but you're having a laugh, aintchya?'

Bull ignored his question and bellowed at the woman who rocked back in her chair and grabbed her chest.

'Ah, Prunes.' Her expression softened, but then turned to stone. 'No! Nothing tonight!'

'Look, I'll pay you double if that's what it takes.'

'No!' She banged a bony fist hard on the desk. 'Nothing tonight.'

'You don't understand.' Bull stepped towards her. 'I can't wait.'

The man inserted himself between them, blocking Bull. 'Hold on right there, mate.'

'Outta my way.' Bull swept him aside and watched him tumble across the floor and crash into a pile of boxes, spilling stacks of passports out onto the floor. Bull lowered his face until he was nose-to-nose with the old woman and could smell chewed tobacco. 'I can pay you. Whatever it takes, name your price but I need them documents tonight.'

Bull retrieved the envelope No-Name had given him from his briefcase.

Frowning, she accepted the envelope from his latex grasp. It was like watching paint dry seeing the old crone first sniff then examine the envelope.

A gnarly hand fished out a sharp knife with a feather on one end. God, who used letter openers, these days?

*Open the damn thing, you old crow!*

Her man picked himself off the floor and carefully refilled the boxes before restacking them. He returned, grim-faced and muttering something about Bull not getting away with treating him like that.

'Shut it. What's she wearing that armband for?' Bull didn't give a toss, but had to find a way to stop himself from busting up the place on account of the snail and her minion.

'If you must know, she had family on the *Marchioness*.'

She finally managed to insert the knife into the envelope. Unable to watch any more, Bull took the envelope and knife from her hands and – *zzzt!*

She glared up at him, snarling and trying not to choke on her tobacco.

Bull fetched a pack of five from his pocket and extracted a Cuban.

Her eyes lit up.

'You're not going to light that in here, are you?' the man said, standing back from him.

'No, I'm not lighting it.' Bull handed the woman the cigar. 'You shout at her that there's plenty more coming her way, if she can rush this job off for me.'

'You can tell her yourself,' the man sulked, turning away.

As though she'd heard him anyway, the woman extracted the paperwork with great care.

'I have done these already. All forty...' The woman set down the list. 'Except one – this one here is new. The rest are done. I may be old, but I'm not uhm...'

'Senile,' her boy added, giving Bull a dirty look.

'I need fresh ones, get me? You're being paid and there's a special bonus in it for you, right,' Bull said, clear and very loud. 'So stop fucking around and get started.'

She sat back, wiping spit off her face and pursing her lips. Her man swiped the papers and scanned down the list.

'This a fackin' joke? The team did this already...twice. Django collected the first batch. Silk picked up a second lot *hisself* last night.'

'Silk was 'ere?' Bull yelled.

'She's deaf, not me...and, yes, Silk was here. You work with him?'

'No, I don't work with— Look, it don't matter, fuckin' do 'em again!'

'Don't matter?!' She leant to one side as though preparing to let one loose in the windowless room. 'Original means one and only one. Two copies of these are out there now. In triplicate – people will ask questions. I'm too old for jail, mister.'

'I need 'em done one more time. Trust me, there won't be no jail for you and I'm the only one gonna be askin' questions.' It was hard to shout and sound reassuring, but Bull'd given it a shot and, for her sake as well as his, he hoped it would get her started on the documents.

She eyeballed him.

Bull was unblinking. For all he knew, Django gave the first lot of documents to the cops. Did Mr No-Name know and was that why Silk was in the picture? If this was a double-cross or fuckin' *triple*-cross, someone would be paying for it in the red stuff.

She blinked.

'You'll be lucky if I even got enough blanks. Can't make documents without blanks.' She pointed across the room. 'Check the boxes over there, Victor. And you check them ones over here, mister!'

Bull shrugged, following her instructions on what to look for. If it sped things up, why not? Besides, he'd see for himself if he checked too. Christ, what's the world coming to when you can't trust a damn thing anybody says, even under pressure?

Between them, well, it was more Victor than him, they piled the blank birth certificates and passports on her desk for twelve West German, eight French, nine Danish, two Greek and three Swiss.

'Keep fackin' looking,' she barked, setting off a coughing fit as she dished out more instructions. 'And you better *pray* I can make an official Medical Organs Release document for that new one without time to practise.'

Victor pointed to the door. 'Wait outside. I'll call you when we're done in here.'

'How long is that?'

Victor turned and shouted. 'How long, Nan?'

She threw both hands in the air, looked up to heaven. 'Nine hours!'

'What?' Bull looked at his watch.

'You heard her?' Victor smiled.

Bull went over to the desk, reached over, and slipped the cigar out of her cleavage, making her gasp. He parted the folds of his five pack from his jacket and slowly slid the cigar in until it disappeared.

'Three hours, by 3 a.m.,' she wheezed. 'No sooner and no later…and bring them cigars…and double what you paid last time.'

Bull shook the entire pack of cigars under his nose, breathing in deeply.

'Okay, same bloody fee. Three hours.'

'Three hours!' Bull walked, patting his breast pocket where the cigars now were.

Victor leant on the lever. When nothing happened, he added another shoeprint to the others on the wall and put his back, gut and whatever else he could muster into it.

'It. Jams. Sometimes,' he grunted.

'Let me?'

'No. I. Got. It.'

'Victor, right?'

Panting too hard to speak, the man nodded at his name. Bull patted him on the head. 'See you at two, aight?'

'But that…is…only…two…'

Bull neither heard nor cared what he was spluttering. He hammered the lever with a fist and the doors yawned open.

'Get movin', you lot. Laters, Victor.'

# CHAPTER 35

Chelsea lay tangled in Egyptian cotton. Her thoughts twisted and turned with the events they'd mapped out, happenings that had placed Jonelle, TK and her, first in 'Grilla, then Brixton, then King's College Hospital and, finally, drinking wine in her hotel suite while being accused by police on TV of being involved in missing children. More importantly, they had been mapping it all to find something, anything, even the slightest hint of a clue, that might lead to Deen:

*They'd all been at 'Grilla on Friday night.*

*It was owned by Bull.*

*And they'd all been seeking Prunes, who wouldn't normally miss a Saturday market.*

*TK had recognised two of Bull's men in hazard suits on his ward on Sunday.*

*Jonelle'd seen a jacket just like the one she'd bought Deen from Prunes.*

*Then there was that Vietnamese girl.*

Would she be able to get the police to listen? What if it was all just a mess of coincidences? She'd been picking at it like a scab, considering the connections, looking for meaning. Their circles had become linked by a logic that both fascinated and terrified her. Who knew what lay in store for them next?

Reaching for her watch, Chelsea toppled the bedside table and sent it crashing to the floor. She froze, listening for sounds beyond the occasional hush of traffic going through Paddington. There was nothing from the lounge where TK had crashed on the sofa after they'd returned from Jonelle's suite. Poor Jonelle had remained in denial as they'd cleaned her up before they'd tucked her in.

After all she'd been through… Well, they would ply her with coffee before facing the Brixton police in the morning. Chelsea scrambled in the dark for the fallen lamp and checked the time.

1:30 a.m.!

Normal people would be asleep, well, except those in clubs and casinos. Dad used to say they were busy all night, offering people a chance of happiness. The Luck Industry, he used to call it. 'Chelsea, forget about luck! All you need to get ahead is right up in here,' he'd say, gently tapping the side of her head with his finger. She touched the spot on her head just thinking about it. She reached for a tissue, but found the box empty so she wiped her face on the Egyptian linen sheet.

Jonelle had said she was fifteen when she was suddenly, terrifyingly pregnant.

Chelsea wondered how old her natural mother had been? The question was one of a chain of enquiries that had dogged her all night. Perhaps her own mother had had a good reason to give her twin babies up? Perhaps she was forced, and the decision taken out of her hands entirely, or maybe there was a tragic illness involved and she couldn't be saved.

Chelsea flung all the pillows off the bed. Listening to Jonelle last night had filled her with guilt. She'd been so happy with her real parents and yet felt pulled to search into a past where she was abandoned.

Jonelle was so brave. She'd done it all alone and was still doing it without anyone by her side. At just fifteen.

Chelsea got up. Plucking the pillows off the floor, she threw them back onto the bed. All this time, she'd been preoccupied with finding her twin brother...thinking that her sibling, if she ever found him, would have the answers to all her questions, but why care about a brother who might not know she existed, and, even if he did, might not want to be found? Better to be grateful for having had parents who had loved her till death and a friend who cared about her enough to do anything to help... And now, well, he needed her help!

She pulled a robe on over her underwear and opened the door into the lounge.

The sound of gentle sawing lead her over to where TK lay sleeping. She stood over him for a moment. Chelsea padded back to the bedroom, stopped and returned to the sofa.

'TK?'

'Hmmm?' He flopped a bony leg from under the sheets to the carpet.

'TK, are you sleeping?'

'Umm-hmm?' The leg returned and he rolled to bury his face into the backrest and mumbled, 'Sausages and rye!'

Chelsea stooped and whispered his name urgently, feeling guilty for waking him, but resolute it was the right thing to do. 'TK, TK, wake up, wake up. Please!'

'Chelsea!' TK sat up so fast the sheets fell away. Chelsea looked down at a pair of legs hanging from his boxers and looked up quickly in case she saw anything else. He raised both arms like a boxer with one ready fist and a plaster cast. 'What's wrong? You alright?'

'I'm fine, TK.'

'Why aren't you in bed, Cee?' TK asked sleepily bringing his arms down to scratch himself.

'Just couldn't. Lot of stuff in my head.' She sank down to sit cross-legged on the carpet. 'I need you.'

'What?' TK seemed to brighten up suddenly. 'Cee, don't you think this is a bit…uhm, sudden?'

'Sudden?' Chelsea cocked her head to one side, thinking TK was probably still half asleep. 'Never mind. TK, I need to ask you something. It's been bothering me – something you said earlier. It can't wait.'

'Okay?' TK said, without making eye contact. To be fair, she'd only ever let him see her once without make-up when he'd come early to collect her.

Her robe had fallen open and flopped either side of her crossed legs. Pulling it together, she tried to retie it. 'TK, tell me again exactly why you can't produce your driving licence.'

'Driving licence?' TK sounded confused.

'Please wake up, TK. This is important. You started to say last night, when we were doing the circles, but got interrupted when Jonelle, you know, got sick.'

'You want to talk about my driving licence?' He looked deflated. 'Now?'

'TK, I know you need your sleep. The hospital said you should rest that arm and everything, but if we turn up without your driving licence… I am really worried what the police will do, especially as they also think we're somehow involved with Deen going missing.'

'Okay. Thing is I couldn't do the driving test to get a licence 'cause I got banned from driving.'

'Banned?' Chelsea moved closer. 'But you've been driving me around and—'

TK hung his head. 'Don't think bad of me, Cee. Sometimes a brother's gotta do what a brother's gotta do, nahumsayin'? I ain't proud o' it or nothingk…'

'Keep going, TK.'

'Long-short? This guy who was teachin' me got pulled over. We was in his motor, nahumsayin'. Cops found ganja under the hood.'

'What?'

'Wasn't the worse thing, neither. The motor wasn't his. Stolen.'

'TK!'

'I didn't know, nahumsayin'? Cops searched me, yeah? Found my licence and confiscated it, see, Cee? Thing is, it was a fake.'

'So the police didn't recognise the licence was fake?'

'Sorry, Chelsea,' TK held up both hands in surrender, 'all I can tell you is they had a long, hard look at it then gave it back. *Aksed* me if I knew about the ganja and let me off with a warning, but banned us from driving... After that I went and lost the damn thing, didn't I!'

She stood, adjusted her robe again and walked away, to the window. 'Did you never think about getting a proper licence after that, TK?'

'Thought about it.'

'But you never did?' She turned to look at him.

He hung his head in his free hand.

'Can't believe I'm saying this, but can't we get another fake, somehow? And then we can get to the station and tell the police what we discovered from debugging the connections.'

'Uhm...you sure about that, Cee?' TK was regarding her intently. 'It ain't legal and you got your business reputation...'

'How do we get the replacement, TK?' She approached and stared at him, unblinking.

'Well, hmm, I guess I can remember where the place is at, where Prunes sent me. But it wasn't cheap, *nahumsayin'*?'

'Let's do it.'

'Now?' TK looked at his bare wrist. 'What time is it?'

'Just gone 2 a.m.'

'I guess it's midday for the midnight industry.'

'Come on, let's go then.'

'Hold up...let me think...' TK raised his cast to scratch his head. 'Ow! Bloody hell! Keep forgetting I got this *effin'* thing on me.'

'How far's this place?' Chelsea walked towards the bedroom. 'Think we can get there and back before Jonelle wakes?'

'Hang on! Hang on!' TK stood to face her. 'Cee, I don't know okay...what if?'

'TK, we've no time now for "what if"?' Chelsea said, firmly.

'But what if they spot it's fake this time?'

'TK, would you prefer to try and explain how come you've been driving for a living *without* one.'

'Nahumsayin'?' TK sounded resigned.

'Look, it only matters that you remember where the place is.'

'Yes, yes, I remember. East End somewhere.'

'Okay, meet you downstairs. Five minutes. In the lobby where the children were playing hide-and-seek when we checked in.'

Ten minutes later, she found him semi-concealed by a large spineless yucca.

'Full make-up, Cee? No wonder you took so long.'

'Well, I'm a businesswoman with an image to maintain,' she said, taking his good arm to lead the way out of the emergency door. 'Plus, I went into the other suite to grab my handbag, in the dark, without disturbing Jonelle or the girls. I felt like a cat burglar.'

All her life, she had been taught to stay on the right side of the law and encourage others to do likewise. Yet, here she was, leading someone astray. Chelsea felt mounting excitement at the very idea.

'We don't have to do this y'know, Cee.' TK looked into her eyes as they strode towards a taxi rank.

'Yes we do.' She felt different and even her own voice sounded strange. It was true that she could turn her back when she was needed, care more about herself than someone else and choose the easy way out. 'I have to do this, TK. I do.'

# CHAPTER 36

Chelsea took a breath before jumping into the black cab. TK ducked in behind her.

'Tower Hamlets,' TK said, slamming the door behind him and pulling at the fold-down seat opposite Chelsea. The vehicle pulled away, sending TK into Chelsea's lap.

'Woah! Sorry, Cee.'

'It's okay.' She helped him roll over to sit beside her.

'You did say Tower Hamlets, right?' the driver called back.

'Yeah. Take Commercial Road, mate. Then I'll tell you where, aight? I need to see a couple landmarks.'

'You're paying.'

The gentle rattle and motion of the taxi lulled her into deep contemplation, generating a strange feeling in the pit of her stomach. TK too was deep in thought beside her or catching up on sleep as they passed St Paul's Cathedral. They'd just trundled past a sign that read Aldgate East when he suddenly came to life.

'Left here, boss.'

'But it's a no entry, mate,' said the driver, slowing down.

TK twisted and turned, bashing his plaster cast against the door. 'Yeah, you're right. Not here, sorry, the next one. Go straight, go straight.'

The driver sighed and continued as directed.

'Okay, turn right at that next road, I'm sure of it!'

TK's instruction came too late, leaving the taxi driver to narrowly avoid a collision with another black London cab.

'Jesus Christ!'

'No, definitely not Him!' Chelsea mimicked her late dad, triggering thoughts of how one misjudgement was enough to cause life-changing consequences.

The cab leant into the turn.

'Stop! This is it, Chelsea! This is the place.'

'You're sure?' Chelsea looked out on a part of London yet unexplored in her own quest.

'Positive!'

The driver thanked her for the payment, and she was just apologising for the small tip when he drove off. She felt certain there'd been more notes in her purse.

TK's attention was on a dilapidated sign, barely lit by a streetlamp nearby. Hindermann's Food and Liquor Import Export Emporium and Haberdashery. Chelsea read the sign aloud to herself, 'Are you sure, TK?'

'This is it, Cee.'

Beneath the sign, the front door opened, and a figure stepped out into the street, lit up a match and brought it to his face.

'No, it can't be. Can it?' TK whispered. 'Shit! It is him.'

'*Him* who, TK?'

'We can't let him see me, Cee.'

The man took a draw of his cigar, tilted his head back and rolled his neck as if to relieve deep tension. He blew smoke at the sky, shoved the matches back into his pocket and started towards them.

Chelsea grabbed TK's good arm and pulled him against her and a wall of graffiti. She'd never thought fake kissing could ever look believable without movie editing involved, but she pressed her lips to TK's anyway and melted into him as the footfalls approached, hesitated, and left them in a cloud of cigar smoke.

'Sorry, TK.' Chelsea pulled away, hot with embarrassment, wiping lipstick off his lips.

'I never thought that would ever work, Chelsea, but—'

'Seems so, TK. Who'd you think he was?'

'I think it was Django.'

'Who?'

'Bull's right-hand man. I'm pretty sure. Positive. Hundred per cent. Maybe seventy-five – haven't seen him in a while, to be fair, and he wasn't at 'Grilla last Friday. But he's always close by, even if you don't see him. People say if you touch Bull, Django feels it.'

'So, what if it was this Django fellow?'

'So? So? Cee, we got *no* business in *Bull's* business, nahumsayin'?' TK looked defeated. 'I'll just take my chances with the coppers. Let's find a taxi back.'

'TK, wait. Didn't you say it was *Prunes* that sent you to this place before?'

'Yeah?'

'So, who cares what this…this… Django wants? They took your money before. Right?'

He nodded.

'Then they'll take it again.'

He shrugged.

*Men!*

'TK, we're here now. Let's go in there, buy you a new fake driving licence and leave. Yes?'

'What if he comes back here with Bull and…nahumsayin'?'

'Then we'd best hurry up.' Chelsea led them across to the Hindermann's Food and Liquor Import Export Emporium and Haberdashery door.

'Stop worrying.' She patted TK on the back. 'We'll be long gone before he comes back…if he's even coming back. Okay?'

A large CLOSED sign hung inside the door.

'Thought you said they worked through the night, this dark economy?' She sighed.

'Chelsea, illegal don't advertise, nahumsayin'?'

'TK, they're clearly closed.' Chelsea pushed on the door to prove it. The door swung open and a loud 'ding' announced their presence.

Chelsea peered in for movement, listening for signs of service. Nothing.

'Let's go in.'

'Didn't go in when I came with Prunes,' TK whispered behind her in the darkness. Chelsea stubbed her toe and fell against something solid and hairy that wrapped around her.

'Careful Cee,' TK whispered, helping her up and untangling her.

Her eyes grew accustomed to the dark, turning the hulking figures into rolls of material as they weaved their way deeper inside. 'This is some fabric shop...' Chelsea ran her fingers along mohair, cashmere, velvet and heavy embroidery, denim and a zipper.

'That's me,' TK said, making her jump.

'Sorry!' She pulled her hand away. 'So, where'd you go for the licence, TK? Shouldn't there be a desk? Shop assistant? Light?'

'Like I said, I didn't come inside last time,' he whispered back.

'What?'

'Prunes made me wait by the door. Someone came out, took my money, gave me an envelope. Job done.'

The door dinged behind them.

An aroma of hot food wafted in.

Ducking into an aisle, she was terrified that her nose would react as it always did in the presence of very spicy food. Soon a familiar flurry of 'th-th-*th kittns*' would commence. While it always embarrassed her, her parents used to say it was cute. She doubted this person would say the same if they were found here, uninvited. Chelsea took a deep breath, clamped both hands over her mouth and pinched her nose.

Instead of ducking down, TK had frozen where he stood amongst the racks, barely hiding his cast under some material. Chelsea could still make out the whiteness of his cast. Surely he'd be spotted?

Still holding her nose, Chelsea peered round. The silhouette at the door had an orange dot for a mouth. The dot glowed brightly from orange to red, before the shadow of a hand flicked it away in a yellow arc.

Chelsea chanced another breath and ducked down as he entered the shop and blended into the shadows.

'Ow – shit! Keep telling that bloody Pam to tie these bloody things back so they don't fall every time a little breeze comes in! Could've damn near broke my bloody neck.'

The front door clunked shut and the aroma intensified. Chelsea tried to ascertain where the man was now. The spicy smell was everywhere.

Unable to hold her breath for much longer, she thought about taking another. Too risky. She tried to hold out…a little…longer, only until…she felt she would pass out. Nearby, she heard a grinding noise, metal rolling on metal.

'I'm back with food. Come eat!' More metallic noise, ending with a clunk.

'Th-th-th-kit'ns!' Chelsea sneezed. 'Th-kit'ns! th-kit'ns!'

'That's so cute, Cee!' TK whispered.

Chelsea rubbed her nose. 'Curry spice does that to *be*!… Stop laughing. What do we do now?'

'Shh!' TK crouched in closer to her.

They listened to metal rolling on metal again.

Then came voices.

'Nan? I still think you should've said no! You need rest… not just food.'

'I lost my appetite when the *Marchioness* took little Asher from us. Plus, I want to buy a good casket for her! Good marble headstones ain't cheap, neither. *Oy-yoy-yoy!*'

'Fine, okay, but at least take a short break, Nan? GP says you must move more, for your circulation. Stop fighting me, Nan? Walk a little, eat a little, use the toilet...'

They paused, inches from where Chelsea hid, spicing the air.

Slap. 'Watch your tongue, boy.'

'Sorry, Nan.'

The chatter continued towards the door with the woman insisting he was just waiting for her to drop dead so he could squander his inheritance, but they agreed to have a harsh word with Pam about tying things back when the shop was open next.

The hinges creaked and the front door dinged shut on their conversation.

Chelsea heard a key turn to lock, then double lock.

'Shit, we're stuck in here, Cee.'

Chelsea stood, waited for her head rush to pass. Without thinking, she felt for material, found cotton, and blew her nose into it.

'Now what?' TK said.

'Money talks. We find someone who will take payment and make you a new fake driving licence so we can get out of here. Fast...those two came from around there somewhere... come on.'

Chelsea found a clear patch where she had heard the grating noises. The wall suggested some sort of service hatch or dumb waiter might be behind it.

Knocking brought no response. Neither did hammering with her fists.

'There's a kind of handle over here, Cee?'

'Maybe we just go in, you think?'

It took all their strength and Chelsea braced a foot on the wall before it began to move. The door slid apart with the metallic rolling noise they'd heard before. They stepped inside and the doors slid shut behind them.

'Jesus.' Chelsea shielded her eyes from the brightness of the room beyond.

'It's like a surgery in here,' TK said.

Chelsea walked over to the four desks in the middle of the sterile room, each having its own magnifier on a stand, guillotine, assorted tools and – what were either archaic bookbinders, cast-iron embossing machines, rusting old staplers or simply paperweights. Further inside, tucked into a far corner, was a small kitchenette, or some form of laboratory. Before she could stop him, TK edged over for a closer look.

There were no windows and no emergency escape that she could see, making those heavy sliding doors their only way out.

Chelsea's heart quickened.

She looked around at the walls lined with shelves and filing cabinets. Large labels suggested a degree of organisation. *DOCS* must be documents, *CERTS* she thought were certificates, *PERMS* she expected had nothing to do with hair, but permits.

'TK. Do you think they've got a copy of your original fake licence. Filed under permits, maybe? Or MISC?'

'Cee, maybe we should have talked to those two, you think?'

The logic had gone through her mind during the panic. 'TK, you said you'd seen this Django, one of Bull's close associates, leave. You also told me you'd not been allowed inside when you came with Prunes before, so how'd they have reacted to us popping up in the dark, inside their shop?'

'Dunno.' TK sounded distracted.

'Hindsight won't help us now...start looking... We find it. We take it. We leave the money and get out of here, right?'

'I s'pose.' TK sounded the way Dad had when he was watching *Columbo* and Mum was talking about carpet paint swatches.

'Cee, look over here. They got jars of dirt from different countries...*dirt*! Paris soil, Rome soil, Stockholm, Washington

DC, Brazil, Jamaica…and there's jars of coffee, tea, baking soda. They…must make some exceedingly good mud pies with all this dirt and…look here…they've got an oven. Friend of mine develops pictures in his dark room with some of the chemical stuff over here!'

'Mmm…yes, very interesting but we've no time to mess around. Start looking for that driving licence. Try that shelf over there…' Chelsea pointed in the direction of *PERMS*, past *PL, BL, TL, HGV* to where the handwritten sign read *DL*.

*Driving licences?*

Chelsea's attention stopped on a section labelled *CERTS*.

*Certificates?*

Her eyes panned down to a subdivision.

*BCs.*

*Birth Certificates?*

Rows of box files dating back beyond the day that she'd heard her parents had perished in the car collision, beyond her graduation, beyond winning her first race in primary school. A box marked 62–63 broke rank from the others on the shelf.

She was born in 1962.

What were the chances?

A yellowing rubber band snapped and stung her wrist as she carefully freed the sheaf of papers. In a strange chronology, some dates under 1962 belonged in 61 and others in 65 and she spotted a couple of 70s.

'Bloody cast is slowing me down,' TK was saying. 'Wish I could just rip it off now.'

Sitting on the floor, Chelsea sorted the box, collating all dates into a pile for 62. If only these were computer files.

'They need a ladder in this place,' TK was saying. 'Come and hold this chair for me, Cee?'

'Give me a second.' Chelsea couldn't believe her eyes as she rifled through the papers, spreading them out on the pristine white floor. She squinted beyond the glare that bounced off the paperwork. So many names and so many dates.

Fake dates of birth?

Perhaps.

For every fake, she imagined there was a real life being lived out there somewhere.

'You comin', Cee?'

'In a minute, TK.' The words felt sharp as they left her lips as she hurriedly sorted the birth dates and names in alphabetical order.

A small earthquake was shaking the floor. Was TK moving something? She had just one small sheaf left to check before going to help him.

'Oh no. No. No...'

Chelsea looked up.

TK was teetering with one leg on an office chair and his other foot on a shelf, trying to steady himself with his cast against the chair back. His good hand was holding a small box, waiter-tray-style, marked T–Z. The wheeled chair was rolling.

'Oh fuck!'

'Ohmygod. TK!'

TK did the splits before falling backwards to the floor, landing hard. The chair shot away, rolling fast to smack into a desk, transferring momentum to a bucket that tipped and tumbled towards Chelsea, spilling its dirt-brown viscous contents across the spotless white linoleum floor and her stack of unchecked papers.

'No-o-o!' Chelsea scrambled to rescue the sheaf, lifting them out of the sludge.

'Shit! Shit! Shit!' TK sat rubbing his behind.

Angry beyond words, Chelsea looked over at TK then towards the sliding door then back to the soaking documents.

'I saved the box, at least,' TK said, trying to pick himself up.

'Why don't you just go out and watch the entrance?'

'It's alright, Cee. I can easily—'

'TK! I can move faster in here with you keeping watch out there.'

It took all their strength to yank the lever to open the sliding door halfway. TK slipped through the gap and fetched a bolt of herringbone to wedge it open.

'Chelsea, anyone comes to that front door they'll see us.'

'A chance we have to take, TK. We're wasting valuable time. Keep watch.'

She rushed back to the papers. 'Shit! Thought I'd got them all out the way.' Chelsea studied a rectangular outline through the liquid and a faint: 'La'.

Using her fingertips, she lifted the corners away from the brown slurry. The tension and penetrating light were making her head ache.

'Blast!' Chelsea looked up in frustration as two corners tore away from the rest as the type-written details and inked markings began dissolving into the staining fluid.

More frantic than hopeful, she spotted a spatula and a pair of tweezers over on the small corner lab. Working fast, against nature and the chances of them being discovered, Chelsea made fresh attempt at lifting the paper from the sludge.

'I think someone's coming, Cee,' TK stage whispered.

*Oh fuck!* Chelsea shouted in her head. *There's nowhere to hide in here.*

'Just a drunk guy!' TK murmured seconds later. 'Sorry.'

Chelsea calmed her breathing, steadied her hands and managed to free the top sheet and start on the one beneath. More soaked than the first, it required more delicate handling. The stark brightness meant she could just make out: *verne*

*La + verne.* Her heart stopped.

Someone had annotated the document in pen and the wrinkle in the paper meant some of the letters were yet to dissolve: *M lt pl b th.*

'Multiple births?' she whispered in her head.

'Someone's coming this time, Cee... I think!' TK said.

'Wait!' Chelsea fought the urge to flee. Could she lift the sheet free, dry it out to take it from here? Her eyes darted around looking for some absorbent paper that she could use to sandwich the wet document. Her scan found the small oven over in the kitchenette-lab where she might warm the sopping paper and dry it out, but there was no damn time to fire it up, so she bent closer and squinted, focusing hard.

*New name:* Chelsea.

Christ!

'Chelsea,' TK said, whispering as loudly as he could. 'I think that guy's back!'

*Gender:* F *New DOB:* 25th December 1962.

What? So, she *wasn't* born on Christmas Day?

'He's having trouble with the key in the door, Cee. Shit, he's going to see the light! Chelsea? Chelsea, you hear me?'

She did, but she couldn't stop – daren't stop reading:

*Ne other:* yce

'New mother: Joyce...maybe?'

'Chelsea! What're you doing? Come on.'

'Hang on!' Her eyes strained at deciphering every bit of information before it dissolved from view. 'Something-something-*w fa h : Lo is...* New father? Louis? Could be *Louis.*'

Dizzy with confusion and conflicted, she scarcely felt the floor beneath her knees. It was a discovery she had method-ically hunted for. Being honest, she'd hoped it would never arrive. How she'd hoped to prove her cousin was nothing more than a vengeful bitch and a liar.

She scanned again where *multiple birth* had been. How many, two, three, five?

'Cee, *we've got to hide...* Chelsea? Chelsea?'

The next line seemed to lift itself up from the sludge into full clarity: *Fee:* Paid in Fu—

'Chelseeee!'

A loud ding sounded as the lights went out.

'No!' she screamed and adopted a fighting stance in the dark, praying her teen self-defence training had followed her into adulthood. Scuffling sounds ended with a bump of something falling heavily.

'TK?'

The lights clicked on.

TK stood next to a switch, wincing. At his feet, a figure lay prone with pieces of TK's cast near his head.

'What happened?' Chelsea said.

'Had to do something, Cee.' TK rubbed his healing arm. 'Hurts like a bitch.'

'He's dead?' Chelsea grabbed her head between both hands.

'Not sure.'

'I just saw his chest move.'

She rushed back to the floor and stooped over the soaked paperwork. 'Is he alone, TK?'

'Only saw him... Leave that, Cee, we've got to get out of here now.'

'Just a minute.'

It was almost all gone, leaving her just enough to make out *father* again. Beside it, she pieced together *Blood Type*. Whose blood type, 'new father' or 'adopted father'? Her eye fell on the faintest *O* in a set of numbers or, perhaps, it was part of a single longer number.

'Jesus Christ!' She felt like screaming as the run of numbers started mapping to the one that had been burnt into her memory, bringing a crashing wave of confusion and anger.

'What're you doin', now, Cee?'

She felt numb and paralysed by what she was seeing.

'Talk to me, Cee?... This guy's growing a big lump on his head that'll fit in with the other three.'

'I rolled him with my foot...he's definitely not the guy

what was with the old lady...he was mixed and this guy's black with no eyebrows. Jesus.'

'I *can't* leave...' Chelsea felt a surge of energy burst in her belly as she looked around and considered the lives touched by this clandestine operation.

'Looks like he might be waking up.'

'That might complicate things. Let's tie him up with something...' Chelsea pointed behind him. 'Help me with that roll of thick tartan.'

They used the fabric to wrap the unconscious man, tightly securing his arms and legs, in case he roused before they were done. Then they dragged their mummified captive away from the door and hid him down a row of material.

'Stuff his mouth too, TK.'

'Where're you going, Cee?'

'No time to explain.'

Chelsea hauled a bolt of cotton into the room and unreeled some to clean the floor, using a small squirt of bleach she found in the kitchenette-lab.

Moving fast and thinking faster, she darted from box file to box file, swapping one set of documents from one place to another, one with one, two with two and sometimes three with three, making sure that every box file contained documents that did not belong there.

'TK! Go check out front...make sure no one's coming.'

She ignored his protests and dashed over to one of the tables where she'd noticed someone had been working on a document headed *Planning Permission*. Speed reading, she stopped at the words '...*do hereby approve the erection of twelve dwellings on the said piece of Green Belt land*...' Beside it was a small ink blotter and little hammers with numbers and letters that belonged in a typewriter. Chelsea used the magnifier to check she had selected the hammer for a zero and not one for the letter O. She touched it lightly on the blotter, once, and then again, until it picked up enough ink. She aimed it gently at the document, lowering it slowly towards her target.

Yes, perfect! Four zeros should get attention!

'Cee,' TK poked his head in. 'It's them!'

'Christ!' She lifted her hand straight up and replaced the little hammer exactly where she'd found it, changed her mind and switched it around with the letter O.

'Just turned the corner, *three* of them. That old lady and two guys.'

'Okay, let's go!' She hoped she'd done enough to ensure no one could tell they'd been here and the papers that she'd tucked under her clothes were misfiled rather than gone missing. She stepped through the opening, hauled the makeshift wedge away, releasing the metal doors to slide shut and plunge the shop back into darkness.

Two tall men and a squat old woman walked up to the front door. As one man put the key in the door, it swung away.

'Didn't I tell you to lock the door, Victor?' The old woman slapped him on the side of the head.

'I did, Nan! I swear!'

The other man chuckled, 'No pocket money for him, Nan.'

'You can talk, Adam, after dripping duck sauce on your shoes. I've a mind to send you home to change but that big black brute'll be back for his documents so we've no time to piss about.'

Far too late, Chelsea wondered whether she and TK should have left the lights in the room on or off. The metal door started rolling open and a widening wedge of light fell from the room beyond.

'What is it, Nan?'

'Someone's fuckin' been in here!'

'How can you tell, Nan?' said one man.

'Place's exactly the way we left it, Nan,' said the other. 'Except I definitely locked the door.'

'I can smell it!'

# CHAPTER 37

The nurse looked out at Prunes from inside one of the containers housing the packages. Once more, he'd stood asking if everything was okay and if she had all she needed.

'You name it – I've got it 'ere somewhere,' he said again.

The floodlights blinked across Prunes' old vans, new trucks and bulging tarpaulin-covered pallets and sent fingers of light reaching through the high chicken wire bordering Prunes' property and into the dense shrubbery beyond. Anyone could hide up there in all that bush, she supposed. Her eyes followed the slope up to the woodland that sat like a crown atop the hilly backdrop of Prunes' emporium. What was over the hill, she wondered? Prunes looked like he'd read her mind and was about to tell her when the lights blinked again.

'Oh God,' Prunes gagged. With a loud click, darkness covered the yard.

'What's wrong?' the nurse asked calmly.

'Someone's ringing at the gate and now the bloody fuse has tripped. Damn this new technology.' Prunes patted himself down. 'And I went an' left my bloody lighter in the— Ah, here it is.'

Sparks flew about his thumb before a dancing flame appeared. Praising his lord, Prunes held it aloft. 'Now who the hell's ringing my gate. Must be nearly, what, two o'clock?

Bull shouldn't be back so soon… No. No. No. Not unless he…
Oh Christ, I'll never be able to do business with them people
again!'

'Calm down, Prunes. I got diazepam.' She always kept
some on her for whenever she ran out of Prozac and she made
sure she never did that. 'Or Maxwell might have a little weed?'

'N-n-naw, I'm a'right. Where's Maxwell's at?'

'Told me he wanted to point Percy at the porcelain.' She
tried not to think about her cousin fussing over his privates
and fretting he might bust his stitches.

'A'right. Get back to work! Stay outtaa sight!' Prunes kept
walking and talking. 'Tell Maxwell to stay outta sight too.
Keep them container doors closed… I bet any money it's
nosy, bloody neighbours complaining about noise and smoke
and all this shit happening on a Sunday… I told them. I told
them…would they listen? Bloody oil drum fire smoking up
the gawd-damn place…treatin' my home like some kinda
ghetto slum *tenniment* yard…'

Prunes' gripes died away towards the corner of the house.
She watched him go, remembering their very first meeting
years ago, long before she'd started working for Bull as The
Nurse. In fact, even before she was *a* nurse at all, she'd decided
to open a Caribbean restaurant in Clapham. While scouting
the markets for a reliable source of ingredients, she'd bumped
into Prunes on his 'luxury' stall, promising the world on a
bargain for what, he'd claimed, meant he'd be practically
'givin' it away' to her.

Ackees, saltfish, callaloo and cow's feet…her customers
would keep coming back for her high-end quality and
imported food, *and* the view, Prunes had whispered, adding
that he had even better stuff 'under the counter' for his 'special
regulars'. She'd declined his offer to make her both special
and regular, along with his promise to rent her a decent place
for her restaurant. In the end, it had never happened because

her nursing career took off and she'd put Prunes well out of sight and out of mind, until her cousin had brought her to meet Bull one 'Grilla night, a year ago.

'You sure we've never met before?' Prunes'd asked her, with Bull looking on, eyeing her up and down.

'Very sure.'

'*Posi'ive?*'

'Positive…wait…perhaps at the VD clinic?' she'd suggested.

'Uhm, maybe not then. No.' Prunes dropped the subject, recoiling.

She noticed the saline drip was almost out. She fetched a new one, set it up and looked down at his tiny sleeping face, which had arrived like a limp lettuce wearing an oxygen mask. Since Bull and his boys'd left earlier, Prunes had been popping in, checking. She'd wondered whether Bull didn't trust Maxwell to prevent more runaways or anything else going wrong. But then Prunes' questions always came round to this latest arrival in the cot before her.

'Anything on my property is my business, get me?' he'd told her when she'd got fed up and asked him why he was making a fuss. Then they'd had the strangest conversation:

'Why're you so interested in this particular package?' she'd asked.

'Quali'y control, aight. Now, what'd you do with that green and gold jacket he was wearing?'

'Got snagged when they lifted him out the container.'

'Bloody clumsy bunch of bloody—'

'It's just a jacket!'

'A perfectly good jacket.'

'Why do you care…?'

'Care? Care? What would the world be if people didn't care, eh? A jacket like that could fetch a good fuckin' price. Second-hand. Anyway, how's Deen?'

'Who?'

'The boy? How's the boy?'

'No, you said a name, didn't you? Deen, I think.'

'I didn't.'

'You did.'

'Did I? Must be coz he sort of resembles someone, the son of someone, one of my special regulars.'

'Really?'

'Naw.'

'Bull know you know him?'

'Who said I know him?'

'You did.'

'I didn't.'

'Bull needs to know, surely.'

'No he doesn't. He doesn't. I said the little guy resembles someone, is all. We all have a lookalike, right? Remember when we met? I thought even you resembled someone, didn't I? She'd wanted some kinda food stall or restaurant and—'

'He's fine,' she'd broken in, 'the boy's fine. In and out of sleep, but all good. Those idiots gave him way too much sedative so that drip there is flushing it all from his system. He'll be himself soon.'

'Oh, I see…'

'You seem disappointed.'

'Naw, naw…if something ain't right wit him, what would happen?'

'I'd sort it, of course. You'd be amazed what—'

'*But* what if he was *really* poorly from all that…that…'

'Sedatives?'

'Yeah, them. Would they just return him and—'

'What? Swap him for a new one? Prunes, he isn't a pair of imported Italian shoes or a Dutch pot.'

'Naw, I know, I know…'

'You needn't worry,' she'd told him eventually. 'Bull's papers say all they want is for him to have two working lungs, strong heart and healthy liver and kidneys and he's got all of them. Just really groggy from the sedative.'

'Wonder why a person'd want all that, eh? They gonna barbeque 'im?' It wasn't funny but he'd laughed. Nervously. And she'd been polite.

She pulled one leaf of the double door, locked it and unhitched the other side and heaved it closed, leaving it ajar a little bit longer to let in fresh air. Her only worry had always been the fate of the little ones and where their little smiles would end up. She smiled, thinking of the little personalities she'd seen forming over the past months. Whenever she was alone with them, she'd whisper in their tiny ears and tell them to become lawyers and bankers and, if they became doctors then they should go private and work for themselves, not the fucking NHS! She'd read statistics about the percentage of all babies that would grow to study medicine and law while others were born for prison and asylums, but – fuck those statistics – her babies would have every chance at greatness!

Maxwell insisted she called them 'packages', 'because that is what they need to be to you, Cuz. It'll make it easier to let go!' Hell, how easy was it for any woman to let go of a child, even harder a baby taken lifeless from her womb to be planted in the ground? She'd wanted to climb into that hole with her stillborn and it had taken a lot of meds to make everyone think she was ready to work the wards again. And she'd been ready, really. Fifteen years in the NHS had taught her how to cope, even if she did need a little help with her chemistry. Her accusers should have understood that. Instead, they'd pounced on her for making a single error in judgement, like that wasn't her human right. Fine, fine, she made *two* mistakes! Only two *silly* mistakes… She'd give them that.

But, in the first place, she'd not technically left the building. Fresh air and a cuddle next to her skin had worked wonders for the struggling little bag of sugar. It had cried when they'd taken it off her and stuffed it back into that soulless incubator. In the second place, just because a person had maternal hormones didn't mean they couldn't be professional. Where did it say that hormones equalled crazy? Mankind existed because of hormones and it was *her* maternal ears alone that had heard the little *babba* wailing on that noisy ward. The wet-nosed school-leaver they'd sent to supervise her had been nodding off into her cuppa anyway. It would have been criminal to ignore the distressed little thing, and as she'd still been lactating – given the research on breast milk and babies – she'd done what she'd had to do. Why had it been so wrong to take it home and give that innocent a few hours of pure maternal love, better than it would ever have gotten from the druggie skank it had dropped out of. Anyway, that was all in the past now.

Behind the container door, the nurse checked her watch in the low lighting. It was time she popped the three pills. She tilted her head back, rubbed her neck and chucked all three to the back of her throat. Her trip down memory lane and the arrival of this new child had stirred more emotion than usual, so she added an extra Prozac. Who would know?

So, had Bull returned?

She smoothed out her whites and started looking around. Everything was done as far as she was concerned. She checked again. She'd done it enough times before.

The nurse's pulse quickened. She blamed the pills. It could also be the fact she knew Bull might have come back already, for his 'packages'.

'Nurse! Quick. Quick!' Maxwell's muffled voice seeped through the steel doors. She pushed it open.

'Get in!'

Maxwell entered.

'I *am* already in! What's wrong?'

'Babylon!' Maxwell gasped and shoved the door closed to engage the mechanism.

'Police?' the nurse said. 'Bull's here with the police?'

'No, stupid woman... Prunes said lock up every damn thing. And start praying.'

'Lock up everything?'

'Yeah!' Maxwell wiped his forehead. 'Prunes said the Babylon can't open the doors from the outside and they'll need a warrant anyway. So, we have to stay put 'til somebody lets us out. Yeah? Good thing we got supplies...can always replace supplies, right?'

'Every damn thing, Cuz?'

She saw the penny drop when his eyes widened. 'Shit, the other container. Bull'll kill me if it's still open and the Babylon stick their noses in.'

'Or more runaways?'

'Oh, my sweet Jesus!' Maxwell cupped himself.

'Nothing you can do now, is there?' she shrugged. 'What's really going on, Cuz? All this ducking and diving...'

'Cuz.' Maxwell looked down the narrow internal corridor and lowered his voice. 'You can't tell nobody this, but this job ain't going down smooth like last time.'

'No?' The nurse tried to sound surprised. Maxwell explained that with all the runaways, Bull'd had trouble with the quota and someone had been feeding information to the Babylon.

'Really?'

'Shush...you hear that?' Maxwell whispered softly.


The silence was accompanied by the occasional gear crunch, the bumpety-bump road noise and tyres screeching. Neither of them had spoken since removing the 'out of commission' sign from the old Panda for the second time and getting it going. Eyes front in the nocturnal traffic on the A23, they watched Brixton become Streatham become Croydon before PC Bailey finally decided he'd break the silence by asking his partner why the place was named Whyteleafe and had she ever seen one. Instead, he just cleared his throat.

Murphy sighed deeply as she accelerated them into Purley.

In their unspoken pact, they silently drove around a drunk stumbling off a pavement into their path, overlooked two street fights and were blind to a small collision between a vehicle and a lamppost. The driver seemed unhurt and astonished as they rolled by.

Sitting there, fiddling with his handcuffs, PC Bailey felt he'd had enough. The Force *was* sexist. Racist too, but the uniform, the badge and their oath to serve the queen and protect her people with impartiality must still mean there was room for fairness? Dammit.

Why the hell were they never being taken seriously and simply just running errands.

Murphy broke the silence: 'If you were paying any attention, you'd notice that we're the skivvies of the department.'

Bailey had always thought women could read men's minds; now he was convinced.

'One token female and a token black. They made us partners so they can pull back the curtains whenever they want the world to think equality exists on the force. Shit. With all the filing, typing and form-filling I do, may as well ditch the uniform and become a fucking bank clerk.'

'What about that murder case Friday night?' he squeezed in.

'Really, Bailey? With everyone else tied up with that Bromley collision, who else was there to knock on doors for witnesses – in the rain! Any idiot can ask people if they've seen anything suspicious, yes?'

He nodded.

'You tell me, Bailey, has anybody followed up on our notes? What did they do after you told them that victim, found dead in her bed, was the very same woman who'd climbed up on you hours earlier?'

'They laughed.' He shook his head and looked down.

'Exactly… I suspect that woman's murder and the double homicide Friday night may be connected, but you know what they'd say…? What they always say!'

'Women's intuition again?' Bailey parroted the guvnor.

'Damn right.'

Bailey folded his arms and looked away. She'd made a good point, the guvnor had batted away his notes and ignored his concerns about the group of seven black guys at that party: *I've no time for your brilliant deductions, Bailey, who the hell assigned you and Murphy to the detective team without telling me?'*

Having refilled her lungs, Murphy opened her mouth but Bailey jumped in quick. 'Look, you – *we* – can't just sit back and take it. We've gotta fight for what we want. Nobody, not even the guvnor, can deny evidence. We're good coppers, same as everybody else. That is how we beat them at their own game. See?'

Murphy was shaking her head. 'Bailey. It's darkness and you think it's daylight. You want evidence? The entire department are right now looking for two people, no, three, that were *our* responsibility that they think are kidnapping kids. Meanwhile…' She added extra mustard to the word. '…we've been dispatched to attend some bloody antisocial complaint filed bloody hours ago that's probably sorted and forgotten by now.'

'But Murphy?'

'Save it. We've arrived at the address.'

She killed the engine, grabbed her chequered hat and truncheon off the back seat and flung the door open.

They walked up to a mighty wooden double-leaved gate in front, blocking their view of the property behind. On tiptoe, he could see two rooftops, but she couldn't. Murphy shone her torch on an intercom.

She jabbed it.

Nothing, apart from a flickering of lights from the other side of the gate.

They waited through a few more presses.

'Loose connection?' Bailey suggested, inspecting the gaffer tape on the intercom. 'That or maybe nobody's home right now?'

Murphy stomped away. He watched her looking at the gap where the gate ended and the high fence began.

Then a noise.

Footsteps approaching.

Bailey adjusted his helmet and his attitude.

Murphy focused her torch on the opening gates. So did he.

A short man shielded his eyes and stepped out to join them. 'Good evening, Ossifers. May I be of help?'

'It's night, sir,' Bailey corrected him and…had he just called them *ossifers*?

Truncheon in hand, Murphy stepped between him and the man. 'This your property, sir?'

'Yes, uhm, yes, it is… There a problem, Officers?'

'Prunes?' Bailey held the torch high and shone it downwards on his face, trying not to blind him with a direct beam.

'Excuse me, we've met?'

Bailey lit up his own face. 'You're Prunes. Brixton Market. Tried to sell me a watch last week and some sort of balm for tired feet.'

'Oh yes, yes, I remember.' The man looked less stunned, but no less concerned.

Bailey felt Murphy impatient for an explanation. 'This man's got a stall in Brixton market. Goes by the name of Prunes.'

'What's your real name, sir?' Murphy asked.

'Prunes is my name, Officer. Everybody everywhere know me as Prunes.'

'And your mother? What does she call you?'

'Prunes, Officer, just plain old Prunes.'

'May we come in, sir?'

'Why?' Prunes shot back. 'I mean, yes. Come in. Come in. Tough day. Long day. Not easy running a business like mine. Was just sorting my paperwork. Follow me.'

Bailey flashed his torch across what looked like three Victorian properties converted into two with a driveway bisecting them and leading through to the back.

'And what do you do exactly, sir?' Murphy asked.

'I buy. I sell. Y'know, officer. Bit o' this. Bit o' tat. Uhm *that*. Anything. Wherever there's a penny or two to be made. Haven't you stopped at my Brixton stall? In fact, there's a new lipstick that I can see would be perfect with your skin tone...'

Murphy's torch washed across the expansive property and sketched the outline of a hillside looking down at them. Behind them, the massive gates whirred shut.

Prunes looked up at them in turn. 'So, Officers, what brings you so far from Brixton?'

Murphy gave Bailey a quick glance and walked away, leaving him to explain.

'We've had a complaint about smoke and noise, sir. It seems some of your neighbours are unhappy about antisocial behaviour coming from your property.'

'I see. Well, as *you* can see, there's nothing antisocial here, Officers.' Prunes started to look less concerned and more edgy.

Murphy aimed a beam at the gap between the houses. Something had been nibbling bits off the corners.

'Nope. Nothing antisocial here at all, Officers...' Prunes followed their gaze. 'That wall? Delivery men. Always in a rush – I'm tired of having it repaired.'

'We've had a complaint about smoke, sir,' said Bailey.

'Smoke?' Prunes looked as though he didn't know what the word meant.

'Yes, smoke. Mind if we have a look around?'

'Yes, of course. But you won't find any fire. No fire, no smoke. See?'

'Take us around the back, please.' Murphy added extra ice.

They followed Prunes along the drive and round to the back of the place.

'Do these lights work?' Bailey shone his torch at a flood-light looking down at them in darkness.

'Yes, Officer,' said Prunes, popping something into his mouth.

'What's that you're eating?' Murphy said, bristling.

'Only dried fruit,' Prunes smiled, nervously. 'Love the way they do them over in California. Want some?'

'No, thanks.' Murphy illuminated the Sun-Maid container. 'I'll thank you not to eat any more until we've left.'

'Sorreee!'

'Would you switch on these lights for us, please,' Bailey asked.

'But, Officer, they're very bright and we don't need to upset the neighbours, do we?' Prunes coughed away something stuck in his throat. 'People can see them from Crystal Palace and Biggin Hill. If I turn them on this time o' night, my nice neighbours will call the police on me, a decent law-abiding citizen.'

'They were on when we drove up, Mr Prunes.' Murphy had her back to him, shining her light all over what Bailey had thought were trailers but now appeared to be two large containers. He flashed his light around the yard picking up orderly fuel cylinders, an array of vans, trucks and what looked like converted milk floats, all neatly positioned in what seemed like three backyards rolled into one. How'd a market trader manage to buy three properties and roll them into one?

Back in Birmingham, he'd met one or two of the Windrush generation who'd bought up properties cheaply from owners relocating to avoid mixing with the 'darkies'. Had Prunes bought this or inherited it?

No, something in his gut told him that was not it.

Not here.

'Prunes, after we rang your bell, they were doing some sort of light show for your *nice* neighbours. We're here because of complaints we've had already. Flick those lights on so we can take a proper look around and leave you to it.'

'Well, here's the t'ing, Officer. Just when you came, I heard a noise m'self and flicked them on. Sometimes foxes attack my chickens and I even get gypsies jumping my fence and grabbing my stuff.'

'And you've reported this?'

'Yeah, man! But the cops always too busy or they tell me to make a note of my losses and come fill out forms down the station. But I'm a busy man. I don't got time fi—'

'Sir!' Murphy stopped him. 'The lights?'

Prunes straightened up. 'That's what I was about to tell you, the circuit's dead – started flashing and then – *bam!* – nothing. Lucky, they draw juice on their own special 'lectric-city ring t'ing – got to call my 'lectrician guy, get 'im down 'ere first t'ing to fix it before—'

'Yes, yes, we get the idea,' Bailey broke in, becoming as impatient as Murphy.

'I can smell smoke,' Murphy said, walking away. 'Sure you've not been burning something, sir?'

Bailey followed her over to an oil drum where a whisper of smoke curled skyward from its mouth. Murphy placed a hand on the outside. Bailey did the same. It felt comfortably warm.

'Why shouldn't I think this was much hotter earlier, Mr Prunes?' Murphy shone her torch into the drum. 'Seems you did have a fire after all, sir!'

The beam faltered.

'Need some bat'ries, Officer? I'm sure I have some in—'

'No thanks.' Murphy banged the torch with the heel of her hand. The beam strengthened to full brightness. 'Now about this fire.'

'Oh, yes, I almost f'got.' Prunes looked irritated. 'One of my stupid employees was burning some old newspaper earlier. Told the fool to take it down the dump and what does he do when my back is turned? Lazy sod! I got him to put it out ages ago. You just can't get good help these days.'

Bailey stood next to Murphy, who was sniffing the air.

'Paper, eh?' she asked.

'Yes, just paper.'

'I smell wood.'

'What? He told me it was just paper!' Prunes looked even more annoyed. 'I have a good mind to sack the idiot.'

Bailey stepped around the drum and returned his attention and his torchlight back towards the containers he'd noticed earlier.

'How did you get those back here?'

'The flatbeds use that gate over there, y'see. That way we don't block the road out front or nothing like that, yeah?' he paused, took a packet from his pocket, looked at Murphy, put it back, and continued. 'Anyway, I sometimes ship things back home for my clients – Nigerians, Trinidadians, Jamaicans – *plenty plenty* people doing that now, say they don't like Thatcher's government and fed up with feeling like criminals when they're just trying to live. Motorbikes, second-hand cars and vans to sell as new or operate as taxis and minibuses – they call them robots back home, y'know? Well, I suppose you do… I pack it all in the containers ready to ship all over the place, well, mostly all over the West Indies. You be surprised 'ow you can pack a person's entire life into one of them things!… I's got all the licences, permits – all the proper documents – if you want a look at them.'

Prunes paused, looking exhausted.

Bailey nodded and asked, 'So you don't only work a market stall?'

Prunes laughed and waved both arms across the scene about them. 'Think I could afford all this just from Brixton market? Come on! Gotta work the angles, know what I mean? *Turn your han' fi mek fashion. Ev'ry mickle mek a muckle an all!*'

Unable to help himself, Bailey smiled. He noticed a confused Murphy observing him with Prunes.

'Mr Prunes,' Murphy face-to-face'd him, 'your neighbours said they have been disturbed by smoke, loud noise and strange goings-on from these premises. Are you saying they've made these things up just to waste police time?'

Prunes shrugged and his robe fell open to reveal he was otherwise dressed in jeans and t-shirt. 'Officer, you can see for yourself, I'm just a man trying to earn a crust without upsetting people. Do you see any *strange goings-on*? Or hear any *loud noise*?'

Rustling from the nearby bushes made them all look around.

'Damn foxes!' Prunes waved a fist in the direction of the fence. 'Sorry, Officers.'

'You stay here, please!' Murphy warned.

Bailey's eyes were following their twinned beams when he caught a sudden glow between the containers. A one-eyed fox or cat was looking back at them, or so it looked for a second. It was there, then it was gone.

Murphy's torchlight split from his and landed on a vehicle.

'See that white van, Bailey?'

'Van?' His torch rejoined hers.

'Looks very familiar.' Murphy sniffed at the air. 'Can you smell sulphur?'

'No, just smouldering wood.'

'Okay, you check out that van.' Murphy was pointing her nose this way and that. 'I'll come and join you in a minute.'

Bailey noticed there was no licence plate, but as it was on private property...

'It's not got no MOT, Officer,' Prunes called over.

The vehicle was similar to the one they'd seen on the hospital video, and that clean rectangular patch on the side looked about the right size for a 'BioHazzard' sign.

'Murphy,' he called to the torchlight across the yard. 'Come and look at this.'

Bailey tried the van doors, found them locked. Trouble was, these transits were bloody common. He spotted a trolley, just like the one Miss Patrick had pushed into that workman in his white overalls. He stooped to look closer and a small glow crawled into his periphery. One-eye again? No. More like a lit cigarette butt, except it was moving, scuttling along the perimeter...scooting across the yard... Bailey shone his torch ahead and illuminated a sign.

*DANGER*

Beneath it, in big letters, the scribbled card forbade naked flames in the area. He saw a third sign, yards from where he saw Murphy now stood, peering into an open container.

*BUTANE FILLING STATION*

He heard himself shout. Felt his voice strain and vibrate and burn but she didn't seem to recognise her own name. In slow motion, she looked around at him, pointing her torch at something inside the container, unaware of the fireball.

As hard as he pumped, he couldn't cover the short distance fast enough and, in his mind, came flashes of his partner telling him about her little girl, showing him the picture she kept with her warrant card.

'Nyreeeeeee!'

# CHAPTER 38

Jonelle trudged alongside infrequent traffic, following signs pointing towards Victoria station. Empty London cabs sped past, ignoring her waves. Up ahead, the Victoria station clock looked down from the red stone building, telling her it was 2:20 a.m.

Her throat felt dry and her stomach unhappy. She huffed into cupped hands to check her breath as she strode up to the first of the vehicles waiting in the taxi ranks before the concourse.

'Brixton?' she said.

'Sorry, luv. Just going off duty.' The driver slid the window shut and drove off, leaving her confused as to why he was there.

She worked the queue, astonished that with so many cabs and no competition she was unable to secure one. The last driver had his head buried in a copy of the *Sun*.

'You working?'

'Yes. Yes. Get in. Get in,' he said, still intent on the paper while he folded it away.

'Thanks,' she said and climbed in.

'Uhm, where to, miss?' he looked around at her, raised his brows and dropped his smile. Did she look as rough as she was feeling?

'Brixton tube station. Please.'

'Brixton? No problem. No problem. But…' A vehicle tooted them from behind as he eased away, slowly. 'I go off duty in ten, y'see, and – well, how about Vauxhall? That's *nearly* Brixton?'

Another horn hurried them along.

'No, I need to get home to Brixton, please.' She couldn't be sure, but the driver honking them looked like the first one she'd asked.

'Fine, Brixton, it is.' His shoulders sagged and they gathered more speed, overtaking a homeless man dragging a blue blanket along the pavement. The taxi picked up the pace and they were soon over Vauxhall Bridge. Westminster became Lambeth and Jonelle felt they had gone deeper into the night, somehow. She also noticed the taxi'd run a few red lights and cut others close. The last time she'd been in a black cab, she'd been travelling to Great Ormond Street Children's Hospital seeking answers for Deen. Back then, the driver had been very chatty and reassuring. This London cabby, apart from asking where in Brixton she wanted to be deposited, focused steadfastly on the road ahead.

*Must you take the corners so fast?* Jonelle kept that thought to herself, rubbed her stomach, and clung to the seatbelt. Her mind flashed back to Friday night, wondering why she was so unlucky with taxi drivers. And men, for that matter!

At last, they pulled up outside Brixton tube station. The £40 charge sent her into shock. Through the half-open window, he told her it was common knowledge that it cost extra to take a black cab across the river into South London – *all them fares I miss out on coming all this way, PLUS I've got to go all that way back empty, see? And it's gone midnight!*

Jonelle felt sick. She opened her purse wide. It was pointless counting the coins under the two fivers nestled inside and creating a scene with Brixton police station yards away, where there were already a host of people hanging about with steaming cups, cameras and big lights.

'Just give me what you got, luv!' the driver said, fidgeting and checking his mirrors and locks.

She emptied the purse into his hands and conjured her sweetest smile. He opened his mouth to speak but shut it again, wound up the window fully and sped away.

She'd have preferred to direct him right up to her door, but vehicles stopping on her road in the dead of night made curtains part. Even she'd been known to peek out to see what other people got up to when shadows ruled, long after bedtime. It held a certain local intrigue and provided juicy tales on laundry day. Jonelle started walking purposefully, head down, praying that neither PC Bailey nor WPC Murphy were out on duty, especially as she was wearing the same clothes that they'd arrested her in. For that matter, the whole world had seen her face and outfit clearly on TV.

At the British Rail bridge, she made a sharp right onto Atlantic Road and swerved around what looked like partygoers straying into her path, avoiding eye contact. With every passing car, Jonelle felt eyes were on her. She quickened her pace, half expecting some observant motorist to honk and yell, 'There she is. There's the child snatcher!'

Jonelle fought back the fear and deliberated over exactly what she was going to do. She pictured the box beneath her bed, the one behind another stuffed with cassettes and assorted vinyl records. The birth certificates she'd come back for were in that small box, in a big brown envelope, hers, Amanita's, Kenyana's and Deen's...and even Tyrone's because he'd insisted that he'd lose the damn thing. There were a few other things in that little box too. Her Barbie doll, a picture of her mum and dad and her baptism certificate tucked inside the little Bible that her godmother had posted to her from Jamaica.

Could she carry the cassettes too? Take it all back to the hotel? Maybe wait until the first train and use the underground? Yes, why not give more people a chance to recognise her? *Jonelle, think!* No. Leave the records and cassettes – maybe only take her faves, the rare ones? *No. You came for the certificates, Jonelle!*

Her thoughts were so forceful, Jonelle looked around to see if she'd been overheard. There was no one left, right or behind.

The documents to a new start for herself and the children. Last night, TK'd said that he knew people and that was how he'd got his driving licence, the one he'd lost and never got replaced.

Yes, she'd just grab the certificates and go…and maybe one cassette…two…three of her rarest grooves, the ones that made her feel alive, strong, proud to be a survivor who can say 'Stuff 'em!' to everyone that ever told her she would fail.

Without looking back, Jonelle quickened her pace and rushed past the Duck & Diva, long shut and emptied of all regulars and irregulars asking questions. She passed Kool Kurls, wondering whether she would miss the wolf whistles and empty propositions.

With her heart pounding in her chest, half running, half walking, Jonelle felt for her key at the entrance to the building. The bloody self-timer landing light didn't come on. Bloody council! She took the stairs two at a time, pausing briefly to almost throw up.

Finally, she approached her front door and noted someone had been using carbolic, probably washing sick off the walls again.

'Jonelle Patrick?'

'Bloody hell!' She jumped back and caught herself on the banister.

'Tyrone?' Jonelle recognised the fancy tone. One too many and he loved everybody; two and he got all posh. 'Nearly gave me a damn heart attack?'

'Best keep your voice down, girl. Normal people're sleepin'.'

Textbook Tyrone.

She felt him watching her trying to open the door.

The key fell.

She bent down feeling about in the dark for little metal teeth.

'You could stop staring and help me out here?'

'Doing fine by yourself.'

She found it, straightened up and lost it.

*Clink!*

Dammit!

She stooped again, following the sound.

'Anybody'd think you been on the booze or something! Give it here.'

Jonelle caught an accent and moved away. 'You're not Tyrone.'

'Didn't say I was. I said keep your voice down, sweetheart… let's you an' me go inside to have a little chat, aight? Let's not disturb the nice neighbours out here.'

'Listen.' Jonelle backed up. 'I got no money. You're wasting your time.'

'Don't want money.' He'd come closer and she felt the darkness thicken. 'Open the door! Go on – it's cold out here in the corridor!'

Passing headlights rolled light across the landing.

He was clean-shaven.

A dresser.

Not a mugger.

Rapist? Jonelle stiffened.

*Jonelle, don't panic.*

'What'd you want with me?' Jonelle said for the benefit of the neighbours who complained whenever she played her music or sneezed or gargled.

His balls were a swift kick away, but her wobbling knees disagreed. Her nose caught a heady mix of something she'd smelled whenever she'd taken Deen into Kool Kurls and… onions? But it was the pub smell that made the hairs on the back of her neck bristle.

'We'll talk in private…use the key or I use your face. Open the *rass-claat* door. Now!'

'No. Not going inside.' Jonelle felt sure conversation was not all he had in mind. 'You got something to say, say it right here!'

The landing window was ajar. They were one floor up. If she could squeeze through, if she could get out and jump, would she break her legs…or her neck?

'I did ask *nicely*,' he grunted.

Fingers clamped around her neck and swung her into the door. He grabbed for the key in her hand. She twisted her body this way and that, trying to get away, struggling. Her key hand wriggled free, came up and raked down the side of his face.

'Aaah! Bitch!' He slapped her hard across her face then pinned her again by the neck.

Perhaps it was instinct, but Jonelle lifted her right leg and felt her bony kneecap smash into the softness of his crotch.

She heard a sharp rush of air, much like a noiseless cough, followed by a sack of something heavy landing on the floor.

Jonelle started to run.

He caught her left ankle.

Jonelle flung her key at the open window, heeled his hand away and started down the corridor.

'One more step – I drop you!'

She'd heard the click in enough movies. Jonelle stopped and turned to face him.

A gun.

He was pointing a gun.

Right at her.

'Go on, try and outrun this!…an' don't think the dark will hide you, neither.'

Terrified, Jonelle forced herself to breathe.

*Oh God! Oh God! Oh God!*

He waved for her to return.

She did, slowly, carefully, wishing she had stayed in the hotel.

'So we won't go inside, then.' He raised himself up on one knee. 'You were at the 'Grilla, right?'

'What?'

'Don't fool with me, bitch,' he said. 'I can go back to Bull and tell him any old thing. Fuck. How'd you like it if I kicked *you* in the balls?'

Jonelle said nothing, trying not to even blink.

He lifted himself painfully, stood in front of her and pressed the nozzle of the gun into her chin. Jonelle kept her head still and he led her to the window. She thought he must have someone down there, outside, waiting.

He looked out and shook his head. 'Fine. No key. No privacy. Talk!'

'W-what?'

'Tell me what you saw on Friday. At 'Grilla.'

'I don't know what you're—'

From nowhere, an angry hand spun her round and slammed her into the window, pressing her against the glass so hard, she expected it to shatter any second and shred her face.

'Look, bitch. I already know your friend Myrna sent you to work her shift, so quit playing. Been waiting two fuckin' days and nights for you. Tell me what you saw in da club! And who you talk to 'bout it! Tell me, right now!'

Jonelle closed one eye, unable to shut the other against the cold, grimy glass as he applied more force to the back of her head with the gun still digging up into her chin. She thought about her girls.

About Deen.

About the doctor, so excited about having answers for her, at last.

*Think! Or you're dead...like Myrna.*

'Okay, I'll talk, I'll talk. Let me go.' Her words dribbled from her squashed lips and ran down the mucky glass. 'I'll tell you what I know.'

'Yes, you will.' He eased back and stepped away. 'Start talkin'.'

She looked about them and so did he.

Nobody. No quick peeks. Not even a curious cat.

'I was at 'Grilla. If I saw puke, I wiped it up. I cleaned shit out the loos and—'

He raised his gun arm level with her head.

'You tell me Myrna suffered for nothin'?'

'It was you? You killed Myrna?'

'It wasn't intentional, but she knew my face, y'see?'

Jonelle tried to stay calm.

'Ho-How could you…she was *good* people!'

'Yeah well, good…bad…all gotta go sometime.' He adjusted something on his gun before aiming it back at her. 'Would you look at that? Had the fucking safety on – *this* is why a man should never drink on the job.'

'Jonie?' Her name floated up the stairwell. 'Jonie, that you up there?'

The gunman moved to look down the stairs. Jonelle acted before she could think and lunged at him.

'Get off me, bitch!' he said on the edge of the step, his free hand grasping for support, his gun hand flapping for balance. Hard as she could, Jonelle kicked the back of his knee.

His foot lost the step.

'Fuck!' he yelled but Jonelle was already running, thinking to break down her door and grab the things she had come to get. No. It was not worth risking a bullet. She legged it past her door to the fire exit, grabbed the handle and hit it with her body weight.

'Christ!' She remembered the man from the Council. *'It's on our fixit list. Top priority. Until then, Miss Patrick, we suggest you and your kids go out the front door for now.'*

Rubbing the pain away, Jonelle looked at the landing window again. Could she fit?

'Jonie!'

'Tyrone!'

'What's going on? That guy down there, he's one of Bull's guys. Style.'

'He's got a gun, Tyrone.'

'He's got a big lump on his head, is what he got, Jonelle. Where're the kids?'

'Tyrone, where're your keys?'

'Keys? You took them from me. Hey, you smell as funky as Style. What's going on between you two? And where're my kids? I got this present for Deen.'

He showed her a metal toy train engine, unwrapped, and even in the low light she saw it'd spent many years unboxed.

'Don't shake your head at me, Jonie. Boot sale bargain – *suh-weet* – no more cassette trains for Deen, aight?'

'No time, Tyrone.' Jonelle stuffed the toy in her pocket and grabbed Tyrone's hand. 'Come on.'

'Jonie, what's up? You? Style?' He scratched his head. 'And I *aks* you to dance for me and *you*—'

'Not now, Tyrone!' She pulled him behind and they descended the stairs.

'But I don't get it, Jonie. You turn down my Gorgon but gone off to 'Grilla. Now you and Style—'

She pressed a hand to his chest. 'Shush! I said not now, Tyrone. We've got to get out of here.'

The words clawed their way from her dry throat. She looked down the stairs expecting to see Style looking up at her. At them. He wasn't. She continued gingerly, leading the way, downwards. The entrance light flicked on to show Style sprawled and motionless at the foot of the stairs, between her and their only way out.

She froze. His eyes were closed. His chest wasn't moving, as far as she could tell. His body lay in an awkward pose as though he'd sat on his legs, raised one arm to allow him to smell his armpit while reaching behind to scratch his arse, only to topple backwards. She couldn't see the gun anywhere.

She looked at the front door and willed a reluctant leg to step over him, her eyes wide for the slightest flinch from the man she straddled. Still expecting to be grabbed, she lifted her other leg over and was quickly at the door.

'I think he's dead, Jonie.' Tyrone was taking a closer look. She saw him jab the man with his foot.

'No, Tyrone, come on!' Jonelle beckoned him frantically towards her. She flung the entrance door open and bolted out towards the communal gate. Tyrone stumbled after her, trying to keep up. 'Faster, Tyrone, we got to get away!'

*Ch-click!* 'Yeah, run bitches. Try and outrun dis!'

They stopped where they stood with Tyrone behind her and Jonelle gripping the cold steel gate.

Jonelle turned. Another minute and they could have swung it open and been halfway to Brixton police station. Her chest felt about to explode.

'Style man, easy!' Tyrone turned. 'Easy with that thing.'

'I know you?' The man limped towards them. A glistening wetness was running down the side of his face and his aim swayed indecisively from her to Tyrone, choosing who should be shot first. 'Don't matter. Get lost. I got business wit' Jonelle Patrick.'

Tyrone edged forward, towards the gun.

'Style? Wait, I know you. What's goin' on?' Tyrone had his hands up, palms towards the gunman. 'Bull even know you're here? Cause 'im and me, wi go way back, seen? Di is my woman, right 'ere.'

Jonelle dared to glance up for curtain-twitchers. Where were those nosey parkers who reported to the Social every time someone spoke to her on the pavement, let alone knocked on her door?

'I *told* you to get lost. Or you want to be some kinda hero? Hol' dis.'

*Blam!*

Tyrone's body jerked and he spun.

'Tyrone!' Jonelle screamed as he fell against her, clinging, toppling them against the gate.

'Run, Jonie,' Tyrone whispered. 'Jonie! Run!' Tyrone's grasp loosened and he grew heavier, slipping from her as her clothes grew wet inside their embrace. Unable to let go, unwilling to let him fall and abandon him there, Jonelle dragged him aside.

'Help us! Somebody! Help! Help!'

From somewhere someone yelled, 'Keep it down or I'm calling the cops, y'hear me!'

'Tyrone, no. No, please! I'm not leaving you…' She lowered him so she could open the gate before her aching arms quit.

'Tell…my kids that…please…please…' The words trickled out on laboured breath, each word less than the last, like a song ending. His eyes closed then popped open to catch hers. 'It's fate, Jonie, you and me.'

Tyrone expelled one more breath before his face settled into an unearthly peace. 'Tyrone… Oh God, no! Tyrone. No!'

'Shouldn't'a get in mi way!' He stood lopsided inside the gate, glaring down at her kneeling with Tyrone on the pavement. Tyrone had called him Style, Bull's man. 'Don't worry. I always hit the heart, quick and clean… Hell, I hate it when bystanders get in my way. Now I have to use two bullets instead of one. Shit! Now stop fuckin' around. Tell me why you was really in Bull's place las' Friday? You spyin' for di Babylon or was you working for dis guy? He got anything to do with trying to take Bull down?'

'You killed him!' Jonelle said through gritted teeth.

'Shouldn't a push me down 'em stairs, bitch. Pain makes a man cranky and impatient. Puts his aim right off, know what I mean? Why was you nosing about at 'Grilla?'

'I was only helping a friend, right.' Jonelle looked at the gun through tears flowing freely down her cheeks and her nose was blocked up. 'Can I blow my nose?'

'Don't care. Talk.'

'My friend, Myrna…she was really sick…and she asked me…' Jonelle felt for a tissue and realised she didn't have one, but her fingers found the gift Tyrone had bought for Deen. She lowered her voice. '…to cover for her, and work for Mr M—'

'Speak up, bitch.' He stepped closer.

Jonelle whipped out the toy train, swung it sharply upwards to ram it home.

'J-e-e-e-e-sus!' He grabbed his groin with both hands, dropping the weapon.

'Not again.' He landed, knees first onto the paving stones.

Jonelle swung the gate open and got to the threshold when he dived for her, grabbing her foot with one hand.

'Get off me.' Jonelle pulled on the gate posts but only managed to drag him forward. She reached for the gate and yanked it, hard, into him.

'Fuckinghell, that hurt!' He let go and lay rubbing his temple.

Jonelle stood over him, willing herself to start running but looking over at Tyrone lying motionless.

'You. Shot. Tyrone. You-fucking-shot-Tyrone.' She swung the metallic gate.

Jonelle closed her eyes tight but kept on swinging.

Something squished.

Something cracked.

Something splashed her.

You.

Shot.

Tyrone.

She felt weary.

Tired.

So sick and so tired.

From somewhere far inside her head, she heard a sound. A vehicle.

'Stop! Stop!'

With her eyes still firmly closed, Jonelle kept swinging and the gate wailed a rusty tune that ended with a thud before she brought it back to swing it again.

If she never opened her eyes, it meant none of this would have happened. Tyrone wouldn't be lying dead. No. He wouldn't. Not the father of her three children, with all he ever was, or all he could ever become, draining from a hole in his chest and soaking the pavement where he lay. Clinging to images of a weedy youth on a bus, embarrassing her, telling her she was the cutest thing and pestering, insisting it was fate that they'd caught the same bus each day.

Jonelle felt the metal being peeled from her grip, finger by finger. Her arms ached.

The world started spinning under her feet and strong hands held her. 'Stop now. It's over. It's all over. That's it. That's it. Come with us.'

# CHAPTER 39

Their frantic torch beams picked a brambly uphill path, darting left and dodging right to finally settle in a pool of light at her feet as they huddled about her, rooted, looking lost.

'I said go…go!' She pointed firmly beyond the trees and raised her voice above a whisper. 'Think of the babies.'

Disoriented eyes looked away from the nurse to the shadowy clutch of trees about them.

Maxwell was such a sweetie for getting her a job with babies. Well, teaching young girls how to care for them. Now they knew how to look smart in their uniforms and keep their little darlings clean and fed and stop them from crying. She'd done the best job, even if she thought so herself. She'd also taught them English, well, stock phrases she'd been given for them to memorise. Yes, she'd trained them well, but it hadn't been too long before she'd figured they'd be redeployed beyond nanny duties and then what would become of their little darlings.

'Listen carefully!' She pointed at her own ear and adapted one of the phrases, hoping they'd understand. 'There is no more I can do for you.'

They looked puzzled. She could see them remembering the many times they'd repeated for her: *Is there any more I can do for you. Anything at all.*

One of them said something in Chinese, which may as well have been Russian, but then the girl stepped forward from the huddle. 'Go? Where?'

The nurse pointed to the gap in the trees at the road beyond. But still they stood there, looking from one to the other. She looked prayerfully towards where the sky was glowing yellow, red and orange as smoke billowed from the yard below.

She addressed their ambassador. 'Explain to them they can't stay here. To go! Find a policeman...tell the police...tell them...whatever you want. They'll help you. There is no more I can do. Understand?'

'They...we...we am scared.'

Broken English or not, she decided, terror sounded the same in any language.

'I know, love. I know.' The nurse grasped the uniformed shoulder of the bravest girl, turned her and gently prodded her in the direction of the road. 'But don't stop, keep going... people will understand. Look after yourselves. Survive!'

Tearful, clutching their little bundles, they started walking, crunching twigs and dry leaves towards the road. The nurse watched them break away, each following the other, stumbling over fallen branches and uneven ground towards the suburban road.

Hot smoke curled into the skies above. In truth, she'd not expected such a large explosion from her little diversion, courtesy of Prunes. Exactly as he had said, he'd stocked everything in that yard, somewhere. The first tarpaulin gave her the wire-cutters and garden shears. She'd lifted another two tarpaulins to find barrels, sulphur wicks and enough rope to run around the yard and terminate at the butane cylinder she'd left gently hissing. Her brief stint in the Territorial Army had not included explosives, so her timing calculation had been as crude as the fuse she'd devised. To be honest, she'd thought the wick might have been spotted as it snaked towards its target. Anyway, thanks to Prunes' enterprise and Lady Luck, she'd got all attention away from their escape.

Through a gap in the leaves and branches she watched them, the most she'd ever helped run away from Bull. They were also the only escapees who could identify her as their secret saviour. She prayed they'd never end up back in Bull's clutches, especially after Maxwell's revelations about him and Style in Brixton. She knew God would have some trouble keeping her safe.

Distant sirens from police and emergency vehicles approached and filled the area. She gently stroked the child's curly head of hair. A tear came to her eye as she looked down at the widest little yawn, his young eyes pinched shut. Still groggy from the overdose of anaesthetic those fools had given him, he could barely stand. She'd carried him up the hill but now he needed to walk to help flush his system.

'Where are we, Mummy?'

'Don't talk, honey. Hush now.'

'Carry me...' he said, making her heart race.

*No, no, no, stop! She must resist...resist...she must resist that tiny egg of a thought hatching into that monster she didn't want to become again.*

Tugging the hem of her white tunic, weakly. 'Mummy, please carry me.'

'Oh, b-baby...you're too heavy to carry, sw-sweetheart.' She'd meant to say, 'I'm not your mum.' She'd felt the shape of the words filling her mouth and tasted their sincerity on her tongue, so why hadn't she...?

'But my knees are hurtie again. My elbones too!' He swayed, eyes half shut, and literally falling asleep against her. 'And I'm c-c-cold, Mummy, and so-o-o tired!'

'No, Deen, d-darling. We can't stop here.' She caught him, steadied him, then quickly slipped off her cardigan, stooped and wrapped his shivering body before drawing him closer, sharing her warmth. His head flopped on her shoulder. It felt good...too damn good!

'Are we going to Aunty Candice, Mummy?'

Rummaging for her medication single-handedly, she slowed, then stopped looking altogether, giving herself a second to enjoy the maternal stirring. In a little while, she'd look again for her pills and they'd help her regain equilibrium, remind her who she was and suppress the urges that had got her into trouble and terminated a career in the NHS.

Now, where were her meds? She thought back to when she'd run the wick along the chain-link fence while Prunes'd gone to the front gate. Then she'd cut an L-shape in the fence so it would appear intact and could be peeled back later. Then she'd tripped the fuse to plunge the yard into darkness and grabbed her meds before leading all the 'packages' through the fence. *Oh shit!* She'd set down the damn meds when she'd lit the fuse.

'Are we, Mummy? Are we going to Aunty Candi…? You smell like her.' He brightened up a little, but then his excitement flickered and his voice trailed away along with the strength in his knees. She caught him and held him close.

'No, Deen. Mummy's not going to Aunty Candice.' She clasped him to her bosom. 'Mummy's staying right here!'


Jonelle felt outside of her own body. Myrna was in her ear, yapping about noises coming from her dentist's chair. 'It was the leather, Jonie, yeah? But he never believed me? Go on, Jonie, you try sayin' "fart" with your mouth wide open! Try it!' Ah, that Myrna, she'd made them all try it and everyone pissed themselves so the launderette got noisier than Brixton market on a Saturday morning, until overpowering traffic noise made the place rattle and lurch about and Tyrone was suddenly standing in the doorway, gyrating, grinning, beckoning: 'Come, dance for me, you lot. Gorgon's the best and 'Grilla can have the rest.'

'What are you doing here?' she yelled, but her words gargled about in her throat and Tyrone only puffed his chest out more, ignoring her words.

'I knew it, Tyrone!' she groaned, above revving noises, 'you asked everyone to be your dancer before me?'

She moved to slap him, but her arms refused to budge – the launderette shook and she found herself instantly in Myrna's front room, glugging Asti with her girlies, taking turns to mimic their men's cum faces.

'Do Tyrone – go on, Jonie-girl. Do Tyrone.' The goading stopped when she screwed up her face, let her eyes roll back into her head as she jerked about as if she'd sat bare-arsed on an electric chair while moaning 'money, money, money'.

Wait! Who's watching the kids?

The thought shot through her as King's College Hospital appeared opposite Kool Kurls where men, young boys, and Tyrone were piled up in the doorway, ogling a woman in a long leather skirt as she walked on by. Her face was as familiar as her own, but Jonelle couldn't quite place it.

'Tyrone, who's watching the kids!'

He just kept watching that woman, ignoring her.

The smell of leather from his jacket grew stronger, as did the cigar smoke in the air around him. Cigar and... rum.

'Tyrone!' At her touch, he spun violently and fell into a basket of whites in the launderette. All the washers and driers were silent. Unable to tell whether she was sitting or standing, Jonelle only felt restricted, looking down on a dot, a full stop, on a white shirt. The red blot spread slowly outwards, turning all her whites red until Tyrone was suddenly standing in the clean basket, near enough to touch and yet beyond her reach, reeking of sweaty leather and dust and cigarette butts, eyes fluttering, his lips still moving but other voices coming out.

'You move di car round to the back yet?'

'Yea, Chief.'

'Wipe all dat blood 'n' shit off too?'

'Yea, Chief.'

'Bring a bucket of ice water in here – can't wait no longer for dis bitch to wake up.'

'Yea, Chief.'

Jonelle's eyes felt pasted down, why couldn't she open them? Where was she? Her fingers tingled behind her. She was lying on them and she couldn't free them. She couldn't move her legs either and her lips felt taped together.

Whiffs of cheap cologne filled the air about her.

'An', Jinxie, go pick up dem papers from that place wot we went to in the East End. And don't take no shit. Use my name. Give that old woman da cigars. Tell 'em their friend Prunes'll settle up. If they give you shit, leave 'em hurting, but make sure yu don't leave wit'out dem papers, y'feel me?'

'Yea, Chief.'

'An', Clint, you go wid him.'

'Yes boss!'

'An' where'd di bloody van get to? Find it and tell di boys to get their arses back here right now. No stopping. And no going back to Prunes' for no reason, y'hear? I need every jack man back here so we can go pay Silk a special little visit.'

'Yea, Chief.'

'Remember, straight back here, got dat?'

'Yeah, mi get it. Mi get it!'

'I t'ink di girl's awake, boss.'

'Did I ask you anything, Clint?'

'No, bossman, I was jus—'

'Too many fucking chiefs. Not enough people doing what's expected of 'em is what's wrong around here…'

'Sorry, Chief. Sorry.'

'Still want dat bucket of ice water, Chief?'

'What for, she's awake, ain't she? I'd get movin' now.'

Jonelle didn't recognise the voices nor the rhythm of the steps hurrying away.

'Wait.'

The steps stopped.

'Bring me back some kerosene, lots of it, understan'? What you waiting for? Christmas?'

A rough yank and her eyes nearly went with the tape.

She blinked to focus. A wetness rolled down to her ears. An upside-down face blotted out the ceiling. She saw fire-and-brimstone in his stare as his fingernails dug into her cheek and ripped away her sticky gag.

Jonelle looked around, her face stinging. 'Who…where am I?'

His meaty hands balled up the gaffer tape.

'Our survey said UH-ERR!' He mimicked the *Family Fortunes* game-show host and tossed the ball away. 'In Bull Manners' house, bitch, I ask, you answer. We clear?'

*'Jonelle, Bull Manners is a nasty piece of work – he don't take no shit…'* She stopped wriggling her wrists and twisting her ankles against their sticky bonds and stayed perfectly still. Shaking his head, he gently stroked wisps of hair off her face. 'All right, here's a good tip. I hate repeating my damn self. So, you ready to answer a few questions?'

'M-May I use the l-loo first…p-please?'

It came from nowhere, a sledgehammer that sent her face reeling to one side and left her brain rattling about inside her skull.

'Now then, who's asking the questions?'

'Y-Y-You!' Jonelle fought the urge to cry and to wet herself. Her lips stung and a metallic taste filled her mouth.

'Tell me your name?' he said calmly.

'J-J-Jo—'

'Fine, take a moment! Clear your head.'

She did as she was told.

'Name?' he asked seconds later.

'J-Jonelle.' She swallowed to keep from choking.

'J-Jonelle what?' he fired back.

'P-P-Patrick,' she said quickly as she could, 'Jonelle Patrick.'

'Now then, Jonelle Patrick, why were you in my place of business on Friday night? Who sent you? What the fuck did you come here for? Who're you working with?'

'Last F-Friday?' Brain fog was making it hard to think.

Wallop!

She felt a sharp wrench in her neck and suspected her left ear was gone.

'You like pain, I think,' he said lifting her easily by her armpits and carrying her across to the room. She recognised the dance floor. On Friday, she'd been mopping up sick right there. Now, without the latest Dub Step for lovers of good music, dance, and semi-clad clubbers rubbing up and copping-a-feel, 'Grilla was looking more like her grave.

Without warning, he pulled his hands away. She crashed to the floor, banging the back of her head, crushing bound hands between the base of her spine and the floor.

'As we're here, how about some music, eh?'

Concussed, Jonelle rolled to one side and wrestled weakly against her bonds.

'Don't waste your strength, Jonelle Patrick. I was a good Boy Scout an' I'm always prepared.' He reached into his pocket and twiddled a flick knife above her, knelt and opened it.

She flinched, pulling back into the floor.

'Easy now,' he said, 'wouldn't want to nick you. I shave with this, y'know.'

Jonelle's entire body throbbed with pain and both cheeks burned. The tip of the knife made a sharp point by her left ear. She felt its movement down her face to the corner of her lip.

'No, don't. Please, I'll answer any-anything I can. Just ask me. Please.'

'Now where's the fun in that? Besides, I need to know you're not playin' fool fi ketch wise, know-what-ah-mean?'

'Please...please...' She turned her head, shrinking away from the blade.

'Ever heard of the Chelsea grin?'

Jonelle's thoughts ran back to the night before in a luxurious London hotel and wished she could go back there; better still, back to when Myrna knocked on her door so she could just say no... Bull looked annoyed. She swiftly recalled the question.

'Chelsea smile? No!' Jonelle shook her throbbing head carefully. 'Wasn't a-a-asking, j-just saying... I-I don't know no Ch-Chelsea smile.'

'Said grin, not smile! There's a difference,' he said. 'I cut your pretty mouth here and there...'

The knife jabbed one corner of her lips, traced the curve of her bottom lip and jabbed into the other corner.

'Then I bash your face in to get those cheeks all puffy so they swell up into one big happy face. The sick fuck who came up with that, eh?' he said, twirling the point of the knife into her cheek.

'Please...' Jonelle pleaded.

He moved the knife down, out of sight, below her neck.

'Now your Colombian Neck Tie, Jonelle Patrick, is not for the squeamish. One little cut, here...'

Jonelle felt a cold touch under her chin.

'...then I yank you tongue through and let it dangle. Let's see!'

He forced her mouth open.

'Bite me and you'll be digesting every one of 'em teeth... Now show me your tongue.'

She obeyed.

'Pretty by the way – you need a mint... As I was sayin', the trick with the Colombian is getting the damn cut just right, get me? Still, we Jamaicans ain't into all that creative shit, we just get the job done. Now, hold still.'

Jonelle froze and felt him grasp the hem of her top and make an upward movement, from her belly button towards her chin. Her top flopped open in two pieces.

'Oops!' he said, dabbing her chin with a severed piece of her top. 'Never mind, I nick m'self almost every morning.'

With one arm, he hoisted her by her waistband and dangled her off the floor. Her head banged the floor and her heels dragged.

'P-Please, stop… Where're you taking me?'

His free hand tossed the knife in the air, blade up, caught it as it fell, blade down and arced it towards her belly button.

She sucked her tummy in and looked away. She felt her waistband go slack as she hit the floor a second time, like a rag doll.

'Hmm, must sharpen this up.' He regarded the blade and continued cutting away her clothing.

'Please…no!'

'Keep distracting the man with the sharp knife.'

She stayed still. He plucked her clothes away, slicing away all resistance until she lay before him in her bra and pants. She felt the flat of the knife against her stretch marks.

'Mmm, not bad for a woman with kids…how many?'

Unsure whether to answer, she nodded nervously. 'Th-Three.'

'Mmm-huh,' he grunted. 'Work out?'

*I ask, you answer. Clear?*

'I-I do run…sometimes…'

'You're thirsty work…'

She rolled her head to follow him with her eyes over to the makeshift bar and the planks on breeze blocks beyond the counter.

'What will you have…vodka, gin…hmmm.' He scanned the sparse collection of bottles. 'Thought you might be a top-shelf sort of girl but now I know about you and Ty…and seeing how you went all prime evil on Style's head… Tut-tut-tut, so much aggression! So, it's Appleton for me…' He reached up for a bottle and then lowered his eyes to the bottom shelves. '…and Bacardi for you.'

He regarded a couple of glasses, grimaced and cast them over his shoulder. 'Y'know, Style took a lot of pride in his looks! Too much, if you ask me. But he was my best shooter and you really messed him up bad…do we need chasers?'

Jonelle hesitated, feeling sick in her stomach. He was coming back. In one hand, he bore both bottles by the neck.

'No chasers it is. Chasers're for pussies. ' He twisted off each cap and tossed them. 'Now. Where was I? Yeah, Style. He could shoot a bee's balls from a hundred yards. Do bees even have balls?'

'I-I-I don't thi-think so!' Jonelle was barely able to hear her own voice.

'So how could a scrawny thing like you take Style out? Who are you working for? Have a drink to loosen that tongue…'

Confused what to say, Jonelle racked her brain as he sat her up, yanked her head back by her hair and started pouring Bacardi down her throat.

'Cheers!'

Coughing and gurgling back alcohol and the taste of blood, Jonelle felt the fluid run into her nostrils, flow down her neck and chest, wetting her bra.

'So, you prefer to spit, not swallow, eh?…' One rough hand clamped over her face, crushing her nose shut. She gasped wide and deep, taking in air and the next mouthful of rum. He held her mouth shut.

'Relax. Open your throat…wide.'

Her body convulsed violently and she writhed against his assault. Convinced she was going to die, just like that – as simple as falling asleep, Jonelle closed her eyes against the neat rum fumes. Her throat burned and she retched.

'Puke it up, you suck it up every drop. Feel me?'

Jonelle nodded repeatedly and watched him take a swig of Appleton.

'Ah!' He held the bottle away, reading the label. 'That just takes the edge right off. Feeling a bit tense after the day and night I've had. Fuck, it's Monday morning, right? Let's have some music to lift our spirits. Stay right there till I get back.'

Jonelle nodded.

'Good.'

He was gone but Jonelle felt no safer. In vain, she tugged and twisted; trying to free her wrists.

Oh, Christ, these people murdered Myrna.

Jonelle vomited into her mouth. She shuffled her body around, in case there was somewhere she could discreetly spit it out.

Someone was on a sofa across the room, near the exit, just sitting there...looking directly at her. Why? There was a second person, who seemed to be taking great interest in his lap. Reading? Asleep? Who could be sleeping through the ordeal she was facing?

'Ty?' she whispered to herself.

'I only got this old cassette on me. Beggars can't be choosers, eh?' He climbed up into the DJ box. 'So many buttons! Sh-i-i-i-t!'

She glanced again at the sofa.

'Yes, they are who you think they are. Well...what's left of Style after you went all loony toons...'

Jonelle swallowed hard.

'That's why you're tied up so tight – more for your safety, know-what-I'm-sayin'? No scrawny little pussy gonna ever whip this big black arse! I ain't Style – seen?'

Had he just asked a question? Jonelle cringed away, blinking, avoiding his glare as he approached. Her legs started twitching involuntarily.

'What's Ty to you, Jonelle Patrick?'

'Ty?' Jonelle mumbled, checking, buying time and quickly realising she could probably not afford it.

He tilted his head the way thick-necked men did in films to prime themselves for action. Crick-crack!

'Did you mean Tyrone?' she asked quickly.

He towered over her.

Jonelle's words spilled everywhere, 'You said Ty. Didn't realise you meant— Anyway, you meant Tyrone, right? Yes,

yes, you did. Tyrone, he's – well, he's my kids' dad. He's wanted me to dance for him – in his new club – I think he called it the Gorgon, something like that – he only comes by to pester me some more about dancing for him, but he claims he wants to see his kids, but I know that—'

'Look a dat. First Miss Tight-Lips, now Miss Motor-mouth!… You say Ty's got kids?'

She nodded furiously. 'Yes, three. Three kids.'

'That womaniser's got kids? Fuck me – think you know a person, eh?'

She swallowed. Bad timing.

'Ever seen one o' these?'

Unable to speak, Jonelle shook her head for all she was worth.

'I s'pose not. Some call it a knuckleduster.' He shrugged. 'I call it my Persuader. Wear 'em when I want people to know they mustn't fool wi' me, yeah?'

Jonelle nodded furiously, praying it was enough.

'You need some Persuader, don't you, Jonelle Patrick?'

'No!' she breathed. Tried to.

'Ty's three kids, what're their names?'

'Amanita,' she gasped, breathing around the pain. 'K-Kenyana?'

'What? Who's idea was that?'

'Ty-Tyrone's. He named our first child too.'

'Amanita, eh? A Man Eater,' he chuckled. 'Lucky the Social ain't all over his arse… By the way, Jonelle Patrick, I only counted two.'

He raised the Persuader.

'Dee-een!' Jonelle called out, turned her face away. Eyes shut.

'Good, if you want to see them kids again…what was you really doin' around 'ere on Friday?'

'Friday? Yes, Friday. I told you the truth… M-Myrna. Sh-She asked me to cover her shift. I swear! She was sick.'

'You left your kids!' He stamped the ground, ready, set, about to charge at her. 'You abandoned those three kids?'

'Y-yes? Uhm, no. No. No. A friend was looking after them. I trust her with my kids. Candice treats them like they're her own…they r-really like her.'

'I don't care!' he barked, raising his Persuader above her head. 'A mother should never leave her kids. What happens when they need you and you're never fucking there, eh? Did you ever think 'bout that? Did you? Did you?'

He looked unhinged with rage. Jonelle scrabbled for something to say, anything, urgently. 'Presents! I-I-I was doing it to buy birthday presents and they were perfectly safe. Th-They were safe!'

She braced herself, unable to look.

'Maybe your kids won't miss you then.'

He held her head like a grapefruit and made her face him. Dizzy and confused, she watched him put away the Persuader and position his knife between her eyes, touching the tip and tracing a line, following the curve of her nose.

'Please.'

He ignored her plea. She felt the blade moving across her lips and down so that if it went any deeper, it would bisect her face and neck and chest. Down it went. Jonelle sucked in her stomach. Tiny touches played around her navel and the tops of her exposed thighs, dancing across her skin.

'Please…d-don't…I a-a-answered your qu-questions.' Jonelle felt too terrified to breathe let alone move.

'Relax, it's just the tip.' He stepped away, took a cheek-bulging swig from the Appleton bottle, and then blew a spray of neat rum all over her.

Jonelle's skin burst into life with a sting that traced the line he'd made from her face to her thighs.

'Rum and cuts, bites like a bitch, but it's a tasty little starter!'

*Jonelle…think…think fast or you're going to die!*

'Say, I believe your shit, why were you in the cupboard when we caught you? And I'd think very carefully before you lie to me, woman.'

'It was Maxwell, he sent me to find a mop!'

He rested the knife along her hip.

'Easy now, it's just the tip...' He held the weapon still with one hand and rested the other gently on the handle, easing it down and down so she felt it ping her knicker elastic, pierce deeper into her until it stopped against her left hip bone.

'Jesus Christ!' A searing pain lanced through her. Tears flowed freely as Jonelle felt her body go numb with shock and a caged scream filled her head.

'Taking the Lord's name in vain?' He turned the hilt and she felt the blade dig deeper, cutting.

'I'm sorry... I'm sorry... I sorry!'

'Look at that. Bet you've never been penetrated like this before?'

Isaac Hayes blasted from the speaker boxes.

She jumped.

Hayes' beguiling voice echoed around her. Yes, who would ever take risks for her? Crazy as it was, she willed Shaft to burst into the room from the giant speaker.

'Shit! Must'a picked the wrong dial...all them fuckin' complicated DJ-ing shit,' he shouted over the music at her. 'You stay here, Jonelle Patrick. I'll be right back!'

Jonelle's head began to swim from the cocktail of pain and rum and terror. Nothing made any sense and the room was starting to spin. She'd only wanted to help a friend.

Her head flopped to one side, making her face the sofa by the exit.

Christ, our kids could lose both parents – become orphans. No, I've got to survive for them. I will survive.

Isaac Hayes lowered his voice: *He's a complicated man... But no one understands him but his woman...*

She heard him coming back.

'Much better, eh? You know, Ty was into the commercial stuff... Oh yes! Fac', this is his mixtape! Was. Fool made it for my birthday, Christmas or some shit like that…back when we was tight. We was partners back in da day, and night. But you knew that already, right, yeah?'

'Partners? You and Tyrone?' Jonelle stopped herself too late. 'I'm sorry, I didn't mean to ask a—'

'Cool, cool…these things happen.' Bull grabbed the knife and gently added pressure, easing it deeper into her. Then he twisted it, just a little bit.

The crunching reminded her of de-boning chicken for Sunday dinner. An electrified sensation burned out from her injured hip into her brain.

Jonelle giggled, gently at first, like she'd remembered a funny story and was embarrassed to say it out loud. It made no sense, but there it was. She couldn't stop.

'You found that ticklish, did you?'

Bull punched down on her thigh, next to the knife. The jolt made her wince and cured her laughing fit.

'Did that hurt?' His words dripped with concern. A meaty hand roughly grabbed her bare right foot and showed her a pair of pliers, waving it back and forth so it looked like a metal bird with a long steel beak flying towards her.

Jonelle reminded herself of his 'no questions' rule, but doing whatever he said wasn't helping.

'Why'd you g-get so mad about me l-l-leaving the kids?' The voice was hers, the mouth too. So was the sense of defiance swelling inside her. 'Your momma know where you are, what you're up to, Mr Bull?'

He looked taken aback for a moment.

'Brave all of a sudden, are we?'

Jonelle's body dangled as he hefted her right foot towards the serrated yawn of the pliers. Her little toe curled pointlessly inside its jaws. Without another word, he squeezed the pliers shut and Jonelle watched her little toe kink off at a wrong angle.

'See, I knew you liked pain. Knew it. But, now you bore me... Why were you at 'Grilla?' He still held her foot high. Blood and pain pooled in her head and her vision blurred in and out of focus. Her damaged foot throbbed. 'Was it Django? Was he in with Tyrone? They send you to fuckin' spy in my business, innit? That double-crossing bastard Django put y'all up to trying to take Bull down – or was it, Silk?'

'Django? Silk? I don't know what—'

'Or that no-name bastard with his fuckin' briefcase?' He rammed her middle toe into the cold, metallic gape of the pliers. 'Not givin' any o' them up, then?… Fine!' He closed the pliers.

The pain that shot through her was beyond giving birth.

'Look, you got a whole other foot and ten fingers to laugh your way through…and then, don't you worry, I got lots more fun ideas for you, bitch. Now, was you working for Django or some other fucker?'

'Django who?' Jonelle screamed at him. 'I-I don't know no Django. Why don't you ask him?'

His forearms bulged in his fancy suit twice more and now only her big toe awaited its turn. He flung her foot to the floor. Jonelle felt a sharp jolt from her hip where the knife remained.

'Was it Silk what sent you?' He yanked her left foot up off the floor and rammed its big toe into place, flexing in readiness. 'Talk to me, was it the bastard Silk?'

Jonelle distracted herself from the hip pain by picturing herself trying to pull tights on over her mangled right foot.

'What? This just one big fat joke to you, bitch?' he growled angrily, casting her foot to the floor and placing her nose in the pliers instead. 'Let's see what you do when—'

SCREEEEE…! Tyres squealed to a stop outside.

'What the fuck!' He walked towards the door. 'I'll be right back… We can have ourselves a good old-fashioned gang bang now my boys're back. You'll find that fuckin' hilarious.'

A metallic creak ended with a slam as Michael Jackson poured 'Smooth Criminal' across the dance floor. Deep bass boomed from the massive bins, vibrating through the floor into the knife in her hip, but it was seeing Tyrone posed on the sofa that brought her more tears. No more would they debate about commercial versus non-commercial music and about blacksploitation and about his Gorgon ambitions.

'Boss! Boss!'

It was coming from the other side of the entrance to the dance floor, about where the bouncer would have stood on 'Grilla night, she thought.

'Jinxie! Cool it!'

Jonelle felt the tape growing slippery on her damp wrist. If only she could wet it more, maybe she could slip right out of it. Having an idea, she looked around the room, but he'd left the rum bottles well out of her reach. Pausing briefly at Tyrone's unseeing eyes, she started to pee. Mid-flow, she lay back into the warm fluid and used it to wet it more.

Christ, she was free!

Her heart raced. She ripped the tape from her ankles, ignoring the pain in her hip and her toes. She listened hard, terrified of what might happen if Bull came back right then. She could just separate raised voices from amplified music.

'What you talkin' 'bout – didn't get them?'

Now, Jonelle, move now.

'Bull, we got to the place. It was shut. Big sign out on the door.'

'Sign? Sign said fucking "Closed" when we was there, idiot!'

'It said shut for business, boss! We pushed the door. It stayed shut!'

'What the fuck!'

*Move your arse, Jonelle!*

'You went to the wrong fuckin' place, didn'tchya?' Bull's bellow drowned the music and she heard strangled objections, conjuring images of his massive hands around someone's throat. She looked down at the knife.

Candice had told her about a big vein in the hip, the same one that caused people to bleed out if it got punctured in road crashes or bad falls, so if an object was stuck in it... Jonelle decided the knife was better in than out...until it was removed with proper help.

She held the knife handle and tried to stand. Gritting her teeth against the effort of the manoeuvre, she tightened her stomach muscles, putting all her strength into not adding any pressure. Letting go of the knife for a second, she quickly tied a double knot in her knicker elastic and almost toppled. Sucking in air and steeling herself, Jonelle waited a few seconds, listening, before trying to step-hop with one good foot and four broken toes.

'Oh fuck!'

Unbalanced, Jonelle stumbled from good foot to bad until she slumped against the sofa knocking the Appleton bottle. She watched it twirl and spin before toppling and scooting across the floor.

'Y'hear something, boss?' came from the door.

'Jinxie, all I hear is you sayin' that you lot ain't worth my investment!' Bull bellowed.

'Listen me! Boss, wait! Me and Clint...all we find was Triple!'

'Triple?'

Jonelle levered herself up using the back of the sofa, avoiding the mess of flesh and bone that was once a face. Tyrone looked as though he was listening to MJ singing, his sightless stare fixed on the dance floor. She half expected that, at any second, he'd turn his head and say something inappropriate.

Then he farted.

Jonelle grabbed her nose in shock and alarm that, even in death, Tyrone could foul the air. The eye-watering stench brought a clear memory of where she'd seen someone hiding in the club.

Bracing against the pain, trying not to breathe too deeply, she took one last tearful look at Tyrone and pushed away from the sofa. Between her left foot and the bony heel of her right, Jonelle hobbled towards the exit to the foyer. She paused at the bar and leant on a stool. The voices grew clearer. Jonelle wondered if they could hear her heart pounding out of her chest, grateful for the distraction of the beat of the music.

*She ran underneath the table... He could see she was unable... So she ran into the bedroom... She was struck down, it was her doom...*

'Aks Clint then Boss... Clint! Clint! Come in here!'

A door opened somewhere.

'Boss, we ring di bell. Nuthin'. Wi look in di glass. Nuthin'. But it was di right place, so wi go down di alley round di back. Dat's where wi fin' Triple. Im was tie' up wi' di garbage. Out back!'

'Yea', boss, out back!'

'So, you two losers're saying I send you for crucial paperwork an' you bring back Triple...and no documents?'

'Erm, yeah, boss!'

'Boss, yeah. Jinxie, 'im was in charge!'

'I don't see Triple?'

'Wi left him in da car trunk, boss.'

'Right. Show me.'

A door squealed open and banged shut with a steely clang. The voices were gone.

# CHAPTER 40

Jonelle edged into the foyer, her left thigh and calves screaming blue murder. A knife lodged in her hip and a broken right foot was not going to stop her getting back to her kids. She scraped the pain from her mind.

She spotted the 'Toylits' sign over the door ahead, leading to the 'Ladys' and 'Gents', both with windows that barely allowed air to escape.

Dead end.

She looked left. The coat check area seemed much bigger now with its empty coat rails. She almost expected to see Maxwell there, scowling, hovering over his shoebox of 'tipps'. Her gaze stopped on the broom in the corner, feet away from the door she knew led to the cleaning cupboard and the emergency exit.

Thank you, Jesus!

Her right knee buckled. She grabbed the door to save herself but only managed to bash the knife in deeper. She covered her mouth and trapped her scream. If only she could sit, right here on this mucky floor, just for a few minutes to close her eyes and rest awhile. Was that too much to ask? Jonelle looked back at the entrance door. Bull or his boys could burst in any time and see her.

A shock of pain shot from her hip and she stumbled onto her left foot. Alert with agony and determination, she propped herself against the nearby wall and used it to inch along until she got to grabbing distance of the broom, stretched for it, turned it brush-end up to use it as a makeshift crutch.

The bristles dug into her armpits and the broomstick felt like it would bend and break each time she put weight on it. She looked around for a cloth, anything, to wrap the bristles.

Nothing!

With her face awash with sweat and tears, Jonelle remembered her Lamaze lessons and started taking long, slow breaths. It wasn't working.

The shouting outside stopped.

Jonelle stared at the main entrance door, unaware she was holding her breath.

Her pain eased, but her lungs begged for air as she came around and started towards the door that had led to the world of trouble she was in. For all she knew, it was now locked. She pushed.

It creaked too loudly.

She froze, looked, listened.

She felt something crawling down her thigh, but this was no time for jumping and screaming. The door was open just enough for her to squeeze through. Angling her body to let the knife into the gap, Jonelle inched through and was almost out when her knicker elastic got caught on the latch. Blood was running down her leg.

Shit!

Steeling herself, she eased the material free and kept going. She saw the emergency exit.

The hill of bin bags remained, but looked higher and shrouded with maggots that made the whole thing seem alive. A cloud of flies rose, disturbed by the rush of fresh air when she eased the door shut.

Slam!

'Triple, when did I ever pay you to think? When?'

From the foyer, Bull's voice vibrated the walls – all that now stood between him and her. She glanced desperately towards the mop cupboard and remembered the wall sliding away.

'And where's the fucking kerosene?'

Jonelle leant on the broom and half hobbled as fast as she could to the cupboard, opened it and waved away a net of cobwebs. She lost her balance. Protecting her side on her way down, she crashed into the pails and mops and cleaning fluids.

It was déjà vu.

*Get up, Jonelle. Now.*

It felt too hard, too much of a struggle, but there were three reasons she had to keep going. She raised herself to her knees and ran her hand against the wall.

*Please be there.*

She heard a loud bang and heavy heels approaching.

*Please be there.*

'The blood's leadin' dis way... Oi, Clint, tell di boss mi find 'er. Him in di dance hall wid Triple! Y'hear me, Clint?'

She thought she felt the lever and pulled. Yes. The cupboard wall slid away but it stopped, barely wide enough for her head to get through.

The cupboard door flew wide.

'Now look at dat!' Grinning, the man half looked away and shouted behind him, 'She over 'ere, Clint. She's in 'ere... Hide 'n' seek is over and you's "it", gyal!'

He looked back down at her, his gaze slithering around her bra size before resting on her soaking wet knickers, tied at the waist.

'Please, please,' she pleaded, keeping a hand over the knife in her side. She used her free hand to feel around for an object, anything to defend herself with. 'Please tell him you didn't find me!'

'T'ink I got a death wish, sista!'

'You can say...say I vanished...or something.'

He stepped back. 'Get out. Let's go!'

'I'm hurt...bad,' Jonelle said breathily, trying to make 'hurt' and 'bad' sound 'helpless' and 'suggestive'.

'Is dat 'ow you jim-screeched Style? Dat won't work 'pon mi! Out!'

'No no no. Look!' she said softly. Fighting pain, she heaved her breasts high, thrust her hips forward and rubbed one bare thigh against the other. Behind her back, her hand rested on a plastic bottle. Practised, like any mother, at doing things one-handed, she unscrewed the cap. 'My foot's broken. At least please help me up...?'

He moved towards her, hesitated, and offered a confident hand. With him in range, Jonelle brought her hand around and threw the fluid contents at him. Then the empty plastic bottle.

'Ah! Jeezass! Wha's dat, y'fucker! Smell like...bleach? Nobody put bleach 'pon Jinxie 'ead, gyal! Y'dead, now, y'hear me? Dead.'

He fell back from her. She grabbed the lever again and yanked with all she had left. 'Open, you bastard!'

'Mi y-eye! Mi y-eye. Gonna cut you, bitch! You goin' fi carry your guts 'ome in a basket, 'ear mi?'

She looked behind to see the man rebounded off the wall opposite, brandishing an implement she'd only ever seen butchers use to chop oxtail in Brixton market. He extended his other hand, feeling his way towards her.

It was truly stuck. Jonelle grabbed at two mops and coupled them.

'Wait till I find you in a minute, gyal. Your mother won't recognise you.' He was chopping at the air with the machete.

Moving as quietly as she could, she shoved the mop sticks into the gap.

'Ah, I hear dat – you just wait where you is.'

Jonelle leaned on the sticks with all her weight and the panel grated open.

'Ah, I hear where you gone, y'likkle bitch. You is dog food now, y'ear mi?'

Jonelle stuffed her body through into a musty gloom that reeked of urine and faeces and talcum powder. A dim red light flicked on to reveal cots and bunks haphazardly crammed into the large space, boxes piled against one wall and windows that had been bricked up.

'Oi, Clint, hurry up! She bleach me, rasta! Clint? Tell di chief that bitch is in 'ere.'

Jonelle searched for some way to block the gap or stop anyone larger than herself from coming through. A large metal cot looked a good bet, but then she spotted another lever and pulled it. The wall started sliding, opening wider apart. Seeing him swivel towards the noise Jonelle flung all her might into shoving the lever in the opposite direction.

'Where you gone, gyal!' He was stumbling, chopping this way and that, kicking into the jumble of buckets and assorted bottles.

'Gotchya now, bitch… I's gonna slice—'

The partition juddered shut. Jonelle pushed the cot under the lever to stop it moving towards 'open', praying she'd got it right.

Bang.

She ducked instinctively and a scream shot up from her belly.

Zing – something parted her hair.

Crying out would surely locate where she'd dropped down low, leaning against the cot.

Thwup – the panel gained another hole.

Jonelle stayed quiet, covered her ears, squeezed her eyes shut and didn't move.

P'zing – a pail or some other metallic thing caught a bullet. Click! Click!

'Fuckit, I'm out. Clint! Where's you, man? Bring me a new clip.'

'Wha' you shoot up di place, Jinxie? What's up wi yer eyes?'

'You never 'ear mi callin? Dat *rass-claat* bitch bleach in mi eye, t'raahs!'

Blood was oozing down her left side and Jonelle felt her sodden knickers slipping down.

'Jinxie, lend mi your cutlass.'

'Why?'

'Nevermin' dat, man, gimme di 'lass...now, back up!... Furder back dan dat!'

Thud!

Jonelle saw a thick blade jut through the solid wood panel. It was gone with a grunt.

Thud!

The force shook the cot.

Thud!

The panel wood split and splintered.

# CHAPTER 41

Of all his regrets, Triple was thinking, the biggest was flying back to the UK, to purchase a second new identity and passport to someplace better than the one he'd picked before; someplace where a crate of beer didn't cost a fortune only to make him slightly merry, where down the road wasn't a million miles from everyplace else, where it wasn't so fuckin' cold all the time, where you could find a West Indian barbershop and, this time, where nobody but nobody would ever recognise him. Worst of all, people kept saying 'sex' when they meant 'six'! How's a man supposed to know?

The lump on his head was itching to buggery, but Bull had warned him not to move a muscle, just like them two on that sofa across the room. Triple did his best to ignore them. One stared fixedly across the dance floor, even though there was no action going on. The other guy looked messed up, like he'd had a discussion with Bull's Persuader, or he'd run into Style, who'd decked him for wearing the same cool jacket Style practically lived in.

Neither moved a toe-tapping muscle, not even to Bob Marley wailing his best 'Roots, Rock, Reggae' from the ceiling-high boxes. Triple thought to ask one of them to whisper what had been going down, before Bull returned from 'killing the damn music', but decided against it after adding one-and-one together and figuring staring-guy had followed Bull's orders and messed-up-head-guy had not.

'G'wan, Triple,' Bull's voice made him jump. 'You was sayin' dat di Babylon was after you?'

'Yea, Chief, yeah.' Triple kept eye contact best he could. Bull'd warned him once already. 'The night we did Django, aight, we walked through a party, aight?'

'Friday?'

'Yea, the Babylon was dere! Right dere. I mean, 'ow they know we was goin' dere? Chief, I was sweatin' that dey was followin' me to get to you. But I outsmart dem, Bull, I lead dem astray...right out the fuckin' country!'

'Out da country?'

'Yea yea yeay!'

'Where?'

'Switzalan'.'

'Switzerland?'

'Shit! No, Sweed'n. I keep saying Switzalan' insteada—'

Bull grabbed his head like a melon and pulled it over the chair back. Triple's throat kinked shut.

'Next you're gonna tell me you chop off all your hair and eyebrows to disguise yourself, aight?'

'Bull, wait, Bull.' Triple leaned back into the chair to let the words out fast. 'They catch up wid me – you kno' how dem have InnerPol?'

'Fuckin' InterPol?'

'Yeah, Chief... Dey try fi get me fi bring you down and be dem new inside man. Yea?'

'Inside man?'

'Yea, Bull,' Triple shrugged, 'I-man never know wha' they was talkin' 'bout! And I tell dem get lost 'cause I ain't no supergrass, crab-grass or no odder kinda grass, seen? Den dey start followin' mi, all over in Sweed'n! I see dem behind tree, in doorway an' in vans...like a stakeout, Chief!'

'Gospel, Triple?'

'No lie, Chief.' Triple tried to make a sign of the cross and got confused so he clasped his hands in prayer. 'Gospel troot. Would I shit you, Bull?'

Triple thought of Django. The lump on his head started throbbing hard. It didn't matter whether Bull believed him or not. He knew the man would sooner remove all doubt than give anyone the benefit.

Did the guy next to Style just move?

'Triple.' Bull moved to face him. Triple eyed the Persuader. 'Why didn't you tell nobody where you was goin'?'

Swallowing was impossible against Bull's vice of a grip and the severe neck bend, let alone spitting out more words.

'Well?' Bull pressed his head back further. 'Speak up, Triple.'

Gargling noises was all he could manage. Bull slapped his stubbly, shaven head and it snapped sideways.

'I want to know why you never tell nobody where you was an', Triple, what the hell were you doin' wrapped in sheets behind the East End shop, next to garbage wit' a note tied on your sorry arse?'

'Would you believe it, Bull, di bloody Babylon was still watching for me. They threaten fi pin Django murder on my black arse if I still refuse fi be dem inside man an' give you up, Chief.'

Bull's nostrils flared and his breath puffed hot down on Triple's head. When he said nothing, Triple swallowed drily and continued. 'So... I tell m'self: any move to go tell Bull would play right into Babylon hands. So, dat was when I t'ink fi a brand-new different new identity fi disappear, aight, Chief? Maybe hide in Brazil or someplace where dem never find mi coz no man was gonna turn me against you, Bull. I ain't no snitch, aight?'

Bull's stare was making Triple's strip search at Heathrow seem not too bad after all. Then his boss's expression changed. Had Bull X-rayed right through to the truth about Django?

Triple's bowels griped as he mentally raced back over all he'd just said.

Blam! Blam! Blam! Blam!

Triple ducked at the sound of each shot.

Bull straightened up and looked towards the door.

Triple heard a faint cry and decided it was Jinxie, except that he sounded in some pain and mad as hell. Clint answered the call from the foyer.

'So, Triple.' Bull returned his attention to him. 'While you was playing kiss-chase with da Babylon, all kinds o' shit hit da fuckin' fan.'

Triple sighed. 'I tell you, boss, it's a weight off mi shoulders now yu know the full story.'

'You still haven't said how—'

'Dey find me wrap up wit' dat note, yea? Dem shots from outside interrupt me, Chief.' Triple knew it was risky, but ploughed on while he had the big man's good ear. 'Is like dis, aright. I went to that place, you know the one where Prunes send me and Django for dem documents, aight? I t'ink one little new passport then grab the nex' plane for Brazil, aight? Easy peasy?'

Triple continued, explained that he'd got to the 'imperium' place but skipped the part about picking the lock to get in. He omitted to mention he'd taken extra cash to buy their silence so that they wouldn't tell a soul, not even Bull, that he'd been there.

'Soon as I go in – bam – somebody bash mi over mi 'ead, innit? Next t'ing I know, Jinxie and Clint was standin' over me and—'

Rrrr!

Engines roared and revved.

Bull raised the Persuader. Triple cringed.

'Follow me.' Bull turned and headed for the exit. 'Must be Likkle, Chigger and George finally back wit' di van.'

Triple obeyed, fast.

In the foyer, they heard the sound of someone chopping wood. Bull aimed a finger at him, then at four jerry cans.

'Triple, grab them cans. Start emptying the kerosene… chuck extra round the two stiffs on the sofa. Watchya waitin' for? Shake a leg – 'less you plan to be holding them cans when I drop the match.'

'Yes, Chief… I mean, no, Chief. Right away, Chief.'

'Soak the back room too, where them packages was – an' tell Clint and Jinxie to hurry the fuck up and ice that Patrick bitch and bring back mi blade from her corpse. I got sentimental ties wit' dat little knife.'

'Yes, right away, Chief.'

'An', Triple?'

'Chief?'

'You an' me can chat some more later over a couple'a Dragon stout.'

'Right, Chief! Right.'


Whenever Triple opened his mouth, Bull knew he'd be sidestepping the truth. Crabs. They were all crabs and Triple was king of the little bottom feeders, if he'd ever seen one. The sonofabitch'd got lucky today – lucky he had no time to loosen his tongue for him and root out the fact of where he'd gone and why. Lucky he was now a man down without Style. And, seriously, what was taking Jinxie and Clint so long in the back and why was they wastin' bullets?

Fuck dat Jonelle Patrick.

Bull tugged his suit, checked his steel, puffed his chest and shook his head at the walls on the way to the exit. *Can't fuckin' believe they brought back Triple instead of the fuckin' documents.*

Bull shoved the heavy doors. They flew open and early morning air rushed at him. George and Likkle should have come in by now, with Chigger hobbling after them – something felt off.

'Bunch-a slow pokes… Oi, Clint, Jinxie, hurry-da-fuck up. We gotta go…now.'

He'd have to make do with five for his raid; five and a half now that Triple was back. He was still their best driver, perfect for a swoop on Silk to swipe his documents outta his hands. Straight in-and-out, no foreplay. That conniving arse-licker wouldn't expect a thing and what a look that No-Name would have on his ugly face when he turned up, like he said he would, with packages, documents and all.

An impatient horn beeped, long and loud. Bull rolled his eyes and promised himself he'd give them a mouthful, after he got Triple to zip them up to Crystal Palace and zap down through Forest Hill into Peckham before that fucker Silk could scratch his bollocks and jerk off his morning wood.

He stomped down the side alley into the gravelly dirt yard where he saw they'd driven the van in and stopped it beside his Beamer. The engine was off, and he made out Likkle and George in the front seat, already waiting, watching him approach. Bull looked around and sniffed the air for some sign of Chigger.

Bull waved a fist as he walked towards them.

'Where've you lot fuckin' been? Stopped for breakfast didya? No matter – turn that fucker round and get outta the driving seat for Triple and where's—'

'Oi, Bull. Likkle and George – they don't take orders from you no more, they answer to me. Right, boys?'

Bull stopped in the naked space, halfway towards his Beamer.

'Silk?'

A lad stepped into view between the van and Beamer. The sun was still half asleep, but in the dawn light Bull noticed a girly familiarity in the boy's scowl, but couldn't quite place it. Silk joined the youth in the face off.

'You got some fuckin' balls bringin' your fuckin' ugly face on my turf.'

'Language, Bull. I got my fuckin' stepson here.'

'You want him to see you get your ass kicked, eh?'

'Just stop right there, Bull.' Silk pulled out a sawn-off shotgun from his trousers and cocked it, ready for business.

'What a relief, Silk, thought you was horny to see me.' Bull knew Silk's weapon, even with the long barrels cut short, could still spurt out enough lead to cause serious damage.

'That the man, Trev?' Silk pointed the gun.

'Yeah, Pop. That's the nigger.'

'Now, now, Trev. What did I tell you about respect?'

'Sorry, Pop.'

'Don't 'pologise to me, Son. It's Bull you insulted. Show him how sorry you are, like I told you.'

The lad disappeared behind the van and returned huffing and puffing and dragging a sledgehammer. He spat in Bull's general direction. Then, with a grunt, he swung the heavy hammer and crashed it into the Beamer.

The side panel buckled.

The windscreen shattered.

The roof caved inwards.

The alloys that had been gold-plated for him specially, chipped and cracked.

The shatterproof tinted rear windows – gifts from Prunes – splintered into shards, all over the yard.

'Sorree, Mister Bull... Sir,' the boy growled, turning towards Silk and sitting his bony arse on the Beamer bonnet.

'You learned him that, Silk?' Bull yawned, looking away but keeping the sawn-off shotgun in his periphery. 'Bring it here, boy. Let me show you how to swing like a man.' *What the fuck was keeping Jinxie and Clint... And, for that matter, Triple. Bull scowled at his men in the van.*

'Yes, they're with me now, old son.'

'I ain't your fuckin' son.' Bull saw that the snubby barrels had lowered towards Silk's feet. He was clearly having trouble keeping anything up after their recent encounter.

'Bull, you buggered my ribs, so this makes us even. Yes?'

'Even? If you ain't got a bunch of passports and documents with you, Silk, you can go fuck yourself with barbed wire!' Bull showed his teeth.

'Shit. I brought fifty of my crew, they're out front waiting. But why fight. I got them papers, you got the goods, let's work together, eh Bull? Maybe I make you my number two, how about that, then? Besides, your guys came to me. Right, boys?'

Bull made a half step, closer to hammer-boy.

George leaned out the van window. 'Chief, we run outta gas in Elephant an' Castle, Chief. We flashed you, right, Likkle?'

'You flashed?' Bull stepped closer to the boy, but kept looking towards George. 'How was I to see that from my back seat?'

'We flashed and flashed,' Likkle added, nodding and making the van rock.

'But you never stop, Chief.' George nodded back at Likkle.

After one more step, Bull was banking that Silk would avoid blasting his stepson to hell and give up the documents rather than tangle anymore with Bull Manners.

'Yeah, we flash and he keep going, George.'

Silk shut them up with a wave of the hand. 'As I was saying, Bull, your guys pushed the van into one of my petrol stations. Hungry, thirsty, no money...'

Bull edged forward, one more step.

'...I gave 'em food and fuel, a few beers and a little weed – and made them the same offer I'm making you, so why n—'

Pumped, primed, and angry, Bull charged, swatted the boy off the bonnet, towards Silk. They careened against the van and a loud boom ripped into the morning sky before the rifle clattered to the ground.

Likkle alighted the van like a cat, a twenty-five-stone cat that pounced between Bull and Silk.

'Move it, Likkle.'

Likkle stayed put. Bull watched Silk crawl on his knees to retrieve the rifle.

'You don't look so good, Silk.' Bull figured he was hurting; he was slow and his aim was shit.

'Get back, Bull.' Silk motioned for him to back up.

'You should do what Mr Silk says, boss.' Likkle stepped forward.

Bull backed up.

'Trev, you hit?'

'I'm okay, Pop.'

Back on his feet, Silk pointed both barrels at him. 'I'll give you one last chance to come work for me.'

George jumped out and joined Silk as the van's side door slid open. Chigger sat looking out. Someone had bandaged his feet.

'Boss,' George said, gun in hand. 'Silk's paying double!'

Bull backed up more.

Chigger nodded at Bull. 'He payin' healt'care too, Chief. And, boss, Mr Silk says we can get plane tickets to go home for 'olidays any time we want at Christmas.'

'Did he?' Bull backed further away, more slowly. 'Maybe I should think about that…when I ice you fuckin' Jud-asses!'

Bull turned and ran, fast.

'Drop him, George!' Silk yelled.

With George aiming at him, Bull knew sprinting for the alley would be iffy, so he corkscrewed to the ground, pulling out his P22 at the same time and popped off a couple rounds back between the two vehicles.

They all ducked and covered while he hauled ass to the 'Grilla entrance. Two slugs pinged off the steel door as he yanked it open and jumped in. Bull felt lucky it was George and not Style shooting at him.

The reinforced door would withstand police battering rams even with just the bolts. Guaranteed. Prunes had sworn that. He slammed the three steel bolts into place. A pinch of metal took a chunk of his thumb as he pulled away. He ignored the pain.

'Clint! Jinxie! Where the fuckin' fuck're you fuckin' fuckers?' Bull's voice boomed off the foyer walls.

'Haven't seen them, Bull.' Triple was backing out of the dance hall with a jerry can.

'What's that stink?'

Triple sniffed and looked worriedly at the jerry. 'Uhm, kerosene, Chief?'

'Not that, y'idiot. Smells really rank in 'ere.' Bull looked over at the open door behind the cloak counter.

'I done emptying the first two, Chief. Still some left in this one to—'

'Gimme dat!' Bull grabbed the kerosene off him. 'Get round back! To the back room… where them packages was!'

Bull finished dousing the foyer as he followed Triple out. He dribbled kerosene into puddles either side of the door and closed it.

'Triple, grab a mess of them bags and pile them against this door.'

'Them bags?' Triple pointed at the garbage mountain and covered his nose with the other hand.

'You see any other bags in here?'

'No, Chief.'

'Hurry up, fool.'

'Yes, Chief.'

Bull found Jinxie sitting slumped against a wall. His face was swollen and the whole area around his eyes blistered and messed up like a motha. Clint was peering into the cupboard, huffing and sweating with Jinxie's machete in one hand and his own beloved .45 Magnum in the other.

'What da fuck? I send you to get rid of one bony-assed bitch with fucked-up toes and my knife in her side!'

'Chief, she chucked bleach on Jinxie's head.' Clint looked round and used his .45 as a pointer. 'She blocked the slidin' wall, right Jinxie?'

'She still alive in there… all this time?'

'Yes, Chief!' Clint and Jinxie nodded to each other.

'Then what're you clowns doin' out here?'

'Di 'lass keep getting stuck in da wood, Chief…and I think she got more bleach to throw, Chief, right?' Clint looked to Jinxie who looked away at the floor.

'Tcho!' Bull kissed his teeth and swatted violently at the flies buzzing from over where Triple was sweating it. 'We got bigger problems!'

'Chief?'

'Silk's outside!'

'Silk, boss?' Jinxie whimpered.

'Bleach gone in your ears, too?'

'No, Chief.'

'You and Clint help Triple finish clearing that emergency door. Get all them bags against the—'

A loud boom announced that the entrance door's bolt had failed.

'Move it.'

Triple sped up, Clint joined in, flinging festering bin bags away from the emergency exit. Jinxie grabbed blindly, casting bags everywhere with Clint issuing warnings. Bull was more concerned that bags were landing in a splash of stink nearby, sending maggots flying like rice at a wedding – right on his Armani.

'Fuckin' watch it!' Bull growled, brushing himself vigorously.

'Sorry, Chief.' The three were in unison just as a dull thud budged the door, freshly braced shut by the festering mound.

'Can't run and hide forever, Bull?' Silk called through from the other side.

'I ain't runnin'…' Bull stopped inspecting his suit. 'An' I sure ain't hidin' from a fucker like you, Silk.'

*Was there any use explaining to a crab like Silk that when a King Cobra rears back, it isn't in retreat?* Bull decided not.

'C'mon, don't make this harder than necessary, Bull. I got you surrounded all round.'

'All round?' Bull bellowed, half laughing. 'You can't surround only halfway round, genius!… Tcho, now you talkin' like po-lice, too, mothafucker! What's next? You want us to come out with our pricks up?'

He motioned, drawing his men to him. Clint made Jinxie drop the bag he was holding and led him over. Triple followed. Clearly, Bull figured, Silk and the army he'd needed to come up against him were busy sniffing each other's butts and paying no attention to the kerosene. It was enough to turn his brilliant plan into a bloody genius idea.

'Gimme a light! One o' you, gimme a light!'

They each patted themselves down and shrugged, one by one.

'Fuck!' Bull cannoned a fist at the wall, dust flew about and a hole appeared in the mortar.

'Woah! Was that your head against a brick wall, Bull?' Silk mocked through the hole, 'My offer still stands! Look, time's up. I'm tired and it's nearly breakfast time.'

'Chief! Chief!' Triple whispered. 'I got an idea.'

'Not in the mood for your ideas, Triple.'

'Oi, Bull?' Silk shouted through the hole in the wall. 'Who else is in there with you?'

Bull laid a not-one-fuckin'-word finger across his lips.

'S'alright, I'll just ask your boys out here, sorry, I should say *your ex-boys*!'

Silk fell silent. Bull made up sign language that sent Triple back to clearing the remaining bags from the emergency door. He beckoned Clint and Jinxie closer. 'Listen me…this is for your ears only.'

'Yeah, Chief.'

'As of this second, you two will be getting their share of the payout.'

'Who's share, Chief?' Clint whispered.

'Chigger's, George's and Likkle's.'

'Why?' Jinxie asked facing Clint.

'Them ungrateful fuckers sold us out...' Bull paused, watching it sink in. Then he thumbed over at Triple, 'You two can split *his* share too, aight? But we gotta get out of this first, you feel me?'

They looked a little confused, but both nodded.

'Clint? Jinxie?' Silk called through the hole.

Bull zipped his lips for them to keep theirs shut tight.

Silk spoke again, 'You tell 'em, George.'

George sounded like he was reading from a script but he couldn't be cos Bull knew Django'd given up trying to teach him to read and write. 'Mr Silk payin' us double, bredren. He says donsah talks, bullshit walks! That okay, Mr Silk, sir?'

'Good, George, you done good.'

'Yea, you keep thinking that, y'traitor!' Bull ground his teeth. 'See if that crab will look after you like me?'

Triple was hefting the final bag with a grunt. Bull looked round at him as it split, releasing slimy, brown sludge down Triple's arms, shirt and trousers. 'Shit, shit, shit!' Triple backed away, slipped and fell against the emergency door handle. Bull expected the steel door to swing open, because that was how emergency exits worked.

It didn't.

'Must be rusty!' Triple started fiddling with the locking system talking shit about slippery fingers and if only he'd had his tools and fuckin' WD40.

The talking from the hole had stopped. In fact, Bull noticed an uneasy quiet from Silk and his bunch.

'Stop, Triple!' Bull waved urgently. 'Leave that latch! Fuckers must be outside there, waiting.'

Triple backed up.

Bull waved them all back from the emergency exit and pointed at the jerry can. 'Triple, you chuck the rest o' da kerosene everywhere, and make sure it run under that exit door, get me?'

'Yes, Chief.'

'Jinxie, you and Clint watch them two doors.'

'B-but. Chief, Jinxie.' Clint pointed to Jinxie's face.

'Fuckit – you and Triple watch then – I bet them buggers're planning to rush us front-n-back. I can feel it.' Bull spoke softly and then he turned up the volume, 'Ain't that right, Silk?'

Bull listened near the hole for a response.

Nothing came from Silk...or anyone.

'Triple, put down the can and take a look through that hole.'

'Now?'

'What the f—' Bull lifted a hammer of a fist.

Triple shuffled quickly towards the hole and lowered his head.

'Oi! Bull!' Silk made Triple jump.

'Yea, shithead.'

'Up yours, Bull!' Silk sounded annoyed. 'Someone here wants a word.'

'Mr Manners.' The sound of Silk's new fuckin' bedmate made Bull's stomach churn. 'I told you before...you're dealing with powerful people... I warned you, didn't I?'

'I knew you'd crawl up some time, you double-crossing, two-faced fuckin'—'

'Mr Manners...we overlooked your earlier "problems" and gave you a chance to redeem yourself. Yes?'

'Wha' you fuckin' flappin' about?'

'You kept on making a spectacle, attracting attention to the operation! You failed – just like I predicted you would. Frankly, I prefer to deal with contractors who are a little less – how should I put this – less crabby, like Silk here.'

'Fuck. You.'

'That's the sort of belligerence I find unconscionable, however,' Bull wished he had his fingers wrapped around the calm voice, 'my employers feel your resourcefulness could still be useful, working under Mr Silk here.'

'I got a better idea. Why don't I stick my dick through that hole so you can all have a suck?' Bull raised his P22 and took aim at kerosene-soaked bags of human waste, but, as he squeezed the trigger the door bulged and busted inwards ignoring the mountain of muck behind it. Likkle poked his head in, looked at Bull's P22 and was gone.

George rolled in over the bags to land in a splash of grime and kerosene and crouched, spluttering with his piece in hand. Bull took aim, but he couldn't see squat for flies buzzing around him. He saw Clint aiming.

'Wha' you waiting for, Clint!' Bull shouted.

Blam!

Clint flew backwards, silent.

Bull popped off a four-shot spread into the swarm, at George.

Blam! Blam! Blam! Blam!

The slugs zinged and ricocheted off the walls, showering the area with sparks. Bull ducked, watching flaming flies rain down on them all. The bags erupted, flinging bits of burning trash everywhere.

'Help!' George stood up, frantically brushing tiny fires from igniting his clothes.

'Drop and roll,' Bull shouted, pretending to care and not see the puddle of kerosene nearby. 'George, drop and roll, save yourself!… Jinxie, you don't move.'

George dropped.

'Jeeeesas!'

Bull shielded his eyes from the sudden burst of flame. 'Fuckin' sell-out. Serves you right.'

'Likkle, help 'im. Quick.' Bull recognised Chigger's voice above George's agonised cries for divine intervention. Wherever

Chigger sent his Bowie, it went, with deadly accuracy. Bull kept his head down, barely making out one large figure beside a smaller one entering the smoke.

'Ra-as! You clumsy fucker,' Chigger yelped. 'Mi foot, mi fuckin' foot!'

Bull ignored the sting of the smoke and aimed at the bigger target. He squeezed off two rounds into the chest of the hulking shape.

'Chief, not nice what you did to George.' Likkle was brushing at the smoke, coming towards him. Bull felt his shoulders being pulled out their sockets and knew what came next. A mother of a head-butt and a bone crushing stomp when he was down.

'Jinxie! Take him out!' Bull shouted. 'Triple, where the fuck are you?'

Jinxie stood, squinting, with his deadly cutlass in chopping position.

'This way, fool.' Bull wrestled against Likkle's grip. 'Turn round, Jinxie.'

Even with a couple of slugs in him, Likkle managed to fist-hammer Jinxie. Bull heard a popping sound and watched him sit back down, hard.

Bull broke free and backed away. He tripped over something... Triple! He was face down and motionless with Chigger's famous Bowie hilt sticking out of his back. Bull grabbed the weapon and pulled it out in a long arc at Likkle and watched him look down as if he'd never seen his own guts hanging out before.

'You know, you ain't nice, boss.' Likkle was trying to gather his insides back inside as he crashed down into a kneeling position.

Whoosh!

'Fuckin' hell!' Bull ducked from the searing flame rushing through the hole in the wall and a massive fireball belched in from the foyer beyond, bringing a screaming chaos in with it.

'Boss?' Clint moaned from somewhere near his feet.

Ignoring Clint, Bull hustled from the fiery furnace building behind him, to reach the cupboard and make his way out. He kicked his way to the sliding door with steam rising from his clothes. His skin felt like it was melting off him. Coughing and breathing into one sleeve, he used his free hand to rip away what remained of the splintered sliding wall. All he had to do was get to one of the bricked-up windows. He'd bash a way through with his bare fists and leave all the crabs to fucking boil in the pot.

The jab to his chest came as a surprise.

It started as nothing much, a small pinch, a gnat bite that grew into a flutter of pain that dived deep and then swam back up from where his heart should be.

He stopped.

'You?'

She didn't run.

She didn't speak.

She stood there and let him grab her twig of a neck. Bathed in the flickering of the flames engulfing the cupboard behind him, he watched her hands fall away from his chest, her bulging stare burning into him.

Her neck felt soft as he juiced the life from it. Relentless heat and dense smoke were hot on his heels, but he was only a few steps away from busting through the nearest window, soon as he discarded Tyrone's whore for good. If only the pain would stop spreading through his chest, gobbling up his strength, loosening his fingers from crushing her throat, and making his legs buckle.

The concrete floor hit him hard in both knees. Looking down, he recognised the knife handle, like a badge on his chest. It was exactly like the one his mother had left him with a note that said it had been carved from genuine Jamaican lignum vitae. She'd told him to treasure it and he had to this day, not because it was perfect in weight and balance but because it made her seem close. He felt happy to have it back.

His eyes followed the flow of red up her thigh to where she pressed her hands on her hip. Blood oozed from between thin fingers. His head was getting heavy as fuck but he managed to lift it and lock eyes with her. The crazy bitch swayed like she was listening to some tune while flames danced in around him. That was a damn funny thing too because the room was feeling cold as hell.

He couldn't hold his head up anymore.

She lowered herself and knelt, looking up at him, her face like a sea of tranquillity as the heat raged in and the air was sucked away. Her eyes pierced into his, taking on a ghostly flicker of contempt that filled Bull with terror.

# CHAPTER 42

'Where're we going, Aunty Chelsea?' Kenyana asked for the fourth time.

'Bristol,' Chelsea said tickling her sides to make her giggle. 'Is this the first time you've left London, Kenyana?'

The child only shrugged and flopped back into her seat. Chelsea looked across at Amanita, who was staring out on the blurred scene flying by the window of the Paddington train bound for Bristol.

'Where's Mummy?' Their eyes met for the first time that morning.

'She wants us to go on ahead. She'll be joining us and Uncle TK as soon as she—'

'He's not my uncle! And you're not my aunt.'

The words shaved pieces off her heart, leaving Chelsea lost for what to say. She reached out to her. 'Amanita, I understand how you…'

Chelsea watched a tear run down the child's cheek. 'Everything will work out, Amanita, you'll see.'

It was as well that she'd bought first-class tickets, Chelsea thought, looking around the carriage. She watched TK returning from the toilet, rocking past a besuited gentleman with his head buried in the *Financial Times* with the bold headline: 120,000 New Homes Approved for Green Belt: PM

EMENTS

and grandmother, from
auty and the burden of
at a little boy when he

ublishing professionals
to those precious indi-
on from the side-lines.
tutors and peers from
rishing my passion for

go to my beloved and
m this tale would have
ntions and best wishes.
laboured over the cover
uce this book for your

Demands Investigation. She wished she'd added one more zero. At least now, with the press on the scent, the truth would come out, the deception exposed, and no more lives would be ruined by those criminals.

Two rows up, on the opposite side, two biddies under large hats were totally absorbed in conversation with each other.

'It's a marvellous day to visit the Cheddar Gorge,' Blue Hat called out to Yellow Hat, carefully hoisting a steaming china cup up beneath her wide lacy rim.

'Yes, George positively loves Cheddar,' Yellow shouted back at Blue, beside her. 'He simply insists on it with lashings of Branston in his sandwiches.'

Chelsea made to say something to Amanita but changed her mind. Since they'd left London, in fact, all the way to the station, the child had looked lost and alone. She had every reason to be upset when the person who'd brought her into the world, who'd nurtured her and kept her safe, whose unconditional love was absolute and dependable had suddenly fallen off the face of the earth.

'It'll be alright…' Chelsea took a chance, pushed away the china crockery and placed her open hand on the little table. 'You'll be alright.'

Time seemed to stand still as the child looked down at the table, rocking with the motion of the train. Lucky for them, the police had insisted, they'd had 'much bigger fish to fry'. So big, in fact, they'd accepted Chelsea's offer to cover all the damages at King's as an end to the matter and dismissed TK with a caution. As to locating Deen, they'd said they were still on the case.

Slowly, Amanita regarded her, contemplating the 'No Entry' sign she hung in her mind, her heart, and the very space about her. Then she unfolded her arms and leaned forward to take Chelsea's hand.

'I'm hungry.' Kenyana thrust her little head into the moment and under Chelsea's arm, breaking the hand-hold.

Hopefully, she'd applied enough No. 5 before checkii
out of the hotel suite.

'Shall I get you a sandwich?'

'Yeff.' Kenyana looked up, thumb in mouth.

'Say "Please",' Amanita reminded her sister.

'Yeff-pweef.' Kenyana looked up again, thumb still ir

'Don't give her cheese.' Amanita folded her arms aga
she has a weak bladder.'

'It's okay, there are toilets on the train. What do y
to drink, honey?'

Kenyana de-thumbed and nestled closer. 'Apple juice,

'What about you, Amanita?' Chelsea summoi
steward and wondered if she'd ever get to call her 'N
Jonelle had done.

'Excuse me,' Bailey blocked the path of a speeding d
the hospital corridor, 'I think we missed a turn. Wh
to ICU?'

'Sorry, Officers, I'm Paediatrics.' The doctor adju
glasses. 'Wait a sec. Is Miss Patrick with you? I have an
for her about her son.'

'We're here on another matter, doctor,' Murphy jun

'No, doctor, Miss Patrick, isn't with us,' Bailey add

'Oh, I see.' The doctor shook off a look of confusio
well, let me find someone – oh, Nurse Brown!'

The nurse escorted them to the ICU, and introduce
to the head nurse, who spoke rapidly before leavin;
Beyond the observation glass, a tiny form lay mumm
burn bandages and attached to intravenous drips b
fluid resuscitation. Masked and gloved, ICU nurses fl
about the sterile room bearing swabs, fresh banda;
hypodermic needles. Monitoring equipment blipp
beeped a chaotic tune.

# ACKNOWLEDC

I am forever grateful to my mother
whom I learned much about the b
womanhood and who never laughe
told them he wanted to write books.

I am thankful also to the first
who urged me to get published, an
viduals wishing me well, cheering n
My gratitude must also extend to n
the University of Chichester for nc
the craft and wonderment of story.

Unreserved gratitude must als
long-suffering Lindsay, without wh
remained buried beneath a pile of ir
So, I thank my wife and the team wh
art, editing, and typesetting to prc
enjoyment and satisfaction.

And thanks to you, dear reader.
Special thanks to:
Copy editor: Nicky Lovick
Proof-reader: Vicki Vrint
Typesetter: Danny Lyle